YA FIC Gong
Gong, Chloe.
Foul heart huntsman

DC - Nov 2023

FOUL HEART HUNTSMAN

ALSO BY CHLOE GONG

THESE VIOLENT DELIGHTS
OUR VIOLENT ENDS
FOUL LADY FORTUNE
LAST VIOLENT CALL

FOUL HEARTHUNTSMAN

BOOK TWO IN THE FOUL LADY FORTUNE DUET

CHLOE GONG

MARGARET K. McELDERRY BOOKS
NEW YORK LONDON TORONTO SYDNEY NEW DELHI

For Tashie Bhuiyan,
whose impact is truly unmatched

MARGARET K. McELDERRY BOOKS • An imprint of Simon & Schuster Children's Publishing Division • 1230 Avenue of the Americas, New York, New York 10020 • This book is a work of fiction. Any references to historical events, real people, or real places are used fictitiously. Other names, characters, places, and events are products of the author's imagination, and any resemblance to actual events or places or persons, living or dead, is entirely coincidental. • Text © 2023 by Chloe Gong • Jacket illustration © 2023 by Skeeva • Jacket design © 2023 by Simon & Schuster, Inc. • All rights reserved, including the right of reproduction in whole or in part in any form. • MARGARET K. McELDERRY BOOKS is a trademark of Simon & Schuster, Inc. • For information about special discounts for bulk purchases, please contact Simon & Schuster Special Sales at 1-866-506-1949 or business@simonandschuster.com. • The Simon & Schuster Speakers Bureau can bring authors to your live event. For more information or to book an event, contact the Simon & Schuster Speakers Bureau at 1-866-248-3049 or visit our website at www.simonspeakers.com. • The text for this book was set in Dante. • Manufactured in the United States of America • First Edition • 10 9 8 7 6 5 4 3 2 1 • Library of Congress Cataloging-in-Publication Data • Names: Gong, Chloe, author. | Gong, Chloe. Foul Lady Fortune. • Title: Foul heart huntsman / Chloe Gong. • Description: First edition. | New York : Margaret K. McElderry Books, [2023] | Series: Foul lady fortune ; 2 | Audience: Ages 14 up. | Audience: Grades 10–12. | Summary: In 1932 Shanghai, exposed national spy Rosalind Lang must rescue fellow spy Orion and find a cure to a dangerous chemical weapon before it lands in the hands of foreign invaders. • Identifiers: LCCN 2023009021 (print) | LCCN 2023009022 (ebook) | ISBN 9781665905619 (hardcover) | ISBN 9781665905633 (ebook) • Subjects: CYAC: Spies—Fiction. | Chemical weapons—Fiction. | Shanghai (China)—History—20th century—Fiction. | China—History—1928–1937—Fiction. | BISAC: YOUNG ADULT FICTION / Fantasy / Historical | YOUNG ADULT FICTION / Historical / Asia | LCGFT: Historical fiction. | Novels. • Classification: LCC PZ7.1.G65218 Fm 2023 (print) | LCC PZ7.1.G65218 (ebook) | DDC [Fic]—dc23 • LC record available at https://lccn.loc.gov/2023009021 • LC ebook record available at https://lccn.loc.gov/2023009022

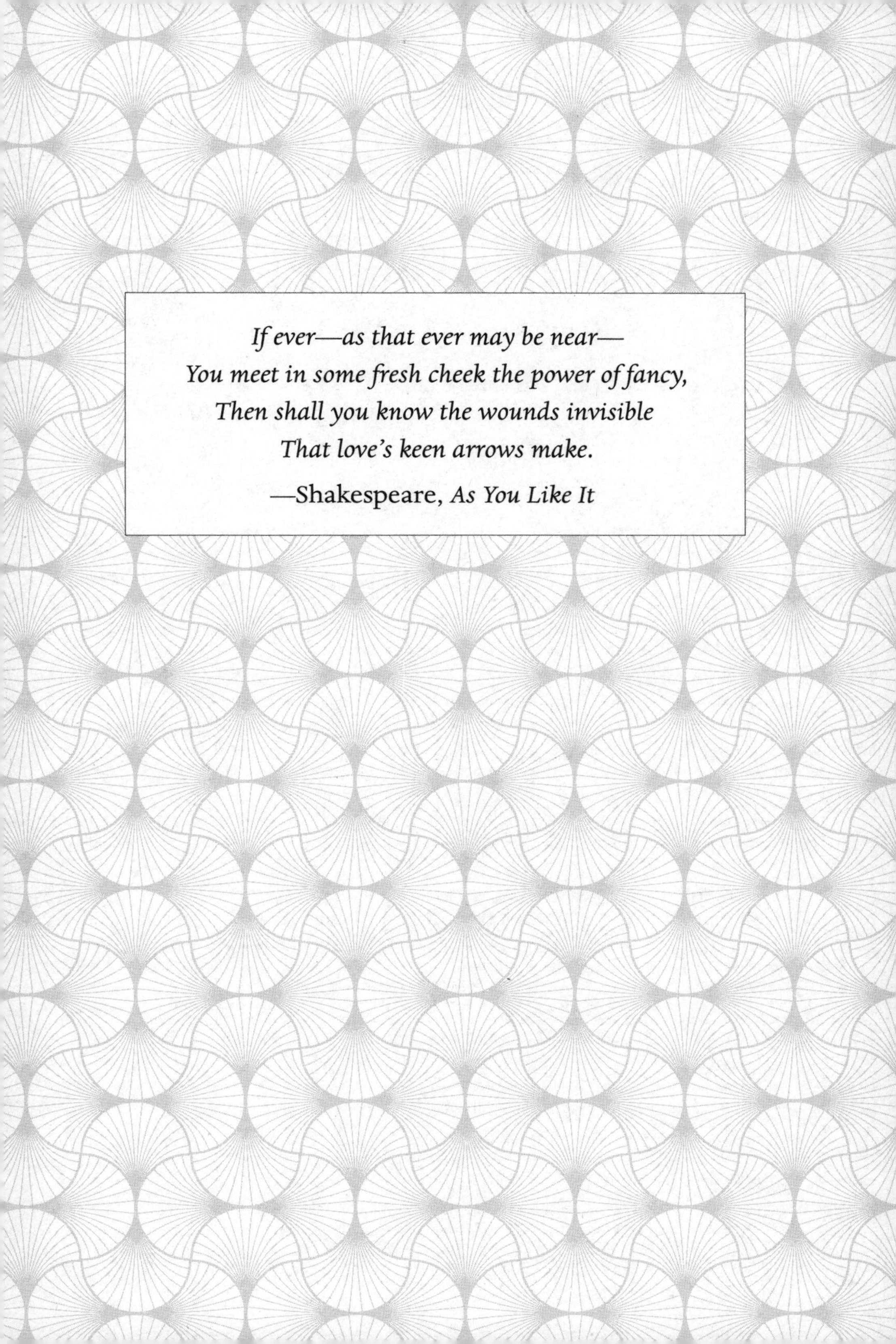

If ever—as that ever may be near—
You meet in some fresh cheek the power of fancy,
Then shall you know the wounds invisible
That love's keen arrows make.

—Shakespeare, *As You Like It*

PROLOGUE

November 1931

The easiest way to disappear was to never disappear fully, always hovering right at the periphery of being caught, responding in an instant when there was movement. It was hard to fall into a trap if you were the one setting the bait. Hard to be taken unaware when you drew the whole game board.

Alisa Montagova poured herself a cup of tea, eyes flitting up to watch the door of the restaurant. The owner had pulled the window panels closed to block out the cold. In the warmer months, they would be left open, and the bamboo leaves growing along the ledge would cast gentle shadows onto the patrons taking meetings or drinking with lovers. This was a relatively small township, somewhere ambiguously to the west of Shanghai. Big enough to accommodate a few city folks for business here and there—which meant Alisa drew no notice while wandering the streets—but not so chaotic that she couldn't find an empty restaurant in the late afternoon, seating herself at a corner table as the hour struck four o'clock.

Alisa was very good at disappearing. She had been practicing since she was a child, lurking in the household to eavesdrop or cramming herself into hidden corners all across Shanghai. It grew to become a personal challenge: hold so many nibbles of information from different places that she could put together corresponding reports and feel crafty by knowing so much. There was no good waiting for conversations to start and then sidling up to them. She needed to be three steps ahead. Already in the cupboard before two distant cousins had an argument in the kitchen. Dangling from the rafters by the time the old lady in the brothel was cursing out the clients to the girls in the back rooms. Only then did Alisa feel at home in her own city. To disappear well was to partake *with* her surroundings, to understand their rhythm and reasons instead of hiding and hoping she wasn't seen as an ill-fitting intrusion. It was moving from township to township while a whole unit of Nationalists was after her, confident at every turn that they would never come close to touching her, because she could pinpoint their arrivals each time and slip away. She had done it twice already. And if the incoming unit made haste today, this coming hour would be the third time.

"Anything to eat today, xiǎo gūniáng?"

Alisa blew on the hot tea. The ceramic cup felt wonderful on her bare fingers after they had turned numb from her stroll here. She hadn't worn gloves once in her life, and she wasn't starting now. Her hands liked being free and unrestricted.

"Can I get that little cucumber dish?" she asked. She waved her fingers about, tapping against the cup. "With the cute chopped-up pieces? And the garlic?"

The owner frowned, trying to work out what Alisa meant. A second later, she visibly brightened, turning on her heel. "Ah. I know which dish you want. It'll be out soon."

"Xiè xiè!"

Alisa slouched on her wooden stool, hooking her ankles onto the stool legs. As soon as the owner disappeared into the kitchen, the whole restaurant fell quiet again, save for the twinkle of wind chimes blowing at the doorway. There had been a bout of very light snow last week, and though none of it remained, the seasonal chill had arrived. It made the residents around these parts duck their heads and turn their gazes down to keep their ears warm, shuffling from destination to destination without much regard for their surroundings. When the scout wandered into the town center earlier in the morning and entered a bookshop, Alisa had sighted him immediately. Or rather, from the second floor of the teahouse, she had noted something off about the way he walked, and as soon as he made his exit, she had hopped out of the teahouse and moseyed into the shop too, where they had told her that he was asking for a girl who matched her description.

The Nationalists were so easy to outsmart when they operated this way. At the very least, they ought to be sending the covert branch after her. But last Alisa had heard from coded radio broadcasts, the Nationalists' covert branch was in shambles, with one of their handlers having defected to the enemy Communists, one of their top agents brainwashed, and another agent kept under lock and key after exposure. It was rough over there. Not that her side was looking any better; she wasn't sure if she had been marked as missing yet, or if the Communists were so used to her disappearing acts that they trusted she was off getting something done.

"All right, here we are. Pāi huángguā. If it's not spicy enough, tell me, hmm?"

The cucumbers glistened with sesame oil and bright red chili chunks. The owner set the bowl in front of Alisa, pausing with bemusement when Alisa wadded up some cash and slid it into her apron pocket before she could retreat.

"Just wanted to settle the bill first," Alisa said casually. In case she needed to run out of here mid-meal.

She assumed that Celia hadn't reported her for the vial currently sitting in her pocket. Otherwise Celia's superior would be contacting Alisa already, demanding that she bring it in. Sooner or later it would leak to her own side that she held the last vial of a chemical concoction unlike anything in the world. One that turned its victims into immortal supersoldiers who didn't need sleep and wouldn't stay injured, who were strong enough to throw an opponent across the room and could take a bullet to the chest without any noticeable effect. When that happened, this disappearing game she played for her own amusement was going to have to end. She would need to run from both factions—and run properly if they sent covert after her—because she sure as hell wasn't handing over a weapon that could completely control the direction of the civil war.

Alisa's eyes flickered to the restaurant entrance again while the owner returned behind the counter. She munched on a cucumber piece. Past the door, the street stayed hushed except for the occasional bicycle bell, ringing to say hello while its rider passed by. The first warning sign that Alisa always listened for was shouting from residents in the vicinity. Soldiers never paid attention to the plants they were kicking or the carts they were shoving aside. Perhaps it was unnecessary to wait for that very moment they were approaching before Alisa started to move, but it was funny to injure their morale if she waited until she was within grasp. She had waved at them the first time while running into the forest. Stuck her tongue out the second time when the car started to drive away.

Munch munch munch. The cucumber was really quite good.

The wind chimes blew against a gust of wind. Alisa took another sip of tea.

Then, without any warning, Jiemin—her former coworker and the head of the unit currently chasing after her—walked in through the door, doing a brief inventory of the place before his eyes landed on Alisa in the corner.

She didn't get up.

"Miss Montagova, you have given me a lot of trouble."

Jiemin sat down at the table, dropping onto the stool beside her as if this had been a planned meeting. Alisa pushed the plate of cucumber closer to him, offering her chopsticks. He wasn't dressed in uniform; nor had he brought any backup. In both manner and attire, he looked exactly as he did every morning when Alisa walked into their department at Seagreen Press, chewing on a meat bun while Jiemin paid no attention to what was going on outside his reception desk because he was engrossed in his book. Knowing what she did now, she wondered if that had merely been a part of his undercover act.

"You move far too slowly," Alisa replied. "It's been over a month since I started running with this vial. A good unit should be closing in at least once a week."

In that month and then some, Alisa was honestly surprised it was only the Nationalists after her. Lady Hong had invented this weapon for the Japanese, but after her son Orion confronted her and Rosalind destroyed the only successful batch, there had been no news along the intelligence grapevine about a replacement being made. The Communists had been watching Lady Hong's movement as closely as the Nationalists: the last sightings put her around Manchuria, reporting in with the Japanese. Perhaps she was lacking some resource. Perhaps she was simply preoccupied in the meanwhile with Orion at her side, his memories erased so that she could use his enhanced strength however she wished until more conditioned soldiers were created.

"I am not moving slowly." Jiemin accepted the utensils, taking a piece of cucumber. "I am moving at a perfectly normal pace. It's just easy for one individual to outrun a whole unit when we're making a racket long before we approach."

Alisa frowned. "Excuse me. This is hardly a task achievable by any individual. It is not only because of the numbers."

Looking rather thoughtful, Jiemin returned the chopsticks to Alisa's side. "I've successfully caught up to you alone, though."

"And yet you alone cannot bring me in."

The owner came to replenish the teapot with more hot water. She poured out a cup for Jiemin. Though her eyes were curious, she didn't say anything before retreating into the back.

"I am not trying to bring you in," Jiemin said when the owner disappeared. "You know what I'm here for."

Alisa's response was immediate. "You're not getting it."

"Miss Montagova," Jiemin urged. He lowered his voice. "A weapon like that cannot be allowed to travel freely. You may think you are helping Lang Shalin, but we are not getting Hong Liwen back. We cannot keep this around in the hopes that it might restore him."

"So you've talked to Rosalind." Alisa resumed eating her cucumber. She wasn't asking a question; she was confirming that Rosalind must have told Jiemin there was one vial left. As far as Alisa could determine, that was the only reason why the Nationalists knew to start chasing her while other factions played catch-up with intelligence.

"There won't be any use stopping Lady Hong's traitorous forces if this vial ends up in the wrong hands," Jiemin continued, pretending not to have heard her remark.

Alisa slapped her chopsticks onto the table. "As far as I am concerned," she said, her tone turning cold, "Nationalist hands *are* the wrong hands too."

Jiemin stared her down. Alisa didn't flinch. It was near impossible to intimidate Alisa Montagova when she had a level of self-importance that inflated up to the sky, and anyone who tried only wasted their time.

Eventually, Jiemin looked away first, his brow furrowing. He seemed to be mulling over something. Seconds later, he reached into his jacket pocket and pulled out a sheathed dagger, offering it forward.

"Is it coated in poison?" Alisa asked warily.

"It is something I hope will change your mind. Remember, Miss Montagova—I came here alone."

Alisa took the dagger. She pulled off the sheath. Though the restaurant was unlit and the afternoon hovered at a cold, dull gray, the metal of the blade flared with its own brightness. It was beautifully crafted, with a thin hollow line down the middle before each side tapered off for a viciously sharp edge. And at the base . . .

Alisa grazed a thumb along the engraving. A small exhale of surprise escaped from her lips. She wondered if she could possibly be misreading the single Chinese character etched upon the metal, but the 蔡 stayed unchanging no matter how long she stared at its glimmering gold.

This weapon was a family heirloom. And Jiemin was certainly not of that family.

Right?

"Good God," Alisa said. "Please don't tell me you're a secret Cai."

Jiemin peered into his teacup. He had relaxed his brow. "What? I—*no*. My surname is Lin if you must know." He nudged his cup away, opting to forgo the sludgy tea. "But you're aware who that dagger belongs to, are you not?"

She supposed she could take a very well-informed guess. And she supposed that meant she could take a guess as to why Jiemin was showing her this. The original owner of this dagger wasn't gaudy enough to pass it around for a token. No—Jiemin had already possessed it and was exposing it to make his point.

Alisa breathed in shallowly, pressing her thumb hard into the engraving. She had suspected, of course. She had caught a glimpse of them in Zhouzhuang that fateful April; she knew exactly where she ought to go if she wanted confirmation that her brother and his lover were alive and in hiding. But she had been far too afraid of learning the opposite—despite knowing Roma was the only one who had the information to be paying her bills every month, despite Celia and Benedikt occasionally slipping up to talk about the two of them in the present tense—and so she had stayed away, living in her blissful hope.

This . . .

This was the first time she had gotten true confirmation. They were *alive*.

Alisa shoved the blade back into its sheath, blinking back the rush of emotion prickling at her eyes before Jiemin could see it. He had better have considered the consequences of telling her this, or Alisa wasn't going to treat him kindly for creating danger.

"I'm going to say this once," Alisa declared, sniffing. "No matter who you secretly work for, you are still a Nationalist. Even if *they* trust you, I am not letting this vial get anywhere near politics." She stood up. Then, politely, she pushed her dish in front of Jiemin. "I will *swallow* the glass vial whole before I let you have it. Bring your forces after me and tear it from my stomach—that's the only way you're getting it. Now, please enjoy the rest of the huángguā, my treat."

Alisa walked off.

"Hey," Jiemin called after her. "At least give the dagger back."

"I have claimed it," Alisa said without turning around. She gripped it tightly in her hand, a smile tugging at her lip. "Go take it up with my sister-in-law herself if you want to argue otherwise."

She stepped out of the restaurant, tucking the dagger into her coat. Right as the first flake of snow drifted onto her nose to signal a new storm rolling in, Alisa set off for the next township, disappearing again until she was needed.

1

JANUARY 1932

Ice had frosted over Rosalind Lang's bedroom window, drawing a bizarre shape that resembled a broken heart—the anatomical kind, with half-severed arteries stretching into the corners. Its edges were starting to melt, though, thawing under the first sunny day they'd had in a while and dripping rivulets of condensation down the glass.

Rosalind was watching the street below. She didn't know how they expected her to leave without causing a fiasco. The media had been relentless for weeks, with different outlets flocking outside her apartment building, hoping to be the first to snap a recent picture of Lady Fortune. Ever since she was discharged from the hospital and told to rest up, she hadn't left her apartment once, relying on her landlady Lao Lao to do the shopping and bring news from the outside. She hadn't needed the rest. As soon as they took the bullets out, her body had healed at supernatural speed, returning her to normal function. If it were up to her, she wouldn't be sitting idle, but her superiors had given her a very stern warning about needing to lie low. Today she had been summoned in at last for a meeting to discuss their next steps. The papers had splashed her entire identity in the headlines: Lang Shalin, former Scarlet showgirl turned Nationalist assassin—not dead as the city had been left to believe but wreaking chaos and killing merchants up and down the country's coast for four years.

With Fortune's real face in the open, she could hardly continue her missions as per usual. She had been pacing her bedroom relentlessly these few weeks, drawing up plans and then tossing them out, knowing she would be barred from acting upon them. She had already made the mistake of telling Jiemin that Alisa held Lady Hong's last vial, a show of good faith while she begged for them to go after Orion, and yet that had achieved nothing except sending the Nationalists on the chase after Alisa. She wasn't going to relinquish the remaining card up her sleeve.

I can help you get him back.
Find me in Zhouzhuang.
—JM.

The note sat crinkled on her desk now. Its words were hardly legible after all her folding and unfolding, but it didn't matter. She had long memorized those three lines; night after night, when she stared at the walls blankly in her version of rest, the note would flash in her mind on every blink. Without even sleep for an escape, there was nothing for Rosalind Lang to do within these four walls but think and think and think.

How was she supposed to get to Zhouzhuang without directly going against the Nationalists? As frustrated as she was, they were still her employers, and she couldn't break away so rashly. Besides, what if it was a trap? What if she fled to the countryside only to find nothing but a dead end? She didn't even know what *JM* was supposed to mean. She didn't know anyone with those initials. A nurse at the hospital had inscribed this note after taking the message on the telephone. Anyone could have made the call. News had already broken about her identity by then. All someone needed to do was locate which hospital was plucking bullets out of Fortune and ask for the message to be passed along. Hell—maybe it was only a reporter who wanted to meet for the exclusive scoop.

Still . . . this was better than nothing. The Nationalists had made it clear that they had given up on Orion Hong. *He is a liability. There is nothing we can do except try to eliminate him.*

"He is one of your best agents," Rosalind had yelled at Jiemin's retreating back when he'd come with instructions to stay put. "How can you tell me there is absolutely nothing to be done?"

He had paused at the doorway. Shaken his head sadly.

"Even if—somehow—we physically remove him from his mother's side, his mind has been altered to follow her every instruction. And if his mind is always going to be under her influence, we cannot trust him on our side ever again. Think of Hong Liwen as having perished in combat. It'll be easier."

A traitorous part of her wished Dao Feng were still here. He wouldn't have told her to stay put. He would have made a plan to rescue Orion. Except her handler had switched sides—or rather, her handler had been on the opposite side all along. The question of whether Dao Feng had truly cared for her or Orion as his disciples was up for perpetual debate.

"Damn you," Rosalind muttered under her breath. She wasn't sure who she was talking to. Dao Feng, maybe. Or the world at large for setting her in this role.

On the street below, a car started to pull up alongside the reporters, stirring interest in the crowd. A girl tumbled out from the passenger seat in a flurry of pink tulle, coming into the building with her key and slamming the door closed before any of the reporters could follow suit. Seconds later there was the sound of heels clacking up the exterior stairs, then the apartment door opening too.

"Sǎozi, you better be dressed already."

Rosalind was not dressed. "You don't have to keep calling me that. I give you full permission to defy cultural terms of respectful fake kinship and use my name."

Phoebe Hong appeared at the bedroom doorway. She propped

her hands on her hips. In stark contrast to Rosalind's lack of preparedness, Phoebe wore a rose-colored dress with a series of complex ribbons down the front, a blot of color suddenly bursting onto a monochromatic scene. She took in the sight before her—Rosalind perched at the edge of her messy desk, her hair spilling down her back and her legs bare—and strode forward immediately.

"Is that my brother's shirt?" Phoebe demanded.

"Maybe," Rosalind replied defensively. The smooth white fabric draped down to her thighs, and she tugged at it, though she doubted Phoebe cared whether she was adhering to modesty. "You're incredibly early. I thought Silas said he was coming at three."

Phoebe went to the dresser and pulled out a qipao. When she tossed it at her, Rosalind barely had a second to catch the bundle of silk before Phoebe was also throwing a necklace, putting together a complete outfit in the most disorderly way.

"You can't be lying around wearing my brother's clothes on today of all days. Go change."

"I was *going* to get ready," Rosalind insisted. She shook the qipao out. Though she stood, Rosalind couldn't help glancing at her desk again, at the note sitting beside her stack of books. The shirt was warm on her shoulders. It felt safe in a way that her own clothes didn't, as if Orion were still around, making a racket through the apartment.

She missed him. Terribly. She had thought him a complete menace while he was here, complained to his face that he was a terror in her space, and he had only ever grinned in return, making an effort to bring her food or smooth her hair down when she was busy writing something.

Now he was gone, and Rosalind felt utterly off-kilter. As false as their marriage had been, Orion Hong had molded himself onto her like an extra attachment of the flesh. Being cut away wasn't something she would eventually get used to: it was an invisible wound that refused to close like her bodily ones did, and the damage had been carved into the deepest part of her heart. If she pulled her ribs open to look at the organ, she could point to its exact site . . . at last, an injury that wasn't healing over at rapid speed. If she didn't get him back, eventually she would bleed out entirely.

Rosalind tore her eyes away from the desk. A terrible sting was pricking behind them, and the last thing she needed was to start crying.

"Go change," Phoebe prompted again, gentler this time. "If we're going to get him back, you need to receive the task."

"Yes," Rosalind agreed absently. "I must receive the task."

The problem was, weeks had gone by and the Nationalists hadn't changed their tune about Orion. For all she knew, this meeting would move her onto a completely different mission—tell her that Jiemin was going to be her permanent handler and then assign her some silly task chasing after an unruly politician—and what then? Did Rosalind have to leave? Give up bettering this city and follow a wild lead into the countryside?

She would. That was the most alarming part. For so long she had only wanted to keep fixing Shanghai, but the focus she once possessed was wavering, loosening its hold and allowing her to crane away. She wanted to love more than her city; she wanted the love that had been wholly hers for that gasp of a moment. Given the choice between the two, she had her suspicions about which one she would run toward.

Except the thought terrified her. And so she had been playing nice these past few weeks, sitting tight instead of outright rebelling. Her employers had a chance to get it right. Let them act agreeably, and maybe Rosalind wouldn't have to go off on her own. It wasn't as if she had done a very good job of that in the past. Her track record was abysmal, in fact.

A loud honk blared suddenly outside the window: Silas Wu, getting impatient in the driver's seat.

Phoebe gave her a prompting look.

"Five minutes," Rosalind promised, hurrying into the washroom.

She changed fast. Too much time had passed since she'd last worn her hair up, and she almost dropped her pin when she stuck the metal into a small plait, pinning the tail end behind her ear. Phoebe was waiting at the front door when Rosalind emerged. She beamed happily, offering a quick clap of approval.

"I should warn you," Phoebe said while Rosalind locked up. "There's been a new article."

"*Another* one?" Rosalind swore under her breath, putting her key away. "How much more can they dig up? I have been in this world for only twenty-four years."

And she had been aging properly for only nineteen of them before disappearing off the grid to live as some shadowy myth. Up until two months ago, people hadn't known whether Fortune was a real person or merely something that the Nationalists had made up to scare their enemies.

"You got on some restaurant owner's bad side in 1926. He had a whole spiel of slander prepared about you and your lack of respect for chairs. Apparently you threw one and broke it."

Rosalind winced. "That was actually my cousin's doing."

"He also said you called his hat ugly."

"Fair. *That* was me."

The only reason this media storm had blown so large was because Rosalind Lang hadn't been some nobody before: Fortune's identity leaking wasn't just the shock of an ordinary girl with unspeakable science running in her veins. When the Scarlet Gang was still around, any gossip column that wanted to slam her cousin Juliette Cai usually dragged Rosalind in too. The city already knew her. They had constructed an existing image of Lang Shalin, a child of Shanghai's gangster elite who fell away when the rest of their system did. For her to arise again as this politician's assassin was absurd, something that felt like lumping clay into a skin of flour and calling it a dumpling.

"Either way," Phoebe said. They paused in front of the building door. Rosalind could hear the rumble of chatter, the reporters murmuring with one another in speculation over when she was going to emerge. "They're hungry for new material. As evidenced by how far back they are willing to dig. The whole country is waiting for a glimpse of Lady Fortune."

"They're going to have to wait longer." Rosalind pushed down on the door handle. "Lady Fortune is away at the moment."

The blinding flashes came immediately. The yelling followed as a close second, voices from every direction demanding, *"Look here, please! Lang Shalin, look here!"*

With weeks to prepare for this moment, Rosalind kept her head down, forging ahead on the driveway. It was only a short distance to the roadside, where Silas's car awaited. They only needed to get through the crowd without stopping.

She was doing so well. Until:

"Lang Shalin, what are your thoughts on Hong Liwen being sighted in Manchuria?"

Rosalind's head whipped up. She sought the voice who had shouted the question, but the flashes invaded her sight immediately, leaving only blots in her field of vision.

"What?" she demanded. "What did you say?"

"You don't need to get information from a reporter," Phoebe cut in, taking hold of Rosalind's elbow. "Come on."

But Rosalind had paused, and the reporters scrambled to take advantage of the opportunity. They had grown ravenous, left out here in the cold for too long. Though the sun beamed high today, it had been rain and gloom in the days prior, some afternoons pouring with fast-falling sleet. Even then they had not desisted, too intrigued at the prospect of being the first to take a photograph to their boss.

"Over here!"

"This way! This way!"

"Lady Fortune, show us your talents!"

Without warning, something sharp came flying in Rosalind's direction, scratching her cheek before landing with a loud *thunk* on the path behind her. Her hand lurched to her face with an instinctive gasp, cupping the painful sting. When she lowered her fingers, she found blood.

Her vision turned red in a visceral, livid tilt. Who dared to *throw* something at her? She could already feel the skin on her face knitting itself back together, healing in front of these cameras, every moment captured under a flash. This was what they had wanted, wasn't it? To turn her into a piece of sensation, put her under a microscope to be picked apart under newsprint.

These damn reporters had forgotten that she was an *assassin,* that they were so interested in Fortune only because she used to be a feared shadow stalking the night, killing people with a mere exhale of poison.

Slowly Rosalind wiped the remaining blood off her face. She had changed her mind. Lady Fortune was here after all.

She lunged forward.

"Hey!" Phoebe cried.

Just before Rosalind could make contact with the nearest reporter, Phoebe scrambled to rein her back, her small frame lifting right off the ground in her vigor to keep Rosalind's arms down. The reporter cried out in alarm. Some around him hurried a step back. Others grew even more excited, yelling for her to come their way instead.

"You really don't want to do that, sǎozi," Phoebe wheezed.

"Let go of me," Rosalind said through her gritted teeth. "Orion would let me tear them apart."

"And that's why I'm being the responsible little sister. Don't make me cry to guilt trip you."

"Phoebe, let me *go—*"

Phoebe gasped. When a second rock hurtled in their direction, Phoebe snatched it right out of the air before Rosalind had scarcely registered its presence, then hurled it back at the reporters. The crowd screeched, shuffling to protect their cameras.

"You're so lucky I used to play softball." Phoebe gave her a push. "Come on, come on!"

Rosalind gave up on her mission to incite a fistfight. With a huff, she shoved through the rest of the crowd, reaching Silas's car at last and flinging the rear door open. She slid onto the seat behind him, her whole disposition locked in a sulk.

Phoebe came around the other side, flopping into the passenger seat and closing her door.

"So, that could have gone better."

Silas turned around to peer into the back seat, checking on Rosalind with concern. Meanwhile, the reporters were already flocking closer to the car, getting their notepads out to record the series of events that had unfolded before them.

"What happened out there?"

"Please drive," Rosalind said sharply. She pressed the heel of her hand into her eyes. When she ran her palm down her face, her cheek was smooth again. "Just drive."

At the front, Silas and Phoebe exchanged a glance, silently debating their response. Before Silas could pull on the wheel, however, there was a sudden thwack on his window, and he flinched in fright, his glasses sliding down his nose.

"Go!" Rosalind commanded. The reporter pointed his camera into the gap where the window was slightly rolled down. "Hurry!"

Silas stepped on the accelerator. Phoebe leaned over to push his glasses up before they could crash from his obscured vision. And

Rosalind watched her apartment fade from view, leaving behind the reporters.

Even as the clamoring noise faded, she hardly dared release the immense exhale that strained inside her lungs. Rosalind only shifted in her seat to face the front again, her shoulders tense and hunched into herself.

The vehicle jolted, passing a bump in the road and weaving into heavier traffic. While Silas and Phoebe resumed their conversation, Rosalind silently reached her hand toward the other side of the back seat, hovering in the empty space there. Then she set her hand down, upon nothing.

2

Local Kuomintang headquarters bustled with busyness, soldiers standing guard to watch the entrances. One of them *tsk*ed at Rosalind when she brushed past too closely at the door, and she glared over her shoulder while she walked away, equally annoyed at their presence.

Headquarters had been on edge ever since General Hong was exposed for conducting his hanjian business within these very walls, summoning his son in to brainwash him under his wife's instructions. If something like that had been allowed to occur, who knew what else might slip in under the radar? They were overcompensating, putting eyes on every corner. Not like it would do much.

Silas was leading Rosalind through the building. He knew the layout better than she did, given how rarely she dropped by. Phoebe, meanwhile, was waiting beyond the gates, barred from entering the compound without official qualifications. From the earful she had given the soldier out front, it was clear that she suspected they were refusing her entry on the basis of her family name.

"Annoying as the reporters are, they're correct," Silas was saying, giving Rosalind the rundown on intelligence he had been receiving. "A unit sighted Liwen in Manchuria."

"Merely a sighting?" Rosalind pressed. "Are they doing nothing?"

"They are not. But even if they did gear up to act, by the time they assembled, Lady Hong would be long on the move."

When it came to Orion, what they ought to do was send covert in, but the Nationalists had no faith in the utility of such a mission. After all, with the abilities Orion possessed, it could blip out what remaining covert agents they had, and covert was incredibly small these days.

"They need to send me." Rosalind plucked at the loose thread on her gloves. "I'm the only one who can do it."

Silas cast her a tense look as they walked, but he didn't argue otherwise. He was too spent to argue, and besides, he had already heard this time and time again while Rosalind was waiting out the Kuomintang's enforced "just lie low until we know what to do" period. Still, it wasn't as if Silas and Phoebe had anything better to suggest. Orion had always been their happy-go-lucky mollifying force. Without him, the two of them shot to the extremes of their mannerisms, which were usually unhelpful—not that Rosalind blamed them. Phoebe practically bounced off the walls at every minute; Silas dropped off the face of the earth for hours at a time while he buried himself in the search for Priest, a mission which he was still greatly dedicated to.

"I shall leave you here," Silas said now. "I believe it was General Yan who would speak to you."

They came to a halt before a long corridor, the linoleum so polished that Rosalind could see her reflection. Something about local headquarters reminded her of Seagreen Press. The newspaper's Shanghai branch had been shut down since Seagreen's head was hauled in for conspiracy toward national endangerment, as were a handful of employees whom Rosalind and Orion had found to be implicated in a chemical experimentation scheme. She doubted they would be punished accordingly though. The Kuomintang government wanted to put protective mechanisms in place but it wouldn't go too far and risk upsetting the Japanese Empire, given the ongoing tensions in the city. Covert had worked so hard to bring Seagreen to justice only for it to turn out that the blame lay with a hanjian traitor of their own nationality: Orion's mother.

"Is he our new handler?" Rosalind asked.

Silas shook his head. "General Yan is more administrative than covert. Jiemin is still handling our mission work."

Then where is he? Rosalind thought. Nerves squeezed at her stomach. If they had kept her waiting for weeks, the least Jiemin could do was organize a proper meeting when she was finally summoned.

"You will be nearby?" she asked Silas.

He was holding a bag of tapes to unwind and clear on the machines in headquarters. His primary method of communication with Priest, according to Phoebe's grumblings during those long afternoons when Silas would disappear and Phoebe would come to Rosalind for company. Though Rosalind doubted there was little that a faceless Communist assassin could do for their predicament, Silas had gotten stuck on Priest's heroic appearance at Warehouse 34, insisting that this could be a method of saving Orion.

"I'll be upstairs if you need me, sǎozi."

Rosalind frowned. "Why are you calling me that now too?"

Silas gave her a sheepish smile, already walking off. "Force of habit. I'm around Feiyi too much."

Which only meant they talked about her behind her back enough that the habit had passed on. At least they were gossiping respectfully.

Rosalind folded her arms, settling against the wall once Silas disappeared. There were multiple doors along the corridor, most of them closed to the sound of low murmurings and meetings ongoing inside. One, however, had been left ajar. Rosalind waited another few minutes. When it seemed no one was getting her anytime soon, she wandered over to that door, poking her nose through the gap. They probably wouldn't mind. If there was something confidential here, they would have posted a minimum of three soldiers.

"Hello?" she called tentatively.

Rosalind nudged the door open wider. It was just an empty meeting room, with a large table situated in the center and various boxes stacked in the corners. Sunlight streamed in through the window, casting a border around the bulletin boards on the walls and the blackboards wheeled in around the table. Every bit of the city's current affairs was plastered on the boards, newspaper clippings and waterlogged telegrams pinned side by side, photographs of politicians and red-pen scribbles on paper scraps occupying the spaces between.

One of the bulletin boards caught her eye, more sparsely decorated than the others. Rosalind sidestepped a box on the floor and made her way over. For a moment, she wasn't sure why that board had snagged her attention; then she got closer and recognized the face on a poster in the center.

Her curiosity dissipated. A surge of rage took over.

WANTED, the poster read. FOR CRIMES AGAINST THE STATE.

Rosalind snatched Dao Feng's poster at once and crumpled it in her fist, erasing his sketched face from sight. She hoped they found him and punished him. She hoped they never found him, that he slipped off into the night and disappeared forever. God—it was an unbearable thought in either direction.

She had *trusted* him. That was what continued to haunt her. It seemed that each time she thought someone was set for a permanent place in her life, that they cared enough to stay, they were secretly plotting otherwise. At least Orion had had no choice in being taken away. Dao Feng had chosen to leave her—had trained her and allowed her to lean on him as a handler, only to be lying the entire time.

Rosalind scrunched the poster even tighter. She had the unreasonable urge to bite down on the wad and rip it to pieces with her teeth.

"Lang Shalin."

Merde. With a jolt, Rosalind spun around, smoothly dropping the scrunched wad of paper and pretending she hadn't been the one to yank it off the bulletin. A young assistant had poked his head into the meeting room, frowning at her presence.

He pointed a thumb out into the corridor. "Ready when you are."

Rosalind nodded. Her blood was still boiling. She didn't say anything as she followed the assistant out of the room and back into the corridor, walking three doors down before he knocked on one of the offices and gestured for her to proceed.

"Thank you," she grumbled under her breath.

She turned the handle and entered the office. Immediately, there was so much sunlight streaming through the four-panel window here that she almost flinched, her eyes narrowing to brace against the onslaught. A man was standing by the window, looking directly into the golden daylight without trouble. General Yan, she had to guess, given he was wearing a Nationalist uniform and standing behind his mahogany desk.

He turned at the sound of her entrance. Gave a fatherly smile and leaned over his desk to extend his hand.

"A pleasure to meet you properly, Lang Shalin. You will have to forgive the circumstances it is occurring under."

Rosalind stayed silent as she leaned forward to shake. Her first instinct was to sweep her memory for whether she might have met General Yan previously at the Scarlet house, but then, why bother? It wasn't as though her past would be helpful here. Not that it had ever been helpful for anything except coloring this idea of her that everyone seemed to have.

"Where is Jiemin?" Rosalind asked. "I would have thought he would be the one to meet with me."

"He isn't in the city at the moment," General Yan replied. He sank into his seat, then gestured for Rosalind to follow suit. She didn't want to. She wanted this meeting to go fast, and then she wanted to act, to stop sitting around waiting for the danger to pass.

But since Rosalind wasn't trying to stir trouble at headquarters, she took a seat. Her hands fidgeted in her lap, folding and unfolding one on top of the other. "Fair enough." Her eyes dropped to the papers on General Yan's desk. What did that say? *Retirement account?* "I hate to busy your schedule further with covert's tasks. I imagine you have plenty of other important business to conduct. While we are at war."

General Yan didn't respond to her half-hearted jibe. He leaned back in his chair, watching her carefully, the room falling silent save for the ticking of the clock on the desk and the sniffle from the assistant waiting by the open door. "We heard from your father yesterday."

Rosalind jerked to attention, her spine turning stiff. "I beg your pardon?"

"He was in contact to express approval for our intended next steps for you. And to communicate that if you need access to your bank accounts, you must return home and obtain his signatures. He says you have not been responding to his letters."

Rosalind wasn't comprehending. Bank accounts? Her father's signatures? What did any of this have to do with her next mission . . . ?

Her eyes fell to the papers again. It occurred to her like a slap across the face, a physical sting that turned her vision completely white for a flash.

"You're decommissioning me."

General Yan said nothing to protest her conclusion. He shuffled through the papers as Rosalind blinked rapidly to recover, her hands gripping the underside of her chair with such sudden intensity that she felt her nails strain on the verge of snapping.

"How can you—"

"This is not an easy decision," General Yan interrupted. "You have done wonderful work, Lang Shalin. But Fortune cannot operate again when the whole country knows about you. The enemies you have made over the course of your career would track your every movement. You cannot go undercover, nor blend in."

"I am an *assassin,*" Rosalind protested. "I don't need to go undercover so long as I am not assigned another long-term operation like Seagreen!"

"And what will you do when you are recognized before you can set your poison? When you are photographed while tailing a target? At every second you would be risking the exposure of the entire covert branch. We must protect our integrity first and foremost."

Rosalind's throat was closing. Her circulation hit a block, her blood stuttering to a halt. Maybe this was it. Her immortality was catching up with her, all the stolen time that had been racking up from the day she was supposed to die. In seconds, she would drop dead on the carpet of this office, her purpose and her life taken with one fell swoop.

"You can't," she said quietly. Somehow, her voice stayed even. "You can't do this to me. What am I supposed to do?"

She was relying on Nationalist intelligence merely to know where Orion's mother was taking him every few days, yanking him along like some plaything of a weapon. Without that, she was utterly clueless.

General Yan slid the stack of papers toward her. "Live a good life. We are paying for your retirement fund, of course. I know covert operated in cash, but we prefer to set up monthly wires, so you're certainly going to need to ask your father . . ."

Though the general continued talking, Rosalind only heard a tinny whine in her ears. She had been exposed beyond her control, and yet they decided to punish her by throwing her away, brushing her tidily under the rug as if she had never existed.

God. She supposed she had always known that this was their method of operation, hadn't she? Get into a little trouble, and the Nationalists would leave her to fend for herself. Do anything that did not fit with their objectives, and she was not needed here anymore.

General Yan had stopped talking. He seemed to be waiting for some sort of response. Rosalind didn't even know what he had last said.

"What about the rest of the covert branch that you are not protecting?" she asked. "What about Hong Liwen, out in the countryside, at the mercy of hanjian?"

Slowly, General Yan set his elbows on his desk. His inspection landed as a heavy sensation, as if he were picking her apart by mere glance and could read her every selfish wish in those words.

Go after him, she wanted to yell. *What good are you for if not to help us?*

"Shalin, you *are* exempt from your previous mission." He laced his fingers together. There was deep concern in the set of his eyes. "He was only your false spouse, after all. I know you have a deep sense of duty, which is appreciated, but there is no need to take the outcome of High Tide so seriously."

For a moment, Rosalind did not understand General Yan's meaning. How could she not take the outcome of High Tide seriously? That mission had consumed her life in the previous few months. That mission had had the safety of the city riding upon it.

Then Rosalind almost laughed, because she couldn't believe his line of argument was that she ought not to care so much because he had only been her false spouse. Maybe the marriage had been fake, but his devotion to her was real. She faulted others for abandoning her, yet it seemed that was all she was capable of doing too. Turning away. Running. Fleeing.

"I reject that," Rosalind whispered. Her voice shook, barely audible to herself, never mind to General Yan. "He loved me, and I left him."

General Yan gave a sigh on the other side of the desk, reaching the end of his patience with her. Rosalind, meanwhile, tried to calm the trembling in her chest. There was surely something to be done. Dao Feng had once told her that if she set her mind on something, no one could force her to back down. If they wanted to retire her, she had to fight it.

"Is there anything else, Lang Shalin?" General Yan asked. "If not, administration can process you. You are also welcome to come back tomorrow instead. I imagine that might be kinder on your health."

Say something. Now. Fight. Her throat burned with frustration. Her fingers itched with the discomfort of her skin growing too tight for her body. "I—"

She couldn't do it.

Instead of arguing her case, Rosalind Lang shot to her feet and walked out of the room, fighting to keep back the prickle of tears.

3

She loathed everything.

The Nationalists, in their offices. The cold weather, temperature plummeting with the sun setting outside. The war, permeating the radio station running in the background.

The imperialists, just for existing within her field of view.

Those matters were not loathed in equal amounts, of course, but she was peeved enough to be silently fuming about everything at once anyway. She stabbed a fork into her slice of cake, biting down on the icing so angrily that her teeth clacked. Meanwhile, Silas returned to the booth, carrying sugar packets for Phoebe's coffee.

They had driven to a café near the Bund, one that was known for having a live jazz band. Rosalind supposed it had been a nice effort on Silas and Phoebe's part to let her decompress at another location before taking her back to her apartment—but when she listened to the trombone, all she could think was that the musician had definitely been fired from a dance hall prior to this job for his lack of rhythm.

Rosalind chewed on her cake. The little bell above the glass doors kept jangling every few minutes, allowing a new blast of cold air to blow through. Red light beamed brightly from the exterior signage, neon wiring in English declaring the café to have the best dessert across all of Shanghai.

"Those are so unhealthy," Silas whispered as he slid along the seat, passing Phoebe her sugar packets.

"Why did you get them for me, then?" Phoebe returned, dropping to a hush too. She ripped one of the packets open and tipped every crystal granule into her drink.

"Don't blame me for your sugar cravings. I'm only warn—"

"You really ought to refuse to get the packets if you are only going to chide me—"

"*Why* are the two of you whispering?" Rosalind interrupted at normal volume.

Silas and Phoebe both froze, twin looks of guilt flashing across their faces as if they had been caught with their hands down each other's shirts. Genuine amusement almost made Rosalind smile, but her next instinct was to look beside her to catch Orion's eye, and then it hit her all over again that he wasn't here.

"You know," Rosalind said before Silas or Phoebe could recover, grabbing her coat in the seat next to her, "upon further consideration, I think some air would clear my head."

"I will come with you," Phoebe said immediately.

"No, please." Rosalind pulled her coat on. "I need some silence to think through this."

"We're here to help you, though," Silas protested. "Three heads are better than one."

By all means, he was correct. Rosalind should have taken her coat off, sat back down, and put her raw, vulnerable thoughts onto the table so that Phoebe and Silas could help her pick them apart. Then she could find their best way forward, be a good friend.

But she was clearly made to be an actively derailing train wreck instead, because Rosalind only gave them a tight smile and said, "No, I mean it. I need to take a walk. Stay here and finish your drinks. I'll be perfectly fine."

She was through the doors before they could argue further.

What was the point of hovering around longer, a sore-sighted tack-on to their two-person outing? If Rosalind had survived this many years with only herself to lean on, then clearly she was doing something right.

The streetlamps droned a weak noise overhead, each gas-lit bulb lighting her way as she picked up her pace. She felt better as soon as she was outside, away from Phoebe's and Silas's kind, concerned eyes. Even as she tugged her coat closer to her chest, combating the cold that drew her breath visible in the January winter, she preferred the bite of the wind over the warm café with its happy laughter.

Rosalind turned off Nanjing Road. Her feet took her deeper into the city, away from the boardwalk and the ocean breeze. She weaved aimlessly into the lesser-used routes, where the shops had started to close and only one or two rickshaws ran by, walking on and on for no other reason than to have something to do while the night drew long.

When she passed the first man in the dark jacket, she didn't think much of it.

When she passed a second man who was dressed the same a mere minute later, with a tattoo on the side of his neck, she started to think that maybe something wasn't quite right.

Rosalind didn't bother disguising her suspicion. She whirled around immediately, tracking where the second man was going. At the same time, the man had turned to look over his shoulder.

Their eyes met.

Now there was no doubt: she had caught on to him, and he had registered her awareness.

In an instant, he raised his arm to give a signal. Shadows stirred from the alleys, revealing three other men emerging from standby. This was a one-way road. A church sat to her left. An instruments shop on the right. Both of those buildings were closed for the night, and none of the residential apartments at their sides looked easily accessible. Somehow, an ambush had organized around her. All her exits were blocked off.

Rosalind made a slow circle on her heel, observing the numbers.

"If anyone is hiding under a car," she said, "now is probably a good time to roll out." Her voice rang clear. Returned with a slight echo, bouncing into the alleys and ricocheting stronger than she had sent it out.

"Apologies for our manners, Lady Fortune." That came from one of the men in the shadows. There was a crowbar in his hands. "We might have invited you over for tea if we had known your identity earlier. But since this is all we're working with on short notice, a street encounter will have to suffice."

The two men she had passed were reaching into their jackets. Their hands emerged again with pistols, fitted with silencers on the barrel. Her mind scrambled to place their faces, but she was drawing a blank.

"What do you want?" she asked dryly. "A ransom?"

The fourth man, who stood farthest away, was holding a large knife. And it was he who lurched toward her the soonest, prompted by that mere question to screech, "Revenge. For my brother."

Ah. So these were the repercussions of her former targets, come to even the scales after years of Fortune's dirty work being hidden behind a persona. She wondered what his brother had done to have landed on the lists passed to Fortune. Whether he had been targeted as a criminal merchant or had been punished for selling out to the imperialists.

Rosalind sidestepped the quick slash. Without really thinking, she pulled one of her hairpins free, sliding the metal across the backs of her fingers for a beat to secure her grip, then dragging the sharp tip across the man's face as he reared back. He grunted.

Though he tried to lunge at her again, the others were moving too. Gunshots sounded into the night. Once, twice, three times. Two hit the pavement, spraying up grit and gravel. The third landed in her shoulder.

Tā mā de, she thought. *I am* so *sick of being shot at—*

The man who received her poisoned hairpin dropped to the ground, his limbs twitching. Rosalind bent down and stole his knife, clutching her shoulder with her free hand. For a moment, she was consumed by mind-numbing pain, her world turning white. She took a deep breath. Staggered forward. Moments later, she could physically feel her muscle moving back into place, stitching itself together and pushing the foul object out. As soon as she removed her hand from her shoulder, there was a sharp *clink* on the pavement. The bullet rolled to a stop by one of the drain coverings.

"Why would you be so *foolish*"—Rosalind straightened up, her jaw aching from how tightly she had clenched it—"as to go after an immortal assassin?"

The man with the crowbar ran forward; Rosalind threw the knife she had retrieved. It missed—rather awfully too—but the flying blade had only been a distraction. She was testing the direction of the wind, watching the knife lift with the breeze and land with a lackluster thud on the ground. Before the man could bring his crowbar down and pummel more injuries into her, Rosalind grabbed a small bag of powder strapped to her leg and shook it vigorously into the wind, particles flying right into her attacker's face. He gasped. Then gasped again, breathing suddenly short.

Another gunshot rang loud. Grazed her arm.

God, that hurt.

The two men with pistols had kept their distance. It messed with their aim, surely, because otherwise Rosalind couldn't comprehend why they wouldn't shoot for the head and kill her at once, blow her brain into chunks and prevent any chance of her healing. Their two fellow revenge seekers were dead already.

"Stop," Rosalind said plainly. Her arm hurt. Her body hurt. "You won't win this."

One of the men opened fire again. This one—it was aimed right into her chest. Sank to where her heart was, already throbbing and raw and red. She had spent these past few weeks locked inside, told to sit in wait while people who hated her circled like vultures, and what was the *point?* Her heart had been hurting long before these bullets. It would keep on hurting even after this bullet was pushed out too, landing as emphatically as a teardrop shaped like death.

Rosalind touched her chest. Softly traced her finger along the hole that had been torn into her qipao, the fabric singed and soaked in blood. Underneath, the wound pulsated. Ran vivid with red, coloring her clothing.

"Fine," she said. She reached into her pocket. Slowly, she started to walk toward the two remaining men, her posture changing. "For old times' sake, since you refuse to leave me alone."

She took her coin out.

A second passed. Enough time for her attackers to register what the object was. When her thumb caught the edge of the coin, sending it up in the air, the man on the left turned and ran. The one on the right, however, remained a beat longer.

Before the coin could finish tumbling through the air, he finally pivoted on his heel, abandoning his mission.

It was too late now.

Now Rosalind wanted blood.

She gave chase, barely bothering to glance down and see what the coin had landed on. There was a voice in her head that told her to stop, to pull back before it was too late and she regressed into that darkness she thought she had left behind. But even self-awareness couldn't stop her from yanking the man's collar when she caught up, wasn't quite loud enough to pull her arm back when she wrenched him to a stop and sank her pin into his neck.

He wheezed for breath. She pulled the pin out.

And the man collapsed.

Rosalind felt a sob claw at her throat. Loathing moved like sludge through her body, clogging up her veins as a poison of her own making. She was supposed to be better than this. She was supposed to have a greater hand on this city, greater than senseless anger in its alleys.

Enough, the voice in her head said. It sounded terribly familiar. Terribly like Dao Feng. *Take a deep breath. This isn't you.*

Shortly after becoming Fortune, Rosalind had been an uncontrollable explosive, as destructive as the one that had shaken through Zhabei and taken her cousin. She had wanted to make amends by causing equal damage, desperate to answer for what she had done, to even the scales in the other direction. Only she was inexperienced back then, weak for an assassin and green when it came to making hits. It was Dao Feng who got the brunt of her rage, an unflinching shock absorber for her tantrums, the hand pushing her on a learning curve and away from being terrible for no reason.

But Dao Feng wasn't here anymore. And after these years of work under her belt, Rosalind could be horrifically terrible if she wanted. If she went out to cause true damage, who would stop her? Who in this vast, vast city had the power to tell her otherwise?

Enough.

With a whole-body tremor, Rosalind tore out of her thoughts. Though there had been no one around to bear witness to the last few minutes, it wouldn't be long before a witness showed up. At once, she hastened to pull the body off the road, dragging him into an alley.

Rosalind Lang walked away from the scene. Looked around the new road she had found herself on, flexing her fingers at her sides. The splotch of blood on her hand rubbed off easily. When she paused at the side of the pavement, her arms stilled in that position: one hand tucked into the inner curve of her elbow, the pad of her palm pressed to the faintest hint of blue where her veins ran.

The former White Flower labs loomed up ahead. Lourens's old labs, where she had been brought back to life.

Dear God—of everywhere in Shanghai, how had she ended up here?

She crept closer to the building. Its windows had been boarded up and the rooms inside abandoned. After the revolution, most facilities in the city that had been under White Flower control were either overtaken by the Nationalists or left in a state similar to this, stuck between ownership debates. There was too much paperwork involved when it came to taking property from a defunct gang that had ruled on connections and intimidation.

"Damn you," she said quietly. She approached the glass, plastered over with newspapers. Much of it looked new, as if someone was coming by and touching up the concealment, putting on a layer every so often in case some rascal walked by and decided to shatter the windows.

Her blood burned. Not in anger anymore but in memory. The feeling of being remade prodded at the crook of her elbow, reminded her how easily she had almost slipped from the world before she was frozen in her final state.

Rosalind exhaled. Her vision fogged, clouded by the warm puff of air. When it cleared, her eyes latched on to the print of the news articles plastered at her eye level, lit by the streetlamp three paces away.

THE WESTERNERS ARE NOT OUR ENEMY!

WE MUST COME TOGETHER AGAINST THE JAPANESE EMPIRE!

Classic propaganda. With each year that passed and each sea change in foreign grappling, the national government couldn't settle on who their enemies were, and neither could the city papers.

Most of the shop fronts along this road had posters plastered on their exteriors, asking the Chinese to befriend Westerners in their fight against the Japanese. Even in the dark, Rosalind could read the bold, red characters printed in attack. Probably the same person or company had put them all up. The next road might have a different sentiment. Then a third opinion one block over.

Rosalind stopped. Looked back to the news article, scanning farther down. It wasn't the content itself that had caught her attention, per se. They were mostly similar in sentiment, urging action against Japanese aggression, attributing atrocities and attacks to possible sources.

Her attention had snagged on the sheer volume of headlines concerned with this matter. Civilian panic was growing. Rosalind was out of touch with the sentiments of ordinary people when she operated so closely to the government. She hadn't realized that it was this far-reaching.

An oversight on her part. And an opportunity.

"'*What we need,*'" she read aloud from one of the papers plastered to the windows, "'*is a way to build morale. We as the Chinese must dust ourselves off and stand up straight or else we will end this decade conquered.*'"

The Nationalists wouldn't send her after Orion because her identity had been exposed and she was too recognizable as Fortune. Fine.

Rosalind would show them just how recognizable Lady Fortune was.

4

Idle work was the strangest part of being between assignments, and each time she sat down to oversee the front desk of a liaison station, Celia Lang wondered why they couldn't just hire someone on the outside for this.

She supposed it would be rather easy to torture a top-secret location out of a regular civilian, though. Maybe they could lie about what function the building served. This liaison station pretended to be a specialized clinic on the outside; they only needed to keep quiet about covert work in front of an outsourced employee.

Celia sighed. But it wasn't like she had anything better to do between assignments anyway. Glorified secretary, it was.

She reached for a pen. Twiddled it around. The Party higher-ups who worked in the offices here had given her a white coat to wear over her dress, ensuring she looked the part to anyone who wandered up the stairs accidentally. There weren't many, of course—most who came into the liaison station knew what they were looking for and gave the code word when they checked in.

It had been a slow day. Celia sighed, then stood up.

The liaison station was located in the north of Shanghai, on a street that saw plenty of foot traffic. The kitchen was incredibly loud when she wandered over, and she spent a perplexed few seconds searching for the reason before spotting the window that had been left ajar. She closed the window, muffling the street vendors and screaming children. It was almost five o'clock. Prime time for bedlam while orange light started to burn onto the sidewalks.

Celia put the kettle on. Fetched a tin of tea leaves, hovering over the table while the water boiled.

This had been her daytime routine for a number of weeks now. Their map-making task in Taicang had finished. The photography shop had closed down under the guise of going out of business. Millie and Audrey were put into new assignments, ones that required true covert work after they had had their training run. Oliver, meanwhile, was between assignments like Celia, since they came as a matching task pair. Nonetheless, Celia hadn't seen him since they said goodbye after the debrief, after they turned in their maps and their reports. If the Communists didn't need him on active work, he went under, and according to the grapevine, at present he was focusing all his attention on being Priest's handler. He had as much as admitted to the role last October, even though he had refused to offer Celia any concrete details.

Celia poured the water into her tea. When she set the kettle back onto the stove, she dropped it too hard, making a loud metallic bang. *Damn it, Oliver.* It was so typical of him to go off the grid without a single note. As if everyone else in the world was secondary to the mission and he got to decide when they were pulled back into his life.

Celia was so focused on bringing her tea out of the kitchen that she didn't glance up when she spotted someone in her periphery, standing before the front desk. The first matter at hand was setting the tea down.

"Hello," she greeted. "Give me one moment—"

The cup made contact with the desk. She turned her attention to the visitor.

And immediately spilled her tea.

"Sweetheart," Oliver said, "you don't have to get so flustered to see me."

Celia scrambled to reach for a towelette, tossing it onto the spill before it could creep any larger and stain the papers. Half the cup had splashed before she righted it. Thankfully, most of the official files were off to the side.

Merde. It was as if she had summoned him by thought. Then again, she was thinking about him constantly with steam blowing out of her ears, so by mere statistics, it made sense that one of the instances would coincide with him actually showing up.

"I was startled," she insisted. She switched to French, afraid that the higher-ups could hear her inside their offices. "What are you doing here? I don't hear from you for weeks, and then you appear out of the blue? Bah, what's wrong with you?"

Oliver tilted his head. His hair had gotten longer at the ends, curling around his ears in a manner that made him resemble his younger brother to a disturbing degree. It wasn't only the hair—he was dressed in a Western suit, too. Celia's first instinct was to suppose that he had just come from trying to blend in somewhere, a costume fit for a social call in the Concessions. But Oliver Hong had been born the eldest son to an elite family. This was how he had looked growing up. She was only accustomed to what she perceived as his usual manner of dress because they were often undercover somewhere rural.

"You sound angry," Oliver remarked plainly. His French in return was equally quick, the easy transition typical of someone who had grown up in Paris. When Shanghai's parents sent their children overseas, this was exactly what they hoped for, every elite circle desperate to endure foreign intrusion by competing against each other on how many languages their offspring could speak.

"You know, Oliver"—Celia slapped her hand down, leaning forward—"it is *really* hard to provoke my temper, but somehow you are incredibly good at it."

The faintest hint of a smile tugged at his lips. "I have missed you quite fiercely."

Celia's heart skipped a beat. Her damn mission partner was impossible. He had declared his love for her, found no good time to talk about it, and then disappeared off the face of this earth. It wasn't as if *she* could have called him. He was the one who went quiet while she was the one located at the same place day in and day out, sitting at this front desk, twiddling her thumbs.

"That's too bad." With a harrumph, she dropped into her chair, picking up a random stack of papers and shuffling them. "I haven't missed you in the slightest."

Lies. A whole mouthful of lies.

Oliver furrowed his brow. "Celia," he said.

She plopped the papers down. "Do you think people should simply languish around waiting to be contacted? Is that how you view your colleagues?"

"Celia," he tried again. "I don't understand. I always go dark between assignments. My risk of being tracked in this city is sky-high."

"Yes—well . . ." *That was before whatever this is between us turned so perplexing.*

She could hardly say that aloud. Maybe Oliver knew what she was thinking when she let the silence draw long.

He straightened his sleeves. There was a briefcase dangling from his other hand, which she hadn't noticed before.

"Don't be angry, sweetheart," Oliver said. "Please?"

Celia thinned her lips. Glared up at him. The expression didn't hold for more than a few seconds before she was relenting, her eyes turning soft.

"Okay. Why are you here?"

"I am very glad you asked." He lifted his briefcase onto the desk. "We have a new task."

Celia hadn't expected this. Usually they were called in together to be posted to their next mission. "And they told you first?"

"They wanted me to bring you the details. They're probably trying to lessen the likelihood of you declining the assignment."

This was starting to sound concerning. "And why would I decline?"

"To be frank, I think they're using you." Oliver opened the briefcase and slid out a large poster. Though it was a sketch, she recognized the subject immediately. Rosalind. "Here is our assignment."

"My sister?" Celia blinked. She tugged a corner of the poster, reading the words.

LADY FORTUNE'S NATIONAL TOUR

This was mind-boggling. First the Nationalists sat her in the corner on time-out. Then they used her for their propaganda.

"Your sister," Oliver confirmed. She didn't think she was imagining the waver in his voice. His own brother was off somewhere outside the city, memory erased and being used as a weapon.

"There's no way she agreed to a national tour. Rosalind cannot stand politics."

Oliver peered over the desk. He plucked up a pen, then flicked off its lid. "Actually, assuming our information is correct, she volunteered. Did you know the Kuomintang were about to decommission her? They leaked her identity to the press when Orion's news went wide and took that excuse to brush her out of the ranks before she caused too much trouble."

Meet the infamous figure you have only heard stories about, the description on the poster read.

"Then what is *this?*" Celia asked, still lagging behind on the information. She hadn't seen Rosalind in two weeks; it was too hard coming in and out of her apartment during the dead of night when the reporters weren't watching. The papers were already shouting that Rosalind Lang was alive and had survived the collapse of gangster rule. The last thing Celia needed was the reporters recognizing her, too, and comparing the sighting to old Scarlet photos, when she was still using Kathleen's name, because if the columns started declaring that Kathleen Lang was alive too, then that was going to start messing with *her* job.

"It's a tactic," Oliver answered. He circled the touring locations. "Your sister gave them something they couldn't resist. Now they have a prime narrative. A Chinese assassin who has been wiping out imperialists and traitors. Builds wartime morale."

Celia crossed her arms. Stared at her sister's sketched portrait.

"We are not even at war yet," she muttered. "Foreign war, that is. I don't think the civil war would get boosted much by this narrative."

Besides, Rosalind had no pride in her work. She didn't see it as a glorious duty. These few years, all she had been doing was punishing herself. So by volunteering for a national tour . . .

It clicked.

"Oh," Celia said. She looked up. Oliver was already watching her. "She's using this opportunity to go after Orion."

He nodded. "And lucky us: while the Nationalists have abandoned Orion, our central command wants him secured. Which means our mission is to follow Rosalind until she gets him, then snatch him away."

Christ. Celia really did have half a mind to say no.

"Surely there are less risky maneuvers?" Her arms tightened around herself. "Didn't we already secure the man from the hospital? The one who received the first successful run of your mother's final invention?"

She had heard about all this secondhand, having been out of the city when the events were occurring. It was Alisa who had taken the man to safety after a brainwashed Orion struck him with the concoction, though she had dropped off the grid afterward. That final man was the only experiment who lived. Everyone else prior hadn't survived, left out on the streets and labeled a victim of the chemical killings before the city realized this was no ordinary serial killer but rather a callous scientific endeavor. Every vial of the successful enhancement concoction created thereafter had been destroyed under Rosalind's hand—except for one that Alisa Montagova was hiding, somewhere in the countryside.

"You haven't heard yet?" Oliver set the pen down. "He was assassinated shortly after we took him. Poisoned. Nationalist hit, obviously."

Celia winced. "Who'd they send with Fortune out of commission?"

"Could be anyone. Plenty of poison assassins in this city."

The Nationalists would rather wipe out assets than let the Communists land them. The Communists were willing to go after assets to the ends of the earth if it meant an advantage on the battlefield. And all the while, their foreign enemies crept farther and farther into the country.

"This is so absurd," Celia muttered, eyeing the poster of Rosalind again. "Do they suppose we have some sort of advantage? That we are likelier to contain our own siblings?"

In the past it was difficult for their side's spies to keep tabs on Fortune because she was an undercover entity. Even if they knew she was Rosalind Lang, the rest of the city assumed Rosalind dead, which meant information traveled about Fortune, not Rosalind. With her identity exposed, there was no escaping the onslaught of information. There was also no chance for Celia to squirm out of this, because she used to claim that Rosalind had disappeared and would refuse communication, but now . . . well, her superiors would know when she was lying.

"I'm sure your sister is less likely to hurt you if we end up in conflict," Oliver answered, ever blunt. "Orion, on the other hand—he was quite happy to throw a punch in my direction *before* our mother wiped his mind."

"Stop that." Celia untangled her arms, setting her hands on her hips instead. "Oliver . . . you cannot possibly be okay with this."

She could stomach merely following after Rosalind. Depending on how their cards fell, it might even be nice to watch out for her and protect her, not that she needed it. The matter became something else entirely when their next step was to capture Oliver's brother for whatever intentions their central command had.

For a moment, Oliver didn't answer, his gaze leveled on the poster. When he looked up, his expression was inscrutable.

"It doesn't matter," he said. "They want us to leave as soon as possible so that we reach her second tour stop before she does. Are you ready? I have the car waiting downstairs."

She wished he would talk to her. Oliver had operated for so long understanding secrecy to be the line between life and death that she wondered if he even knew that he was *allowed* to talk to her.

"I need to pack a bag," Celia said. "Drive me to the safe house first?"

"Of course."

Celia put up a BACK IN TEN MINUTES! sign. She would not be back anytime soon, but these liaison stations were used to agents swapping out frequently. Someone else would be by in the next hour.

"What is it that they say about siblings?" she grumbled, waving Oliver along and gesturing that they could hurry now. The sun was going down soon. Night falling in cover for operatives to fetch their battle gear and return to the intelligence field. "We can't pick the ones we need to chase across province lines."

5

To nobody's surprise, Phoebe Hong was not a big fan of her house these days.

Voices echoed too loudly in the hallways. The bedrooms had started developing a rancid sort of smell no matter how much she opened the windows and aired out the space, as if the carpets were sensing their lack of use and had started to languish on their own. She used to love the way the chandeliers twinkled at full brightness. One of her earliest memories, long before leaving for London, was an occasion when her mother had put her in a sparkly dress, and she had twirled and twirled under the lights, spinning so fast that everything blended into glitter and blots.

Now the hallways were so empty that Phoebe was afraid to go to the kitchen at night for a glass of water, reverting to a child again fearing some monster in the dark corners. So many bedrooms and yet only two were being used.

It was a matter of time before someone came to collect the house as an asset. Her father had been imprisoned. Her mother was a national traitor. Her eldest brother publicly worked for the enemy faction, and her second brother wasn't even himself anymore. Sooner or later, the government would find an excuse to seize everything under the Hong name for national security. She supposed she and Ah Dou had to enjoy what limited time they had left in this vast space.

"I'm heading out!" she called.

The elderly housekeeper was dusting a vase in the foyer. He dusted a lot these days—possibly because there was nothing better to do. Phoebe had her meals outside the house, went about most of the day prancing around this big city and returning only when night fell and she needed a place to sleep. She almost felt guilty sometimes, abandoning Ah Dou to suffer this silence alone. Even the last maid had left. What was once a whole household staff had dwindled to one white-bearded man keeping up a constant stream of tea from the kitchen.

"Don't return too late," Ah Dou called kindly.

Phoebe shut the door after herself. Silas was waiting in the driveway, having parked his car and clambered out in the time she had taken to get ready. His hands were in his trouser pockets. His whole frame was slouched, his ankles crossed, leaning on the front hood and staring off into space.

"Have you been waiting long?"

Silas jumped at the sound of her voice, his eyes snapping in her direction. It was odd to see him distracted. Attentiveness was one of Silas's most discerning traits.

"Not long," he said.

The pinkness of his nose indicated otherwise. Phoebe stopped in front of him, then reached up to flick his cheek. "You had the warmth of your car, and you chose to stand outside? It's freezing."

Temperatures had been plummeting these last few days. Usually, the garden would smell fragrant, its rosebushes and magnolia trees waving with the wind and greeting every visitor coming up the driveway. Today there was only the scent of *cold* and the threat of snow that could shake out from the skies at any moment.

Silas smiled weakly. He pushed off the hood, then started toward the driver's seat. "I needed the air. Ready?"

Phoebe opened the passenger seat. Grimaced. There was a bag of tape recordings already hogging the seat.

"What's on your mind?" she asked.

"You mean other than Rosalind sending herself on tour so she can chase after Orion alone? Only the usual."

It was still strange to hear her referred to as Rosalind in English. For the entire time they had known her, Orion's pretend wife had been named Janie Mead. Then the arrests had happened at Seagreen, and while their government hauled in the imperialists contributing to a conspiracy that killed numerous people on Chinese territory, Orion had been taken in as the prime perpetrator, and Rosalind had been exposed for her true identity.

"I don't know. You look a little more intense than usual."

Phoebe lugged the bag into the back. She recognized where these tapes had come from. She was careful to keep her face neutral.

"Do I?" Silas was already pressing the ignition, his voice sounding distracted too. "I am scheming. I don't like Rosalind taking on the entire responsibility of doing something."

They had had this conversation multiple times since the news of Rosalind's tour went public, but they weren't getting anywhere with it. This flailing, helpless feeling between them had been even worse back when Rosalind was stuck under house arrest, because Phoebe and Silas *weren't,* and they should have had plenty of schemes up their sleeves. But what could they really do except mull around and complain? This wasn't a fun jaunt to sneak into a bar. This wasn't Silas and Phoebe plotting as children to pull a fast one over Orion's head when the three of them lived in London.

If anyone played their hand wrong here, this was international war.

Phoebe slid into the passenger seat. It would be a short drive into the International Settlement, where they were going to see a film. On the outside, they were making an ordinary excursion, one that Silas had suggested so they could get their mind off Orion's predicament. In reality, Phoebe knew that Silas was dropping off a correspondence in his work as Shepherd: a triple-agent publicly associated with the Nationalists, pretending to defect to the Communists while reporting back with the intelligence he acquired. He hadn't told her much about his continued work trying to draw Priest out into the open. But there was a letter addressed to Priest waiting in his pocket.

Phoebe knew this because *she* was Priest.

"There is something I should tell you," Silas said. He pulled onto the road. "We got confirmation today that your brother Oliver is Priest's handler."

The car drove over a bump. Phoebe stilled. It was as if he had heard the direction of her thoughts, but she knew Silas didn't suspect her. He was only telling her this information out of concern over her connection to Oliver.

If he suspected her for so much as a second, they wouldn't be having this conversation at all. Silas had grown obsessed with trying to find Priest in these few months. Before everything went so wrong, it had only been his assignment. His mission—an aspect of his work life that he could set aside on his off hours.

"Why are you telling me this?" Phoebe asked, a hint of animosity entering her voice. Perhaps they had discussed over and over again their inability to save Orion, but they had disagreed even more over Silas's foolish plan to combat their stasis. After his best friend and her brother got yanked away, Silas had decided he had one course toward a solution: Priest. Now there was no waking minute where he wasn't hunting this mysterious assassin down. She hated it. Not because he was anywhere close to discovering her secret identity, but because Silas didn't feel like Silas these days.

He cast a glance over. Silas's expression remained composed even while Phoebe bristled, though his attention promptly returned to the road when a light changed red ahead.

"I know you don't believe me, but Priest must have some stock in this. Remember what Rosalind said?"

"Yes," Phoebe huffed, "I remember."

Priest had shown up to the final conflict at Warehouse 34. Had taken out all the soldiers there and left Rosalind and Orion alone, even though she was a Communist and they were Nationalists. Instead of making important hits for the civil war, she had disappeared into the shadows.

To Silas, unveiling Priest would mean finding and recruiting some powerful entity who could single-handedly save Orion.

If only he would realize it wasn't that easy. That sometimes mysterious assassins kept their identities hidden under ten layers of security not because they were all-powerful fighters but because they had signed on to the opposite side only to protect older brothers who were intent on working the covert branch for the Nationalists.

Now Phoebe had lost Orion anyway.

Some protective little-sister assassin she was.

"I don't understand what your resistance to this is," Silas said. The light turned green. He pressed forward on the accelerator.

"My resistance"—Phoebe heard the clatter of the tapes in the back seat falling over one another—"is that you are putting far too much trust into an operative you know *nothing* about. An enemy who has every reason to kill you if you slip up and your true loyalties come out."

"She won't," Silas replied in an instant.

Phoebe's temper flared. *She* knew that she and Priest were one and the same. But Silas *didn't*. What was it about Priest that deserved his unwavering belief like this?

"I just remembered that I need to get fitted for a dress," Phoebe said abruptly. "Can you let me off?"

Silas blinked. "What?"

"Right here," she insisted with a flounce. "The shop is the next street over, but it's a one-way road. So you can let me off here."

The wonderful thing about Silas was that he rarely argued. Or maybe that was a terrible thing, because he was so quick to agree with anything Phoebe said that she never quite knew what was going on in that head of his.

The only thing she couldn't seem to get through to him about was Priest.

Silas stopped the car, pulling close to the pavement. Phoebe inhaled tightly. They sat for a moment, the car's engine fading quiet.

"I didn't bring up Oliver to upset you," Silas said. He had misattributed her reaction. "It is only that if we can use whatever we have available at our disposal, we can help Orion."

Pit one brother against the other. The little sister caught in the middle. That had been the last four years of her life, and Phoebe was endlessly tired of her own family being the epicenter of a war.

"It's not . . ." She turned to Silas, trailing off with frustration. His eyes were wide, deep brown behind those thick glasses, a barrier keeping back the swirl of unrest that she might have been imagining. Without thinking, she reached to push his glasses up, sliding them along his nose in a familiar move.

Her hand lingered. She wasn't sure what she was doing. A weightlessness had started in her chest.

Phoebe made a fist, yanking her arm away. "I will call you," she said. "Thank you for driving me."

Before Silas could say a word in protest or agreement, she got out of the car and hurried off.

The orphanage located at a small church in the French Concession had become Dao Feng's hideout. By virtue of that fact, it had also become his communications base, and since Dao Feng had been assigned as her second handler since his official defection to the

Communists, that was where Phoebe went to find him. Oliver had said goodbye to her a few days ago to begin a new assignment. He was handing over all duties to Dao Feng.

Phoebe's shoes clacked loudly over the path, coming around the church building into the backyard. "We need to boot him out."

Dao Feng looked up from where he was sitting, a straw hat on his head and gloves on his hands. He had a block of wood squeezed between his legs, working with a little penknife to shave out what appeared to be a carving of a dragon. So far it was looking more like a garden-variety lizard.

Phoebe paused, her brow furrowing before Dao Feng could answer. "And are you not cold?"

"I have braved elements much fiercer than the cold," Dao Feng replied. His shirtsleeves were cuffed at his upper arms. He looked nothing like a high-ranking covert agent and more like an aging film star on a retreat at his holiday house. "Who are we booting out?"

"You *know* who." Phoebe's skirts puffed as she stomped her foot. "Silas. Wu Xielian. Shepherd. *Magician.*"

Throwing out his second code name seemed to scare the trees. They sprinkled down a thin smattering of ice, all the dew that had collected in the night and frozen in the morning. Diamonds dusted the backyard grass, settling into place while the wind blew at the tire swing hanging from the nearest tree branch. No one within the Nationalists knew about Silas's Communist code name after his false defection. It was a way to make sure he didn't get caught as a true triple agent in the event that he was suspected.

Anyone who knew was a Communist. Like Phoebe.

"Whatever for?" Dao Feng asked calmly. "Last you reported, he was nowhere near your identity."

"But he is getting closer and closer." With every time Priest needed to respond to a correspondence to feign that nothing was wrong. With every time Phoebe had to listen to him piece together what he thought were clues: her feminine voice on the tapes, the scuff marks on the bags, the delays in getting back to him. "He needs to be shaken out of our ranks and his communication with Priest taken away. In a way that is natural, so he does not think Priest was ever onto him."

"Hong Feiyi," Dao Feng said. He flicked off a piece of wood shaving. "Do you want central command finding out that he is still a Nationalist? Because that's how you get central command aiming a sniper at his head."

"Not necessarily—"

"What excuse do you have for restricting his access to Priest? Short of suspecting his loyalties. Go on."

Phoebe's mouth opened, ready to argue. Seconds later, it snapped closed again, because she had no answer. Central command needed explanations for the decisions their agents made. They were at war, and there was no room for messing up, or else their entire faction would be obliterated.

Phoebe pinched the bridge of her nose. Her eldest brother, Oliver, chose his loyalties by following what he believed. Four years ago, shortly after he walked out on the family, he offered her the chance to join him, and she was won over easily because she had liked the allure of having the other side's information by *becoming* the other side. It was a brilliant way to stay one step ahead, to keep them from harming Orion if she occupied enemy lines watching for missiles locking upon him. In that time, she had foiled two attempts on his life simply by messing with the directive when it moved along the command line. Oliver kept her identity protected. No one suspected any foul play from secret family members.

Some nights Phoebe did wonder why she played such a complicated game when it would have been easier to sit out and let her brother look after himself. He was smart enough to escape attempts on his life, surely; not every assassin was as good as she was. In truth, though, her work had started because she missed her mother, and the last promise Phoebe had made her was a child's vow that she would look after Orion. And somehow, because fate liked laughing in her face, it was her own mother who had then resurrected from the assumed dead and caused Orion the most harm.

Phoebe swung her arms along her sides suddenly, filled with fretful energy. So there was nothing to do. Nothing except for Phoebe—for *Priest*—to do everything in her power to avoid capture.

"What if I just told him?"

Dao Feng's penknife stopped. He almost hacked off his garden lizard's tail. "Say that again. I think I may have misheard you."

"I am spending all this time keeping my identity from Silas while he investigates on behalf of the Nationalists," Phoebe elaborated. "What if I told him? What if I asked him to give up on his search?"

Another gust of wind blew more ice onto the grass. Dao Feng set his miniature carving knife down. He laced his fingers together, then rested his arms upon his raised knees.

"Then I have a question in response," he said evenly. "Do you have full-hearted trust that he would defy everything to follow you instead?"

No.

The answer came quickly. Phoebe winced, too stubborn to voice that one word upon her tongue. But indeed, no—she couldn't claim that he would follow her, because if she was already having trouble convincing him to lay off this search for Priest, then who was to say whether he would listen when she told him her reasoning? For as long as there was the slightest risk that Silas would turn her in to the Nationalists after she admitted the truth, she couldn't do it.

"I think he could," Phoebe said weakly.

"*I think he could* is not the same as a firm *he would,*" Dao Feng replied. "Trust me, Hong Feiyi. It is difficult to keep people in the dark, I know, but it keeps them from having to make difficult decisions. And more often than not, you won't like the decision they end up making."

Her handler turned back to his wood carving. She wondered if he was thinking about Rosalind and Orion. Two of his charges, whom he had abandoned when his identity started to slip. Would either of them have reported him for being a double agent? It was hard to say. Loyalty was a complicated thing. There was nothing stopping Dao Feng from reporting Silas to the Communists himself. They didn't need to wait for central command to find out; if anything, it made them bad Communists to fail to report a spy in their midst. But people were more complicated than how political allegiances looked on paper; people protected one another in ways that made no sense and held on to larger beliefs even while committing smaller infractions along the way.

"So I must keep stringing him along."

"Dear girl." Dao Feng leaned back. Up on the tree branch, a bird cawed into the weak daytime sun. "In the grand scheme of this war we are fighting, it could be much worse."

"Yes," Phoebe agreed. "It could be worse. It could be that my brother is out in the middle of God-knows-where, and I can't do a thing to help him while I am being chased down from every side by a friend who thinks I can."

Dao Feng's expression twisted. He finally released the log of wood from between his legs and let it roll through the grass, the collected shavings and dust sprinkling back into the garden.

"How is your latest assignment going?"

Phoebe frowned. Was he trying to change the subject?

"We hit a wall, but I'm still looking," she answered nevertheless. "He may have caught wind of his buddies getting sniped and fled."

"Put that on pause, then." Dao Feng drummed his fingers on his knees. "I have a suggestion."

Phoebe hurried to sink to the ground, sitting beside her handler as though he were going to tell her a bedtime story. There was something about his tone that incited immediate intrigue. It didn't seem like this was an official task allocation. This sounded mysterious.

"If you are going to tell me that Oliver has been assigned to track Orion, I know," Phoebe said. "Perhaps it would be wise for me to follow . . . ?"

Dao Feng shook his head. "No, Feiyi. What more would you contribute that Oliver isn't already handling? There's another route you can take instead."

Phoebe had clearly already been curious, but now she was almost to the point of bursting.

"The way I remember it," Dao Feng continued, "your mother was recruited into the Kuomintang's earliest experiments because she had previously done work on that front. She led the endeavor, and then, when the Kuomintang's higher command cleaved the resources from her, she tried her next round on Orion. What does that tell you?"

"She wasn't afraid of it failing," Phoebe answered easily.

"Right." A bird landed beside Dao Feng. He tossed a blade of grass at it, and the creature fluttered off. "Why? How much had she already advanced? What more is there hiding behind this?"

Phoebe understood now. If Oliver was on the chase for Orion, then there was only one critical path left for her to cover.

"You want me looking into my mother."

"I know you work with targets more than you do intelligence, never mind historical background intelligence, but I think you could do it." Dao Feng paused. "Let people see what they need when you go digging. Find what they're hiding when their guard goes down. You'll do great."

Phoebe beamed. Sure, she was no intelligence operative, but people letting their guards down around her was her prime specialty.

She had been making use of it all her life, had been exploiting the way the world saw her since the moment she was born.

"Yes, I'll do great," she echoed.

Dao Feng nodded. "Do a search into your mother's past, see what comes up," he went on. "Even if your eldest brother is successful, I fear it is not that easy to reverse something strange in the mind. If at any point this seems too much, though—"

"No," Phoebe cut in. "I accept the mission."

6

January's winter sees Manchuria frozen over in the daytime and arctic in the night. The faraway horizon blows wind through the plains. The mountains shiver, shake down clumps of frost that harden into place and build an encasement of ice over the world. Heat is a luxury that the soldiers planted up here will not be offered. The military base the Japanese have built is biting, dry. If one doesn't keep moving their feet, the ground stakes its claim. Opens a crack and swallows a soldier in for food.

Most of them aren't of the mind to complain, at least. The moment they think to protest their unsavory conditions, a silent chemical command slithers into position, scrubs away the words before they can leave their tongue. It keeps them loyal. Compliant to their leaders. Not every soldier needed to be given this fix, but since the science exists, it may as well be generously used.

One traitor has done too much work to hear arguments otherwise.

Inside the military base, she's of the few who need to bundle for warmth, a threadbare blanket pulled over her shoulders. The facility isn't large, built for surveillance instead of true offensive capabilities. Its perimeter is tucked inside a hill, and the hill is tucked inside a valley. When a rumble of thunder moves through the clouds, its echo booms tenfold, rebounding again and again and again. With each passing hour the temperature drops, but she doesn't show that she's bothered. Even if frost seeps through her ribs and crawls into her heart, she won't display discomfort lest the ambassadors see her as weak, lest they pivot their investment and choose another avenue of interest.

A rumble of activity clatters outside the office. The traitor doesn't yet stir, eyeing the blackboard stretched along the wall. Very little is ready. She is immensely behind. They asked for the concoction to be complete before winter scratched its fingers on the chains of their tanks. She promised she could do it. She had pulled out her research files, pointed to two separate concoctions that had proved to be possible—albeit with faults—and claimed that the perfect science was in their complete merge. She only needed the right ratio. Easy.

Footsteps enter through the door. She doesn't turn. The birds that have stolen over the base's perimeter cluster around the window like civilian witnesses, peek their small heads against the glass. Maybe blood will spill. Maybe this is the point where she will be punished, having pushed their mercy too far. Who would know if they were to dispose of her?

"You said this week at the latest."

Mr. Akiyama is one of three ambassadors that she has been in contact with. He's a quiet man, with very little patience for nonsense. According to the pictures in his wallet, he has two children, both of whom have barely learned to walk, but he never mentions them in conversation. He frowns upon uncouth behavior, and he is never late to any place he is expected. When he was summoned into this country, "ambassador" was a loose term for his role. Others might call him a "government official." Or a "diplomat," on assignment to survey relations and determine prospective goals for an empire that requires resources. Regardless of what other definitions may be used, "military general" is the only title he is not. Though the soldiers here operate under his command, he will not be claimed by his empire if anything goes south. They will insist he was an individual actor. Anyone asked will put a finger to their lips; anyone trying to find evidence will have to rummage extensively under the table, beneath cover after cover.

The traitor slowly pulls the blanket off her shoulders. She folds it in half. Then again. The birds watch her, forming a tighter line.

"There are many moving parts to this invention. It needs more time."

The days have been long, but the nights have been longer—when the units pause in their movement and take inventory of their progress. At a certain date, they must move into Shanghai, awaiting a signal from the top. At a certain date, they will proceed with or without her, and if it is the latter, then she is useless, gaining absolutely nothing out of this arrangement.

"How much more time?" Mr. Akiyama asks plainly.

Enough time to make and combine the two parts again. There's the first half of the concoction which provides strength—that's straightforward. She invented it on its own at first, but it doesn't last long, eating away at the body it occupies unless there are new doses. In a war, there's hardly time to be checking in on a soldier every few days as though they run a nursery.

"Another week," she decides shortly. It might not be enough. There is a lot to create from scratch again. In that brief moment before evacuating Warehouse 34, she had turned her back on her successful invention to secure transportation, and the assassin the Nationalists call Fortune had destroyed everything. Her papers. Her progress.

"That's too long."

She tosses the folded blanket onto the table. Her patience snags, catches a tight knot. The second half of the concoction is much harder—*that's* what she needs time for. A science entirely new . . . but one that will finally balance her invention of strength, change a body so that it shall be everlasting and won't be eaten up without new doses. It will provide the ability to heal any wound, to never require sleep. It will halt the cells at every stage and freeze a subject in its present form. Her classmates at Cambridge heard the hypothetical proposal and called it immortality, but that's not entirely true. A soldier might still take a bullet to the head, blow his brains out without recovery. True immortality is something for the hands of gods. She doesn't need to play God. She just needs something so undeniably powerful that the Japanese will perceive her as one.

"I *had* it," she says tightly. "I told you I had it when we were still using Seagreen as a middleman." Before Seagreen had gotten caught. Before her husband was hauled in and her son tried to break away from her. "The final product had been perfected. The ratio worked. We know it is possible; we know it can be done—I only have to do it again, and that takes *time*."

Silence.

The birds peck at the glass. Beg to be let in. Each of the traitor's brittle words forms clouds of breath in front of her.

"Won't it be worth it?" she continues when she gets silence in response. "Think about what is within reach. These are soldiers stronger than any man on earth. They can heal any wound. They require no sleep. What other asset in this coming war will match up? Once you have this, who will bring something better up the chain of command?"

Mr. Akiyama considers it. He turns to look out the window, and at once, the birds flee, soaring into the night. In the time she has been working with him, she has never seen anger cross his manner. Only carefully measured neutrality, occasionally furrowing his thin brows. It's never too late for rage to erupt on the scene, though. That's something to remember about men: the trickiest ones know how to hide their temper, so one should never assume the absence of anger equates kindness.

"Very well," he says. His expression never changes. "Another week."

Orion.

At the farthest side of the military base, a voice whispers through the soldier's room. The soldier startles awake, launching off his sparse mattress and barely catching himself before he strikes the concrete floor. Very few items occupy the room with him. His uniform. His weapons. Dust, coating the walls and coating his world like a curtain before his eyes.

Orion, Orion, it's me. It's me.

A terrible ache presses at his head. There is no one else in the room with him, no one to attribute to this voice, waking him from his dreamless sleep. It is only his own mind, calling him by a name that isn't his.

"Get out," he whispers. The concrete is painfully cold on his skin. The floor beats with the sound of his own telltale heart, buried six feet deep.

Orion, please, please—

He slaps his hands over his ears and screams.

7

The first tour stop was in Shanghai, because the media vultures at home were the most important.

And the most vicious.

"Lang Shalin, what have you started here?"

Jiemin pushed into the dressing room. Outside, the clamor was reaching a fever pitch, the lobby of the hotel filling up beyond capacity. There was a whole flurry of activity each time the door opened, and yet Jiemin managed to look bored as he came closer, waving off an assistant trying to give him a schedule.

"How nice of you to show up," Rosalind replied, mimicking his indifference. She was standing over the small sink in the corner, scrubbing at a blotch on her palm. Now she turned the tap off, water trickling along the sides. "I was wondering where you had gotten to. Didn't manage to catch Alisa out there, did you?"

Jiemin frowned. He sidestepped a second assistant hurrying around with a bundle of forms in the crook of her arm—someone at the hotel had wanted their own photographer on the scene, and now the group of assistants in the corner were arguing over whether they had permitted a front-row seat. It was an important matter. The Nationalists had chosen a location on Bubbling Well Road, a hotel that was smack-dab where the members of the highest social status usually mingled.

A few of the elite were hovering in the lobby when Rosalind

poked her head out. It was easy to pick out the men in suits and the women in qipao among the reporters who flocked close to the podium. Though they weren't the primary targets of the tour, there would be plenty of intrigue among civilians. Rosalind was counting on it. Their interest made her indispensable. Their interest stitched her into the papers in a way that would cause an outcry if her employers tried to tuck her away in retirement and bid her to hush.

"You can imagine my surprise when they yanked me back and made you my charge again," Jiemin said.

"Really?" Rosalind used her wet fingers to slick back a strand of hair. "Because you asked for me to be decommissioned?"

"I had nothing to do with that."

Back when he worked undercover at Seagreen as well, Jiemin always looked vaguely distracted, which was certainly one way to avoid being perceived as a threat. Rosalind could see now that it wasn't a front: he was always like this, even while dressed in uniform, holding a position legions above what was expected at his age.

"Regardless . . ." With a harrumph, Rosalind walked over to the vanity mirror, then brushed off some excess powder on her nose. "I don't need a handler for this. You can rest easy."

"Of course you need a handler," Jiemin returned. "You cannot truly believe you are doing a public service, Lady Fortune. These reporters will tear you apart if given the chance."

"I am *well* aware." The room suddenly fell quiet. Her voice bounced back in echo, its loud volume cutting through the other hubbub. Patience lived paper-thin inside her these days, always one wrong fold from scrunching into something unsightly. Her anger itched to turn ugly, begged to be let out at the slightest provocation.

One of the assistants cleared her throat. "Shall we—"

"Do you think," Rosalind interrupted, "that I'm foolish enough to believe any of them out there *like* me? They would desire nothing more than to see me break into pieces so they can snap a picture and make it a headline: 'What Finally Kills an Immortal Girl?'"

She could see her reflection out of the corner of her eye. When Rosalind turned to look, every snarl was plainly written on her expression. At once, she hardly recognized herself and saw herself more clearly than ever. She wasn't enough of a fool to believe that she could have the world's love, and yet she was enough of one to stick around wanting it anyway.

"Not a very creative headline," Jiemin said drolly.

The clock struck three in the afternoon. It chimed rapid-quick to the rhythm of her thudding heart, each beat striking hard against her ribs.

"It doesn't really matter what they write, does it?" Rosalind tried to smooth her rage away. "Until I am dead, I am still immortal and larger than life—larger than every single one of you within the Nationalists. If I say get in line for a sound bite, then the reporters will get in their little lines and let me speak."

A knock came on the door. An assistant poked his head in, looked around to see the tense situation, and dropped his voice to whisper, "We're ready."

Rosalind ignored him. As did Jiemin. In silence, they only regarded each other until Jiemin said, "You've changed, Lang Shalin."

The assistant cleared his throat again. Microphone feedback screeched once outside.

"I haven't," Rosalind said. "I have always been like this. I merely forgot who I was for some time."

She brushed by, stepping through the door and into the lobby. The assistant led her out, arm extended to show her the path. Sound hummed around her like white noise. Soft golden light fell in all directions, beaming from the patterned light fixtures on the high ceiling and the crystal flower bulbs craning their necks in the corners. The thick support beams that dropped to the floor were made of polished marble and cut in perfect straight formation, blocking out parts of the crowd until Rosalind walked past them and came around the podium, realizing that the whole picture was so much more gargantuan than she had estimated. Though a grand piano sat in the middle of the lobby as a piece of functionary decoration, it was entirely swallowed up with flocks on its every side.

A bulb flashed. Rosalind smoothed down her qipao.

"Thank you for coming," she said. Her voice boomed into the microphone, squealing against the speakers for a moment before clearing. "It has been such an endeavor to get before you today, but I pleaded and pleaded to the powers that be. Better this than hiding away inside windows some of you have tried to climb."

Scattered laughter moved through the crowd. Her smile turned wider. Here was something else Rosalind Lang had forgotten: she was a born performer. Before she was an agent, she had been a dancer. Before she was an assassin, the stage had been hers.

"Lady Fortune, why are you under their control?" someone yelled out.

Rosalind looked toward the voice. She didn't know who had said it, but the approving mutter in the front-most rows meant it didn't matter—it was everyone's question.

"Listen very carefully," General Yan had said when he'd agreed to her plan. "We have accepted your proposal for the well-being of the nation. But for it to succeed, there are certain criteria you must follow."

"Very well," Rosalind had returned evenly. She didn't care about telling a few lies here and there. She didn't care about anything as long as they sent her out.

"Most primarily"—General Yan leaned forward on his desk—"Lady Fortune emerged out of your own volunteering. Forget that there was ever sickness. We take Lourens Van Dijk out of the narrative. You became an agent for the Kuomintang, and you took on these abilities."

Rosalind had nodded. Walked through the rest of the list of matters to memorize and change. Discarded what they told her to discard and adopted the lies they wanted told. Though she had always considered Fortune a part of her, Fortune was now being presented to the world just like another undercover identity, formulated for a purpose and designed for an end goal.

The microphone screeched again as Rosalind adjusted it. She leaned in closely.

"Control?" she echoed. "Let me clarify how my work began. . . ."

They were enraptured by her narrative. The questions went on and on. At some point, Rosalind felt the approach of a presence behind her, and she knew that Jiemin had come along to signal the close of this session and find an opportunity to withdraw her from the reporters. Clearly, they were not eager to let her go. They asked about her opinions on the city and her opinions of the foreigners. They asked how much truth there was to the collapse of the Scarlet Gang and the downfall of the White Flowers. No answer out of her mouth was the complete truth. Nor did any qualify as a full lie. Only a story, woven from fractured pieces.

Rosalind pointed at one more reporter.

"What about Hong Liwen?"

The lobby grew brighter. Her hands tightened on the podium.

Jiemin cleared his throat. "I think it may be time to finish up now—"

"The media has had a dozen different sources, but I know he's innocent," Rosalind answered. "In fact, the reason he's even anywhere near the imperialist effort is wholly because his traitor mother has captured him. Lady Hong used him to experiment with a concoction that will aid the Japanese in their invasion, and I still have the last vial of it—"

Her microphone cut off. Jiemin took her shoulder and dragged her away from the podium, gesturing quickly for the assistants to hold the reporters back as they surged forward in excitement.

"What do you think you're doing?" Jiemin demanded under his breath. Rosalind barely caught his words. He marched her across the lobby at breakneck speed, cutting a line through the people and heading toward the front doors. "You said you gave the last vial to Alisa Montagova."

"I did."

Rosalind left it at that. She didn't bother with smug, didn't lift her nose. The single seed was planted. Now it needed to sprout before she got self-congratulatory.

Jiemin turned a brief glance at her. It was hard to read his expression.

They exited the hotel, greeted by another wave of flashbulbs and a gust of winter air. Rosalind flinched, but Jiemin yanked her shoulder roughly and pushed her into a waiting car. Seconds later, Jiemin got in from the other side. The chauffeur glanced back, saw that he had acquired his passengers, and pulled away from the sidewalk.

"Whatever you're trying," Jiemin said slowly, carefully, "you're playing with fire. You're not on assignment anymore."

Rosalind stayed quiet. What could she say in her defense anyway? Her ulterior motive was rather blatant.

Jiemin, after a few seconds, seemed to realize that telling her off was not only a lost cause but embarrassing for both of them. The Nationalists weren't going to pull the tour when they knew how useful it could be. Any threats he made were empty. Any promises Rosalind made were lies. The car turned the corner onto Seymour Road.

"You ought to be very careful," he eventually concluded. "We begin traveling in two days. I'll be accompanying you on the journey."

"All right," Rosalind replied.

She shifted her gaze out the window. Shanghai shimmered in the afternoon light, mounds of dirty sleet collecting on some corners and hefty trash bags filled with excess stacked up on others. Each shop front winked an eye of mischief under the golden haze; hawkers ducked under their stall covers when the wind blew too cold, huffing into their palms to get their fingers moving again in the city winter.

Rosalind's own hands curled in her lap, burrowing into her qipao skirt. If her plan succeeded, at some point in the countryside, Lady Hong would come after her with Orion in tow.

And then Rosalind was going to snatch him back where he belonged.

8

"You can take first choice on the rooms."

Oliver pushed the door open as he spoke, the key to the inn suite dangling from his fingers. When Celia stepped through, the carpet made a peculiar crunching noise—and it wasn't as if she were stepping very hard, wary as she was about not making too much noise in the corridor. Early morning had barely crept over the horizon. They had wanted to get settled before the town started rumbling with activity . . . and before Rosalind's tour arrived. Blending in was critical when it came to being successful tails. If the Nationalists found out that two Communists were shadowing their movement, Celia and Oliver would get a bullet between their eyes faster than they could blink, sibling relations to their highest agents be damned.

"Oliver," Celia said dryly, closing the door after herself. "There's only one bedroom."

"What, you don't like having the illusion of choice?" He tossed his bag onto the table. They adopted the same routine whenever they were on these sorts of missions: going in and out of different towns to follow a target. Get the cheapest suite at a shabby inn, which usually meant one bedroom. Celia would take the bed. Oliver would insist he loved sleeping on the hard living room carpet, that she was doing him a favor. Instead of just admitting that his sense of chivalry would give him a heart attack if she so much as suggested taking turns on the bed, he claimed floors improved his posture and toughened up his back.

Celia shrugged. When her bag moved up and down with the motion, Oliver reached out quickly to take it from her, placing it on the table too.

"I *suppose,*" she said, indulging him, "that I will choose this one."

She walked into the bedroom, making a quick inventory. It was a narrow box of a space, barely enough walking room on either side of the small bed. One wooden table in the corner, with a lamp plugged into the wall. She turned the light on. Then she drew the curtains tight and shivered.

"I'm going to take a look around the perimeter before the day begins," Oliver called over. He rustled about in the living room, moving the furniture into a more secure formation. "Something felt off on our way here."

Celia had sensed the same. Being spies meant growing sixth senses triggered by the faintest brush of notice. She had felt watched while walking in. And though Celia had looked around thoroughly, eyes scanning the nearby tree line and searching the hazy morning for movement, there had been nothing.

Orange light pricked through the curtains. Sunrise, creeping higher.

"Do you want me to accompany you?" Celia asked, returning to the living room. It was rare for trouble to arise so early in a mission. Usually, though, when they were assigned to travel, they were only gathering intelligence. Drawing conclusions on soldier units or passing messages for other agents who needed to make contact but couldn't go into the city. For a mission where they were directly in the Nationalists' line of sight, anything was possible. Maybe they had already put people here to prepare for Rosalind's arrival. Maybe it was already too late.

Oliver shook his head. "Stay here. I doubt it's anything."

"All right." She wandered over to the dresser. Spare sheets in the first drawer. Towels in the second drawer. "I will search for hearing devices." Celia pulled out one of the mold-ridden sheets. "Though I'd be shocked if someone can get equipment in here when they cannot even get fresh laundry."

"Oh, sweetheart, don't say that." Oliver, meanwhile, was shaking a second scarf from his bag. It wasn't as cold here as Shanghai's below-zero wet freeze, but enough to warrant bundling thickly. "I don't want to think about sleeping on mold."

Celia tossed the sheet onto the floor. "You're out of luck, then."

"None of them?"

She tugged forth another sheet. Then another. "Would I ever lie about moldy sheets, Oliver?"

"I know you have a magic touch. Summon one that is clean."

"Unfortunately, my magic has its limits." She tossed out the final sheet. Now there was a mountain on the floor and nothing more in the drawer. "Each and every one of them is moth-bitten in some shape or form."

Oliver made a theatric sigh. He stuck a hat on. Both to brace against the cold and to shield his face.

"How much will I have to plead to be invited into the bed instead?"

Celia blinked. Turned around slowly.

Wait, what *did he just say?*

The silence drew on. She needed to say something. She needed to say something right now.

"I'm . . . going to check in there for listening devices."

Promptly, Celia walked into the washroom, then slammed the door after herself.

WHAT IS WRONG WITH YOU? her reflection bellowed.

I don't know! she mouthed back.

THAT WAS YOUR CHANCE TO TALK TO HIM!

"Be careful," Oliver called from outside. His voice was entirely level, with no indication of concern over her behavior. He was joking, after all, in that terribly sardonic way of his. No reason to believe otherwise. "I will return shortly."

The main door closed after him. The suite fell quiet. And Celia was arguing with herself in the mirror.

With a huff, she stormed out of the washroom, feeling absolutely ridiculous. She had been brooding for weeks about his silence, and at the first opportunity that presented itself for her to throttle words out of him, she turned in the other direction instead. The problem was, even if she did summon the willpower to demand an answer, what was she to say? In truth, Oliver had spoken everything he needed to say. It was on her now.

Celia kicked the mound of sheets.

How was she supposed to accept this? She had grown up convinced that romance would skip over her. As though it were a great hand from above counting its darlings, and when it reached her, it would only grimace and cover her up with a blanket of invisibility. Instead . . . instead she was pulling that blanket over herself, scrambling for excuses to keep the comfort. She had spent years ignoring whatever it was that was trying to bloom to life between them, so why did Oliver have to go *tugging* at it—

Tap-tap-tap-tap.

Celia froze, her foot halting halfway through another kick. She had been so lost inside her own head that she was only just hearing the sound coming from the bedroom.

At once she reached inside the slit of her qipao and pulled out her gun. Maybe she ought to start carrying blades around instead, because if she needed to fire a bullet, it was going to be loud. Then again, if she had to fight with a knife, the only person she would be stabbing was herself.

As quietly as she could manage, Celia slid around the bend of the wall and entered the bedroom. It was brighter than before. The sun was climbing higher. Where had the sound come from? Was it Oliver surveying the perimeter?

Celia waited, listening. Though the sound didn't come again, her attention gravitated firmly toward the window. When she'd pulled those curtains shut, the window had definitely been closed.

So why was the fabric billowing now, letting in a faint breeze?

She crept forward a step. Another.

Then, before her very eyes, a small hand stuck itself into the room, groping around the wall.

Celia's heart leaped to her throat, but she didn't waste time with the scream that lodged itself on her tongue. With one frantic motion, she hurtled to the window and grabbed the hand, pulling the intruder into the room. She was pointing her gun at them before the tumble of motion stilled at her feet.

"*Oof!*" Alisa Montagova peered up, her hair tangled around her face. She gave a sheepish smile. "Hello."

"Oh my God." Celia tossed the gun away quickly, then scrambled to haul Alisa upright. When the girl was standing again, she patted along Alisa's arms, making sure nothing was broken. "You scared the *crap* out of me!"

"Sorry." Alisa winced, rubbing her shoulder. "I was trying to make a sly entrance. I didn't think you would hear me undoing the latch."

Celia frowned. "Is the front door too ordinary for you?"

"Yes." With the trickiness of a house cat, Alisa slinked away from Celia, tugging out of her grip and prancing around the room. "I won't stay long—the Kuomintang are still after me. I just needed a moment with you once Oliver left."

Of course it was Alisa who had been watching them as they came into the inn. Alisa and her creepily keen stare.

"What is your objection to Oliver?" Celia asked. She couldn't hold back the slight hitch in her voice.

It had been the same that night in October. Alisa had been about to give her something. Celia hadn't known it at the time, but Rosalind told her later it was Lady Hong's last vial—the chemical concoction that she had been killing civilians to perfect. When Alisa spotted Oliver in the house, she had turned on her heel and run. Celia hadn't seen her since then.

Alisa folded her arms. Twisted her lips, which had gone almost entirely white from the cold outside. "It's not an objection to him," she answered. "He's loyal. If anything, I am looking out for his interests so that he's not making a hard decision."

Celia considered the answer. She hauled the blanket off the bed and, without bothering to wait for approval, draped it over Alisa's head to warm her.

"Are you and I not loyal, Alisa?" she asked quietly.

Alisa let the blanket settle around her head. Her dark brown eyes pulled wide, her hands clutching the covering.

"I have to report to you, but you can't report back," Alisa said in a hush. "Or report up, I suppose. Or . . . whatever—you can't report in any direction, including Oliver."

"I am technically *your* superior," Celia countered. "I do still have the right to handle any intelligence you pass me on my own call."

"Yes, but I'm not telling you because you are my superior." Alisa squirmed deeper into the blanket. "I'm telling you because you are Rosalind's sister. Two very different matters."

So this was what it was. Celia felt a breath snag in her throat. "Tell me."

"I think there's an ambush coming for her." With a waddle, Alisa hurried to the window, peering out into the yard. The curtains had been left disturbed, with a gap that spilled sunlight into the otherwise gray room. This inn was located in a less populated part of the town, surrounded by the woods on one side and a carefully cultivated scenic view on the other. The innkeeper had planted bamboo shoots that framed the stone walkways. Dug a little pond into the dirt, its water providing a drinking station for the birds that flew near the lotus flowers.

"I don't know how soon," Alisa continued. "When I move around, I don't go any farther north than Nanjing . . . which, I know, is still very south. But whispers travel through major cities faster than they do through the townships. When Shanghai's papers are constantly writing about Lady Hong's traitorous forces, people are going to be looking for her too."

"Lady Hong has been spotted," Celia guessed. "Hasn't she?"

Alisa turned away from the window. "I stuck my nose into our own grapevine last week. We have a few safe houses left in Nanjing that are receiving underground reports. There's been mobilization in the Shandong region. Lady Hong is heading south, very quickly. She must have seen Rosalind's tour route and decided to intercept her, especially now that Rosalind has run her mouth lying on the very first stop, claiming to have the vial."

Rosalind did what?

Celia's head was starting to hurt. She couldn't keep up with the papers quickly enough while traveling.

"I don't think the Nationalists know that Lady Hong has left Manchuria yet. It's hard for them to determine which units are theirs and which units are her brainwashed soldiers wearing Kuomintang uniform," Alisa went on. "But . . . but our side might soon. We have been observing for long enough to tell the difference."

A thud came from upstairs. It was unrelated, only other guests waking up, but Celia stiffened nonetheless. They needed to wrap up this conversation. Oliver would be returning at any moment.

"You know what my mission is at the moment, don't you?" Celia asked. "We're *supposed* to want Lady Hong to come after Rosalind. That way we can grab Orion."

"I know. I figured Rosalind wanted that too the moment I saw the tour poster." Alisa tapped her foot on the floor. Its echo was loud, like gunshots, like a gavel striking death sentence after death sentence. "I wanted to give you a warning, nonetheless. Because if the objective comes down from central command . . ." A pause. "What if Oliver is instructed to grab his brother without any regard for Rosalind in the middle?"

Celia reared back. "You are not trying to imply Oliver would *kill* Rosalind for our goals."

"I absolutely did *not* say that." Alisa sighed. Her shoulders slumped, and then the blanket fell off too, crumpling in a semicircle on the floor. "I am only saying that we're fighting a war, and I don't want you to be taken aback. If it were my sister, I'd want to raise my shields early. Be careful. The battalion is arriving any day now."

With that, Alisa hurried to the window again, clambering up onto the sill. She turned back. "I will be close by. Give a shout if you need me—"

"Wait."

Celia stepped into the living room briefly and lugged her bag to the bedroom. From a side pocket, she pulled out a trinket she had bought just before they left the city, a tiny ox with a blond fringe that covered its eyes. It had reminded her of Alisa, so she'd held on to it on the chance they might run into each other.

"For you," Celia said, pressing it into Alisa's hand. "Happy belated birthday."

Alisa beamed. She held the ox up to the light. "I haven't been keeping track of the Western calendar anymore. This is adorable."

"Looks a little like you, don't you think?"

Alisa snorted, but her expression was one of delight. "I will treasure it forever and ever. See you soon."

She hopped off the sill and disappeared. The glass pane swung with her momentum. A bird started to sing outside. A chorus soon followed.

Quietly, Celia closed the window, then gathered up the fallen blanket and threw it back onto the bed. She picked up her gun and put the safety on. When she tried to shove it into her bag for safe-keeping, the weapon slipped from her grasp, landing on the carpet with a small thump. Celia sighed. Its shape was hideous. As would be the shape of knives in her bag too. Or wires, or poison bottles, or anything they needed to use in this war.

Goddamn. She had always known a day like this would come: when it became apparent that she and Rosalind were working for different sides. She just didn't think it would get this complicated. An enemy sister who was utterly committed to putting herself in danger. A mission partner who always felt ten miles away, no matter how much she wanted to trust him.

Oliver walked back into the suite at that moment. When he stepped near the bedroom entrance and saw her, he stopped in his tracks. "Sweetheart?"

Celia looked up. Her heart twisted. "Yes?"

His brow furrowed. "What is your gun doing out?"

For a moment, she considered telling him the truth. *Alisa showed up. She thinks the ambush is coming any moment. Can you promise not to harm my sister? Can you do that for me?*

Maybe that was why Oliver chose to operate in silence with his information, why he would rather withhold than tell her what he had been tasked to do. Let them flip the table—let her stand here wondering if she ought to ask for his input, and she clammed up in an instant. It felt so much worse imagining her requests denied. Instead, she could let them hover forever in ambiguity, in that space where she was neither accepted nor rejected. If she never asked, she wouldn't have to face the possibility of a terrible answer.

Celia kneeled to pick up the gun, breaking from Oliver's gaze.

Her father had been the one to teach her that lesson. There were so many moments in childhood when she would have been better off had she asked fewer questions. She would be bearing far fewer scars ripped into her heart if she had written her own narrative and just stuck with it. Instead, she fumed around the living room during that first month back in Shanghai, unaccustomed to the sounds and sights after so long in Paris, nothing better to do than to hover around her father all day. She wanted to press him to a breaking point, as if that might make him reconsider whether it was *really* necessary that she take Kathleen's name. Why were they pretending a different sibling had passed away from illness in Paris? Did they think their relatives so unforgiving that they would rather believe Kathleen Lang had always looked like this than that the sole Lang son had come back a daughter?

Celia had pushed it. Kept pushing it. Finally, she had said: "I wish you would hear what I'm saying. Don't you care about how I feel—"

"No, I don't!" her father had interrupted. "You shouldn't have this much to say about it to begin with. *I* wish you'd go back to how you were born, but apparently that's not an option, is it?"

Celia had reared back with such shock that she hadn't known how to react. Not until she was telling Rosalind about the conversation later that night while they were tucked into bed and the sobs started, unbearable bubbles of grief floating up from her stomach and into her throat.

"He doesn't know what he's saying," Rosalind had spat fiercely, wrapping her arms around her. "I love you like this. I love you as you are."

Pretending to be Kathleen during those years in the Scarlet Gang was a compromise. It was safe. It kept her protected. But after that day with her father, the matter was always going to grate away a small bit of her insides each time she considered her circumstances. She had asked too much, and instead of happily believing that her father was only looking out for her, she knew without a shadow of doubt that this was the only option he would allow, that if Kathleen had been alive—if her sister had never died in Paris and left her identity for the taking—then Celia was the one who would have needed to die instead.

"Sweetheart."

Celia snapped out of her thoughts, blinking back to attention. She wasn't there anymore; she had long cut herself free from the Scarlet Gang and, by association, the need to protect herself from their judgment.

"I was only moving it, don't worry." At last she put the weapon into her bag. Oliver had come into the room with a certain air about him, the smell of winter cold and a metallic sting. She slowly stood, taking him in and reading his manner. "Nothing concerning around the perimeter?"

"We seem to be in the clear. But . . ."

The moment Celia was level with him again, Oliver grasped her chin. The contact was benign—as casual as a prod of the shoulder if he were trying to move past her in the hallway—but his eyes were narrowed. Suspicious.

"You're certain that you are all right?" he asked.

Celia's breath locked in her lungs. She only needed to ask. Except what then? In the scenario that she feared, he would go against her outright. In the scenario that she wanted, he would choose her, and then he might throw everything away, might act against what he believed in for *her* sake, and how could she ask that of someone?

She needed to let this play out. She needed to save her sister without getting in his way.

"Celia," Oliver prompted.

"Yes," Celia said firmly. "Never better."

9

"Once you get those papers signed, we can send someone to the bank in your stead," Jiemin said, rustling through the transfer forms. "Apologies for the inconvenience otherwise. It didn't seem right to send an assistant for this part."

"It's fine," Rosalind replied wryly. She was sitting in the passenger seat while Jiemin made a whole orchestra of noise plucking papers out of the envelopes in his lap. They were leaving today. A row of military vehicles was parked behind them at present, engines stalled to await Rosalind's predeparture task before they exited city bounds. "He probably wouldn't sign something an assistant brought him anyway."

To be fair, Rosalind wasn't sure he would sign these forms when she brought them herself, either. She hadn't seen her father in almost a year, and that last time had been entirely by chance because she hadn't known he would be attending a function where she was working undercover. Before the news headlines revealed her to be alive, the rest of Shanghai believed Mr. Lang was mourning the loss of all his children. Mr. Lang, however, had always known that Rosalind and Celia were out there in the city; it was only that neither of them wanted anything to do with him anymore, and in their line of covert work, disowning your parent was a rather easy task.

Until Rosalind's government employers suddenly required official bookkeeping outside the covert branch and needed her bank accounts transferred to her control from her guardian, apparently.

"Ten pages," Jiemin said, passing over the stack. "Get initials on all of them too. This is a British bank. They're fussy about that stuff."

"Yeah, yeah, I know."

Rosalind was quick to step out of the car. She continued grumbling while she walked a short distance down the stone alley and, already familiar with her surroundings, pushed open the large wooden gate into one of the apartment blocks. She hadn't been here in a long while. It was her grandmother's residence, technically, but her father had been living here since the Scarlets merged with the Nationalists, opting to put some distance between himself and the family business. Lady Cai was his sister: she had probably wanted him farther away once the Scarlets started to lose control, and her father—ever the man to take the easy way out—had been happy to oblige.

Rosalind entered the courtyard. By all means, her grandmother's residence was not shabby. The Langs were already members of elite society before her aunt married into the Cais. It was only that they were incomparable up against a family that had possessed the might of royalty, one so tethered to the city's economy that tides rose and fell on their command. In that vast shadow, every Lang in that household was always going to be a forgotten tack-on.

We should have stayed here instead, Rosalind thought. Her head tipped up; her eyes took in the four-story apartment building. It wouldn't have been a bad life. If they had never stepped foot into the Cai mansion, Rosalind might have turned out an entirely different person. Perhaps she wouldn't be living with regret hanging off her body like a second shadow, wouldn't be frozen immortal in the last state that house left her.

With a frustrated sigh, Rosalind finally knocked on the front door. A maid opened it at once, eyes already round and startled. She had been standing right in the foyer, waiting. Rosalind's presence was expected.

"Xiǎojiě," she whispered. "It's really you."

Rosalind thinned her lips, making her best attempt at a polite smile. "May I?"

The maid stepped aside quickly, ushering her inside. The papers rustled in Rosalind's hand. She had always remembered her grandmother's place to be cozy, but it didn't seem that way anymore. The ceilings were chipped and the carpeting scuffed. There was a peculiar dripping sound in the distance, or perhaps it was from inside the painted brown walls, the pipes springing a leak. The building was aging, she supposed. As most things did.

Most, but not all.

"Through there, xiǎojiě," the maid said, pointing ahead to the double doors. That was her father's office. What he did in there every day was anyone's guess. Back when the Scarlet Gang was still functional, Rosalind should have been called Mr. Lang instead, given the amount of his work she'd taken on. She had answered so many of his missives. Balanced so many of his accounts.

Her grip tightened on the papers.

With a nod at the maid, Rosalind pushed through the doors without bothering to knock.

"I almost didn't expect you to come," her father said from his desk. He was writing something.

It was much warmer inside the office than the rest of the residence, a fireplace burning beside the desk. Rosalind started fiddling with the cuff of her left sleeve immediately, rolling some of the thick fabric, giving herself room to breathe.

"Why not?" she replied. "I said I would."

Mr. Lang looked up. His pen stilled. The years had worn on

him—she could see that starkly. At the Nationalist function, she had gotten the briefest glimpse of him before hightailing it out of there, pretending she'd never made that contact and ignoring all the letters he had sent her way thereafter. Now, face-to-face, she saw every wrinkle and every whiter patch of hair, the heaviness under his eyes and the weariness dragging at the sides of his face.

"You have not answered a single letter, Shalin. The only way I even knew you were *alive* was through the Nationalist grapevine."

It was a bit late to be showing fatherly concern. Before the revolution that caused her rumored death, he wouldn't even check in unless there was something he needed. As if he cared that she was alive. As if it didn't make his life easier that all his children were presumed dead, because then their actions couldn't affect his standing in society, and nothing they did could have any bearing on his place with the Cais.

"I never got them," Rosalind said dryly.

"Never got them?" her father echoed. He reached into his desk drawer. Grabbed a handful of lined notepaper—letters—and slapped it upon the surface of the desk, a gradient of blue and black ink staring up at her. "This would say otherwise."

Rosalind recognized the handwriting in an instant. These weren't her father's letters. These were the replies he had gotten back.

"He was *answering* you?"

She set the transfer forms down with a clunk, grabbing the first letter from Dao Feng on the pile. Rosalind flipped through sheet after sheet, scanning lines at random. She didn't slow down to read closely—they all seemed to carry the exact same sentiment anyway.

Your concern is appreciated, but Shalin will be well taken care of in Kuomintang lodgings.

If there's anything you need, contact me instead. . . . She's doing better by separating from her old life. . . .

I assure you there's no need to ask her to return.

She's doing well. . . . Work keeps her busy. . . .

Rosalind's breath felt shallow in her lungs. These were all so much kinder than she would have been. He reported on her progress like a father might, concerned about her health and well-being even though each of Mr. Lang's letters were demands that couldn't care less about what she was actually doing as an operative.

Rosalind paused on the last letter. It was yellowed at the edges. An older one, dated from two years ago.

She stops at nothing to do what's right. I'm proud of her. I think you would be too.

Before she realized what she was doing, Rosalind had thrown that letter into the fireplace. She thought it would bring satisfaction to erase those words from sight, but regret struck the moment the paper started to burn, singeing the center before the red-hot color moved outward to turn everything to ash. The bottom of the paper was the last to go. She had the impulse to plunge her hand into the fire and save what she could while Dao Feng's sign-off remained, but it was too late. She watched Dao Feng's name disappear.

"Excuse me," Rosalind said, already backing out of the office. "I need to use the washroom."

She turned a corner. Her hands shook. This was such typical behavior for her. Let anything land in her grasp, and she turned to the fire without thinking. As much as she had suffered from Dao Feng's betrayal, those words were real. There was no other reason to write to her father, to keep him sated without letting any of the burden fall to her.

The thought didn't make her feel any better though. On the contrary, she felt so much worse knowing that her handler *had* loved her—he had cared about her enough to write those words and mean them, and he had still left. What more did it take, then? What hope did any other love in this world have?

Rosalind nearly stumbled into the washroom. She took a ragged breath in. A ragged breath out.

"Calm down," she whispered to herself. "What's wrong with you?"

Her heart hammered in her chest. It was a beating war drum, albeit screaming about an attack still miles away. The house groaned around her. It carried the same cadence as the reporters' cameras, rapid clicks echoing along the walls as though they were shutters. She could feel their eyes creeping in under the doors and pressed up to the windows as invisible ghosts. Watching, and waiting, just hoping to find a single detail that they could spin into sensation. They'd catch her crying over her handler's letter and accuse her of being a national traitor too.

Rosalind leaned over the sink. When she tried to take a breath, she gagged instead. Once. Twice. Nothing would come up. Her stomach turned. Her hands shook. The blades of her shoulders shuddered and swept a cold sweat down her back. It was all a phantom sensation—there was no need to be sick. Her system only knew that something was wrong and it wanted some way to expel its hot panic, but the poison wasn't an illness in her body; it was an exhaustion in her mind.

She was so angry. She was so *sad*.

Her forehead drooped down, hot against her arm while she rested on the edge of the sink. Slowly her heart stopped shrieking its battle cry. Her pulse turned weary, quiet as a bird without wings.

It was so tempting to stay like that forever. She could reroute the course of her life, bend time to start walking backward and grow up in this house instead. If she became frozen immortal like that, no one would care about bothering her. Fortune would never exist.

A knock tapped on the washroom door. Then:

"Xiǎojiě? Do you need anything?"

Rosalind snapped upright immediately. The maid's voice cut through her self-pity as if a switch had been turned. She imagined herself from the door, imagined seeing herself moping and pathetic at the sink, and her hopelessness turned to rage turned to fuel. There was too much riding on her shoulders to wish for another life. If she weren't Fortune, she never would have acquired the competency she needed to get Orion back. He was depending on her, and she was going to save him.

Rosalind swiped a hand at her eyes. In a blink, she looked normal again. She walked to the door and opened it. Outside, the maid had her fist raised in preparation to knock again.

"I am well. Excuse me."

The maid shuffled aside with a nod, letting Rosalind proceed back into the hallway. Suddenly this whole visit seemed excessive, some charade performed for falsities that no one cared about. It wasn't as though the banks would notice if she forged his signatures. It wasn't as though her father was one to protest in the event that they contacted him to confirm his transfer of ownership. Her father, after all, had merely written her letters to complain that she should come home. Not once did he think to get up and find her himself.

When Rosalind entered the office again, her father was sifting through the transfer forms.

"My apologies," she said. "Allergies."

He looked up briefly. "You are allergic to seafood, no?"

That had been Kathleen. But Rosalind didn't expect anything less than an utterly arbitrary mix-up.

"That too," she lied. "I won't waste your time further. If you could release control over my official accounts, that would be swell."

"In proper society, Shalin, a young woman shouldn't be controlling her own accounts."

"In proper society, I wouldn't be killing people for a job, either, but I suppose we can't be fussy during times like these."

Her father turned a sad look on her. Rosalind didn't feel a pinch of guilt. She had been at the receiving end of this for years: there was no pity where it concerned her health; there was only concern and fear as far as her actions went. Lang Shalin—she would be carrying his name wherever she went, and her father never let her forget it.

"On the contrary, I have given you the choice many times over." He flipped to the last page of the forms. "There is no need for you to be doing what you do. And now look what you have caused. Your face is splattered on every newspaper in a hundred-mile radius."

Rosalind's fists tightened under her sleeves. Before she could snap a terrible response, the maid poked her head into the office, carrying a tray of tea. It gave Rosalind a second to compose herself, shaking her head when she was offered a cup. The maid proceeded forward and set the tray down on the desk.

"What would you rather have me do?" Rosalind asked. "Shall I be the one to bring you tea at every strike of noon? Let that be the most exciting part of my day?"

"Don't be deliberately facetious, Shalin."

"Stop calling me that." Her demand tore out without thought.

Her father narrowed his eyes. "Should I call you Fortune instead?"

She wished he would. Then she would be entirely free, untethered to this past and this ache.

"Yes, you may." Rosalind walked forward. Perhaps she should have played this smarter, possessed some sort of pretend piety so she could appease him, but she couldn't find it within herself to summon the energy. "Will you sign this?"

Her father leaned back in his chair. That was answer enough. Rosalind scooped up the forms, holding them to her chest. She was her own guardian; she had always been her own guardian. She already knew how to forge his signature anyway.

"Shalin, I urge you to—"

"Lang Shalin is dead. Please don't contact me again." Rosalind's voice hitched, but she blamed it on her movement, the swish of her hem and the rustle of her coat as she pivoted and walked for the door. "Besides, no one will be answering your letters anymore."

The house hissed what sounded like a farewell. A good riddance from the corridor, expelling something that was no longer welcome.

"Adieu."

When our operatives leave the city, it begins to stir.

It has been inching toward a breaking point for quite some time now, public sentiment climbing and climbing in the direction of a colossal scream. Every covert branch is starting to heave under the weight, pieces breaking out into the countryside to get all ends in order, but it doesn't take an operative to tell you that. Ask any civilian on the street. Ask the elderly lady who sits at home watering her plants. Ask the schoolboy who holds his auntie's hand when she walks him past the gates of the academy.

They came for Manchuria first. They will come for Shanghai next, swallow up the coastal city where they have already been allowed land and law. The empire across the sea is small. And when this is an age of expansion, they will claim that invasion must be performed in self-defense, that it is a necessity while their people grow hungrier, a population with mouths to feed and feet to plant.

Isn't that how it always goes? Their people are real people.

Our people are not real people.

Give it a decade, and maybe the sides switch. Give it a century, and maybe the power moves.

But here, now—the worst of it begins.

They have chosen to push Shanghai, so Shanghai pushes back. This is a city with an open artery gouged through its middle, feeding off the running leak instead of losing lifeblood. For so long, ships have poured in, commerce piling onto the piers that act as grafting for a wound. Banks and hotels with soaring domes, plugged along the riverside like tumors. An automobile crashes into a barrier; a rickshaw screams its fare. Foreign power glistens and crowds together under the golden spotlight, but what is any of it without the feral body it grows on? They push, and demonstrators crowd the streets. They push, and Shanghai clears its shelves of Japanese products, for the businessmen know how to fight too, using the same capital ichor that brought these ships in to drown air out of their lungs.

Protests rise up and down the country, but the city that feels everything right underneath its skin emits a different fury. September sees Manchuria snatched in the north. So January sees a volatile readiness storming fast along Suzhou Creek, snarling at Hongkou, where the Japanese Empire has put most of its residents. For every push, there is a riot. Shops close. Japanese residents go home. It's not enough. It won't stop until one side breaks.

Hit me, the city screams. *I dare you. I'll show you what I'm made of. I will expel you all.*

So they do.

They do.

The calendar opens to January 18. In Zhabei, an incident is unraveling directly on the streets, within view for any civilian in their homes to see, and if it feels too obvious, it's because they have been sent in. *I heard there are monks parading,* the whispers pass on. *Someone said they were chanting slogans. Someone else said they were calling for Japan to rule over all of Asia.*

The people mob out into the streets. A push deserves a shove, does it not? A scream demands a battle cry, does it not? If the Japanese are to occupy this city and ask for it to be swallowed up, then the people here can surge forth too, light their torches and stake their ground. If they are to be swallowed, then let them choke.

You can't have me, Shanghai says. *I was never made to be controlled.*

The Chinese beat one monk to death. Wound two others. Hours later, Hongkou stirs with its own mob—Japanese—marching to a Chinese factory in retaliation. The Japanese set it aflame, causing two to burn to death inside.

Shanghai managed to keep civil war outside its borders, pushed its own grappling away from the foreigners. International war is a whole other matter.

The Japanese have their excuse, just as they did when the train tracks exploded in Manchuria. Their consul general goes to Shanghai's mayor, asks for the arrest of the mob who killed the monk, asks for an end to this boycott of their goods and products.

"This is justice. Get your city under control."

The whispers move. Rumor mills and truth wrapped in shadows. The mayor deliberates how to perform to the demands, and war lurks at the ready when he answers wrong. Cruisers and destroyers enter the river. Marines land in the International Settlement.

"What is happening?" the streets mutter. "What has caused this?"

"Haven't you heard?" others whisper back. "The empire has made its threat. *You have ten days to meet our demands. Or else.*"

10

"Why are we going south?"

Rosalind's question cut into an hour of silence. At the wheel, Jiemin seemed to startle, as if he had forgotten that she was sitting next to him. "I beg your pardon?"

They were three days and three stops in. After Rosalind's stunt in Shanghai, Jiemin was closely monitoring her answers, ready to pull the microphone at any moment if she started talking about Orion. So far she had been adhering to her usual answers—she rather enjoyed slamming the concept of imperialism anyway, so it was far from an unenjoyable job. These stops tucked between the more populous areas didn't draw large crowds, so she was being smart about how often she annoyed Jiemin, in case he really decided to pull the tour entirely. Only two or three reporters showed up at each stop, writing for their township distributions. The rest were usually townsfolk or villagers attending out of mere curiosity.

"South," she said again, pointing to the window. The sun's position in the sky and the current hour told her the direction of their route. "We have been driving down a while now. At first I thought you were only trying to avoid traffic, but this is definitely not the way to our next stop."

The Nationalists had drawn a northwestern route. Though the posters broadcasted a *national* tour for sensationalism, the truth was that this was very much a regional tour, targeting the rural areas that received Shanghai's news most. If they crept too close to other major cities, the people in those surrounding areas wouldn't care much about Lady Fortune anyway. Perhaps they had heard of her, but war moved differently through the country, changed the ways that the papers talked about its saviors. Rosalind's prime targets were nearby. Or what constituted as nearby in a country so large.

"It is only a small change of plans," Jiemin replied. He took one hand off the wheel and rested his elbow to the side. His fingers tapped the window glass, betraying a hint of nerves where none showed on his face. "We will rest up at the next town and keep touring, don't worry."

"Which town?" Rosalind asked. "The next stop was supposed to be right outside Nantong."

And since Nantong was a small city—small compared to Shanghai, anyway—it was going to be the next place she went rogue. It would have drawn a crowd. It would have drawn media outlets that spread her claims wide and wider.

"We're going to drive awhile until we're closer to Suzhou," Jiemin replied.

Interesting, Rosalind thought. He hadn't answered the question.

She turned to face the back, peering through the rear windshield. The passenger seat rumbled beneath her, the engine on the car puffing hard from their daily movement. The Nationalists, to their credit, weren't working *her* very hard. Jiemin always drove slowly because they were a five-car procession. At any moment, his modest car was followed by four enormous military vehicles, jammed with soldiers who guarded every stop. Each traveling leg of the journey took about three hours when they set out in the morning; under normal circumstances Rosalind suspected the drive would be faster, but Jiemin would navigate on the more winding roads, his eyes glancing to the rearview every so often to watch for trouble. Once they arrived at their destination, Rosalind was given her own room at whichever inn was the best in town, and she was left to her own devices to read or brew poison by the crackling fireplace until she was needed in the early evening.

"We aren't being tailed or anything?" she asked.

"Of course not." Jiemin's gaze stayed on the road. "Don't be ridiculous."

"How am I being ridiculous? This is a public tour. We're a constant target for attack." They had soldiers guarding their route, after all. Though Rosalind found no reason to poke the bear and mention the Communists during the media questions, some reporters had asked nonetheless. It would only be good warfare to ram a car into her while she was touring and take a propaganda figure away from the Nationalists.

"Well, there's no attack coming." Jiemin, as usual, maintained his monotone. "So relax. Sit properly, would you?"

Slowly, Rosalind adjusted herself to face the front. Since Shanghai sat on the very eastern coast of the country, there were only two choices for traveling outward: northwest or southwest. The tour route started north, going until they reached Nantong, right at the mouth of the Yangtze River. Then they were almost following the river's flow, moving westward until Nanjing, curving south until Hangzhou, then east until they were home, performing a loop around Lake Tai. Rosalind had been making calculations the moment she traced their proposed path on the map. If luring Lady Hong out didn't work as her first plan, her second plan was to slip away a few days from the end, when they were close to Suzhou. Because Zhouzhuang was nearby and, by then, she supposed she would be desperate enough to trust an anonymous note.

But now . . .

If they were heading to Suzhou *now,* they were going in the opposite direction entirely. What happened to the original northward route?

"I noticed you whispering to one of the soldiers at the last stop," Rosalind said carefully. "And as much as he's eyed you up, I doubt you were merely organizing a rendezvous. If we are not being tailed . . . are we avoiding something?"

What report have you received? she was asking instead. *Has intelligence sighted Lady Hong coming to attack us?*

"Lang Shalin," Jiemin said dryly. "Perhaps I think Suzhou is nice around this time of the year. There needn't be a reason why we are doing the tour in the other direction instead."

"Do you think I'm a child you can lie to?" Rosalind shot back. "I am *older* than you. By five years, at least."

Jiemin shot her a sidelong glance. "I thought it was one year."

"I am frozen in time."

"Then that doesn't count. You're still nineteen."

Rosalind threw up her hands. "It is remarkably clear that you are lying about your reasoning right now, so—" The thought occurred to her like a flash of lightning. Suzhou. Zhouzhuang. That letter Jiemin had been writing back when they were working together at Seagreen. "Wait a minute. Are *you* JM?"

Jiemin frowned. "I beg your pardon?"

"JM," Rosalind said again. "The person who left me that note. *I can help you get him back. Find me in Zhouzhuang.*"

And at once Jiemin went pale. "*Who* left you that?" he demanded.

What sort of reaction was this? He both seemed to understand and not understand what she was talking about.

"If I knew, I wouldn't be asking you, would I?" Rosalind said nastily.

Jiemin still looked like someone had stomped on his foot. He peered over the wheel, eyeing an upcoming turn. He didn't speak again until the gravel crunched under the vehicle, clearing as they proceeded straight.

"You said a JM summoned you to Zhouzhuang?" He switched to English. "*J* for 'jester,' *M* for 'mountain'?"

Now she didn't want to confirm it, because she had just put Jiemin on high alert for that location. Rosalind went for a non-answer instead. Give him a taste of his own medicine.

"What part of this confuses you?"

"The part where this note exists at all." Jiemin shook his head. "Either way, it's not me. I promise you that."

But he clearly held some stake in it.

"Why did you react so affectedly?"

"I was surprised to hear you mention Zhouzhuang." Jiemin's expression had leveled again, returning to his usual bored temperament. "I have friends there. It's very small."

"You weren't acting like that," Rosalind insisted. "You sounded horrified."

"Maybe I'm horrified about why you possess something like that. Who is that note referring to, Lang Shalin? Is it Liwen?"

Rosalind went quiet. If she said one word more, then she would get the very same spiel from Jiemin that she had already heard. Orion was a lost cause. Orion was never coming back. Orion was a traitor to the nation, and even if the Kuomintang did catch up to him, it was no rescue mission; it was an assassination. Jiemin had cornered her into the end of this conversation, and he knew it.

"None of your business," Rosalind grumbled, leaning back into her seat. She folded her arms. "I don't—"

Jiemin slammed suddenly on the brakes. The whole vehicle screeched, and Rosalind barely kept herself from launching forward into the windshield. *What the hell?* Even for him, this was an overreaction—

"Stay here," he commanded, pushing his door open.

Rosalind blinked. Oh, so that wasn't for her? Maybe she was getting egotistical. As quickly as she could, Rosalind hurried out of the car too.

"I thought you said we weren't being tailed."

"I thought I said *stay* there." Jiemin had stopped two paces away, looking warily into the distance.

"Don't tell me what to do." Rosalind pulled out a hairpin. She observed their surroundings too, following Jiemin's line of sight as the rest of their retinue pulled to a stop. They were no longer driving on a proper paved route, but rather a half-cleared dirt road, proceeding down the length of a field alongside a wire-linked fence. Two parallel lines in the frosted-over grass marked their path, just enough to accommodate the four wheels of a vehicle, still leaving the tuft of grass in the middle. Where Rosalind stood, the grass tickled her calves, icy blades running against her stockings.

The wind blew against her cheeks. She shivered.

"If you're going to stand there in the open," Jiemin said tightly, "cover your head. I don't want to have to explain to upper command that you got sniped."

Rosalind threw her arms over her head obediently. She wasn't too concerned. Most people weren't very good at making headshots from a distance, and if it was actually going to kill her, they needed to shoot point-blank and blow her apart on a level she couldn't heal from. From here to the distant tree line, she could see only open ground.

"Why are you concerned that . . . ?" Rosalind trailed off in the middle of her question, finding the answer for herself. Only three vehicles had come to a stop behind them. One was missing. Jiemin must have noticed through his rearview mirror and pulled them to a halt.

Was Lady Hong already here? Rosalind had expected an appearance at an actual tour stop—not somewhere along the route. Lady Hong would always be moving with a large number of soldiers because that was where her power force came from, so how was it possible that she could find them while they were journeying between stops, especially when Jiemin had been driving in a new direction for hours . . . ?

A fourth vehicle rolled into view.

Jiemin drew his pistol. Their backup in the other vehicles got out too, hands to their hips and braced on their weapons.

Then the vehicle got closer, stopped, and one of the familiar-faced drivers stuck his head out from the window.

"Sorry, sorry!" he bellowed from a distance. "I was only helping out a lost couple from the city. We're clear!"

The other soldiers grumbled, clearly irritated about the disturbance. Jiemin, on the other hand, put his pistol away with only a stony nod. He gestured for Rosalind to return to the car.

Slowly, she lowered her arms, her eyes narrowed. Even after Jiemin returned to the driver's seat, closing his door after himself and starting the engine again so they could be on their way, Rosalind remained.

What kind of couple from the city came all the way out here?

"Lang Shalin," Jiemin said, rolling his window down. "Let's go."

Rosalind nodded. She traced her gaze along the horizon once more, then finally got back into the car.

With a breath of relief, Celia leaned back in the passenger seat, watching the soldier drive away. They were parked under the shade of a large tree, having pulled over to feign confusion about their route when the soldier stopped and approached them.

Is there anything I can help with? I noticed you close behind.

We're a little lost, Celia had lied. She leaned in as hard as she could on her Shanghai accent, patting Oliver's arm. *Poor dear doesn't know how to navigate. Can you point us north?*

"Oliver," she said now. In that one word, she communicated her entire rebuke.

"Yes, yes, I know." He opened the door to the driver's seat, using his foot to kick it wide open. "Fine, you can take the wheel instead. I *might* have a habit of following too closely."

11

Ever since her father was arrested, Phoebe had stayed out of his office, thinking he might feel her presence in there even while behind bars, under Kuomintang watch. Then again, she didn't have a reason to go into his office anyway. It wasn't as if she cared about the administrative work he was doing there.

Until today.

Phoebe stepped through, waiting for the dust to settle around her. Ah Dou had stopped coming in to clean. What was the use when they didn't know when General Hong would be released—*if* he would ever be released? On the slim chance that the Kuomintang decided to let him free, it wouldn't be to this house, and it certainly wouldn't be back to the life he had before. The countdown had started on how long Phoebe and Ah Dou could remain here undisturbed.

So she needed to make a good search now.

With her fists clutched around her skirts, she hurried up the thin stairs two at a time. The wide spiral curved around the office, the steps ending at eye level on the ground before smoothing out for an elevated platform. Bookcases lined the walls as soon as the platform started, curling along the spiral up and up until it reached the high glass-dome ceiling. Some of these books had been here longer than Phoebe was alive. She had never bothered asking about their contents. This was her father's office: any normal girl would assume they were boring textbooks or accounting inventory.

It was almost a little astounding. She and Orion were both fully trained operatives by the latter years of their parents' treason. How had they not noticed what was going on? She supposed Orion couldn't be entirely blamed—her brother had been under chemical control from the very beginning, so even if he had raised a question, maybe their father had simply told him to forget it. Phoebe, on the other hand . . . What was her excuse?

She ran a finger along one of the spines, a poetry collection with leaves drawn onto the edges. Though Dao Feng had sent her to perform intelligence work on her mother, this wasn't intelligence gathering in the traditional sense. She didn't have to locate anything, lie her way onto the field, outrun pursuers chasing her away from critical findings.

No, all she needed to do was turn inward and look at what had been waiting under her nose this whole time. She had spent four years working for a faction that directly opposed Orion, thinking she was so smart, and for *what?*

In a fit of anger, Phoebe smacked one of the bookcases. It didn't make her feel any better; it only stung her palm.

Protecting your family is the most important thing, her mother had said to her that very last time she visited London, when they were walking through the park together on their usual mother-daughter outings. *Don't tie yourself in knots trying to discover what you ought to do in this world. At the end of the day, every job is the same, but you only have one family.*

Those words were the very reason Phoebe had become Priest. Those words flashed in her mind each time she trained her scope onto a target's forehead and fired without hesitating, spraying blood and grisly, fleshy, pink brain matter into the air.

Phoebe Hong, grand protector.

God, she couldn't even protect her secret identity from Silas. She was so obtuse to think she could keep this up forever.

"Xiǎojiě, where did you wander off to?"

Phoebe leaned over the railing. There was only one rung and empty space below it, so she was careful not to slip and tumble right off the platform.

"I'm here, Ah Dou," she replied, raising her voice so it would carry. "Bàba's office!"

The housekeeper's hard slippers clacked down the second-floor hallway. He shuffled in, hands behind his back, craning his neck with a grimace to search for Phoebe hovering above.

"Lunch will be ready in half an hour."

"Okay," Phoebe chirped.

She was careful to sound relaxed. Although Ah Dou was very good at keeping his mouth shut regarding affairs around the house, she didn't want him to get suspicious about what she was doing in here. Phoebe, to the world, came across as nothing more than a vacuous girl. She liked it that way. It made her feel as though she had control over herself. Over how much she was giving away and putting down.

Though he had been dismissed politely, Ah Dou stayed where he was standing. He cleared his throat.

"Feiyi," he said. "Is there something you're looking for?"

"I am only perusing," Phoebe replied. She scrambled to come up with an excuse. "I've come to the realization that I don't know much about my parents, which is quite startling."

Ah Dou didn't say anything in response. The silence drew long. As Phoebe resumed scanning the spines, she almost thought the housekeeper might have left. Then, in a gentle manner, he said:

"If you miss them, xiǎojiě, you can always ask me."

Phoebe's hand halted on the shelf. That was true. She *could* ask him outright. Ah Dou had started working for the household the moment her father inherited this mansion. He had been here since before her parents got married, three years prior to Oliver's birth. Even if Ah Dou didn't know about the tricky parts as they were occurring—like the treason—he *was* still a good resource.

"It's only that"—Phoebe whirled away from the bookcase, laying it on thick as she splayed onto the rail—"I feel like I have an entirely false conception of the world now. My parents weren't who they say they were. My parents are liars and . . ." Though she was exaggerating her excuse for Ah Dou's sake, the hurt in her words was unfeigned, the sorrow clawing a sharp nail at her insides. ". . . and I don't know how to handle that I do still miss them. I want to look back into the past—see how I didn't catch any of the signs. I want to know how much was real."

Her mother was the one who taught her to aim. Her father was the one who allowed her to have high ambitions. What was it all for? If Orion had been plucked up to be used, would Lady Hong come for Phoebe next, inject her too and manipulate her for gain?

And if Lady Hong didn't come—if she actually didn't care at all to come . . . then was that even worse?

When Phoebe glanced down, Ah Dou looked terribly sad.

"I suppose there is little help I can offer for that," he said. "They did love you, though. Of course they did. People can be capable of terrible things and hold love in their hearts at the same time. That's the complexity of mankind." Ah Dou straightened his sleeves, then pointed a finger up. "Your father stored photo albums at the very top shelf. They're hidden behind the medal display. Hopefully there's something in there that proves it. Lunch in half an hour. Don't snack before then."

He shuffled out of the office. Phoebe's gaze shot to the top shelf, hurrying along the spiral and grabbing her skirts again.

"Behind the medal display," she muttered in echo, searching the very end of the platform. She needed to watch her step. The glass dome was right above her, and taking a tumble from this height would most certainly break her neck.

"Aha."

There it was. Phoebe rose onto the tips of her toes, grabbing the medal display at its sides and easing it off the shelf. It was heavier than expected, the rectangular frame tilting dangerously. The medals swung on their hooks. On the left side, one dropped entirely.

"Tā mā de—" Phoebe shifted in an instant, adjusting to hold the frame with one hand at the base, her other hand shooting out to catch the medal before it could slip off the platform and smash to pieces. She breathed a sigh of relief. Set the frame down.

Exactly as Ah Dou had said, there was a whole stack of photo albums waiting behind the frame, covered in a thin layer of dust. Phoebe's arms hurt a little as she went to grab them, twinging from her close save, but she ignored it.

"Let's get to work."

12

Rosalind was growing increasingly suspicious.

The outskirts of Suzhou were fish farms and fields, villages situated around lakes and townships running with canals. Jiemin had practically driven in circles before they arrived at their next town, slathering the wheels of his car with mud. Perhaps that could be explained as him being careful, but Rosalind stood now in front of a podium taking questions, and though the hour hadn't drawn to a close yet, her superior was wandering off, something catching his attention at the side of the town square. It was bizarre. He had made it his mission to supervise her answers. Wasn't he afraid that she would start talking about forbidden topics again? There were still at least ten minutes left of questions.

"—mobilization?"

Rosalind started. "I'm sorry." Her microphone screeched with feedback. She searched the crowd for the person who had been talking, then realized she hadn't even noted it to begin with. Though it wasn't getting dark yet, the hour hovering somewhere past four in the afternoon, the skies were gray and heavy, signaling a downpour to come. The whole town square was vaguely foggy. "Could you repeat that?"

The tour was moving in a new direction, and it was avoiding major locations. If Jiemin thought Rosalind wouldn't notice, he was sorely mistaken. They could have cut a line straight through

Suzhou. Instead, they had pressed as close to Lake Tai as they could get, curving north to south like a half-moon.

"No, of course there's no threat to our safety at the moment," Rosalind answered after the audience member repeated their question. She was still searching for Jiemin. He had disappeared. "Besides, you can trust that the Kuomintang are snuffling out threats before they ever reach your ears. Next question?"

Hands shot up. Small as their locations were, the crowds were getting bigger each time.

"Can you show us your powers?"

Rosalind barely stopped herself from rolling her eyes. "Unfortunately, unless you want me to bleed all over this podium, I will have to refrain from doing that."

The man at the back wasn't satisfied with that answer. "Come on! There are hardly any photographs of the immortal Lady Fortune in action."

"I don't see the relevance of that request."

"You can understand the people's curiosity. How do we know this isn't some invented scheme by the Nationalists?"

"If you believe that, then—" Rosalind stopped dead. While she scanned for Jiemin, she had caught movement on the other side of the town square. A glimpse, and then nothing, disappearing behind the teahouse on the right.

Orion. That was Orion peering around the corner.

At once, without a second of hesitation, Rosalind pushed away from the podium, jumping off the raised stage. The reporters exclaimed aloud in curiosity; the ordinary townspeople raised their eyebrows, perplexed over this turn of events. She didn't pay them any mind. She performed a hard swerve in the crowd so that it was clear she wasn't heading over to strike the man with the outrageous question, breaking from the audience and running for the teahouse at the edge of the town square.

"Orion!" she called. Rosalind skidded around the bend. The pathway was empty. *No*. "Orion! I know you're there!"

"*What* is going on?"

Someone grabbed her shoulder and spun her around. She came face-to-face with Jiemin.

"I saw him," she said. "Orion. He's here."

It was a flash of bewilderment that crossed Jiemin's expression first. Then—*pity*.

"You probably just saw me," he said. "I was looking around the perimeter."

He thought she was imagining it. That she was mistaken.

Rosalind yanked her shoulder out of his grip. Behind him, the other Kuomintang soldiers were shutting down the press event, waving for the attendees to scatter.

"He was wearing something entirely different. He was dressed in black. *I saw him.*"

Before Jiemin could give her another excuse, she spun on her heel and ran down the pathway. She didn't know where she was going; nor did she know exactly what she was looking for. She took a left, and then she scanned her surroundings; she gasped in a breath of air and moved through a thinner alley, peering into each window she passed. She'd seen him. She knew she'd seen *something*.

Rosalind kept running. Kept searching. She almost collided with dozens of townspeople minding their business, but she couldn't stop herself from continuing, even as she wandered so far from the town square that she knew she was on a wild-goose chase. She finally brought herself to a halt at the corner of the next wide road she came upon. Her pulse was pounding so intensely that she could feel it in her teeth, each vibration thudding from her neck right into her mouth.

"Damn it," she whispered to herself. "Goddamn it—"

A car pulled up in front of her. The door opened from the inside: Jiemin, pushing it wide and sliding along the back seat.

"Get in. Now."

Rosalind exhaled in defeat. Though she wanted to dig her heels into the ground and refuse to move, she got into the car, her hands clutched tightly before her. She always did. Wasn't that the problem?

Jiemin didn't say anything at her side. It was a very short drive. When the car stopped in front of the inn, Rosalind clambered out, itching at every bend of her limbs.

She slammed her door. "This is the end of today's event, yes?"

"It is," Jiemin replied. He was close on her heels as she walked into the lobby, going up two flights of stairs to her room. "I do request a word, though."

"What?" Rosalind snapped. She pushed in through the entryway, tore her gloves off, and shed her coat. Even though her room wasn't well insulated and her qipao was short-sleeved, she could barely feel the cold. Her bones might as well be made of poker irons, burning red from contact.

Jiemin caught the door before it could close in his face. He grimaced, stepping through and shutting it properly. "If you need time away from this tour . . ."

"I don't need time away," Rosalind hissed, spinning around. "I need to know what the hell you've been concerned about these past few days and whether it has anything to do with Orion *showing up*."

A howl of wind blew outside, shuddering the windowpanes. They had come into the inn right on time: rain poured down in an instant, hammering a staccato tune upon the roof. Something was shifting into place here. A thousand different explanations ran through her head over how she could have seen Orion, half of them being that he needed help, and she couldn't do a single thing to save him.

"I think you might have misunderstood." Jiemin, still holding that grimace, walked to the table in the adjoining kitchen and leaned against it. "Fine. Yes. There have been warnings coming through covert about your tour. It has nothing to do with Hong Liwen. We received an alert about Communists trying to put a stop to it."

What?

"For what reason?" Rosalind demanded.

Jiemin shrugged. The motion looked entirely too casual for the topic at hand. "We don't know yet. Our spies are hard at work trying to figure it out. Right now, all we can conclude is that they have sent people in, so we're on high alert and changing our routes to minimize the chances of sabotage. That's it. I promise."

"You promise," Rosalind echoed. She scoffed. "You just as much as admitted that our information pipelines aren't functioning very well. Lady Hong is nearby. We need to take advantage of the opportunity."

"It is highly unlikely," Jiemin insisted. "She's moving with a military force. Any conflict with us would be an international incident."

"Domestic."

Jiemin paused, taken aback at her quick correction. "I beg your pardon?"

Rosalind examined her hands, pacing a small circle around the room. Winter always used to roughen her palms and crack her knuckles, but these days her skin stayed perfectly unmarred. It didn't look right. "She's in collaboration with the Japanese and passing her research to them for resources and money, but technically it would be a domestic incident. She's a Kuomintang asset gone rogue. It would be infighting."

"Infighting for another country's agenda. Therefore an international incident."

"No, that's impossible to prove," Rosalind returned. "The empire could deny it every step along the way. She has never been a Japanese agent. She has always been serving her own interests, following where her research goes. It is no different from a militia group starting a coup against its warlord because someone else offered to buy their loyalty. Domestic."

And when the coup succeeded, Lady Hong would be rewarded, and she would have the resources she needed to continue experimenting in the name of research. In a way, this was easy to understand. Everything she did against her country, she did for herself. It just so happened that the Japanese Empire was also benefiting while she worked, and Lady Hong didn't care that she was helping cause harm.

Jiemin seemed to give up on arguing with her. He stuck his hands into his trouser pockets, still leaning against the table. The rain poured on. They listened to it fall for a long moment. Then:

"We're not in the age of gangsters and warlords anymore, Lang Shalin," Jiemin said. "This is the national government. Please leave the battle plans to the generals and lieutenants. You are one agent. You have one task, and it's not Lady Hong."

Sure. The generals and lieutenants. As if they weren't the ones who let this build into what it was now. They had dismissed General Hong the first time around. They had failed to find Lady Hong even knowing she was armed with resentment over her project's shutdown.

"How can I do that?" she asked tightly. "Right now, their battle plan is ignoring her and hoping she goes away."

"Right now, their battle plan is keeping an eye on the empire funding her. We have bigger problems than one woman."

When Jiemin tipped his head back, stretching his neck and letting his gelled hair shift from its combed line, he looked his age for once. Eighteen years old and handling national decisions. Eighteen years old with sway on the fate of hundreds upon thousands.

He pushed off from the table. His hair fell back into place.

Rosalind tucked her fingers into fists. She stopped pacing, hovering at the edge of the kitchen.

"You should get some rest," Jiemin said now, walking for the door. "We're starting early tomorrow—"

"You are underestimating her." Her words stopped Jiemin just as he was reaching for the handle. "You have to know that. This isn't your regular rich elite turning hanjian for more wealth. She's working with science that you cannot begin to imagine." Rosalind reached for the knife block on the kitchen counter.

Jiemin swiveled around rapidly, just in time to see her draw out the sharpest one and press the blade into her arm. "Lang Shalin, what are you—"

"Have you seen my powers before?"

Rosalind cut a line from the inside of her elbow to the inside of her wrist. The blood ran immediately, rushing into her palm, running down her open fingers, dripping to the floor. Pain followed seconds later—sharp, searing pain—but by then Rosalind had prepared herself enough not to react.

Though Jiemin's eyes turned wide, he held his tongue. His lips thinned; his posture was as stiff as a board.

"You haven't," Rosalind answered for him. "So look. I will show you. A few seconds more and—oh, how nice. Bleeding has stopped." She set the knife back onto the countertop. Wiped the crook of her elbow to clear some of the blood there. "All my wounds knit together from the inside first. If anything gets caught deeper, in muscle or near bone, the injury won't heal until it has pushed all debris out, so the skin is the last thing to smooth over. And just as I say that . . ." She stretched her arm out. The wound was gone. As if it were never there.

"Were you making note of the time?" she asked.

"Less than a minute," Jiemin answered. He had schooled his expression to impassivity again.

"Shoot a soldier with these abilities, and he heals that quickly." Rosalind went to the sink. She put her arm under the tap. "Make a strike that should have been critical, and before you can take a step away, he's already recovered. That *one woman* has the power to start a large-scale hostile takeover. If you don't get Orion away from her and stop her from experimenting further, she could blow a hole in the government just to prove that she can. What then? What's the point in preparing to fight the Japanese on the battlefield if she's killed everyone before you can even lift your weapons?"

Rosalind slapped the tap off. The water stopped running, swirling down the drain in a muddied brown fashion. Her arm was clean once more.

Jiemin heaved a sigh, scrubbing his hands up and down his face. The rain poured on.

"Okay," he said eventually. "Okay. I will talk to upper command. We can formulate a better plan." He pulled the door open. "In the meantime, *please* just try to prevent getting snatched by the Communists before we finish this tour. Meet me in the hallway in the morning for our next stop."

Jiemin exited the room. Once Rosalind was alone again, she walked to the window, peering out at the dull gray. Everything looked the same. The low buildings, the shop fronts. The heaving, crying skies and the slick, paved street. She missed Shanghai. Everything outside the city had a sleepy quality during these hours because their lights went dim so early. Though Shanghai was blinding at times, its heart pulsed electric no matter what time of the night it was.

Rosalind pressed a hand to her mouth. She had missed a bit of blood at the tip of her finger. She ignored it.

Had she been mistaken? Even if it was a trick of the eye, she had seen someone peering around that corner. She couldn't possibly be so lost in her own head that she was conjuring Orion out of nothing.

A cold tremor crept down her spine. She turned around suddenly, moving away from the window. What had that driver in their traveling party said? *I was only helping out a lost couple from the city.*

"Mon Dieu."

Who looked nearly identical to Orion? Christ. Rosalind couldn't believe the thought hadn't occurred to her until now. Especially after Jiemin *just* said that the Communists were meddling with the tour.

Rosalind caught sight of a telephone plugged into the corner. She hurried over, picked up the receiver, and dialed headquarters.

"Can you transfer me?" she asked when the line connected. "To Shepherd."

"May I ask who's calling?"

Rosalind hesitated. Little point in using code names now. Not when her face was splattered on posters across the city. Still, she said: "Fortune."

The click was immediate. A few rings later, Silas answered, his voice hoarse. "Wéi?"

Rosalind frowned, looking at the clock. "Were you sleeping? It's five o'clock."

"Why am I being judged for my sleeping schedule?" A rustle echoed over the line—probably Silas adjusting the telephone cord. They had both switched to speaking fast English, which didn't entirely protect their conversation, but it did make it harder if there were spies tuned in. "There are underground meetings I attend late at night. Nothing wrong with catching up on rest ahead of time."

Rosalind wouldn't know. Rest had become a foreign concept to her.

"Do you know anything about Oliver out on the field?"

A beat passed on Silas's end. Rosalind hadn't bothered with a prelude to her question, so Silas needed a moment to process what she was asking.

"I haven't heard about any specific mission," he replied, "and trust me, I've been looking extensively into Oliver. Why?"

"I think he's following me." Rosalind paused. *A lost couple.* Although she was certain that Celia was likely to be close by too, she left her sister out of this. There was no need to implicate her or risk any information leaking to the Nationalists about her presence. "I think he's after Orion too."

Silas took another moment to consider the matter. The thing about Silas, Rosalind had noticed, was that he never mused excessively—he digested, he drew his conclusion, and then he verbalized precisely that.

"He must know," Silas said aloud, arriving exactly where Rosalind was. "When you encounter Orion, he's going to swoop in."

Rosalind swallowed down her curse. "I can't let him do that. Can't you put some words in undercover? Get the Communists to withdraw?"

"I'm not high up enough for that. Oliver makes most of his own decisions."

Damn it. Rosalind was at a loss. He and her sister were most definitely going to make an appearance, but as to whether they would harm or help . . .

"Okay. I'll figure it out," she decided.

Silas made a curious noise. "What's that mean?"

It meant she ought to get ready. Though she was never going to hurt her sister, she would do whatever else necessary when the situation arose.

"If they're going to combat me for him," she said, "I'll return fire."

Celia returned to their inn an hour after Rosalind's press meeting ended. She entered when another group did, appearing natural by fiddling with her sleeve and looking distracted so that no one within the group would wonder why she was walking so closely. The receptionist at the front desk didn't notice her come in. Good. Silently, she parted with the group at the stairwell and climbed to the top floor.

Inside their room, Oliver was playing with a piece of string. He didn't immediately turn when she walked through the door, but the legs of his chair made a scraping noise against the floor, pivoting the rest of him to face her.

"I was about to start worrying."

"I didn't want to go in when there was no one there," Celia replied. She took her coat off. There were flurries of ice collected on her collar. "Small town, smaller telegraph office."

When Rosalind's press event ended and the Nationalists ushered her away, Celia and Oliver had signaled to each other from their hiding places before Oliver slipped away from the scene and Celia went off to send a telegram to central command, updating them on their mission progress. Oliver had been waiting for some time now.

"So the missive has been sent?" Oliver asked.

"Of course. I updated them on where we're going next." Celia finally took a deep breath, relieved to have returned. Maybe the concept of safety was a mere illusion in their lives. All the same, this—the doors locked and the curtains drawn tight, a candle flickering for light and Oliver sitting vigilantly in the corner—was close enough. "What have you been doing?"

Oliver gestured behind him. A dress of hers was hanging off another chair. "I finished restitching the hem half an hour ago."

"I'm talking about that." She pointed to the string he was still flicking back and forth.

"Oh, that." In a flash, Oliver had tied the string around his armrest, securing it in a looped knot. "Practicing a one-handed restraint technique. Impressive, no?"

Celia reached for a cup in the kitchen. She filled it with water. "You tied a pretty bow, Oliver. Whoever you are trying to restrain like that is going to free themselves in about ten seconds."

"It is only a temporary method. Don't have such high standards, sweetheart."

He stood up. Wandered over to the counter too, propping his elbows on the granite. For a good minute, she and Oliver listened to the rustling of the inn and the night outside singing with crickets. The rain had stopped. Oliver, eventually, broke the lull to say:

"She was calling for Orion."

Celia took another sip of her water. "An easy mistake to make," she replied, her voice quiet.

"I didn't think she would see me. I was rather far away."

Meanwhile, Celia had been situated on the third floor of a building overlooking the town square. At first she had risen quickly when Rosalind plunged into the crowd, pulling away from her surveillance out of personal concern. When she'd realized it wasn't danger that her sister spotted but rather a case of mistaken identity, Celia had forced herself to duck low behind the window in case the Nationalists started looking around and saw her.

"Be glad that she *did* mistake your identity and didn't yell *your* name out loud," Celia said. "The Kuomintang can shrug off her imagination running wild. They're going to be much less inclined to shrug off confirmation of our presence."

Oliver folded his arms. He leaned lower on the granite, his head lolling before rising suddenly.

"How often did you speak to your sister after she went on assignment at Seagreen?"

Celia almost dropped her cup of water. "Why do you ask?"

"Only curious." Oliver straightened up, then returned to his chair. "Don't sound so concerned."

Alisa's voice echoed through her head. *What if Oliver is instructed to grab his brother without any regard for Rosalind in the middle?* It was a valid question. And Celia hated that. They had already formed a plan, and the encounter today with Rosalind confirmed that it would certainly work when the time came. If Orion were to appear, he would be wearing a Nationalist uniform as part of Lady Hong's disguised forces. That meant it was easy for Oliver to dress exactly like him and incite confusion, which also meant it would get most of the attention off Orion for Celia to grab him.

"I can offer no help about her time at Seagreen." Slowly, Celia walked across the room too. She opted to remain standing, her arm brushing the curtains. "Everything she told me was about her personal business. Not her work."

"Good," Oliver said. "That's exactly what I was wondering about."

"Her personal business?"

A pause. Oliver reached for the dress he had left hanging on the other chair, prepared for her. He smoothed the fabric against his fingers.

"Is she in love with Orion?"

This line of questioning was entirely unexpected. Celia was most definitely not up to date on that. She hadn't even known that Rosalind and Orion had infiltrated Seagreen pretending to be married. As close as she and Rosalind were, it was only natural that information slipped through the cracks if they were separated for months on end.

"I . . ." Celia scrambled for an answer. "I don't know. I hardly thought to inquire in our letters."

"But it's not something you need to inquire about outright. It must have shown in the way she spoke about him. In the matters she mentioned."

"I don't know. Really. Believe me or don't believe me."

"Okay, okay." Oliver raised his eyebrows. "Don't bite my head off. I'm not trying to be an irritant on purpose."

"Hmm." Celia took another drink of water. She let their conversation peter off, then peeked through the window. When there appeared to be nothing interesting on the street outside, she turned around again. "All right, why are you asking about Rosalind like that?"

"I am only curious," Oliver said again. "When we encounter her . . . it is information that is good to know."

When they met in conflict. When battle broke out around them.

"Well, for her sake, I hope she's not in love with him," Celia muttered. "It can only make everything a dozen times more complicated."

"For Orion's sake, I hope she is," Oliver countered. "Maybe it'll save him when nothing else will."

Celia paused. Digested his words. He had sounded completely matter-of-fact, but she knew him well enough to spot that waver at the end, a signal that the truth had squirmed its way out despite Oliver's best efforts.

"And do we want that?" she asked carefully. "Orion saved?"

Central command wanted him as an asset. Central command had sent them after Orion Hong to secure a resource, either to be used or to be wiped out on their terms. If Oliver went against this, he was going against them.

"The first step is saving him from my mother," Oliver replied evenly. "Everything else comes next."

"But then *what* happens next?" Celia kept pushing. "Let's say we successfully yank him away from her when he shows up. What if the only way to save him is by giving him back to the Nationalists?"

Oliver was quiet for a moment. Suddenly, he stood up, stretching his arms wide.

"How about we consider that when we get there?" He walked past, brushing her shoulder. "It's dinnertime. I'm starving. What are you feeling?"

Celia held back her sigh. Just as she thought she was getting through to him. "Dumplings. You're on duty to go get them."

13

The first time Silas had spoken to the agent Priest, it had seemed like some sort of fever dream.

Not because he couldn't believe he was in contact with her or anything along its technical aspects. He had slowly been winning the trust of the Communists and they had been talking about his proper recruitment, so he had known the opportunity was coming. They had talked about where he would fit in, whether covert needed more hands doing its grunt work . . . which—though they used pretty words and circled around saying it outright—meant they needed more assassins. Silas had leaned into that as hard as he could. He had asked about tutelage. Confirmed that he possessed the skills necessary and only needed a guiding hand who was already an expert in the way their faction functioned to show him the ropes.

When the Nationalists assigned him to work as a triple agent, their instructions were clear. It didn't matter how long he ultimately went undercover, but he did need to show progress or they would put him on something more useful. Silas thought he had been making plenty of progress. First the approval to try him around covert. Then the communication tapes from Priest that had given him tasks to complete and people within the Communists to speak to.

While Orion and Rosalind were still working at Seagreen, Silas had secured a phone call. It was the next logical step. To officially designate himself into the role.

"I am confirming my acceptance of central command's proposal," he had opened the call with. "I will operate under you, if you would have me."

"That's a little presumptuous."

Her voice had sounded more feminine outside of the tapes. The cover-up technology didn't work as well when it was nothing except a phone line between them.

"I beg your pardon?" Silas asked. He thought he had said something wrong. Or that someone in the Party had moved him elsewhere, so he was about to lose his contact with Priest. In a fit of panic, he had leaned an elbow on the phone booth door, then almost tumbled right out of the phone booth when the door started to move.

"Usually it takes a bit more wooing before I let people operate underneath me." A beat passed. "That was a joke. Now is your cue to laugh."

Silas, meanwhile, was scrambling to right himself and pull the door closed again, tangling the phone cord around his wrist. He processed the words.

"I—huh?"

On the other end, then, Priest was the one to laugh instead. It was an unfathomable sound. Silas had heard her voice already, for months on end with the two of them exchanging recorded tapes at drop-off points around the city, but not this. Not spontaneous reactions, a quick back-and-forth that instantly erased the idea of a mysterious assassin in his head and replaced it with a girl. A laughing, tremendous girl.

So he stood by it: the conversation had felt like a fever dream.

The tapes had sounded different after that. As had the few letters. There was something that turned him practically *abuzz* during his communications with Priest, but ever since Warehouse 34, she had gone unusually quiet.

Silas lifted the rock. Underneath it, the hollow still held the same tape he had put there three days ago. He had dropped a letter at a more secure location too, the back of a letterbox at a cinema in the International Settlement. There had been no reply.

She was taking longer and longer. The responses, too, were becoming more and more vague.

With a frown, Silas pushed his glasses higher up his nose, then hurried to his feet, brushing the dirt off his knees. He left the cemetery, his breath visible ahead of him. The pavement was slippery this morning, and his parents had warned him to watch his step when he left the house. Not that the warning did much until he actually almost slipped getting out of his car. He was warier now, his polished shoes coming down on the pavement with care. Some of the shops in these areas were still decorated with Christmas ornaments in the windows from the previous month's festivities, but most of the city did not care about the Western holidays. He hopped over a bundle of silver tinsel that someone had torn down and tossed on the streets. The last of the shops would be tearing down their decorations before January's end, tossing them into the trash to glimmer amid rotting food and burnt cigarette ends.

Orion's house was nearby. It was part habit that had Silas getting back into his car and driving over—because he was accustomed to seeking out his best friend at the drop of a hat. Orion, though, wasn't there anymore. Orion was out in the countryside, and when Silas arrived at his house, it was Phoebe he sought for company instead. He liked to act as though she needed him. He liked to imagine himself as a steadfast auxiliary, the net waiting below at every moment to catch her if she slipped.

The truth was that *he* needed her. At every waking moment, if there was nothing dependent on him, then he might crumble into dust and ash.

"Feiyi?"

He thanked Ah Dou at the door. The Hong household was as familiar to him as his own: the chandelier in the main atrium and the vases at the foyer, each one dusted and polished at least twice before the day's end. Though there used to be a time when he had wondered why expensive paintings kept disappearing from the walls, it had taken only one accidental glance at the unbalanced account sheets that General Hong had left out to determine the answer.

"Feiyi," he called again.

"In here!"

He entered her bedroom. She was surrounded by photo albums, seated in the middle with her skirt puffed out. She was dressed in yellow today. Like a daisy sprouting from her pale blue bedspread.

"What are you doing?"

"Indulging in some nostalgia," Phoebe replied. She waved him near. "Come look. I was so cute."

Silas wandered over compliantly. When he peered at the photograph she was holding out, he found a black-and-white page of a much younger Phoebe dressed in an oversize nightgown, knee-high in garden grass.

A smile jumped to his face immediately.

"I remember when you looked like this."

"Do you?" Phoebe moved the photo closer. "My cheeks were so chubby."

"As is fitting for a six-year-old." Silas scanned the rest of the albums around her. Many were open to images of her parents. Each had little descriptions written at the bottom. The years they were taken or the locations. "Where did this all come from?"

Phoebe shrugged. She set down the album she was holding and

reached for another. "My father's office. I figure if he hid so much from me already, I may as well have a look at what else there is. My mother conveniently marked all the information I need. Oliver's first steps. Orion's first tooth. Phoebe's first throw-up."

Silas grimaced.

Phoebe's eyes flickered up, her lip quirking. "The last one was a joke."

"I sincerely hope so."

In London, Silas used to spend hours upon hours having the most inane conversations with Orion. They would sit in the study during the half-hazy evening hours, their heads tipped up at the ceiling, books open on the floor under the guise of completing their coursework. His unflinching friendship with Orion was what kept him sane. Orion would talk about his family. Silas would talk about his. The difference was, terribly, that Silas missed them more and more with each passing year, but Orion had started to notice that something wasn't quite right with his.

While Phoebe continued flipping through the photographs, Silas picked up an album at random. It opened to a wedding picture: Lady Hong, dressed in a red bridal qipao.

"My mother is not like yours," Orion said once. The stars were bright that night. Easily traceable for their constellations. "She cares for me in a way that seems like there is an ultimate purpose. Like I mustn't slip, or else some invisible strike will be made against me on a scoreboard I cannot see."

"I'm sure you're imagining it," Silas had returned. "It makes more sense that you are imagining it than it would if it were true."

Orion had hummed. Then, simply: "I do think you're right."

"Which one are you looking at?" Phoebe asked in the present.

"Your mother," Silas replied. "It's a little strange that she's your age in this picture. I feel like I can't look directly at it."

Phoebe grinned. "Don't be shy. Good looks run in the family."

He tried very hard not to blush. He failed. With a huff, Silas flipped farther into the album and skipped ahead to a picture of Lady Hong holding an infant. Not Oliver. The year marked at the bottom was 1909. This had to be Orion.

Silas had wondered, over the years, if maybe it was Orion he was in love with instead. Maybe Phoebe was only a stand-in until Silas could digest the minutiae of every feeling that lived within him. He was certainly invested enough in his best friend to ensure his health and heart and happiness. It would make more sense when he knew everything there was to know about Orion. Phoebe, on the other hand . . . well, he knew plenty about her, too, but there was always *something* about her that was slightly harder to reach.

The more he had mused on that possibility, however, the more he knew it wasn't true. As much as he had the capability to be in love with Orion—despite the fact that Orion was a goddamn menace—his attitude toward his best friend was that of family. He wanted to offer his help until the end of time. He regarded Orion as one of his favorite people, the one who smoothed over the pit of emptiness that opened inside Silas every once in a while.

A hand closed on his elbow. Silas jumped, taken aback, but Phoebe didn't even react to his awkward lurch, more focused on leaning in to see the photo he had opened to.

"What is *that?*"

Orion was not Phoebe. Orion was a comfort.

Phoebe was . . . He didn't even know how to describe Phoebe. An ever-expanding supernova. A hurricane that changed worlds and remade them.

"I believe that is your brother as an infant."

She took the photograph. A corner was blurred from movement at the time of capture, because even though the Hongs could afford a camera that would capture these images, it was not easy to freeze the moving world onto film, especially not for a kicking infant.

Phoebe remained quiet for a moment. Something seemed to have occurred to her; she only went silent like this if there were matters she didn't want to say aloud. In the hallway outside, Ah Dou clattered back and forth, mopping the floors.

"Phoebe," Silas said. Her name tasted illicit on his tongue when he switched to English. "What's the matter?"

Her head snapped up. Her ringlets shifted along her shoulders. "Just thinking about how I wish I could show this to him," she said. She let the album fall closed in her lap, the pages shuttering one after the other. Phoebe jostled a knee, and then the album went to join the rest scattered on her bed.

Silas thought about Priest again. If only he could *find* her, then they could help Orion, and Phoebe wouldn't be sitting sadly like this.

"You can when he's back," he said.

"Careful," Phoebe replied. She prodded his arm, and he felt the contact from his elbow to his spine. "Don't make promises you can't keep."

A *tap-tap-tap* echoed from her window. When Silas looked over, he found a tree branch nudging against the glass, a coat of ice around the bark sharpening the sound. He went over at once, taking it upon himself to open her window and snap the branch right off, tossing the loose piece down into the gardens. Phoebe was right. There was no point in making hollow promises. Nor was there any use wishing about a matter, as if that might cause something to come to fruition.

"Do you want to come with me?" Silas asked suddenly, closing the window. "I have a lead."

Phoebe shifted onto her knees. "Excuse me?"

"On Priest." Silas felt the urge to hurry to explain. Phoebe didn't like his search for Priest because she thought he was wasting his time. She didn't seem to understand how *close* he was to some answer. He could practically see the horizon in grasp; he just needed to strain as hard as he could to get within reach. "Last night, I went through every tape I have from her. Twice. And I finally caught something."

"Silas . . ."

"No, really, it's promising." He dug into his pocket quickly, pulling out the scribbles he had made. "On one of the more recent tapes, I heard the briefest interruption in the back. I couldn't figure out what it was until I listened again and realized it was music."

Though Phoebe took the scribbled note, she didn't look very impressed by his list.

"Priest records each message from a radio station," Silas concluded. "Someone opened a door at just the wrong time. Or the right time, I suppose. If she has to go to a location to use its equipment, someone must have seen her. Someone real who I can talk to and get information from."

"And have you thought about how suspicious it will appear when you're asking every radio station whether they have seen an assassin?" Phoebe replied. She pressed the note back into his hands. "Have you thought about how the whole station is probably a hideout for Communists? That the moment you poke your nose in, it gets back to her, and you are exposed for being a plant? *God,* Silas, use your head."

Silas stepped back.

Phoebe's expression crumpled. "Wait, I'm sorry. I didn't mean—"

"I do have another idea," he cut in. "But I'm not sure if you want to hear it."

There was a moment suspended where Silas almost hoped that Phoebe would be enthusiastic, a drawn-out second where the tide could have turned in any direction, and he might get the Phoebe who jumped on board with every one of their outrageous plans. But when Phoebe only blew out a breath, Silas had his answer. Very well, Phoebe thought this work was useless. He had hope in it. Once he brought her proof of his progress, maybe she would believe him then.

"Silas . . ."

"I have to go." He turned away. He didn't know that he was capable of doing that to Phoebe until he did it. "See you tomorrow?"

Before Phoebe could respond, Silas hurried out. No matter how foolish it might be, he was intent on putting his next steps into action.

Phoebe picked up the phone. Waited for her line to connect.

"It's Priest," she said, pinching the bridge of her nose. "Shut down operation at the Mei Sound and vacate the premises immediately. The Kuomintang are onto us."

14

In the middle of the night, a different telephone rings loudly across the makeshift base. Where a warning was passed within the city earlier today, this one stretches outside of it, carried by a trickier player and containing a premonition instead. The *brring-brring* echoes and crackles, each pulsing second filled with static, each imminent word crawling underneath Shanghai's borders instead of over, hiding from the view of prying eyes.

"Hello?"

The traitor answers. She uses English, because it could be military leaders along the line of command, checking in on the progress of the concoction. Their plan, at the very least, is shaping up nicer than its pitiful state in Manchuria. The mountains shield their movement south; the mountains watch their frantic speed, dressing the militia in play-pretend clothing, arming them with weapons that she is loath to need, because she *should* have given them something better by now.

"I have a bargain to make with you," the voice on the other end says, wasting no time.

She listens.

Five minutes later, she hangs up.

That is how she's still standing when Mr. Akiyama comes in through the door. He makes his rounds at this hour, wanting progress reports before retiring for the night. They will be moving again tomorrow, as early as they can manage. The shadows of mountains are hostile to traitors, and each moment spent here is another where frostbite nips at her fingers and whispers curses down her spine.

"I have to let my son go," she announces frankly.

Mr. Akiyama frowns. "I do not understand."

"He isn't useful here anymore. There's another purpose for him so that we may acquire something better in exchange. It would speed up my experiments drastically."

"I am yet to see the problem. Let him go, then."

"The problem is that he is my *son*. I do not wish to let him go." There's a crack in her voice. An uncharacteristic display of emotion. "He should travel with me. By my side."

Mr. Akiyama shakes his head. He grabs the last of the boxes that awaited in this temporary base, making one last glance around to ensure they haven't left anything behind. They cannot waste time when sunrise comes. Their lodgings are always temporary. Until they start their invasion properly, it will not do to get surveilled by the domestic forces governing this country. Much too complicated.

"Let him go," he instructs again, and he's already out the door by the time he's calling back: "And don't forget, you're a scientist, not a mother."

The mountains snatch those words like gold. Their shadows rush in, giggling, looming tall over the traitor and laughing at her misgivings. *Do you see what we witness?* they say. *Don't you see how foul you have played it?*

She grabs her bag for departure. Regret is an emotion reserved for the powerless. There is no need for it here.

15

At the very least, going southward meant it was less cold.

Rosalind breathed into her gloveless hands, trying to spread warmth along her frozen fingers. She had opted to go without that extra layer because it made a nicer image in photographs. Still, even though the temperature was bearable, she felt the sting each time the wind blew.

"We're getting in position around the perimeter," Jiemin said from her side, his hands behind his back. He wasn't wearing gloves either, but Jiemin didn't look like he was bothered by the cold. A wire looped around his ear, which he would tap anytime he was trying to communicate with the other soldiers. Judging by the number of times Jiemin had shaken that thing around, Rosalind suspected the Nationalists didn't have very good prototypical technology. They might as well yell loudly across the teahouse gardens.

Then again, Rosalind supposed that wouldn't be very effective if the soldiers spotted anything unsightly in the crowd and needed to give a warning.

"Okay," Rosalind said.

Jiemin cast her a glance askew. "And no more running off this time. I had to do immense damage control convincing the reporters not to write you up as a lunatic."

"You should have let them."

"Upper command would not like that."

"There was no thought of pleasing *them* when—"

Jiemin's look of warning intensified. Rosalind cut herself off, biting her tongue. He was getting distracted by his wire anyway, listening for a moment before swiveling and saying, "Then check for uniform. Our own people are . . ."

He marched in the other direction, his voice fading. Rosalind, meanwhile, remained where she stood, smoothing out her coat sleeve. She rubbed her hands again. The temperature would get better once they left the vicinity of Suzhou, where there would be less water bringing a damp chill into the air. Maybe she also needed to suggest that they start doing these interviews in the daytime instead of the evening. The sunset was impending, the sky cast in orange and pink.

"We're ready for you, Lady Fortune."

The man on the elevated stage gestured for her to ascend. Rosalind barely held back her frown, pasting a smile in its place.

Fortune. It's just Fortune—my goodness, where did this Lady *ever come from?*

"Thank you," Rosalind said. She stopped behind the podium. The crowd stretched to the edges of the gardens, piled out onto the pavement. Wind chimes sang from the teahouse behind her. A camera flashed in the front row. "I hope—"

Rosalind stopped suddenly, her gaze locking on one point in the crowd. Jiemin probably thought she was going to make a scene again, because he waved from where he was standing, signaling for her to continue.

Did no one else see the metal object rolling at their feet?

Rosalind rose onto the tip of her toes, trying to isolate its shape. It came to a stop in the middle of the crowd. Still, no one stirred, their attention fixed on the scene before them: on her, at the stage.

That looked like a damn grenade.

She lunged for the microphone. "*Everyone move*—"

The world went up in smoke.

Rosalind choked on her gasp. On instinct, she threw an arm over her face as she flinched, taken aback by the sound. It was not fire that erupted but opaque clouds, cloaking her surroundings at once and making it impossible to see anything more than her own two hands. She waved at the smoke furiously. The crowd was screaming—from alarm, not pain, but it was hard to tell.

"Lang Shalin! We're retreating!"

That was Jiemin's voice. She had no idea where he was.

"Retreating from *what?*" Rosalind called. A cough scratched at her throat. If the Communists were behind this, it was absolutely not the enemy party's usual style. *Smoke bombs?*

The wind blew a gust, clearing certain parts of the gardens for a brief moment. The tour had only brought along ten or so soldiers, stationed around the perimeter for safety. Now it looked like there were more than twenty.

And they were fighting each other.

Rosalind ducked behind the podium at once, shielding herself. She allowed herself the barest sliver of view. The smoke swirled low, irritating her nose.

Those aren't our people, she thought. Each part of that realization floated within reach slowly, in the way that dreams dragged at one's running speed. Then, at once, the only possible conclusion slammed into place, as if she had startled awake to find herself going at a dead sprint.

There were costumed soldiers on the scene. Which meant . . .

When Orion emerged from the smoke, he was holding a knife in his hand.

Merde—

Rosalind's grip tightened on the podium, her knuckles turning white. His mother followed behind him, her shoulders straight and her white coat fluttering with the wind. At that moment, their resemblance couldn't have been starker. Maybe it was their expressions: Lady Hong's determined frown and Orion's blank eyes. Maybe it was the synchrony of their appearance, breaking from the midst of the smoke like gods birthed out of chaos.

Rosalind couldn't move. She had plotted her steps, had coated each of her hairpins with sedatives and prepared to grab Orion when he arrived. Yet now, faced with him before her, she stayed frozen behind the podium.

He was dressed in Kuomintang uniform. The sleeves weren't right. The badges were fake. Even if the disguise fooled anyone, that absent gaze would certainly give him away.

A soldier dove at Orion. He stabbed his combatant and tossed him away as though it were nothing. The blood oozed a puddle into the grass. Turned it from green to slick red. While the smoke was clearing in small amounts with every gust of wind, there was still enough opacity to incite confusion, drawing short distances long and long distances short.

Orion took three strides forward. Scanned the gardens.

When he spotted Rosalind, her heart dropped to the bottom of her stomach. She wasn't afraid *of* him; she was terrified that she wasn't going to get him back, that he had been pulled too far away to reach. In her plans, she had envisioned rescuing Orion to be as simple as meeting his eyes and convincing him to leave with her.

Judging by their circumstances at present, that was probably not happening.

"Okay, okay," Rosalind whispered under her breath. "You got through to him once. You can do it again—*Jesus Christ!*"

That last exclamation came with Orion leaping onto the stage without warning. One moment he was still maintaining considerable distance, and the next his grip was closing on her shoulder. The stage suddenly felt miles away, swallowed up by the smoke clouds and shadowed by the gray skies.

Dimly Rosalind knew that this moment was dangerous. He could tear her apart. He *was* poised for attack, and yet her aching heart could only circle around *Oh, he's here.*

Oh, he's—about to stab her.

Rosalind gasped, twisting her shoulder out of his grip and avoiding the slash of his blade by a hairsbreadth. There was an acrid smell in the air when she inhaled, like rubber burning in the distance. Before she could overthink her circumstances, she swiped a leg at Orion's ankles to take him off-balance. He wavered unsteadily for only a moment. Still, it was enough for Rosalind to roll herself away, coming to a stop by the stage corner and scrambling to her feet. Smoke blew hard into her eyes. She thought she heard Jiemin yelling for her.

Rosalind held her hand out. As if that alone might keep Orion back.

"I know you don't remember anything," she started carefully. Her voice was hoarse. "I know this must be incredibly confusing."

Something passed in Orion's expression. It was gone just as quickly.

"Where's the vial?" he asked.

"Listen to me." Rosalind took a step away, teetering at the very edge of the stage. Her eyes flickered left, keeping his mother in her periphery. Lady Hong was observing the scene. There were no other soldiers nearby. "Orion, listen."

"Stop calling me that."

Rosalind stilled. Anger lurked in his command—or, rather, anger that spilled out of frustration, sharpening his words and contorting them away from that monotone.

All right. This was something to work with.

Orion lunged forward, and Rosalind feinted before skidding left, letting the blade whistle through the air. When the metal caught light, it reflected back a faint purple color.

"That's your name," she gasped. "Orion. Hong Liwen."

The blade swung again. This time Rosalind wasn't quite fast enough. She felt the knife make contact, cut a shallow line at the highest point of her cheek.

"The vial," Orion demanded. "Give it to me."

Her cheek stung like hell. One bead of red started to drip down her face in slow motion, like some color-inverted tear track. When her hand went up to wipe it away, her blood felt sticky on her palm.

The teardrop kept growing larger. Of course. That purplish glean on the blade was poison. Lady Hong knew better than to arrive with an ordinary weapon—it needed to be something that actually worked on her.

On his next strike, Orion slashed up, his blade making an underarm arc. Instead of swerving away, Rosalind caught his wrist with every iota of her strength, narrowly avoiding a puncture in the chest. Before he could recover and push harder, she kicked him back, her heel making a noise when it struck against one of the metal badges on his uniform.

The kick didn't seem to affect Orion much at all. It was only a distraction anyway before Rosalind had grabbed a handful of his hair and swung herself onto his shoulders, securing a grip on his throat.

"Do you know who I am?" she demanded. "You called me Rosalind. You said you wanted to call me Rosalind."

Orion threw her off.

And though Rosalind could have rolled to absorb the impact, she was so shocked that she fell face-first, barely putting her elbows forward to protect her nose before hitting the stage. She heaved for breath. Okay. Maybe provoking him wasn't working.

"You are nobody."

"Excuse me?" A wave of irrational anger overrode the pain of her landing. "I am your *wife.*"

The knife flashed. Orion stabbed down. Rosalind caught his wrist again, but only after the tip of the blade had already pierced her throat. They held in that stalemate for three seconds, five, ten. She could feel his pulse hammering where their skin made contact, pounding at such speed that she couldn't tell it apart from one long continuous war cry.

Rosalind's strength at full force was quickly about to give out. The small trail of blood already running from the tip of the knife would not stop anytime soon. Lady Hong had done the same with the bullets she shot at Rosalind back at Warehouse 34, had likely used the same poison. A lethal wound from this knife would kill her. She wouldn't heal from it.

"Orion, listen to me," Rosalind gasped. "You cannot be that far gone. Whatever you have been brainwashed to believe, you can break out of it. Orion, *please.*"

A shudder quaked down her spine. Her words tremored. She was trying to convince herself as much as she was trying to convince him: It couldn't be permanent. It *couldn't.*

Rosalind's grip slackened. Though the natural next action would have been Orion plunging the knife exactly where it had been poised, dead center in her throat, his hand suddenly jerked to the side, a flash of hesitation stilling his expression. The blade sank deep—into her shoulder instead.

Before he could yank it out and try again, a bag came around his neck.

Celia couldn't see a thing through the smoke.

She coughed lightly, waving the tendrils out of her face from where she was lurking. Most of the chaos was occurring in the teahouse gardens, and Celia had situated herself around the corner to avoid being sighted. They were prepared. They had been prepared for every stop along the way—it just so happened that at last, chaos had finally erupted.

"Christ," Celia muttered under her breath. *Had* Lady Hong arrived? The yelling would suggest the affirmative. As would the smoke bomb rolling out to interrupt Rosalind's event, obscuring the orange evening and turning everything into an impenetrable haze.

Celia surged forward, coming around the corner. Oliver had been stationed on the second floor of the building next to the teahouse. He had a ladder that spilled out the window and a fast-track route into the gardens in the event of an attack; he was the counter-distraction, and she was the agent who needed to improvise the best way to grab their target and filch him from both adversaries. There was no way to draw up a plan with further specifics. They went where the tide took them.

Celia choked on a half cough. But how was she supposed to grab Oliver's brother with all *this?*

"Where the hell are you?" she hissed aloud.

She caught sight of movement a few paces before her. Without time to spare, Celia backed up, her shoulder hitting a tree that she could use to take cover. There was no sign of Orion Hong, but that *was* an authentic uniform. When the figure in the smoke yelled out, raising his arm and calling for his forces to move forward, Celia identified him as Rosalind's newest handler.

Shit. She reached into her sleeve. Pulled a knife into her palm, just in case. Lin Jiemin—they had sent along a folder with his information, detailing his early education in the military and transition into covert intelligence. Celia scanned the scene again, waiting for another gust of wind to blow. A loud clatter came from the north end of the gardens. Then a shout.

Rosalind.

Jiemin surged forward. "Lang Shalin!" he bellowed. "Did you hear me? Retreat! Now!"

Wait, wait—

"Sweetheart." Just as Celia was about to follow, a hand closed on her shoulder, a whisper of breath coiling against her ear. She identified Oliver's presence behind her by feeling; he was going too fast for her to turn and confirm. He held her only long enough to hiss, *"Orion's with her. Get him,"* before he was moving again. Celia pivoted left instantly, merging deeper into the smoke. A cluster of soldiers were on Oliver's pursuit, being led away.

But Jiemin was still heading in the right direction.

Celia tore off her coat. Then her hat.

"Jiemin!" she yelled into the smoke. Her hair unfurled down her back, half loose and the other half pinned.

Celia had mulled over their plan of action dozens of times. In fact, she had spent most of their time on the road calculating how on earth she could intercept someone who had been enhanced beyond human, how she could possibly take him unaware short of shooting him until he went down.

Movement swiveled ahead. Jiemin turned in confusion, trying to locate what sounded like another Rosalind.

This part, Celia hadn't told Oliver. She knew he would ask the question she didn't want to answer: whether she was actually improving their plan or plotting to help Rosalind from the sidelines. Whether she was even working toward the ultimate endgame of securing their asset, or if she only cared to make sure the soldiers weren't impeding her sister.

Celia tugged at her qipao collar. "I'm here!" she shouted at Jiemin, taking a step back. "I'm over here!"

16

Rosalind heaved for breath, throwing herself onto her side. Half a second—that was how long she allowed herself to pause before she scrambled to her feet again, her hand clamping down on the blood spilling from her shoulder.

A few paces away, Orion threw off his attacker and tore the bag from his head. Alisa Montagova winced as she landed on her back, rolling to get out of the way.

"Alisa, go," Rosalind demanded at once. "This is dangerous."

"Yes, I *know,*" Alisa said, her voice dripping with attitude. "Hence why I've arrived to help you."

"Alisa."

Orion, in his hostile state, slowly looked between the two. As soon as he processed the intrusion, he was going to attack again. Rosalind's shoulder wasn't healing. With every second she wasted, another gurgle of blood rushed to the poisoned surface and seeped down her arm. She couldn't pull the blade out, either, because keeping the weapon there was actually stanching most of the blood flow.

"Do you think you're going to win this fight?" Alisa hissed. "You were two seconds away from getting stabbed right in the—"

Click. Rosalind's attention whipped toward the smoke. She hadn't forgotten that Lady Hong waited there, but she had hoped someone else would engage her in combat or pull her away. Instead, Orion's mother stood calmly by an overturned outdoor chair, pointing a gun with the safety off. She was growing tired of the argument, it seemed.

"Allez," she told Orion.

Go on.

Orion started forward. Rosalind's shoulder throbbed.

"Arrêtez," Alisa snapped in response, reaching into her sleeve. She was not talking to Orion. She had turned to Lady Hong. "Is this what you want?"

When Alisa Montagova tore out the vial, its liquid practically glowed green, neon with the promise of its might. The hastening dusk brushed the glass, touched up against its strangeness and flinched away.

A furrow of confusion sank into Orion's expression. Lady Hong, meanwhile, lowered her weapon. This was the last remaining vial of her final experiments: a merge of Rosalind's immortality and Orion's strength. The one that Orion had tested citywide in his brainwashed state until they finally got to its finished form. The one that Rosalind had given Alisa for safekeeping in case it proved useful for reversing whatever had been done to Orion. Before, Rosalind still held hope they could take back his strength, let him be another ordinary civilian walking the streets without the power to turn the tide of a war. But now his memory was a whole *different* matter, and where did they even start, with or without the vial?

"Alisa, don't," Rosalind whispered. Slowly, she reached up into her hair and withdrew a pin. "It's not going to be enough for her."

A series of bullets rang through the gardens. The smoke, however, proved still too thick to shoot accurately, so the sounds faded shortly before they could hit their own side.

"This is what you have come for, no?" Alisa went on. "Or you wouldn't have moved so fast."

Lady Hong's expression turned steely. Rosalind was paying more attention to Orion, whose eyes were fixed on the vial. He had been told to grab it. Now the one who issued the instruction was holding on standby too. Even in his altered state, Rosalind thought she could read him: he wasn't sure what to do.

"Miss Montagova," Lady Hong said. "Hand it over. You won't like it if I have to force you."

This time Alisa didn't offer a retort. She turned slightly to her right and met Rosalind's eyes. *Sorry, Janie,* she mouthed. Then: "Grab him."

Rosalind reared back. "What?"

Alisa smashed the vial to the ground. The glass split down the middle with a single fracture and parted the vial into a clean two, releasing the concoction inside. Though smoke swirled low around them, there was enough visibility to watch the green liquid seep into the grass and disappear into the brown soil.

For a moment, Rosalind could only stand gaping in shock, unable to believe that Alisa had destroyed their primary bait. It was gone. What were they to use as a lure now?

Grab him.

But if she was fast enough, they wouldn't need further bait at all.

Rosalind lunged before the chance could slip away. The pin was cold in her hand. She knew to duck to avoid Orion's immediate defenses; she knew to feint left, one arm coming behind his back to loop around his neck.

The time for softness was gone.

"Good night," she whispered.

She shoved her pin into his neck. It pushed with resistance, battled with her strength as if the very act of hurting Orion repelled her hand. Before she could scarcely finish the slash, Orion grabbed her arm and tossed her over his shoulder, the motion so fast that Rosalind flew across the gardens and thwacked against a tree trunk.

Her head spun. She suspected that awful crack was her collarbone breaking.

"Over there!"

Rosalind groaned, trying to rise onto her elbows. Her shoulder continued dripping blood. Her collarbone screamed in pain while the pieces reached for each other, trying to smooth back together. In that one throw, she had been hurled far enough from the stage that she couldn't see past the smoke anymore. Though her sight was veiled while she staggered upright, sound carried well across the gardens, and clear as day she heard Lady Hong command: "Get in contact about the bargain. We will accept the terms."

A bargain?

"This way! This way!" That came from the other direction. Nationalists. Sooner or later Jiemin was going to find her, and she needed to wrap this up before he could interfere. With a pained grunt, Rosalind stood properly, her shoulder pulsating hot and her cheeks red with exertion and rage.

"What kind of poison did you put on this?" she muttered, gripping her shoulder hard. Her collarbone seemed to have healed. It didn't hurt to rotate her other arm anymore, but even the slightest brush of her coat edge was irritating the blade in her shoulder.

Rosalind pivoted. A figure broke out from the smoke suddenly, coming to a prompt halt before her. In shock, the two of them stared at each other, waiting a beat in case the scene was a mere illusion.

"No," Rosalind said in lieu of a greeting. "You're not snatching him away."

Celia spluttered. "Calm down. That's not what I'm doing." She gestured at Rosalind's shoulder. "Do you want me to pull that out?"

Rosalind shook her head. "Poisoned. I'll bleed to death."

"You'll have to stitch it closed."

"Yes, *thank you,* mèimei—how could I forget to stitch my wound closed in the middle of battle?"

Celia frowned at her. Rosalind resisted the urge to press her palm to her mouth and blow a raspberry. They were having this conversation to the backdrop of men scuffling and what were likely knives clanging in the smoke. Someone was going to stumble onto them at any moment if they kept this up.

"What are you doing here?" Rosalind asked.

Instead of answering, Celia hurried forward, tugging Rosalind's coat around. She barely had a second to give her sister an annoyed look before Celia was yanking her sleeves down.

"Give me this."

"I beg your pardon?"

Celia took her coat. Rosalind's confusion overrode her suspicion.

"Go," her sister said. "I will handle this. The nearest hospital is in Zhouzhuang. Go there."

Zhouzhuang. There was that name *again*.

"How do you know that—"

Celia spun on her heel and disappeared.

"Wait, what are you doing with my coat?" Rosalind bellowed after her. She waited a beat. Celia wasn't coming back. With a huff, Rosalind lurched in the direction of the stage, her arms now bare in her short sleeves. Just as she was wondering whether she was going the right way, Rosalind slammed into another figure in the thick of the smoke.

"Sorry, sorry," Alisa hissed, reaching forward quickly to steady her. "Come on, I have a way out."

"I'm not leaving without—"

"Orion is collapsed on the ground over there. Your poison kicked in."

"Sedative," Rosalind corrected quickly. Following the direction Alisa was pointing, she waved frantically at the smoke before finding her way to the stage, muttering a curse under her breath. Orion was lying on his side. His head had lolled into the grass. Her pin was still sticking from his shoulder.

"Oh, darling," she whispered. She plucked the pin out. He didn't stir. If she ignored the roar of the gardens at war, Orion looked so normal before her, as though it were only another afternoon on the couch in her apartment. Flipping through files together, then declaring he was only going to rest his eyes for a minute before falling asleep in her lap.

"Rosalind! Get ready!"

Rosalind whirled around. She had thought Alisa to be directly behind her, but now her voice was coming from elsewhere, echoing through the smoke. Where had she gone?

"Alisa?"

And where was Orion's *mother*? Her best weapon had been left here, unguarded and weak. How could she let that happen?

Rosalind tossed her pin away. She pulled another from her hair, this one coated with proper poison, squeezing until her grip tightened to the point of pain. A section of the smoke had cleared to show silhouettes. By some instinct, Rosalind was certain that Lady Hong was one of them, departing the scene.

She hesitated. She didn't know what protocol to follow. Leaving Orion might mean exposing him to danger. Letting Lady Hong slip away meant the potential demise of the very country.

What do I do? she thought, frantic. *What do I do what do I do what do I do—*

As though it were a real voice blown across the gardens, Rosalind suddenly heard Dao Feng in her ear, each of his training lessons tugged out of her memories and spoken into the wind. She flipped through the earliest days of her work, through Dao Feng's made-up scenarios and his step-by-step instructions when they would walk through every worst-case possibility during an assassination and how she was to get out of it.

Yet all those lessons flashed past her mind's eye without taking root, each occurrence unable to be used at present. Instead, the one memory that clawed forth from the others hadn't even been spoken directly toward her. The loudest piece of her former handler that suddenly echoed into the gardens was: *She stops at nothing to do what's right. I'm proud of her.*

Rosalind lunged forward.

"Hey!"

Someone grabbed a handful of her hair.

"Oh my goodness," Rosalind said at once, coming to a quick halt. "Alisa, what's wrong with you?!"

"Sorry, sorry, I panicked." Alisa let go quickly. She examined her hands, sniffing with distaste, then seemed satisfied when she was sure that she hadn't accidentally pricked herself on any poisoned pins. "What were you doing? Let's *go.*"

"Lady Hong is about to get away—"

"Let her," Alisa said. "Your Nationalists are going to home in on us if you don't get Orion out of here in the next minute. Do you want that?"

She very much did not. With a curse under her breath and the bitter acknowledgment that Alisa Montagova was correct, Rosalind reached down to help an unconscious Orion upright, grumbling for Alisa to hurry and help.

"This way," Alisa instructed once they had Orion between them. She was inclining her head into the smoke.

"What?" Rosalind wheezed.

"I have a car. Come *on.*"

Alisa didn't wait for Rosalind to finish processing the instruction—she yanked Orion's other side hard and started to lug them forward. Three strides through the smoke revealed a small civilian vehicle, its engine still running and its tires mowed over the low garden fence, leaving the entire north side of the fence collapsed.

"Did you drive over that?" Rosalind hissed.

Alisa shot her a dirty look. "I couldn't *see.*"

She opened the rear door. In tandem, they pushed Orion onto the seats.

"He dropped unconscious shortly after fighting with you," Alisa reported cautiously, nudging the headrests away to get more space. "I heard Lady Hong tell her men to leave him here. Orion, I mean. It looked like she was trying to exit the scene as soon as he went down."

That didn't make any sense. His mother had to be planning something. As soon as Alisa finished adjusting the back, Rosalind clambered in too and reached for Orion, balancing her knee on the leather seat. She grabbed his jaw, turning him toward her. This was him. From the arch of his brow to the mole behind his ear, this was Orion—not some lookalike placed to play tricks on her. Still . . .

"Something's not right." Rosalind swallowed hard. "But we can figure it out later."

"What about . . . ?"

Alisa trailed off, tilting her head toward a new chorus of shouting. Though Lady Hong had presumably departed the scene, many of her soldiers remained, fighting Rosalind's side. A gunshot tore through the smoke, and they both flinched. The night grew darker. It was impossible to see where the bullet had landed.

"I'm going with you," Rosalind decided firmly. Her priority was Orion. The foremost matter at hand right now was getting him out of here.

"Okay," Alisa said, already moving. "Get in."

Rosalind scrambled into the back, her heart beating a cacophony in her chest. Alisa, meanwhile, tumbled into the driver's seat so fast that she slammed the door closed with half her hair caught outside.

"Ow, shit." She yanked her hair in through the door.

"Language."

Alisa spared a second to roll her eyes. "You think you're so funny." She put the vehicle into reverse. Stepped down hard on the accelerator. "Hold tight."

The car screeched, pulling away from the gardens. For a moment, they seemed suspended, hovering in the smoke with the same opaque nothingness on every side. Then Alisa grumbled more curse words under her breath and jerked sharply on the wheel, putting them on the road with an aggressive bump over the sidewalk.

In a matter of minutes, Rosalind had abandoned the tour—and the Kuomintang at large.

17

Dense forestry rushed past the windows in a blur, the trees turning all-consuming the farther out they went on rural land. They had only left the scene moments ago and had quickly exited the town, but Rosalind didn't feel like they had made a getaway.

It didn't help that Alisa was . . . not a great driver. On the third time Rosalind got tossed around in the back seat, she realized with rather decisive certainty that Alisa didn't actually know how to drive.

"So I have bad news and good news," Rosalind said, recovering from the rough bump and glancing out the rear windshield. As long as they didn't crash, she supposed she didn't need to be fussy.

"Good news first," Alisa said from the front.

"I'm bleeding at a rather steady rate, so I'm not dying for another half hour, give or take."

Alisa turned around at once. Rosalind yelped, her hand flailing to clutch the seat while the car almost pivoted off the dirt road. Her life flashed before her eyes.

"Sorry, sorry!" Alisa took control of the wheel again. "That's the *good* news?"

"The bad news is that we're being pursued."

"What? But there's no car—" Alisa squinted into her rearview mirror. Rosalind caught the moment Alisa spotted them too: five, maybe six soldiers. Running. They had to be enhanced by Lady Hong's experiments in some manner or other, else it would be impossible to keep pace with the car. And they were keeping pace very closely. "Oh, surely you jest."

"I don't think they jest. Can we lose them?"

Alisa shook her head. "Not here. There's no path anywhere but forward."

The trees were too dense on either side of the dirt road. Their only alternative was going by foot too, and they most definitely did not have the means to outrun the soldiers, especially with Orion knocked out.

Rosalind inched closer to him. She was afraid he would bolt awake when she touched his face, her every paltry movement ginger as if she were treating a wild animal. There were multiple bruises where his neck met his shoulders. Too many to have been caused by her one hairpin, and besides, she had stabbed into muscle to avoid harming him. These were older. Her finger traced the edges of the purple mottling, her inhale held inside her lungs. She could feel his heartbeat thrumming directly under his skin, soft and wild.

His mother was still experimenting on him. That was all Rosalind could conclude in a red-hot fit of rage, but how did this make any *sense*? Lady Hong had been present at the scene herself. She could have easily issued her instructions there, commanded that her soldiers haul Orion back the moment he collapsed under the sedative. Instead, she had disappeared into the smoke, no one had come to combat Rosalind, and the thick of the battle had been with the Kuomintang in a whole different section of the gardens. Now there were soldiers running after them, but why send people after the fact? Why let them have him at all?

"The nearest township from here," Rosalind said, "is it Zhouzhuang?"

The car jerked again. Alisa's eyes flashed fast to the rearview mirror, catching Rosalind's gaze for a brief moment before she course-corrected. It had been too fast to determine, but Rosalind swore she caught surprise in Alisa's expression.

"No. That's slightly farther out," Alisa said. "Why?"

"Celia said it's the nearest hospital."

"*Celia?*"

"Oh, you didn't notice her in the smoke?"

Alisa removed one hand from the wheel to pinch the bridge of her nose. They started to veer left. "What the hell is she talking about? There's no hospital in Zhouzhuang."

Rosalind frowned. "I don't suppose she's just trying to kill me. She's had nineteen years in the same household as me and five years with an enemy faction to try."

The car veered even farther. Noticing their diagonal driving, Alisa quickly adjusted the wheel again, her attention flicking up to check on their pursuers.

"Tell it to me straight," she said. "Do you need medical attention right now?"

Rosalind hesitated. "No."

"Miss Lang."

"No. I told you, I'll be fine."

For half an hour. If the poison didn't take her out first.

It was as if Alisa could hear that silent addition. She raised her brow into the rearview, and Rosalind stared back.

"We're stopping," Alisa decided. "Celia probably knows better than I do."

"What?" Rosalind exclaimed. "They'll catch up the moment we stop."

"You can't argue with me on this. It'll do no good if you end up dead."

"I'm not going to end up dead."

"Do you *see* how much you're bleeding?"

"*Yes,* Alisa, I clearly see it when it's my own blood."

The car fell silent. Her tone had sliced forward razor-sharp, weighted with every bit of panic in her stomach. Alisa flinched, drawing her shoulders up to her ears. Rosalind felt her tongue curdle in her mouth.

"Wait, sorry," she hurried to say, her volume lowering. For most of her life she had trained as a dancer, and yet she still seemed to walk through the world with horrendously clumsy feet, stomping on the toes of every person she passed. "I didn't mean to sound like that."

"It's fine." Alisa scrunched her nose. Her tone genuinely matched her response, brushing off the matter without any hint of bitterness. "You have to admit that I'm right, though. We can't keep driving into oblivion. We're more likely to run out of fuel before these soldiers get tired."

Another bump in the road sent the car flying for a flash of a second. Rosalind tightened her grip on Orion's arm, a lump building in her throat. If Jiemin had anything to do with that note from *JM*, stopping in Zhouzhuang wouldn't bode well. There might be an ambush waiting. She might be walking right back into Nationalist hands.

Yet Alisa was right—what was the alternative? The back seat reeked of a metallic smell. She was keeping her shoulder as still as she could, but even with the blade plugging up its wound, small rivulets streamed nonstop from either side of it.

"Drive faster," Rosalind said. "They're catching up."

"They only build engines that go so fast," Alisa muttered. She made a hard right at an upcoming bend, then stomped harder on the accelerator. When her gaze returned to the rearview this time, it only inspected their pursuers for a moment before lowering onto Orion. "Should we tie him up?"

"What?" Rosalind curled her hand around Orion's arm, holding him steady against the rocking car. "Why would we do that?"

"He's the one who stabbed you."

"It's fine."

Something had gotten through. Whether it was memory or not, it had changed the direction of his attack, even if he couldn't stop himself entirely.

"I'm not even going to pretend to understand," Alisa muttered. The sunset had almost disappeared over the horizon. It would be pitch-black in a few minutes, which wasn't great when there weren't any streetlights on these rural routes. "The exit to Zhouzhuang is coming up."

Rosalind turned to investigate the rear window again. "The moment we stop, I'd give it twenty seconds before they're on us."

"Then we'd better move fast." Alisa swerved a fast left. Suddenly, she was on a proper paved road, driving toward a set of town gates with lights shining at their base. "You keep them back; I'll shoot."

Rosalind blinked. "Don't you know hand-to-hand combat?"

"Miss Lang, please." Alisa started to press on the brake. "My side has a resource shortage. Covert agents go into the field untrained. Or bringing whatever skills they already possess."

"I mean, I knew *that*." Rosalind shifted in her seat, pressing closer to the door in preparation. "I just thought, with the way you grew up . . ."

"The gangs dissolved when I was *thirteen*."

"All right, all right." The car skidded against gravel, joining two other vehicles parked by the gate. "That's my mistake."

At once, Rosalind and Alisa pushed out into the night, meeting a fierce gust of wind. Their doors slammed closed. An unconscious Orion remained inside. With the light around the gate, it was harder to see movement coming by the tree line, but Rosalind knew they would be approaching.

Alisa clambered onto the top of the car. Her gun clicked with the sound of the safety coming off.

"There they are."

Quicker than Rosalind could have imagined, the soldiers arrived.

"I'd better not regret this."

Rosalind yanked the knife out of her shoulder for a weapon, then used it on the first soldier lunging at her. She turned to the next immediately, moving on after one deep slash. Alisa's gunshots were terribly loud. Though Rosalind winced with apprehension that it would draw out the townspeople living in Zhouzhuang, there was no time to dwell on the matter: three new soldiers were on her at once. And despite Rosalind aiming well when she made her next slash, her knee grew weak when she pivoted, sending her off-balance. The knife skittered to the gravel. She was empty-handed.

Rosalind could ignore the pain, push her shoulder wound to the recesses of her attention. But she couldn't ignore her rapid blood loss once she'd pulled the blade out, her vision spinning faster and faster. White dots danced in her periphery. Loomed larger.

When the soldier grabbed her, she barely had time to take a breath before he was trying to drag her away. They must have been instructed to take their subjects alive, or this would hardly be a fight. The soldiers weren't trying to kill; they were trying to capture.

"*Christ.*" Rosalind kicked. It did nothing. She dug her heels into the ground. Still nothing.

"Rosalind, do something!" Alisa screamed. With one yank, she was hauled off the top of the car and roughly onto the gravel. "I'm out of bullets!"

"I'm"—Rosalind grasped frantically through her hair—"trying!"

"Try harder!"

"Alisa, that is *so* unhelpful!"

Rosalind finally released herself, stabbing her last hairpin into the soldier's wrist. Even with that momentary freedom, another had ahold of her in an instant, an ironclad grip around her upper arm. She wheezed, making a count of their opponents. No one was going for Orion in the car. Why wasn't anyone going for Orion in the car?

There was no way Rosalind was getting out of this. Whatever Lady Hong's intention was sending these soldiers after them, she must have wanted Rosalind captured. It was over.

Then a sudden gunshot tore through the night. Rosalind pivoted fast, still flailing in protest, eyes searching for Alisa. The soldier that had been holding Alisa collapsed on the ground, a bullet in his forehead.

"How did you do that?"

Alisa looked up with a start. "That wasn't me."

"What? Who would—"

The night came alive in a flurry of motion. Before Rosalind could scream in fright, another figure was on the scene, leaping onto the soldier holding her and slashing his throat. A woman—clothed in black with fabric pulled across her face. As soon as she was on the move, she threw something to the side, and then a man was there too, catching the knife she had passed on. He was dressed the same.

And he was just as fast, two bullets to weaken another soldier before his blade slashed into a rib cage.

Who are these people?

Rosalind scrambled to steady herself. She yanked her hairpin out from the body on the ground to keep the last soldier back, but the woman was on it before she could do much. Though the soldier landed a punch, the woman smoothly took the attention and absorbed the attack while the man finished the killing blow on the soldier's back. Down he went.

The night finally exhaled.

The two strangers exchanged a glance. Turned around.

Rosalind's hand went up to clutch her shoulder. In the silence that followed, she was trying to stay vigilant despite being close to passing out, because if the purpose of this rescue was to intercept the asset in the car and take it for themselves . . .

Alisa let out a shriek. Rosalind stiffened, except when Alisa ran forward and launched herself at the stranger, she realized it wasn't a sound of alarm but sheer delight.

"Oh my God," the man said. He wrapped his arms around Alisa tightly, holding her up. "Oh my God, Alisa, you're so big now."

He was speaking Russian. And his voice sounded . . . familiar.

Slowly, Rosalind turned to the woman.

Holy shit.

She was seeing ghosts.

The woman yanked the square of fabric off her face.

"Biǎojiě," Juliette Cai said, grinning. "Don't you recognize me anymore?"

Rosalind released her shoulder, losing all feeling in her fingers. Before she could say a thing in reply, she crumpled to the ground.

18

The smoke was starting to fade. Celia had been fumbling around for some time now, pitching her voice like Rosalind's to keep Jiemin going in circles. Though she was all the way at the southern end of the gardens, she had just heard the screech of tires, then the loud echoes of Nationalists calling instructions to one another. Someone had left the scene. Either Rosalind had made a getaway, or Lady Hong had.

Celia pressed up against a tree, considering her next move. Even with the coat on, she and Rosalind didn't look *that* alike up close, not in the way that Oliver was nearly identical to Orion. If she moved fast, there was a chance that the Nationalists would follow and continue thinking she was Rosalind from a distance, buying her sister time to get away. There were safe houses in this town. One that was nearby, according to the map she had scoped before the event. But then her own mission . . .

Large swaths of the smoke cleared with a new gust of wind. For a brief moment, Celia glimpsed Oliver up ahead, engaged in combat with soldiers who looked to be Nationalists. It was hard to tell. This whole affair was a fight between true Nationalist soldiers and fake Nationalist soldiers wearing costumes. It could have been either side.

Celia hesitated. She couldn't wait until the smoke cleared to find out. That was a fast-track method of getting killed.

As soon as Oliver finished disarming a small group of soldiers, Celia surged forward and grabbed his wrist. "We're going."

Oliver blinked, twice. The first time was in surprise; the second time was at something over her shoulder. He said, "Duck," and Celia acted on command, dropping to the ground just as Oliver threw his jacket over the head of the soldier running at them. The moment his opponent was blinded, he took Celia's elbow and hauled them out from the thick of the battle.

"Where's Orion?"

"Yeah, about that."

The fence was completely flattened. Someone had driven a vehicle into the gardens, then reversed with little care about what they were running over. Those tire tracks didn't look like the military vehicles Lady Hong must have charged onto the scene with. It looked like a civilian getaway car.

"Over there!" a soldier bellowed from behind.

Celia stifled a gasp. The Nationalists had almost cleared the scene amid the last wisps of smoke. What remained were either bodies from both sides collapsed upon the grass or Lady Hong's soldiers being held captive. Perhaps the Kuomintang had plans to bring them back for information, but she doubted any of these men had much of their minds left intact to give up anything of value.

"Run."

Oliver didn't hesitate. He did, however, look rather confounded, casting another glance at the tire tracks before they circled around and skidded onto the street past the teahouse.

"Do continue," he said, as if they were maintaining polite conversation over a light platter of snacks.

"Rosalind has him," Celia huffed. She had no confirmation, but she was willing to bet on the guess. "Assuming she follows my instructions, I know where they're going next."

Celia cast a glance back. The Nationalists were mobilizing on their chase much quicker than she would have expected. They needed to deal with this first before worrying about finding Rosalind again.

"This way," Oliver said, noting the same and signaling left.

They swerved into a side street. Celia spotted a door into a pavilion and hurried them toward it, closing the entrance after themselves just as a few soldiers ran by.

"Confirming report. Spread out and search . . ."

". . . operatives Hong Lifu and Lang Selin on the scene . . ."

At once Oliver and Celia froze, their gazes colliding with shock. There was no reason they should have been identified already. For all that the Kuomintang could see from a distance—from the only context they were working off—they were Orion and Rosalind.

"That doesn't make any sense," Oliver muttered. "I look just like my brother. At no point did they see us both. How would they know?"

Not only that, but they were calling her Kathleen again. For her entire time as an agent she had been identified among Nationalist enemies only as Xiliya—*Celia*, but its transliteration into Chinese, spreading among operative circles like a code name. Her sort of intelligence work meant she swapped into new code names too often to let one be her general identifier, so by nature she and Oliver slipped their proper names into the field. And since she never chose herself a new Chinese name, Westernized it was.

She supposed that since Rosalind's identity had gone public, information was starting to cross streams. Rosalind was being slapped front and center on the papers, so it was only a matter of time before Celia joined her, before people farther along the Nationalist chain of command recognized her photos and put two and two together that the Xiliya they knew used to be the city's Lang Selin. They would believe Kathleen Lang to be the real person and Celia Lang to be an adopted identity—when, in reality, it was the other way around.

But how could they have seen through the mix-up between *Rosalind* and Celia that quickly, unless they had already suspected that Oliver and Celia would show up? It sure as hell wasn't Rosalind giving them the warning when she hadn't even known Celia would be there, so . . .

Celia bit too hard on her lip. She tasted metal in her mouth.

"We better find an escape route as soon as possible," she whispered. "I suppose we're not really fooling them anymore."

Oliver squinted beyond the pavilion wall. "Might be better to take shelter first. Isn't that the safe house?"

Celia followed his line of sight. The apartment was three houses away, rising slightly taller than the other buildings on this block. Its east-facing window was visible from here, reflecting the gleam of the low moon.

"It is," Celia said. The soldiers were still shouting closely enough that their voices echoed back, albeit faintly. It was a tricky maneuver, but Celia could trace the exact route to the house, even from her lower vantage point. "We could climb our way there. It'll be less conspicuous than using the streets."

"My thoughts exactly. Let's go."

Oliver hoisted himself onto the top of the wall, then reached his hand down. While Celia scrambled to hurry, her shoes weren't doing her any favors when it came to balancing. She squeaked, almost pitching right off the top of the wall before Oliver slid an arm around her waist to hold her in place.

Celia stilled. Her balance was recovered, but she was off-kilter in a different way.

"You okay?"

A nod. She didn't trust herself to speak. The building on the left had a small ledge on its side that they would need to leap onto, and she focused her concentration on that instead.

"Go first," Oliver whispered.

"All right." Celia stood shakily, listening for the soldiers' voices below. "Don't scream if I fall and splatter in the alley below."

"Don't *say* that," Oliver chided.

"Too late."

With a barely held wince, Celia jumped, clutching a pipe while she secured her foothold on the ledge. Oliver followed suit, entirely without struggle. They circled the exterior walls, one foot in front of the other on the precarious ledge, then repeated the process to get onto the next building. This one had to be an inn. When Celia pressed up against a window and eased across it, she heard snoring inside.

"There!"

Celia froze, her hand still gripping the top of the window frame. The call had come from below, at the other side of the building. Seconds later, a gunshot rang into the night. She didn't dare look over. If they had been seen . . .

"False alarm! Keep moving!"

She breathed out. Beside her, Oliver released his exhale too.

"We're almost there," he whispered. "How are we going to get through the window?"

"It looks like it's only a latch on the inside," Celia replied, inching along the exterior wall again. Her shoe kept threatening to slip, but she was cautious, making sure each foothold was secure and at no risk of sliding around before putting any weight down. "Do you have anything thin we can get between the panes?"

"I would pat my pockets, but I shouldn't let go of this wall." Oliver paused. "What about the pins in your hair?"

"I don't wear—" Celia stopped. She was about to say that there were none, but there were three perfectly good pins sticking out of her hair that she had put in to mimic Rosalind. She was surprised Oliver had even noticed them. "That might work. Get me up?"

As smoothly as they could manage, they jumped onto the restaurant building, hovering just below the window that would be their entrance. Footsteps thudded closer and closer, and when Celia glanced down, she saw a soldier surveying the alley right beneath them. He had his back to them, going in the other direction.

But that way was a dead end. He was going to turn around as soon as he reached the wall.

"Putain."

"Mon Dieu, surveille ton langage."

"Watch your surroundings," Celia retorted. "Hurry!"

Oliver lifted her smoothly, putting her at direct eye level with the window. It took a few seconds of fumbling before Celia could push the pin in, then it was *just* too short to smoothly hit the latch. She shoved against the pane. Yanked the pin up. Again.

"Another soldier has entered the alley. . . ."

"I've got it!" Celia declared, the latch swinging off. "Come on!"

She pushed the window, its hinges squeaking obnoxiously. Though she intended to hop over the sill smoothly, she practically threw herself in, lying flat on the floorboards. Oliver scrambled in too, ducking down just as the soldiers turned around to continue their search.

A few minutes passed. It sounded like they had left the alley.

The safe house groaned in greeting. Night was a blanket of safety, but it was also an extra veil of risk. Anything could jump out when they weren't watching.

Celia rose to her elbow carefully. They had landed in some sort of small room. A few boxes were stacked tightly to their left, but otherwise the space was dusty and unoccupied, leading toward an open door.

"The whole place should be empty," she said, still slightly short of breath.

Oliver clambered to his feet. "It can't hurt to make sure."

They entered the dark hallway, waiting for a reaction with each step they took. The safe house wasn't large: it was an unoccupied residence above the restaurant, so the only proper access was through the stairs in its back kitchen, leading up to the hallway, which then split into two rooms, one on each side. Celia peered down the stairs, listening. No doors or barriers blocked them off from the restaurant. She could hear the soldiers shuffling around outside.

"These rooms extend a bit farther than the restaurant itself," Oliver observed. His volume was quiet, as though he was talking to himself more than actually intending to speak aloud.

"Maybe a passageway?" Celia suggested. "For another exit."

It didn't look like there was any other way out except for the stairs, unless they wanted to climb through a window again. Oliver entered the second room wordlessly. Celia trailed in after him, letting her eyes adjust to the darker space. With less moonlight coming in through the smaller window, she could hardly tell what the shapes in the corner were until Oliver went rummaging around, kicking at the tarps draped over the furniture until something metallic clinked.

"Hmmm," he said simply.

Celia sneezed.

"Shush, sweetheart."

"Sorry," Celia said nasally. "Let me just plug up my nostrils. What was that noise?"

Oliver pulled the tarps off. One dresser. A mirror. Nothing useful in the slightest—no radios or telephones hooked up to the walls. "I'm not sure. Do you still hear it?"

He rustled the tarps around, trying to re-create whatever he had done to prompt the metallic clinking. All he did was produce more dust, and Celia pinched her nose to prevent sneezing again. A groan reverberated along the floorboards. The curtains to the window were folded at the top, a pale fabric color that was gathering spiderwebs from its sides.

"I don't hear it." Celia stepped closer to the furniture pieces.

The cheap wood and chipping sage-green paint looked like they hadn't been touched in eons, put up here and left forgotten. As if they were decoration pieces to another era rather than real, usable pieces, and Celia nudged her foot against the corner of a mirror stand, trying to push it against the wall.

It scraped against the edge of the rug. The clinking noise came again.

Ah.

"It's the floor," Celia said. "Something is beneath the rug."

Oliver got to work immediately, shifting the furniture pieces off the rug. Now that Celia's eyes had adjusted to the dark, she could see the patterns on the yellow rug as each segment was cleared, the ends stretching to take up half the room. The border was faded, as were the symmetrical whorls and floral details, but it still looked like something that had been rolled right out of the Qing Dynasty.

Celia grabbed one corner. Oliver grabbed the other. Underneath, there was a circular handle attached to a panel in the floor, barely larger than the window they had climbed through.

"Well, it's not an exit." Oliver lifted the hatch. Inside, the space was miniature, likely built to store food. Whether the original intent or not, it could also store fugitives in the event the safe house was intruded upon. "But it is a hiding spot."

He let the panel fall closed. The metallic handle clanked once more.

"That's the whole safe house," Celia said. "I don't think we have any way to communicate with central command from here."

Oliver made a contemplative noise. He walked to the window, peering out.

"Let's check the restaurant," he decided. "And if there's no telephone . . . then I suppose we wait until the coast clears outside."

19

Something cold was brushing across her face. A cloth, accompanied by a gentle hand poking around and moving her hair out of the way.

Rosalind's eyes snapped open. Her body jolted once, then stilled in a frantic scramble to make sense of her surroundings. She was lying on a couch. Her fingers touched a rough material beneath her. If she could see a ceiling directly before her, then she was in a house, and if she was in a house, then . . .

Rosalind turned to face her side. Traced the hand up to the person it was connected to. Perhaps she had fainted from blood loss earlier, but she might have fainted anyway from sheer shock even if she hadn't been bleeding from a hole in her shoulder.

"You're awake sooner than I thought," Juliette said, her focus directed on brushing away a piece of Rosalind's hair at her neck. "Don't move too much. I stitched you up as well as I could, but Roma said it looks like I attempted abstract art on your shoulder."

Rosalind struggled for words. Her cousin was dead. There was a grave for her and everything, flocked by mourners every year on the anniversary of an explosion that had devastated a whole street in Zhabei.

"Thank you," Rosalind whispered, because she didn't know what else to say. Where did she even begin? With a wince, she eased herself onto her elbow, taking a proper look around. They were in a living room, a fireplace at the wall and a large mantel curving over its stone.

"I have a few antidotes lying around, but I couldn't figure out what poison was on that knife," Juliette went on. "Better to let it leave your system naturally instead of risk disturbing the wound further. You'll heal when it's gone, right? Then we can pull the stitches out. Oh, and I left the knife over there."

When Rosalind stared at her silently, Juliette gestured to the desk at the far side of the room, where the aforementioned poisoned knife awaited, its metal cleaned and glimmering. Her cousin was chattering so casually, as if this were an ordinary evening visit. As if Rosalind was staring in awe because she wanted a medical report and not because, last she heard, Juliette was *dead*.

Rosalind suddenly lurched, pulling at her stitches. "Where's Orion?"

"In the bedroom. Don't worry," Juliette replied immediately. "He's still out. He might be out for a while. Alisa has been checking on him every ten minutes."

This was the very definition of an impossibility. Juliette and Roma had emerged from beyond the grave. And with such valiant heroics, with timing so precise that Rosalind could believe they might have been waiting . . .

Hold on.

"Did you *know* we were going to show up?"

Juliette's lip quirked. "Jiemin gave me a warning. The moment you fled the scene, he figured you might be en route. He's not very happy with you, by the way."

Rosalind must have misheard. Jiemin—her temporary handler, the Nationalist—had contacted *Juliette* to tell her that Rosalind was on her way? But . . .

"He's more my operative than he is a Nationalist," Juliette explained, seeing the confusion on her face. "So long as his first loyalty is here, he gets fed information from us that he often needs for his larger work."

"This is . . ." Rosalind trailed off, uncertain which adjective she was looking for.

Dear Bosses, Jiemin had been writing into that envelope addressed to Zhouzhuang. Then, in the car, when Rosalind had asked him about a *JM* . . .

Oh. *Oh,* how could she have not realized?

"I can help you get him back," Rosalind quoted. "That was you. You had already been waiting for me to find you."

Juliette Montagova. Arisen from the dead and bearing a solution.

"I had to stay vague. Every correspondence into the city is a chance of getting caught." Juliette reached forward, giving Rosalind's wrist a small nudge. "But I knew you'd find your way here."

The house was illuminated by candlelight. It had to be late, the hour creeping nearer to morning. A kitchen was adjoined on the left, the shadows of two figures sitting at the table. Alisa and Roma Montagov, passing something back and forth at each other. Rosalind was positively circling her disbelief again, incomprehension so thick that she felt it dripping off her skin like molasses. By now she had inspected every aspect of her surroundings, so there was nowhere else for her attention to turn except back to Juliette, who was folding up her cleaning cloth.

"Biǎojiě," Juliette said eventually, breaking the silence. "You're looking at me like I grew a third arm."

Rosalind couldn't help herself. The term "biǎojiě" wasn't even accurate anymore.

"Because you're so . . . old."

Juliette's brow shot up.

"No, wait, that's not what I meant to say," Rosalind rushed to clarify. She suddenly felt like *she* had grown a third arm and it was flopping all over the place, making a scene. "You just look different, and I haven't seen you grow into this difference. Obviously, Celia is different too. It's just me who's not different, so it feels as though everyone else has drastically changed—"

"Rosalind." Juliette's tone was gentle. She set the cloth down. "It's fine. I get it. Twenty-four is practically retirement age in Shanghai."

Rosalind leaned back. She pressed her fist into her forehead. First she couldn't find a word to say; now she couldn't shut up. And even though her cousin was cracking a joke, Rosalind felt terrible.

"I used to be more well mannered than this," she muttered. Her hand dragged down her face. Before she could help it, tears were welling in her eyes. "And then you *died*."

"Oh God—" Juliette plopped onto the couch, setting herself at Rosalind's side. She had changed since their brief encounter outside, swapping out the black clothes for a white dress. It wasn't quite a qipao in the same way that Rosalind's was, the collar lower and the sleeves frilly. "I'm sorry. I'm sorry to have done that to you."

Rosalind wiped at her eyes. What was her cousin doing, apologizing to *her*? Rosalind was the one who needed to apologize. Rosalind was the one who had been wanting to apologize for five long, long years, wishing she could open a door into the afterlife and obtain some chance to beg for forgiveness. Maybe that was what had taken her aback most of all: that this whole time, she hadn't even *needed* to seek the afterlife—

"Stop that." Rosalind sniffed. She had never been a crier, and now her eyes were leaking like faucets. "It's my fault that you died to begin with."

"What on earth are you talking about?" Juliette gave her a rough shove. She had forgotten how indelicate her cousin was, and the reminder drove back some of the tears when her stitches complained. "The fault is my own. When we ran"—Juliette's gaze rose above Rosalind's shoulder, looking into the kitchen—"I knew what we were choosing. Ourselves over everything else, and though it is terrible to be selfish, I did it anyway. I left you behind. You should blame me for it."

"How do I blame a dead girl?" Rosalind asked quietly. It was a serious question. She was relieved beyond anything she could put into words that her cousin sat beside her. When Rosalind reached out and closed her fingers around Juliette's wrist, she felt solid blood and flesh, warm and beating with the steadiest pulse.

But Juliette was dead to the city. And never returning to Shanghai—never returning *home*—was still a heavy matter that Rosalind was responsible for. There was no blame here. Not when it was the deserved outcome of how viciously Rosalind had betrayed her.

"If we're talking selfishness, then I was a thousand times worse," Rosalind went on. She could barely smooth down the tremor in her voice. "I tore through the city like an exit wound, ripping damage wherever I went."

The past shimmered between them. Dimitri leading his men. Those last days in Shanghai before the revolution came. Those last days before the explosion blew hot and tall, marking the moment that ended gangster rule.

"That *a thousand times worse* wasn't your doing," Juliette countered. "You got used, Rosalind. What is love if you are not cared for in return? It doesn't matter how thoroughly you choose it."

Rosalind looked down at her hands. "Yes," she said. The past stuttered, lost its color. And in its place came the thought of Orion, filling up the broken fissures. "I know that now."

Her tears started again. Years and years of them, desperately making their way out.

"Hold on, hold on—I have a handkerchief."

Juliette retrieved a smooth square of fabric from underneath the table. It looked like the same black cover she had been wearing over her face. Rosalind took it anyway and patted the tracks down her cheeks.

"I'm sorry," Rosalind sniveled. She didn't know what exactly that was directed at. An apology for messing up the handkerchief or a general apology that wanted to cover every wrong she had done.

She pulled the handkerchief away. Stared at the blots she had made.

"The only reason I left so fast that night," she said, the safe house in Zhabei materializing before her eyes, "was because I didn't want you to see me cry." She could feel Juliette watching her carefully. "And after you were gone, I realized that would have been your last memory of me. Walking out on you—not a single goodbye exchanged, only a decision that we would never see each other again."

"How long have you been carrying that?" Juliette whispered. Her eyes were watering too. "You couldn't have known what would happen."

"Neither that conversation nor the city's events would have happened at all if I hadn't made so many mistakes," Rosalind returned. "I betrayed you—"

"And I forgave you," Juliette cut in, her hands coming around to grasp Rosalind's shoulders, "a long, long time ago. Even if I *were* dead, you made a mistake, and then you needed to pick yourself back up to live for me. What else is there to do? Do you expect to repent forever?"

Rosalind took a ragged inhale. Then another. "You're going to make me start crying again," she whispered.

Juliette laughed, throwing her arms around her in a tight embrace. When Rosalind hugged her cousin and exhaled, it felt like she was breathing differently for the first time in five years.

20

"Ow!"

Alisa tried to yank her wrist back. Her brother gave her a stern look, his grip tightening.

"Don't be such a baby," he said, bringing the swab to her wound again.

"Personally, I think I have the disposition of a reasonable toddler," Alisa replied dryly.

They were sitting at Roma's kitchen table, her left arm stretched over the dinner place mat like it was being prepared for surgery. She had gotten badly scratched in the scuffle just outside Zhouzhuang. Her palms were an angry shade of red, and despite her attempts at hiding the damage, some of the deeper wounds on her arms needed cleaning. She had tried her best to insist that she would be fine, that she had suffered worse throwing herself out of a window once. After Roma had gone back out to check the township for more pursuers, he had returned to give the all clear alongside a giant bottle of alcohol.

For disinfectant, that was. He hadn't found it very funny when Alisa opened her mouth and gestured for him to pour. She barely got a chuckle out of him—only a tut and the demand to sit down immediately so he could inspect the wounds.

"How did this even happen? We got there so quickly," Roma muttered. He scrunched his nose, leaning in close to peer at the mark by her elbow after he finished cleaning her forearm. "Goodness, Alisa, there's a whole chip of gravel in here."

Alisa leaned in as well. That bit of her arm *did* hurt a little more than everywhere else. "Squeeze it out."

"*What*? No. I'll get it with a small knife. Juliette?"

"First drawer!" Juliette called from the living room, already overhearing their conversation. Rosalind, meanwhile, had gone into the room to observe Orion.

"The needlepoint ones?"

"Um . . ." There was a beat of silence. Then a clatter as Juliette moved around, opening the living room cupboards. "I don't know if I ever got those back."

"Did you lend them out?"

Juliette mumbled something under her breath. Alisa only heard "not my fault," but Roma clearly caught the full sentence, grimacing quickly and not chasing the topic further. He reached for the first drawer. Alisa's eyes followed his movement, then skated along those drawers and higher, scanning the entire kitchen. Her pocket itched. At some point, she needed to deposit the item she was carrying, and it seemed as good an option as anything to leave it with her brother, who was in hiding from the rest of the world.

The only trouble was that this household was far too pleasant. Everything was neat and tidy. When the morning came, it would be sunshine and well-lit corridors. No hiding places in sight. Bleugh. She thought they were supposed to be former gangsters.

"Here we go," Roma said, wielding a knife from the drawer.

Alisa lurched back. "Are you trying to butcher a cow?"

"Now you're just being dramatic. A cow would break this knife."

"Roma."

"Give me your arm, Alisochka."

Warily, Alisa offered her arm again. She watched her older brother take the tip of the blade to her scratch, then flick his wrist just enough to get the gravel out. His hand was astonishingly steady—she barely felt the knife. That shouldn't have been a surprise to her, but it was and it wasn't, just as it was and it wasn't strange that the two of them had fallen into their rhythm so easily despite almost five years apart.

In truth, Alisa had always known he was fine. He was paying her bills. He left signs everywhere, from the magazine subscriptions with inanely obscure educational topics that showed up at her apartment to the mysterious, anonymous presents resembling his taste every Lunar New Year. All the same, it would have been nice to confirm that she wasn't only imagining him everywhere, that she was correct to put together those clues and hadn't overstepped her usual confidence into outright delusion.

Roma made a noise under his breath, retrieving the swab again and running more disinfectant over her scratches. He used to hum like that anytime he was pondering a trivial matter—such as whether he wanted to eat a meat bun or a vegetable bun. Serious matters were accompanied by utter silence. If she stuck her finger into his ribs and managed to draw a noise from him, that always meant the matter wasn't *that* bad.

He had changed so much over the years, and yet he hadn't seemed to have changed at all.

Alisa couldn't hold it in anymore. Finally, she had itched for long enough to blurt out, "Why did you never contact me?" at the very same moment that Roma also sighed, demanding, "So, why did you never go to Moscow?"

They blinked at each other. While Alisa held still so that the disinfectant would dry on her cuts, Roma drew back and propped his elbows on his legs, every bit of confusion written starkly into his brow. They had always possessed the same expressions, though painted with different color palettes.

"How could I?" Roma said first. "You're working for the

Communists. There is no group more heavily watched in the city right now. If I sign my name on a letter to you and a Nationalist spy finds it, I sign my own death warrant. If I send a messenger and they're stopped and interrogated, my location falls into the open."

"I know *that,*" Alisa grumbled. Logic still reigned supreme in her mind. But her sudden surge of grumpiness didn't adhere to logic, as was the case with most emotions. "Still . . ."

She trailed off, not really knowing what alternative she could offer. Besides, it wasn't malice curling between her tongue and salting her words. It was only the dim sort of loneliness that came from spending so many years alone, vigilant and independent and putting so much effort into marching forward without knowing what exactly she was marching toward. After the revolution, she had turned fourteen, fifteen, sixteen—each year passed in anticipation of something grand that was about to slip over the horizon if she could *just* wait another year longer, just keep doing her job without flaw and await the reward at the end. She had thought that the best course of action was to hold strong. Maintain a place in the city however she could. Because in truth . . .

"I saw you, that day," Alisa said quietly. "Celia brought me here in April after the revolution, and I saw you with Juliette on that boat and it had to be you, but I stayed put, Roma. I stayed put." A lock of hair fell into her eyes. "I couldn't keep tugging your sleeve my whole life, and I couldn't bear it if I had lost my mind entirely. So I went back to Shanghai and I imagined you out here. I went back to Shanghai and I never left, because if I left, how the hell would you be able to find me when you returned?"

Her gaze shifted up. In the other seat, Roma was entirely unmoving for a long moment. Then his whole chest quavered, shuddering with his inhale.

"I would have found you anywhere." He reached forward. Tugged that piece of her hair, then tucked the curl behind her ear.

"Across the world and under it. No matter how well you hide. It doesn't matter where you go. I'll always find you. Understand?"

Alisa choked back a twist in her throat. Though she smiled, the expression suddenly felt watery, threatening to press past her eyes.

"If I had gone to Moscow, would you have contacted me earlier?"

"Yes. *Yes,* of course. Benedikt and Marshall have known for years. The only reason they were forbidden from saying anything to you was that it was dangerous knowledge inside city borders." Roma grimaced. "We're never going back, Alisa. At least not permanently. Wherever home once was, it's not there anymore. But I didn't want to influence you on where *you* needed to be."

Give it two seconds more, and Alisa was going to start crying. She did the only thing she could to stop herself: she pointed her index finger and shoved it hard into her brother's ribs.

"Ow!" Roma exclaimed, jolting in his seat.

She was filled with glee in an instant. "I have to use your washroom," Alisa declared.

He waved her away. "Down the hall, you terror."

Alisa scuttled off. She passed Juliette in the living room, whose eyes flickered up from the desk to offer a friendly wink before Alisa disappeared into the hall and through the washroom, closing the door behind her.

She didn't go to use the toilet. She scanned the small space, opened the cabinet above the sink, sniffed at the various medicines inside. Hmm. It was too empty. Too easily searched.

Alisa closed the cabinet and turned around, perusing the rest of the washroom. There was a medium-size clawfoot tub in the corner, squeaky clean on the inside and ornately decorated along the exterior. Moving quickly, Alisa peered around it, crouching low to examine the space where the bathtub brushed the wall, the ridges of the porcelain enamel chipping away some of the green paint.

Alisa stuck her finger into the hollow between the ridges and wiggled it around. There was very little maneuvering room against the wall because the tub was so heavy. Perfect.

With a glance at the door to make sure it remained closed, she brought out Lady Hong's last vial—the true one, not the fake she had duplicated for the purpose of smashing it—and hid it behind the bathtub.

Midmorning felt strange on Rosalind's face, bright with the low-hanging sun. As was the stillness of sitting at the canal with nothing to do except wait, listening to the birds cawing with the cement warm under her legs. While she was unconscious, Juliette must have hauled her from one end of Zhouzhuang to the other, because this looked to be the edge of the township, running into a larger lake in the distance.

Rosalind peered up. She shivered a little from the breeze, but otherwise remained seated, kicking her feet. The house stood right beside the canal, where water lapped forward carrying dried leaves and twigs in its current. She had been watching the current for some time now, which wasn't so bad as far as distractions went while she twiddled her thumbs for Orion to wake up. Her sedative was strong. Most times, it wouldn't wear off for a full day, maybe more. There was no use hovering around anxiously.

"There's something I should warn you about, though," Rosalind had said when she and Juliette were standing over the threshold into the room. Orion had been placed on the bed. His face was pale. Military uniform torn and bloodied, one sleeve pushed up unkemptly.

"He's under control, isn't he?"

Rosalind blinked. "How did you know?"

Her cousin folded her arms, her hands disappearing into the

ruffles at her bodice. "The papers said you two uncovered a scheme to do with the Japanese Empire conducting chemical experiments in Shanghai. I figured if Hong Liwen was then suddenly deemed a national traitor, then perhaps it wasn't voluntary." Juliette shrugged. "My guess wasn't entirely uninformed either, though. A similar set of experiments have been happening here, too."

"Here?" Rosalind repeated. "In Zhouzhuang?"

Juliette hesitated. "I suppose it's more accurate to say the subjects fled here. They were experimented on elsewhere. By Lourens."

Rosalind's elbow started to burn at the mere mention of the scientist's name. Why was Lourens everywhere she went? Why was he everywhere, yet, at the same time, absolutely nowhere to be found?

"The incidents here have all blown over now, don't worry," Juliette went on. "But while the matter was ongoing, Roma and I came into possession of a neutralizing agent. It's supposed to free subjects from their conditioning."

Rosalind swiveled so quickly she created a breeze in the hallway. "That could fix Orion."

"It could," Juliette confirmed. "We should wait until he awakens before we give it to him, lest something goes wrong and his body doesn't respond right. But it's ready for him. That neutralizing agent is the whole reason why I summoned you here. *I can help you get him back.* To himself."

Rosalind allowed herself a sigh in the present, reaching to pluck at a vine growing through the cement cracks. As soon as Orion woke up, it would all be resolved. They could get him back. Return him to himself.

At that very moment, the sound of smashing glass echoed from inside the house. Rosalind whirled around, eyes flying to the front door.

"We might have a situation!"

Alisa's voice. Was Orion awake already?

Rosalind clambered to her feet immediately, running back into the house. She skidded to a stop in the middle of the living room, dread slick down her back. There was already something in motion. Down the hall, the washroom light was on, and Juliette was rummaging in the cabinet above the sink.

"Roma!" she called. "Syringe!"

"I've got it!" Roma replied from the kitchen. "Alisa, keep him—"

Alisa tumbled out of the bedroom, hitting the hallway with a groan. She stayed down, looking annoyed. "I will *not* be flung around like a rag doll. Rosalind, you get him in order."

Orion was most definitely awake. Rosalind hurried around Alisa and entered the room carefully, hands up. There was a vase at her feet, shattered into three pieces. Orion was standing at the center of the room. His eyes—though they were wide, glancing around the house in confusion over how he had gotten there—were still blank.

He had had all his weapons removed from him. Surely he couldn't do too much damage.

"Are you still after a vial that doesn't exist anymore?" Rosalind asked calmly, as if this were a natural conversation. "Or did those instructions have a timed expiration?"

Orion frowned. He didn't seem to be comprehending her sarcasm. Or maybe he was, and he was fighting within himself to figure out a response.

"The vial . . . ," he echoed.

Rosalind's eyes flickered to the sheet that had been thrown to the floor. And, before Orion could decide to attack again, she lunged for the sheet and threw it over him.

Juliette was at the door suddenly. While Orion snapped into action, yanking at the sheet hard, she hurried in, surging right past him and going to the window, pulling a length of rope in. Juliette threw; the rope whipped toward Orion's arms, unfurling like a serpent before the end curled itself around his wrist tightly and snapped into place, some magnetic mechanism making a loud click.

"Maybe we should have done this when you were asleep," Juliette muttered under her breath. She drew her pistol. Orion sprang toward her in defense.

Rosalind started forward. "Wait, wait, don't hurt him—"

"He'll be fine," Juliette said. Her eyes flashed up, the motion barely perceptible. When Rosalind turned around, Roma was in the room too, something small glinting in his hand. In a blink, he had it pressed into Orion's neck.

Roma removed the syringe.

Orion sank to his knees.

"Orion!" Rosalind dove forward, putting herself eye to eye with him.

"Be careful. The effects might not have wholly faded yet," Juliette warned.

Rosalind didn't care. She grasped his arm, searching his expression desperately. When Orion looked up again, she could have cried in relief, because his dark eyes were full of life again, emotion and intensity and bewilderment lurking in their depths.

Only then:

"Who are you?" Orion whispered.

21

Phoebe had been skipping school for months now, to the point where she didn't know if she was even on the registry anymore. Surely when the academy saw her parents plastered on the front page of the news as national traitors, their board would have quietly erased her name from school records.

"All right, I found you in the registry. Go on through."

Phoebe jumped. She clutched her folder closer to her chest, a line of purple ribbons on her dress rustling from the motion. "Wait, really?"

The gate guard frowned. He stood up inside the booth, leaning against the window to peer out at her. "Is there a problem—"

"No! No problem at all!" Phoebe sidled in through the walking entrance quickly, waving her farewell before the guard could step out and offer to escort her. "Thank you, kind sir. My apologies for not arriving on time before the gate closed. It won't happen again!"

It was high noon, the sun beaming from the apex of the sky and casting blinding white onto the cold day. If she had actually come to attend class today, she was more than just late; she had missed half her lessons. Her overall attendance on her record was probably *so* bad.

Phoebe skirted around the classroom buildings, sticking close to the fence that made up the academy perimeter. Ivy crawled on the metal bars, resembling ropes tying the bars together.

Class was in session, so there was no one around as Phoebe hurried across campus grounds. She stomped past the shoveled snow mounds, then ascended the steps into the library. It was immediately warmer inside, the radiator in the corner chugging with effort. Light streamed through the stained-glass windows, casting pink and green shadows on the foyer floor. Phoebe scuttled to the front desk, tapping the bell rapidly.

"Hold your horses, for goodness' sake," the librarian called. Her voice was coming from the room behind the desk, wherein the door was propped open by a stack of books.

"I can't. It's a very big horse."

The librarian poked her head out, her expression mildly puzzled. Her silver hair was piled in a bundle at the top of her head, a feather sticking out from the middle. A chain of pearls was looped around her neck.

"What a strange comment," she remarked. "Shouldn't you be in class?"

Phoebe smiled primly. "I have special permission to be out doing a research project. I'm looking for a book."

She shimmied the folder onto the desk and opened it. Inside, Phoebe had brought along the bottom half of a photograph, plucked from one of the earliest albums in her father's office. She had cut away the other half. She didn't want the librarian to recognize her mother's smiling face and get suspicious as to why Phoebe was looking for a book that Lady Hong had owned.

She had been glad to snip away most of the photo, to be honest. Her mother looked so young. The more Phoebe stared at it, the stranger she felt, prickled by a sense of nostalgia for something she herself hadn't experienced. If asked, she would have said that her mother was happy back when the Hongs were still a family. That things had changed only after their family had started to crumble—that the happy days were happy days, and Phoebe wasn't mistaken to recall them so brightly in her memory. Phoebe held those moments in her heart still. She and her mother were always giggling with each other over jokes that the boys didn't understand, were always stepping out together to skip around the neighborhood in the evenings.

Yet as she flipped through those photo albums, she was seeing an entirely different mother. She was seeing Lady Hong with her eyes crinkled, occasionally captured in laughter with the entire image blurred. Carefree in a way that Phoebe had never seen in childhood, a wholly different person from the mother she knew. Somewhere along the line, her happiness had faded and left someone else behind. Phoebe had convinced herself her mother grew capable of doing such terrible things in those years apart, that of course Phoebe couldn't have known it to be a possibility when she was an ocean away in London, but maybe, actually, her mother had been this way all of Phoebe's life. Maybe Phoebe had always been in acquaintance with the traitor, and this laughing, blurry woman was long gone by the time Phoebe came into the world.

"Here," Phoebe said. "This one."

The librarian picked up the photograph. Lady Hong was holding the book in question while she lounged on the living room couch, her pregnant belly visible over the top. Oliver was soon to be born. That placed the photo sometime in late 1905.

Was it the world? she wondered. Did everyone overlook her mother again and again, push her to her limits? Phoebe supposed she could understand that. As much as her brothers were suffering worse consequences as a result of their respective infamy, she knew what it was like to be treated as someone discardable, the tack-on to a family merely because of the outward image she presented.

Or was it us? She swallowed hard, pushing the photograph forward. *Was it us who weren't enough for you? Enough to keep you?*

"You are searching for this book right here?" the librarian asked.

A thread of alarm curled up Phoebe's spine. She didn't like the doubt in the old lady's tone. "Yes."

"What is the nature of your project?"

Phoebe didn't give herself time to panic. She wound a finger around a ringlet of hair. On her next blink, her eyes glazed over entirely, misted with annoyance.

"Ugh, don't even get me started. I'm tracing the origin of these images. An assignment from a historiography unit."

The explanation seemed to suffice. The librarian's frown was more directed at the image itself than at Phoebe.

"I could be mistaken, but I believe this belongs to a collection. You see the logo at the bottom?"

She tapped the photo. Phoebe leaned in, squinting, and though it was blurry and barely visible, she did catch a symbol that marked the book's spine. "I see it."

"That signifies Kuomintang archives. Give me a second."

The librarian disappeared into the back room again. Phoebe mouthed a silent curse, because she had hoped she might find the book here and glean some idea about where her mother's work started. If this route of investigation was unsuccessful, she had very few other paths to follow. There weren't any more clues conveniently lying around the background of her father's old pictures. Half the time it was Phoebe's big face taking up the whole frame.

"So the collection this book belongs to is stored at the Shanghai East Library," the librarian reported, returning. "The Kuomintang have it under lock and key."

"In the Shanghai East Library?" Phoebe echoed. She couldn't hold back her disbelief. The area surrounding the Shanghai East Library—or, rather, the Dōng Fāng Library to the Chinese and the *Oriental* Library to the more annoying foreigners—had been the site of fierce grappling during the revolution. The White Flowers in

Zhabei had fought through the whole night trying to hold the territory before it fell to the workers in the morning. "It's still run by the Commercial Press, isn't it? I'm surprised the Nationalists haven't shut down the whole building for fear of spreading Communist doctrine."

In the aftermath, after the Nationalists severed their alliance with the Communists, they had arrested a whole swath of Commercial Press employees to suppress Communist movement. The ones who had been loud about their loyalties either were forced into exile or rapidly buried themselves undercover in Shanghai.

The librarian eyed her, unimpressed. "I'm sure anyone sensible can understand a library must stand regardless of ruling party."

Phoebe shrugged. She took the chiding. "Do you know who I should see to hunt it down?"

"Oh, darling." The librarian dropped into her seat, ordering the stacks at her side. "Again: lock and key. The Nationalists haven't let anyone in for years now. The librarians over there aren't happy about it."

"You're telling me the collection is kept in a restricted-access room?" That definitely sounded suspicious. And it sounded like it could be exactly what Phoebe was looking for. "How *many* years has it been locked up?"

The librarian frowned. "That building was only finished in 1924. Not that long ago. They moved their materials in around the time the library was established and closed the room shortly thereafter."

It matched up. Her father was investigated in 1927. Her mother must have contacted the Japanese a few years earlier to begin working for them if the paper trail was what got her almost caught, which meant "shortly thereafter" 1924 was exactly when the Nationalists shut down her experiments and put her research materials away.

"Isn't the library open to the public?" Phoebe continued pushing. "Surely if I ask—"

The librarian was already shaking her head. "Do you think you can *ask* your way past a Nationalist lock? If you want to get in, you're going to have to find a Nationalist."

"Dao Feng!" Phoebe shouted, barging through the back door of the church and coming into the yard of the orphanage. "Dao Feng!"

Her handler looked up, in the middle of raking leaves. Sister Su was truly putting him to work. There was a ladder nearby and a tin of paint, too, as if he had been touching up the church exterior before. "What's the matter?" he asked calmly.

Phoebe ground to a halt before him. Some of the leaves scattered from their neat piles. "Who shut down my mother's experiments?"

Slowly Dao Feng wiped the sweat from his forehead, considering the question she had fired back at him. Again, he wasn't wearing a coat despite the freezing chill. "No one in particular. It was a higher-level decision approved along the line."

"Okay, okay, so—" In her excitement, Phoebe had practically started trembling, trying to keep up with the speed of her thoughts. "Who was responsible for getting rid of her research? She must have submitted findings while she was still working for the Kuomintang. I imagine it was confiscated."

"Let me think." Dao Feng tutted and waved her away from the leaf pile, scraping the rake along its edges to neaten the circle again. "If I remember correctly, her confidential materials were burned and destroyed. Getting rid of their possibility of harm also meant getting rid of the knowledge they held. Which is a shame, because if we kept anything around, it would be coming in very useful now."

"But what if some parts remained?" Phoebe asked.

Dao Feng stopped. He set the rake down. "What did you find?"

"There's a room in the Shanghai East Library that the Nationalists keep locked." Her hands fluttered, working off her excess energy. "Do you know what's inside?"

"Sure. Rare books. Don't tell me *that's* what you're excitedly after."

"My mother was photographed reading one of those books—it cannot possibly be a coincidence."

"If there was anything of hers that the Nationalists took away, it must be because they lent it to her initially. They wouldn't keep around her findings. The risk is too high."

"Yes, *but*—" Phoebe jumped a step forward. Dao Feng winced when she messed up the leaves again. "My mother was very fond of annotating. They might not have *known* she left her findings in there."

A bell started to toll from the church building. The children filed out, taking their playtime in the yard. A cluster ran straight for Dao Feng and jumped into his leaf piles, but now he barely paid the matter any mind. He was finally beginning to look convinced.

"All right," Dao Feng said. He gave the squealing children a wry look but let them continue.

"You approve these next steps?"

Phoebe held back her smile when Nunu clambered out from the leaf pile and offered a handful. Phoebe accepted the dead leaves. The little girl ran off laughing.

"Approved, Feiyi. But you may wish to hurry." Dao Feng seemed to consider his words. Afternoon clouds were rolling in, dimming the sun. "We got a report yesterday saying your mother made an appearance. The eyes on the field haven't sent an update yet on how it played out, but the preliminary account suggests that Liwen fell off the radar."

Phoebe needed a moment to process her handler's words. Orion fell off the radar. Meaning he wasn't with their mother anymore, because their spies never had trouble following Lady Hong's militia. Her force was strong because it was big, but being big also meant she couldn't hide. This should have been good news, only Dao Feng didn't sound happy.

"He's . . . he's still alive, right?" Phoebe asked, her stomach twisting.

"Yes, I believe so," Dao Feng replied, and Phoebe released her breath. Her handler continued. "The matter that we are concerned about is . . . well, it almost unfolded a little too easily on Lady Hong's front. The soldiers on Shalin's tour responded to Liwen's appearance, but Lady Hong didn't send more men after her first round was defeated. Your eldest brother was at the scene, but he certainly didn't do anything to cause that."

"Maybe my mother is just weak now," Phoebe suggested. "It can't be easy gathering forces while on the run."

"She is stronger than ever, Feiyi," Dao Feng corrected. "She's taking refuge at Japanese bases and communicates with their highest generals. Perhaps she doesn't have the final concoction to alter her soldiers with Fortune's healing, but she can continue enhancing them with the strength and mind control she gave Liwen."

So something was being planned. Perhaps her mother had offered Orion up on purpose. Perhaps she simply didn't need him anymore. This whole affair was giving Phoebe a headache. She needed to get in touch with Oliver on her own soon, and she could only tell herself over and over again that he would remain safe while on mission so that she didn't worry herself into paralysis.

Phoebe stood up straighter, tossing her ringlets back. "I will resume investigating if there is nothing more. I think the library is promising."

"Go on, then. You might be able to get a key by sneaking into headquarters."

Phoebe scoffed. In an instant, she lost her operative tone and switched right back to speaking like Phoebe Hong. "Are you kidding me? I'm getting into that room fair and square."

22

Who are you?

Rosalind could feel everyone watching her. Concern and confusion spilled into the room, each pair of eyes fixed wide on the scene. *Who are you?* He wasn't under his mother's control anymore, but he still didn't remember her. She should have known that Lady Hong wouldn't make it that easy.

Rosalind grasped for something to say. Anything. Where there had been forceful hostility before, now Orion was looking at her like a kicked puppy, appearing utterly baffled. Maybe there would be some way to jolt his memory back. Maybe she only needed to say the magic words to trigger something in his mind, and he would recollect all that had occurred, fighting through everything the chemical conditioning had induced.

But that probably had to start with answering his first question.

"I . . . I'm . . ."

Your mission partner? Your wife?

"I'm your friend," Rosalind settled on softly. It was the truest answer she could find. No matter what else existed in the twist of her throat and the swoop of her gut, care and regard and friendship wrapped a steady hold around her hand, and when she held her palm out to help Orion up, it was that which she offered.

He got to his feet. Hope swelled in the hollows of her chest.

"Do you remember your name?" Alisa asked from the doorway.

She was rubbing her temple, grimacing over the hit she had taken.

"My name," Orion echoed. "My . . ."

His eyes rolled back without warning. Before Rosalind could scarcely finish her gasp, Roma had swooped in to prevent Orion from falling, grabbing him from his other side.

"He's fine, he's fine," Roma assured them, cutting in before anyone could yell with alarm. "Let me just—*by God,* why is he so tall?"

Roma transferred Orion's unconscious form back onto the bed. In an alarming next move, he put his fingers on Orion's neck to check his pulse, and Rosalind locked up entirely, having failed to consider that the solution they'd injected into him might just kill him instead. After a few seconds, though, Roma removed his hand and nodded, seeming to find Orion's pulse still beating.

Nevertheless, fear had seeped in, iced over Rosalind's form and frozen her bones.

"What happened?" she rasped. "Why doesn't he remember anything? I thought that was supposed to be a cure."

Juliette came forward slowly. She sidled past Roma, peering at Orion as if she might be able to pick up an answer by sight alone.

"Has his mother given him anything else?"

The room fell silent. When Rosalind tried to clench her fingers, she couldn't summon any strength.

"I don't know," she said. "All his experimentation happened away from me—"

She stopped. No, that wasn't true, was it? She had seen that final scene in Warehouse 34. After he had broken free from his orders and held himself back, after he had let Rosalind go despite his every instruction otherwise, Lady Hong had injected him with something burning red. Prior to that, he had fallen into a trance only when he was needed. He hadn't been erased entirely.

"I think the cure you just gave him erased the earliest

brainwashing his mother put in him," Rosalind said quietly. "But the memory loss is new. A different test tube full of chemicals."

Just as his strength was its own thing too. After all, Lady Hong's experiments had been going on for a while now—twenty-two years of time to change Orion however she liked.

Juliette looked immensely thoughtful. She was staring at the floor, and when Rosalind traced her cousin's gaze, she spotted the syringe, rolled to a stop beside the bedside table's left leg.

"If Lourens's cure worked for the earlier strain of brainwashing," Juliette said slowly, "what are the chances he can cure this amnesia, too?"

"We can't just *find* Lourens." Rosalind's tone came out sharply, far more than she had intended. A thin layer of sweat had broken out on Orion's forehead. Those few minutes of being conscious had already taken a physical toll on him. Still, she couldn't summon the nerve to reach for him. "He's disappeared off the face of the earth."

"Actually," Juliette said, "we have his address."

You . . . what?

"I suppose using him as a solution is a fair point," Roma added, exchanging a glance with Juliette. "He knew how to reverse one concoction; he must know how to reverse others, too. They cannot possibly be that different on a chemical level. We should summon him in."

This was absurd. The conversation had stepped on the accelerator, steamrolling in a direction Rosalind wasn't sure she was willing to risk. She had spent *months* searching for Lourens. So many sleepless nights scanning the national papers and sitting on the rooftops of train stations trying to catch a glimpse of a former White Flower scientist moving about the dark. Wherever he had disappeared, he had done a good job, because she hadn't come close to catching his trail, and with all that time wasted, being told now that Lourens could merely be *summoned* . . .

"I really doubt it's that easy."

Maybe they pretended not to hear the slight sneer entering her voice. Maybe Rosalind caught it before it seeped in fully, bit down on her bitterness until it slid back against her tongue. When she swallowed, there was a lump in her throat: fierce as a shard of glass, lodged tight with no means of removal unless she tore the skin right open and let her blood run free.

She was so tired of herself. Even if she clawed and clawed with the assurance that no amount of damage would kill her, the blood would run and the wound would heal, but still she wouldn't be rid of this sensation. She had always been like this, since the burlesque clubs swallowed her up, since she offered her heart to abandon, since she'd betrayed her own cousin—no matter how she attempted to leave behind the girl from the Scarlet house, the fact of the matter was that she was stuck in this frozen state, so how could she ever go very far?

"It might be exceedingly difficult," Juliette agreed evenly. "But don't you want to try?"

The daylight rose higher and higher through the window blinds, drawing gold across Orion's face. Even unconscious, he looked so tortured, his brow drawn tight.

Of course Rosalind wanted to try. But if it was going to end up crumpled in her hands anyway, it would feel so much worse than if she had never wished otherwise.

"Fine," she managed. "Fine, summon him in."

It was almost approaching three in the afternoon. This was growing ridiculous.

"Any change?" Celia asked, redoing her hair. She had untangled her small Rosalind-esque plaits, wincing each time one pulled painfully behind her ear. Her scalp heaved in relief once she gathered everything at the base of her neck again, wrapping a ribbon into place.

Oliver was observing the scene outside the window. Arms folded across his chest, his expression as mean as it could go.

"I swear they're standing guard there," he muttered. "Don't they have anything better to do?"

"Better than catching Communists?" Celia said, coming up to the window as well. "Certainly not. They must know we couldn't have gone far."

Even after Celia and Oliver waited out the night, thinking the Nationalists might be summoned away to tend to another important matter, there was no luck. The streets were crawling with soldiers on the search. When morning broke, more had arrived in their rumbling, green military vehicles, and for a sleepy little town, that meant the two of them were barricaded in even worse than before.

After their extensive search, they had concluded there was no telephone in the building. No way of communicating outward. What a terrible design for a safe house.

The soldiers below were pointing around while in conversation with one another. Though sound didn't travel far enough for them to hear what the soldiers were saying, it wasn't hard to take a guess. They must have made note of each route exiting the town and put eyes at each point.

Oliver started to pace again. His shoes scuffed up against the rug, which they had pulled back into place.

"We could make a gamble at nightfall and proceed to the car," Celia suggested. She hesitated. "But we need to get an update back before then, especially if we don't manage to get out tonight. We cannot leave the operation in silence."

"We hardly have a way of sending a message out. Unless we want to use a homing pigeon."

"There's a telegraphy office just down the road. I saw it on our way here."

Oliver stopped pacing. He regarded her carefully. "If you are about to suggest going alone . . ."

"They will pay less attention to me." Celia pointed to the wardrobe, where a few ordinary qipao were hanging. "Especially if I change. It's debatable whether I would be identified even if they stop me. You, on the other hand, are wholly recognizable by face."

Oliver was tight-lipped, looking like he was scrambling for an argument.

"It's dangerous," he said eventually.

"What other option do we have?" Celia reached into the wardrobe, picking a bland gray qipao. Perfect. "Help me with these buttons."

The trees are cold.

In the countryside, they shiver at every gust of wind. Daylight filters away from the scene early, filched up into the clouds as if an almighty suction is sapping all color. When there is only miles upon miles of greenery, it's easy for ice to curl in and out to its leisure, latching where it wishes, undisturbed until the season changes.

They take temporary lodgings at a base some distance away from the nearest town. The closer they get to cities and urban bases, the more careful they must be. Mr. Akiyama will be arriving soon to check on her progress: he travels on a safer route, unlike the traitor on a chase southward. She may move as she wishes with the militia given to her, as long as she has results to show for it. She will. She won't accept any alternate option.

"Get the telegram machine out," the traitor snaps, hurling her coat off when she enters the building. Some parts of the ceiling are made of straw. She can hear the rustle of the trees that grow directly overhead, long leaves drooping upon the exterior walls. The sooner they get out of these makeshift facilities, the happier she will be. She wants her warehouses. She wants tall ceilings and endless steel.

They bring her the machine. Her heart hammers in her chest. She has always known that it isn't possible to produce this enhancement substance en masse. There is a very limited amount of a key ingredient. Even if they do perfect the formula, the core element needs time to replenish.

But really, she needs to create it only once to prove that it is possible. She needs to hand over only one successful test subject, and then she has done her part. She can take the innumerable funds, disappear somewhere with her family, continue studying what she wishes. Once she has invented what they call *immortality*, no empire can tell her she has not done enough.

She's quick to compose her message, tapping with efficiency. It's a simple correspondence, because this exchange, too, is simple.

> ***It's your turn. I will be making contact when I enter the city.***

23

Birdsong flitted up and down Baoshan Road.

Silas kept his distance from the creatures rather nervously, their beady eyes following him as he walked. He swore more of them were swooping off the rooftops just to greet him as he passed the row of Commercial Press factories, either diving right onto the grassy ground or perching upon the stone fences that lined the facilities and kept them cleanly divided. The birds were louder than any human person on the streets. Perhaps that was only because there were so many of them and hardly any passersby. People tended to steer clear of volatile areas in the city if they had the choice.

"Silas, are you keeping up?"

Phoebe was a few paces ahead, proceeding directly toward the East Library. At five stories tall, the library loomed larger than everything nearby, its perfectly rectangular exterior standing as solidly as an immovable brick. They were north of the city, in what was technically Zhabei. Still, the moment they started walking along the factories, their surroundings had turned quieter than what Silas was used to, as if the pavement were listening to every footstep. The land here had its own feeling to it, separate from the residential streets with their chatter and rumble. The land here knew that war was coming again before the rest of the city did—or maybe it was wise enough to remember that war had never left.

"How do I keep up when you practically scuttle on those legs?" Silas replied. His instinct was to kick one of the birds. He wasn't a violent person, so it wasn't like he wanted to hurt the creature. Perhaps just give it a little whack and send it farther away.

"Learn to scuttle too!"

Phoebe had insisted on coming to the Shanghai East Library, one of the few in this city that was not only Chinese-run but accessible to the public. She had said that some of her father's writings had been stored away in one of the Nationalist-governed rooms, and *please, please, please, Silas, make a phone call and get us in?*

It was possible that Silas had a problem when it came to saying no to Phoebe Hong. At the very least, this hadn't been a hard request. The Nationalists barely asked a single follow-up question when he put in the call for the room to be opened. He imagined that whatever it was they kept under guard couldn't have been that important, so there was no harm in spending a day there with Phoebe. Better this than to feel like he was being utterly useless.

Up ahead, Phoebe let out a whoop, approaching the tall building. Silas turned away from the birds and, without time to realize where he was walking, suddenly collided with another man on the road.

"My apologies," the man said quickly, gaining his balance before Silas did. He was dressed like one of the Commercial Press employees, in a clean suit and tie complete with a gray hat.

"No, it was my fault—"

The man was already hurrying away. Silas peered over his shoulder, confused. The road was enormously wide. Perhaps Silas had been too distracted by the birds to watch his step, but the man had been charging right toward him, so how had he not realized . . . ?

"Silas!" Phoebe called. "Aren't you coming?"

She stepped in through the gate. Just as Silas resumed walking, the thought occurred to him that perhaps it hadn't been an accidental run-in at all. He reached into his jacket, rooting around every place that might have been accessible during that brief second of contact.

In his inner-left pocket, his fingers made contact with a slip of paper. He closed it into his palm. Pulled it out without exposing the paper, then opened his hand in front of him as if he were only stretching.

> ***MAGICIAN:***
> ***North Railway Station. 14:00.***
> ***—PRIEST***

His heart started to pound in his ears. Though Silas didn't break his stride, he did wince as he checked his wristwatch, the time reading twelve minutes to two o'clock. Driving was too burdensome, especially when it came to finding a place to park by the station. Walking would take around twenty minutes, though he could cut it down to ten if he managed to hail a rickshaw. But that meant he needed to leave now, and immediately. After such a long period of silence from Priest, maybe this contact would serve as an explanation.

Phoebe had paused right outside the library, waiting for him to catch up. Silas scrunched the note tightly in his fist, putting it into his trouser pocket as he approached. He considered saying outright that Priest had summoned him, but he didn't want to upset Phoebe if she thought it meant he was choosing the meeting over her. She had already gotten upset after he mentioned the radio station clue. There was no use risking an unnecessary debate until Silas received concrete information, and he *would*.

"Will you be all right to go in alone?" he asked. "I have an errand that I need to check on nearby. I should be able to finish up right as you're finishing here."

"Of course," Phoebe replied instantly. "As long as they still let me in without you present."

Silas waved a hand. "It'll be fine. I already told them I was bringing you as my primary guest."

The clock was ticking. He felt every passing minute, each second tracked with the rustle of the spindly branches growing in front of the library. All their leaves had fallen off from the cold weather.

Phoebe mocked a salute. Her pink lips curved into a smile. "I will be fine. We can meet at the car."

Silas imitated the salute. He turned to go.

"Wait, Silas—"

Just as he pivoted to face her again, Phoebe threw her arms around him, the embrace so sudden that Silas entirely short-circuited, his brain signals frying into oblivion. This close, he could smell every layer of her perfume, from the initial wave of jasmine to the deeper traces of something heavy like whiskey.

"Thank you," she said, her words muffled against his chest. "I don't know what I would do without you."

He lifted his hand, settling it on her back.

"That's okay," Silas said. His voice was steady in a way that he absolutely wasn't. "This is far from an arduous task."

"All the same"—Phoebe drew away—"I appreciate that you indulge my little searches. I know it isn't relevant on the greater scale of matters these days, but I really need it. So thank you." She stepped through the library's main doors. "See you at the car!"

The East Library swallowed her in. Silas allowed himself a few seconds to get his breathing under control. Then, with a glance at his wristwatch again, he hurried off in search of a rickshaw.

Phoebe felt like she was using him.

Well, she was. That part was unquestionable. Friendship consisted of reciprocally using each other with love, after all. But she was clearly using Silas with malice, manipulating him into thinking she was flitting around looking at her family files when really she was performing covert work.

She *did* need to find her family files, technically. She couldn't help it if her family was heavily involved in the current state of their country's politics, and because she didn't know what she might find, she'd sent Silas away, using the one piece of bait that she knew he couldn't resist. Still, she hadn't needed to lay it on so thickly.

I appreciate that you indulge my little searches.

Ugh, she was awful. Only a few days ago, she had told him that *his* searches were useless.

"It's right through here," the librarian said, unlocking the room. "Wu Xielian isn't coming along?"

"He had a bit of work elsewhere," Phoebe said, already glancing around the treasure trove. Floor-to-ceiling shelves lined the four walls, while the middle of the room had three aisles separated by shorter shelves. The space itself was rather small. Everything in the room was within sight on one preliminary glance. No windows.

The librarian nodded. "I will lock the door so that you are undisturbed, but you can always open it from the inside. Find me on the first floor if you need anything."

"Tài gǎnxièle," Phoebe enthused, flashing a smile.

The door closed. She got to work.

It didn't seem like the room had a sorting system. Tang Dynasty poetry was ordered right beside an Italian calendar. A German manuscript that looked entirely frayed and tattered sat atop a stack of Shanghai periodicals from 1923. Everything here had been shoved in wherever there was space.

Phoebe hummed under her breath, dropping to a crouch and scanning the bottommost row of the middle shelves. Fortunately, despite the lack of order, she was looking for something particular, so she'd know it when she saw it. The collection of books would surely be lumped together, and they had distinctive spines. How hard could it be?

Phoebe kept shuffling along the shelves.

She found posters. Figurines. Large stacks of government-mandated textbooks, many of which were likely first print runs that contained mistakes if they had ended up in here instead of out in the world.

At random, Phoebe started to pull out the cardboard boxes shoved into a middle row. On the third one, she finally hit the jackpot.

"There you are," she whispered beneath her breath, spotting the five gold-spine books. Her mother had been holding only the first one in the photograph. Phoebe plucked it out and, with a flip of her hair so that nothing was falling into her face, she seated herself comfortably against the shelf.

There was no use reading its contents closely. Though it was written in English and Phoebe had a much easier time comprehending her primary language of study, half of the book was gibberish to her, going from advanced principles of meiosis to new theories of chromosomal replication. Instead, Phoebe riffled through the pages rapidly in search of markings; as she told Dao Feng, her mother was an avid annotator, and if she had read anything, she had likely left her marks within its spine.

Phoebe didn't find any sign of the usual notes that her mother would make, though. She saw numbers instead.

"What *is* this?" Phoebe muttered. Zero, one, two, and three were written frequently at the side of the columns. Zero appeared the most often. Three barely appeared at all. Phoebe reached the end. She moved on to the second book immediately and found the same. She supposed she ought to have expected this, because her mother wouldn't leave incriminating evidence in books that she would eventually have to give back. Still, Phoebe had anticipated something cryptic that she might have been able to decode, not *numbers*. This could mean *anything*.

The fifth book fell closed in her lap. For a while, Phoebe sat unmoving on the floor, her attention wandering off into space. Somewhere along the library floor, a grandfather clock tolled loudly, the sound reverberating through the walls.

She looked down again.

The photograph had captured her mother holding these books before Oliver was born. Yet Lady Hong hadn't had these books taken away until her experiments were shut down, which meant they were relevant in some way, or else surely they would have returned to circulation. That gave at least twenty years in which she had been reading through them and making notes.

Just how early had she *started* her experiments?

The way I remember it, Dao Feng had said, *your mother was recruited into the Kuomintang's earliest experiments because she had previously done work on that front.*

Phoebe peered into the rest of the box. It wasn't only books. There were miscellaneous objects, too. She recognized the stethoscope in the corner because, as a toddler, she had almost choked herself to death on it while running up the stairs with the medical instrument looped around her neck.

This whole box must have been confiscated from her mother when the Kuomintang pulled the project. Curious now, Phoebe picked up a leather journal, giving it a shake to make sure the pages weren't loose. When she undid the latch, the first page opened to a medical log: what looked to be blood pressure readings. Two columns. The left side showed normal results; the right side appeared to be for someone wildly unhealthy. There was no biographical information in accompaniment. No patient description nor reason noted for why the readings were being taken. As Phoebe flipped farther, she did find writing at the bottom of the pages, describing what looked to be symptoms. *Dizziness. Nausea. Chills.* This was her mother's handwriting.

"What does any of this *mean?*" Phoebe whispered to herself.

Lady Hong had not been a doctor. Besides, the Nationalists would have noticed people coming and going from the household if her mother had been treating patients there, which meant she would have been under suspicion much earlier.

Phoebe stopped at a page in the middle.

I don't remember the ten minutes directly after today's round, but this is impossible to record properly on my own.

"Wait a minute," Phoebe said suddenly. These readings were of Lady Hong herself. At once, Phoebe flipped to the beginning of the logs again, looking at the date. *October 16, 1903.* More than two years before Oliver was born.

Phoebe didn't know if she was jumping to conclusions, but a journal like this resembled the *before* and *after* records of an experiment. There was nothing explicit here that stated so, because if there were, the Nationalists would have long burned it. Yet Phoebe couldn't shake off the feeling.

Her eyes wandered back to the archival books. Their contents spoke of science that she couldn't even begin to understand. Maybe someone with more studies under their belt would have been able to comprehend the technical aspects. All Phoebe had to work with were the numbers scribbled onto the side.

Zero, one, two, three.

Oliver, Orion, Phoebe.

"Holy shit," Phoebe whispered. The three never appeared much, after all. But the zero did, again and again, in faded ink that might have been made twenty years ago. Had her mother's first experiments been on *herself*?

It was half past two. Silas glanced at his wristwatch again, his other hand tapping the bench beneath him.

Either Priest wasn't showing up, or he was late and had already missed her. The rickshaw had pulled up to the North Railway Station at two minutes past the dot. Surely she wouldn't have left the meeting with only two minutes for leeway. Then again, Silas didn't know what sort of parameters top-secret Communist assassins kept.

He chewed his lip. If he didn't get back soon, Phoebe would start to worry.

The railway station screeched every few seconds, whether from the doors slamming open or a passenger hurrying to board their train. Though Silas remained alert, not a soul had looked in his direction in the time he had been sitting here, facing the departure board and pretending that he was waiting for an arrival.

In a frenzy of motion, the departure board changed, updating to the newest times. Silas sighed, finally deciding to take his leave. Maybe something had gone wrong. Priest could have been followed and needed to reconvene, especially given the heavy presence of Nationalist soldiers guarding the station perimeter. The threats of war were increasing day by day. Why would she choose a train station for a meeting place anyway? That was possibly the worst place as far as Kuomintang surveillance went.

He stood up. Dusted off his jacket and headed for the door. Or maybe it was his fault. Maybe Silas was the one going about this the wrong way, and each proper path he followed was only going to take him in circles upon circles. Wasn't that what the papers were always criticizing the Kuomintang for? That they hardly got anything done in their desperation to follow order and keep waters calm? Perhaps Silas was making the very same mistake, jumping when Priest said jump, tucking tail in the hopes that she would choose to offer information out of the kindness of her heart.

"Xiǎo huǒzi! Wait!"

Silas frowned, his step halting. An old man had called out to him from the bench he had just departed. This couldn't possibly be Priest. . . .

"Is this yours?"

The old man pointed to a small object on the bench. Silas hadn't seen it before, so he must have been sitting right in front of it.

"It's not mine," he replied, walking closer. "I'm sure someone dropped it as they were leaving. . . ."

He trailed off. It was a tin case, perhaps to hold cigarettes or mints. Drawn upon the surface, however, was a top hat. The long, comical sort that people pulled rabbits out from.

"Never mind. That's mine indeed," Silas said, taking it quickly. "Thank you."

The old man nodded. Silas hurried out of the station with the tin case tucked close to his chest, pushing out from the crowds of passengers—and the pervasive smell of roasted chestnuts from the street stalls surrounding the area—before he paused and opened the case.

Inside, there was a single negative panel from a reel of film. Silas held it up to the light, incredibly perplexed. It looked like a building. There was no way to discern anything else until he had a copy made and enlarged, but at least this meeting wasn't a complete bust.

He put the film panel into the tin case again and hurried on his way back to Baoshan Road.

Phoebe ran down the library's stairs, clutching her skirts so she could descend faster without the layers around her knees. The building was quiet around her, only a few other patrons working on the other floors. Scholars, probably, flipping through the collections and taking notes. The windows at the sides let in plenty of sunlight. The thick carpeting on the staircase softened her footfall, preventing her from disturbing the work going on in the vicinity.

"Did you know your mother was an academic?" Rosalind had asked a few days after Orion was taken. Phoebe had been bringing food, hovering around the room while Rosalind stared out the window at the reporters gathered below. "She did research at Cambridge. I looked into it yesterday: there was only one paper in Shanghai that mentioned the completion of her thesis. Nothing else."

"I suppose that makes sense," Phoebe had replied. "No—I didn't know, though. She never talked about that part of her life before us."

"She seemed to blame high society for that." Rosalind crossed her arms. "No one cared to know, and so she brushed her education under the rug."

Phoebe didn't know if she agreed with that or not. Her mother was a strong-willed person. Matters were known if she wanted them known. Hidden if she wanted them hidden. At that moment, maybe Phoebe had spoken out of hurt because there had been so much going on within her family that she hadn't been privy to, but she hadn't hesitated to declare:

"I think she kept it from us because she didn't want people to realize the harm she could do. She knew she was capable of something terrible, and she did it anyway."

Phoebe skittered onto the first floor now. She headed quickly for the information desk, rising onto the tips of her toes to get the librarian's attention while he was processing returns.

"I closed the door after myself," Phoebe reported in lieu of a greeting. "Where is the natural sciences section? Biology, to be specific."

The librarian raised his eyebrows. "Second floor, the shelves to the left of the stairwell. You found everything you needed in the room?"

"I'm suddenly interested in general knowledge too!" Phoebe

called over her shoulder, already hurrying for the stairs again. She didn't waste time. Silas would be heading back as soon as he found the tin case that another operative had left for him, once he realized Priest wouldn't be showing up at the railway station after all.

Phoebe stopped in front of the biology resource books. Some were educational and written for students; others were academic findings, collated together from theses and doctoral dissertations. With a silent apology to the other patrons on the floor, she yanked the whole shelf at once and dumped the stack onto the floor.

"Sorry," Phoebe whispered, flinching at the sound. She immediately pushed aside the books written in Chinese. Her mother had studied at Cambridge, so it was most likely that she had observed her research in English. Phoebe started to pick through the remaining foreign books, scanning down their tables of contents. She was quick to toss away any volume the moment she saw French or the occasional Dutch. Even with her attention reserved solely for those written in English, her pile of discarded books grew higher and higher as she perused through one useless volume after the other. Phoebe was almost ready to relent, acknowledging that this had been a shot in the dark. Then, on the second-to-last book she picked up, she stopped short the moment she read the table of contents.

She had found it.

```
Section 6: Jiang Lei—SERAMORINE:
A HYPOTHESIS ON BLOOD MUTATIONS AND
GENETIC TRANSMISSION
```

Her mother's maiden name. Phoebe flipped to the corresponding page at once. Though her shoulders were trembling with her agitation, her fingers remained steady.

"First Presented to the Faculties of the University of Cambridge, 1901," she read aloud. The paper was lengthy. Fitted with diagrams and

charts. But as Phoebe read the abstract alone, she figured she might have found everything she was looking for.

> *. . . The invention of seramorine will change our understanding of mortality and humanity as we have come to know it. Science itself as a practice will have to re-shape entirely if we are to pursue utterly revolutionary findings that could defy death. . . .*
>
> *Before the active elements of seramorine can be stabilized, it requires successful mutation on an original host, followed by transference into a second host via genetic replication during meiosis. With the presence of genetically diverse blood, further advancements can be made in the creation of concoctions . . .*

Phoebe needed to make sure she wasn't misunderstanding.

"Dictionary, dictionary . . . ," she muttered, lunging up and bee-lining for the reference section on the other end of the second floor. The first English dictionary she pulled out looked too thick and complicated. She tugged out another that was aimed at children.

> *MEIOSIS: (noun) the process of cell division to provide genetic material for reproduction.*

Phoebe stared at the definition. She wasn't misunderstanding. In fact, she had understood her mother's writing exactly as intended. The very root of her experiments began with herself, in that small journal the Nationalists had tucked away, thinking nothing of its contents. She had changed her blood to host something strange, turning it into an ingredient for a concoction she would soon create.

Then she had only needed the next component: the blood of her offspring, carrying her altered genetics.

24

Celia had found a shopping basket inside the safe house, which gave her something to fiddle with as she passed the soldiers outside the building.

She kept her face inclined down. She knew Oliver would be observing from the window, so she didn't look until she had made her way around the building and put herself out of view, afraid that she would be giving up their location if she so much as glanced in that direction.

A soldier watched her turn the corner. Celia resisted the urge to flinch, though she did reach up to tug her qipao collar. Maybe she should have taken her pendant off, on the chance that the soldiers had been told to look for it. Surely too many years had passed for anyone to remember the details of Kathleen Lang's usual state of dress in Shanghai. Then again, Celia hadn't thought anyone would start calling her Kathleen again, and yet the Nationalist channels were probably abuzz with her dead sister's name. It could have been worse. It could have been the name her father wanted her called at birth—and thank the heavens he wasn't anywhere near involved with this.

Celia stepped into a small fruit shop. She needed to look natural. As though she were merely running errands before stepping into the telegraphy office. Her attention moved from the apples to the apricots to the men standing guard on the other side of the street.

She bought a bag of apricots. Once she placed it neatly in her shopping basket, she stepped out, eyes on the telegraphy office.

"You there!"

Celia's stomach dipped. She paused, glancing behind her shoulder to source the shout. As soon as she saw that the soldier was only stopping the man behind her, she let out a low exhale, resuming her path as if the interruption hadn't been anything strange. In reality, her heart was pounding so hard that she didn't hear the door close after her when she entered the telegraphy office, its thud adding to the drumbeat in her chest.

There was a customer at the counter already. With only one clerk taking messages, the office was quiet save for their confused back and forth regarding the price of sending two telegrams to two different locations. Neither the clerk nor the other customer paid Celia any attention as she went to the table and set her basket down. She tried to even her breath. Her handwriting shook as she picked up the pen attached to the tabletop and scribbled a message.

She set the address for a safe point that sorted all mission communications incoming and outgoing to Shanghai. It was too dangerous to contact liaison stations in the event that a physical location was exposed and communications were traced. Safe points, on the other hand, did nothing except move messages back and forth.

Which was why, when the other customer finished and Celia took her missive to the counter, the clerk took one look at the intended address and said, "Oh, there's a message that came in from this location too. Is it yours?"

"An incoming message?" Celia asked. Who would be contacting *them*? They hadn't gone silent long enough for central command to be worried yet. "When did it arrive?"

The clerk leaned to look behind the counter. After someone at the office translated the incoming Morse, they placed the missives onto the shelf—he scanned the topmost row for a moment before identifying the right one and plucking it out.

"Half an hour ago. It's only addressed to a Mr. Yin. We were about to start looking through the records to find a registered recipient."

The safe house was under a Mr. Yin, undoubtedly. Celia just couldn't figure out if it was actually a missive for her and Oliver—that someone was sending it to their last-known location and simply assuming they might be residing at the nearest safe house—or if this was intended for any operative nearby to pick up.

"Yes, it's my father's," Celia said. "I will receive it."

She paid for the outgoing message and took the incoming envelope, thanking the clerk. The exterior of the envelope provided no further clues to the mystery, no markings or indicators as to what might be inside, so she slipped it into her basket with the bag of apricots. Just as she was coming down the steps of the telegraphy office, two soldiers hurried by, and though Celia ducked her head again, intensely focused on making sure the apricots were sitting right, they barely paid her any heed.

". . . vehicle identified. Rope it off."

"Oh no," Celia muttered. That was probably their car. This was bad. Very, very bad.

She slinked through the shadows, walking the final block to return to the safe house. As soon as she was outside the building, Celia dropped the shopping basket and picked up the envelope, shoving it into her qipao. They had to go. There was too much risk waiting for nightfall now.

"It's me." Celia knocked frantically on the door. She kept knocking until Oliver opened it, and then almost bowled him over when she barged through. "We're leaving."

"What?" Oliver demanded.

"They found our car," Celia said in a hurry. "It's as good as confirmation that we are in the vicinity, so we need to flee immediately."

"*Without* a car?"

Celia found a lumpy-looking scarf in the wardrobe and shoved it at him. "We'll walk on foot until we find a vehicle to take hostage."

"We're in the rural countryside. We'll collapse before we find a transportation method to take over."

"I am very aware." Celia found a second lumpy scarf and looped it around her neck. "However, we're out of options."

At that moment, a rumble of activity sounded below, and both Celia and Oliver hurried to the window, concerned. Soldiers filed through the alley, half entering the neighboring building and the other half coming into theirs.

Merde.

"They're going door to door," Oliver stated plainly. He didn't sound panicked enough for Celia's liking. She knew that he was an internal person, but a small showing of hysteria for their terrible situation would have been nice.

"Rooftop?" she asked.

Oliver shook his head immediately. He pointed to the trapdoor beneath their feet. "We must hide."

"*Hide*? While they come in?"

"I don't like this either, but as you said before: we're out of options."

There were three exits that were within the realm of possibility. The front door, though it would be impossible to navigate the rest of the building when the Nationalist soldiers were coming from that direction. The window next to them, though there were soldiers directly below on the two ends of the alley. And, on the other end of the safe house apartment, there was a window in the washroom, which led out a different dead-end alley that the Nationalists would have no reason to guard, although Celia had peered along it earlier, and it didn't look like there was any way to scale down the wall.

All to say, there was no way out. How had they gotten to this point?

With a muttered curse, Celia yanked a corner of the rug back; Oliver pulled the trapdoor open.

A door slammed on the first floor. When Celia jolted, her inhale was ice-cold, a physical sensation gliding down her throat.

"Go, go," Oliver said in a rush.

With a stifled wince, Celia stepped through the trapdoor, entering the hideout. It wasn't quite right to call it a cellar when it was jammed between levels, but it felt close enough to one. The restaurant below was built with attic storage, which meant there were gaps in the floor plan that the apartment above could fill downward. There was only enough space for Celia to be perfectly kneeling while Oliver needed to keep his head ducked when he stepped through too. One water pipe ran along the side, gurgling in greeting.

"Wait, listen." Celia's whisper was sharp. She grabbed Oliver's elbow, stopping him from closing the trapdoor. The rumble downstairs seemed to be . . . lessening. Or perhaps dispersing, voices spreading in a way that made them hard to track.

Then there was a burst of footsteps thudding into the apartment, and Oliver reached to yank the trapdoor closed, its click echoing. Needle-thin light filtered through the gaps in the floorboards.

Celia realized two things at once. One: there was blood on the floor—a large stain in the corner that had sprayed droplets onto the wall too, illuminated in the faint light. Two: there really shouldn't have been any illumination coming through the hideout space in the first place. Because if there was light filtering through the floorboards, that meant the rug wasn't pulled over the trapdoor and its lines were visible, and they would have no way of pulling the rug back into place while they were hiding anyway.

Which culminated in making her realize, three: if there had been an encounter here in the past and someone had gotten shot, then maybe the Nationalists already had this safe house location on their radar.

"Celia," Oliver said suddenly. With his tone alone, she knew he had made the same guess.

"It's going to be fine," she assured him before he could continue. "They won't find us."

Footsteps came up the stairs. Soldiers, calling instructions and reports back and forth.

Oliver pivoted quickly, searching the small space. "Is there something on that pipe?"

"The pipe?" Celia echoed. She shuffled over two steps. Her knee scraped against the rough floor. "Not that I can see."

A thud traveled down the corridor outside. Though Oliver had asked the question, his gaze was turned to the trapdoor. She knew that look. He was about to do something terrible.

"If they're checking every building, they will not be making a very thorough search," Celia whispered. "It is mere logic. It is not hopeless."

Oliver turned to her. His mouth opened and closed, and then Celia grew even more concerned, because rarely did Oliver look alarmed, but this was as close to it as she had seen him. As if he were already resolved to the fact that a soldier was going to find the trapdoor and lift it.

"It might be around the other side," he said.

Celia didn't comprehend. "Excuse me?"

"Help me check," Oliver clarified, reaching for the pipe himself. He ran his hand along the side closer to the wall. Rather puzzled, Celia hurried to search too, but her fingers only brushed dust.

"There's nothing here."

A call—getting closer.

"Please don't be angry at me," Oliver said suddenly, "because this might be the last chance I have to do this."

Before Celia could ask what he was talking about, before she could so much as grasp the meaning of his words, Oliver slid a hand along the side of her neck, then kissed her on the mouth.

She froze.

Utterly and entirely, a statue made of warm contact and incomprehension. Perhaps it would have taken another mere second for her to snap out of it and kiss him back, but she would never know: there was the sensation of something sliding around her wrist and the tightening pressure of string.

When Oliver drew back, he had already used that time to tie her to the pipe.

"Don't you dare," Celia immediately hissed. She pulled against the string. It was secured around her firmly, a double knot holding her in place. "Oliver Hong, I swear—"

"Please don't yell," he said. "Don't make this for nothing. Please."

"Oliver—"

He opened the trapdoor. Celia yanked as hard as she could on the string, but she couldn't tear herself away from the binding.

"—stop!"

The door closed. As soon as he put the rug into place above ground, the light faded, and Celia was left in complete darkness.

GODDAMMIT, OLIVER, YOU SELF-SACRIFICING PIECE OF—COMMENT OSES-TU ESSAYER—PUTAIN DE BORDEL DE MERDE—

He had said not to yell, and Celia was logical enough to abide by the request, releasing her violent anger with only the barest thump of her fist against the pipe. It wasn't anger, though, not really. Beneath it was terror, because he had just given himself up to keep her safe, and no one survived being captured by the Nationalists. Her breath came short. Her lungs were deathly tight.

In all their time together, she had always known that allowing someone to care about her would result in this. Throwing themselves into the battle head first, acting counter to what was right.

She hated the world at that moment, but she also hated herself. She had caused this. Her.

Don't, don't, please don't— Come back—

His footsteps moved to the window. Celia heard the glass pane being opened, then Oliver's steps heading for the direction of the door instead. Whether he was trying to create the illusion of Celia having already fled, she didn't know. All she knew was that she needed to clap her other hand around her mouth when an involuntary sob tried to make its way out, narrowly drowned out by the sound of soldiers rushing in.

One gunshot. The room erupted with shouting, so loud that no individual voice could be made out. Celia's every impulse crowed for her to scream, to give up her location just for the sake of it, but she was an operative, not a child; she needed to emerge unscathed if Oliver getting caught was going to mean something and give her the chance to escape. They wouldn't kill him, not yet. The soldiers would be forbidden from making an easy execution shot on someone like Oliver. Their superiors certainly had firm instructions for these occurrences: Bring the enemy back—and bring them back alive. How else would you torture out information about the rest of the resistance cell?

Another gunshot in the room. Celia clamped on her mouth harder. Her cheeks were damp, chillingly cold with every passing second, but she could barely move to wipe the tears away. There was a cascade of movement above ground, shouting and instructions and a rumble of footsteps that disturbed the floorboards so ferociously she had half a mind to believe the trapdoor might cave in and reveal her anyway.

Then she heard a voice, cutting clear through the pandemonium:

"To Shanghai. Let's go, let's go, before his backup falls in!"

Take him to Shanghai, where the prison cells and the war generals were. Where they could celebrate their catch, eliminate every point of internal opposition against their power, one by one by one, never mind what lurked at the external borders.

The footsteps cleared out. The voices, too, were now discernible enough to catch that they were demanding Oliver be led away.

Slowly Celia summoned the nerve to lower her hand, no longer at risk of making noise. She tugged her entrapped arm once more, and at last the string on her wrist snapped, releasing her from the pipe. It hardly mattered now—Oliver had only meant for it to be a temporary bind, and there was no use following after him when she could hear the soldiers exiting the building.

Celia listened. Her fists were clenched to the point that she could feel her nails cutting into her skin, drawing sharp pain along her palms.

The safe house had fallen silent. Celia waited another minute to be sure that they were gone, that there were no more eyes left on the room.

Please don't be angry at me, because this might be the last chance I have to do this.

"God*dammit*—" Celia wiped at her face harshly, clearing the tears. If Oliver was resolved to become their torture subject, Celia was going to raise a damn battalion to insist otherwise.

She lifted the trapdoor. Swore under her breath, punching away the rug that tried to lift alongside the latch.

"I'm going to kill you," Celia muttered, clambering out from the floorboards. "I'm going to save you, and then I'm going to kill you. Cut you into tiny *chunks*. I'll feed you to the *fish*."

The safe house was quiet. As was the building when she carefully entered the hallway. Celia felt like she had left the house and forgotten to put on clothes. Like she had marched into war without a shield. Oliver missing from her side was an appalling feeling.

Celia finally emerged outside. She shivered, wrapping her scarf tightly around her face. The first matter at hand was finding transport. Then she needed to fetch help, which happened to have been her next destination anyway.

Zhouzhuang.

25

Night hung heavy in the water-filled township. The shadows were as dense as smog, hovering low along the canals.

Orion was awake again.

This time, he seemed better recovered, remaining conscious past just a few minutes. Though Rosalind had been viciously on edge when she was called back into the room—her attention latched on to his every move in the fear that he would either collapse again or, worse, suddenly snap and have this confusion turn out to be an act that Lady Hong had put into place—it didn't take long before she started to relax.

Orion didn't listen to any of their insistences that he ought to sit and recover. He made it his mission to poke around the house while asking a dozen questions per minute, flying through everything from why he was here to why he was wearing a military uniform, and no question could be answered easily. While Rosalind tried her best, Orion wasn't paying full attention anyway. He flipped the light switches on and off and poked around Juliette's things, much to her confusion, and Rosalind had tried her best to assure her cousin that it was a habit of Orion's to prod around his surroundings. His behavior had to be genuine at that point, because even if a brainwashed Orion was a good actor, there was no chance he could mimic the look of sudden sheer delight when he found a grenade in one of the wardrobes. With horror, Roma had immediately plucked it out of his hands, chiding that it wasn't a toy.

Orion had come back—or at least partly. She could see his quirks in every swing of his arm and every quick crouch. When he wasn't paying attention, she basked in the sight before her, breathless over how he would perform a regular task like pulling out a kitchen chair.

The missing memory was certainly a problem, though. Orion might have been freed of his mother's directives, but he wasn't the same if he couldn't recall his life or remember who anyone was. There was no sense of urgency in his manner; he didn't know that his older brother was after him and his younger sister was in the city fretting over him, that his best friend was infiltrating deeper and deeper into the enemy faction in an effort to find a solution, and that Rosalind . . . well, Rosalind wasn't sure what she was to him, so maybe that was a problem all on its own.

"I don't understand," Orion said. He tapped the piece of paper in front of him. "How do you know me so well if this began less than five months ago?"

They were sitting at the kitchen table. Rosalind had needed to get him into a chair before he broke more items around the house, or heavens forbid, started playing with another grenade. Then, in an effort to help him understand their present predicament, she had started drawing on a piece of paper, tracing out every person he knew and how they were interconnected.

"We lived together," Rosalind replied. Admittedly, she was skating over some of his questions. "I picked up a lot."

Orion made a thoughtful expression. "And Alisa also had so much to say because . . . ?"

"Coworker," Rosalind supplied with a wince.

A small snicker came from the sofa. Juliette, who was sitting with a bowl between her legs, sharpening her knife on the base. Some things never changed.

Orion nodded his understanding. His attention had been drawn by Juliette's snicker too. "Then Juliette was a part of the Nationalists like us?"

"Oh, absolutely not." With a sigh, Rosalind tried to direct his attention back to the paper, where, if he had paid attention, he would see the absence of her name. "She's been out of the city for years. So has Roma."

As if summoned by his name, Roma opened the front door then, ushering Alisa through first before he stepped in too. They had gone outside before to make a telephone call, with Roma assuring them that he knew exactly how to summon Lourens and Alisa immediately hurrying on his tail, wanting to accompany him. On the sofa, Juliette glanced up from her knife sharpening, raising her eyebrows once to ask Roma a question and getting a nod in response.

"Then how do we know them?" Orion, meanwhile, kept pressing.

"You don't. I do."

"What?"

"Juliette is my cousin. Roma is her husband."

"And also Alisa's brother?"

"And also Alisa's brother."

"Why do we know Alisa but not Roma?"

Rosalind resisted the urge to throw her arms into the air. "Listen, Orion. Roma and Juliette are somewhere out here"—she motioned at the outer corners of the paper, beyond the web she had drawn—"and we need your focus in here." She tapped the pen to the center, marked with a big star that said ORION. "Those two are backstory. Forget about them."

"Ouch," Roma said at the door.

"We're sensitive," Juliette added.

Alisa snorted. She hurried over to the kitchen while her brother joined Juliette, his head inclined so that the rest of them couldn't hear what he was saying into Juliette's ear. It seemed Alisa was bringing her own report anyway when she bounced to a stop by the table and asked, "Can I interrupt?"

"I doubt you need our permission for that." Rosalind set her pen down. "What is it?"

"We have people bringing Lourens in," Alisa said plainly. "But it'll take more than a week. Roma wants us here until then."

Rosalind almost gasped out loud. "A *week?*" she demanded. "Why on earth would it take a week?"

"*More* than a week," Alisa corrected, as if that were the matter Rosalind was shocked about. "And it's because we need to send my cousin to find him first. Benedikt—you remember Benedikt?"

Rosalind pinched the bridge of her nose. Orion peered at the paper in front of him, making a frantic search.

"You didn't mention a Benedikt," Orion muttered.

"He and Marshall are on their way now," Alisa continued. "I don't think we can trust anyone else to convince Lourens successfully, so we need to wait on them from Moscow."

Orion lifted the paper entirely. "Now, who is this *Marshall?*"

Rosalind and Alisa both ignored him.

"Phoebe and Silas are probably worried sick," Rosalind said. "Once the Nationalist presence lessens in the last town, we need to leave." She paused. Suddenly, she felt like an absolute blockhead. "That is—Orion and I absolutely must leave. I am in no authority to tell you what to do."

Alisa rolled her eyes. "Stop being so soppy. I can always come back. They can't get rid of me now."

"Yes, we can," Roma called from the living room. "I'll give you the boot at the first hint of attitude."

"Nevertheless," Alisa continued, pretending not to hear him, "a week is hardly a long time in the grand scheme of matters. Phoebe and Silas are understanding people."

That was a blatant lie. Or maybe Alisa and Rosalind had very different interpretations of what the word "understanding" meant, especially when it came to Phoebe.

"Lady Hong is still at large," Rosalind said. "We don't know what she's doing, we don't know what she's planning, and we don't know why she just left Orion at the scene like that without guarding him ferociously because you would think that if she needed him—"

Rosalind cut off. Orion had put his hand on her arm, fingers curled around her wrist. She stared, and then he jolted too upon looking down, as if he hadn't realized what he was doing. While she was trying to stir his memory, she had been making small bits of contact with him: an elbow grazing past his shoulder when she reached for paper, a hand sliding against the edge of his, fingertips brushing when passing a pen. She needed to make sure that he wouldn't disappear, that he existed before her in real form. This, suddenly, was too much—*too* real, invading her senses at once.

Orion let go. "Sorry," he said abashedly. He winced. "I suspect I must be missing something here, though. Are we still on active mission?"

"Us?" Rosalind clarified.

A nod.

Rosalind hesitated. "No." Her gaze dropped, focused intensely on a little crumb on the table. "I mean—my only mission was touring the country, and I abandoned it. You, technically, are a fugitive."

"Right." Orion looked at the sheet of paper. It included everyone they knew. It didn't include every detail, every bit of wrongdoing he committed under his mother's control. "I killed a lot of people."

Before Rosalind could assuage him, could prompt him to remember that it wasn't *him,* that he had been used as a tool when he should have been safe with someone he trusted, his gaze flickered up again, and he asked: "If neither of us is connected with the mission anymore . . . who assigned this need to stop my mother?"

The ticking clock on the wall grew excruciatingly loud. It was the metallic clang of a train passing faulty tracks, each second echoing with the clangor of a carriage at risk of derailing.

"No one *assigned* it," Rosalind said, turning defensive. She wasn't sure why. "But she's on a forward march to give the Japanese Empire incredible research, and if that succeeds, there's no winning any future war. We may as well put up our surrender flags today."

"I understand that." Orion ran a finger across the piece of paper, trailing the web of names. "But are there no other operatives on this mission?"

"There are many people keeping an eye on her," Alisa contributed. "Whether there's anyone actively making the effort to stop her?" A shrug. "Debatable. Besides, she hasn't given the Japanese government anything yet. All she's done is experiment on her own men—whether filched from the Nationalists or borrowed from the Japanese—and if we're just talking about hanjian to arrest, there are a *lot* of those in this country."

Orion stared at her. Then at the paper. "So she *doesn't* need to be stopped?"

Rosalind tutted. "If you saw a candle burning underneath a curtain about to catch on fire, wouldn't you move it?"

"What if it's not a candle?" Alisa returned just as quickly. "What if it's a pipe that overheats in the winter and can't be plucked out without renovating the whole house?"

"Then we should renovate the whole house," Rosalind countered.

"But you're not a renovator," Alisa said. "You don't have a renovating license."

"You might as well just safely fireproof the curtains," Orion added.

Silence. The tack-on was so ridiculous that neither Rosalind nor Alisa could continue without scoffing, and then it became rather hypocritical because, really, his suggestion wasn't any more ridiculous than what they had already been volleying back and forth. Juliette and Roma were listening now, too, their attention turned toward the kitchen. Rosalind couldn't understand why this was even a debate. Dao Feng would have agreed with her. Dao Feng would have issued this as a proper task, let her stop—

Rosalind leaned back hard into her chair, crossing her arms over her chest and forcing her line of thought to come to an abrupt stop. Dao Feng wasn't here. Because instead of being her handler, he had swapped sides, and regardless of which faction in the war was right or wrong or neither, what did it matter what he would have approved? He clearly didn't care enough about what impact she made as Fortune.

No one was controlling Fortune anymore. Her throat restricted on her inhale, then further on her exhale. The house had grown stifling. When had it grown so stifling?

"Rosalind . . . ," Alisa said.

"Give me a minute." Rosalind was lurching to her feet and walking toward the front door before she had finished her sentence. "I need some air."

From where she stood, the water looked entirely silver.

Rosalind might have been inclined to believe that the sheen on top wasn't a reflection of the moon but rather pure metal poured over its surface—only then she crouched along the edge of the weed-filled lake and dipped her hand in, fingers slicing through the cool water. Not metal. Not an impenetrable surface, only another fragment of nature waiting for her to lean down and break the illusion.

Rosalind inhaled the cold night.

Now that she had calmed down, she could admit that they were right. It *was* smarter to stay here. Lie low for a week, wait for Lourens to arrive and figure out how to restore Orion to normal. Yet the very thought threatened to drive Rosalind mad; she had already wasted weeks upon weeks holed up in her apartment to no effect. Even if they helped Orion here, his mother was going to come after him eventually. Why hide away, why risk a false sense of security if the world could crumble beneath their feet the next day and take him away?

Rosalind picked up a rock and threw it into the lake. It sounded with a hollow *plonk* before cutting through the silver surface.

One person alone couldn't keep the city from falling. She knew that. It was too complicated a matter, something vast that extended a thousand hands at once, and she couldn't possibly hope to shake them all. Politics moved as fickle as a breeze in a storm, spinning whichever way the tide turned and hurling ships against the coast by chance. But even if she knew that she had little power here, that didn't stop her from wanting to try. When she could see a path, shouldn't she take it? Find Lady Hong, stop her, save the world. How else could she protect everything she cared about?

She threw another rock. Hurled it, really. The next *plonk* wasn't as satisfying.

With a huff, Rosalind turned away from the water and started back toward Juliette's house. She didn't want to cause any worry, and she had been standing out here for a while. At least she hadn't gone far: anyone who peered around the other side of the house would have seen her standing in the distance, gazing off into the watery nothingness. She wondered how her cousin had gotten used to living in a place like this—if she could truly be happy so far away from the city's beating heart. Zhouzhuang was so quiet that her ears were starting to hallucinate noise.

Rosalind picked her way around the bend. Just as she was heading for the door to the house, her gaze lifted up the path to a large weeping willow tree, where there was a shape at its base.

"Orion?" she said immediately. She hurried closer.

He was asleep. His back was against the tree with his head lolled forward, hands placed neatly over his stomach. Carefully, Rosalind crouched down, poking a finger at his chest as if he might only be pretending. He had been bundled into a borrowed coat, the collar thick and furry around his neck. His breathing was heavy and even. He didn't stir when she poked his chest a second time, harder in case the coat fabric obstructed her jab.

Instead of shaking him awake, Rosalind sighed and sat down next to him. The night air blew, and she leaned her head against the tree trunk too, letting herself feel the cold breeze against one arm and Orion's natural body heat against the other.

"You are such a pest, you know that?" she said to him.

He only responded with a light snore. Rosalind pressed her hand to her mouth, and suddenly she was struggling to hold back an outburst, struggling to keep herself composed when she wanted to scream until her throat grew hoarse.

"I was doing perfectly fine before you," she snapped, and then she couldn't stop the words from slithering out, placing blame where blame didn't deserve to go. "I had a purpose. There was no one in the city I needed to answer to, and no one in the city cared to answer to me. All I had to do was report to Dao Feng. Then there was you. Asking for my opinion on the most foolish of things. How many people need to collect a poll on whether to wear a black tie or a blue tie, Orion? Just you, apparently."

Above, the leaves of the weeping willow rustled, as if it were giggling in response to Rosalind's remark. She wouldn't be surprised by the turn of events if the trees somehow sprang alive for no reason other than to laugh at her. Nature was acting witness to her confession, jotting down her words onto its tree bark, and maybe someday, centuries later, those who looked hard enough at the weeping willow could bear witness to her wrongdoings too.

Rosalind clutched her arms together. Her ire burned down to embers, quick to flare to life but quick to die too. She knew what she was truly angry at, and it wasn't Orion.

"It was nice to be asked, actually," she whispered in defeat. "It was nice to be all that you needed, even if it was for one moment, for one decision regarding a mere tie."

Orion's breath changed. There was a stutter—as if he was stilling in his dreams—before his posture relaxed once more. She waited. Her own breath escaped before her in a cloud of opaque white, misting the air around them.

"Do you want to know what I think?" She looked down at her hands. Blood-lined, terror-inducing hands. "It's easier to save the world, actually. Easier than saving myself. Easier than trying to save you. I'm not trying to prove a point by going after your mother. She's just the only threat I can fight. Everything else . . . Everything else feels like a lost cause most days. Eventually I'll destroy myself. Eventually you're going to leave."

All of a sudden, Orion lifted his head, his eyes wide open like he had never been asleep. "I'm not going to leave."

Rosalind squeaked, rearing back with fright. "I thought you were asleep!"

"I was," he replied smoothly, not a flicker of guilt in his expression. "But then you started talking to me, so I woke up."

How *long* had he been listening? Rosalind started to get to her feet, an incoherent half excuse mumbled under her breath. In a snap, Orion reached to stop her, his hand closing on the edge of her coat to hold her still.

"I was waiting for you," he said quickly. "I didn't want to startle you, so I was waiting for you to come back. Don't go."

It was terribly strange speaking to him directly. This was Orion in front of her, and yet it wasn't. This was Orion's expressions and mannerisms and his face, so beautiful under the silver moonlight that it hurt, but there was none of his attitude. Before they'd started getting along, they had exchanged jibes and mockery for sport, sniffing out each other's sore spots like bloodhounds out for a kill. Like it or not, she knew his humor as well as the back of her hand, and here she could only find the replica of it—formed in the shape of Orion but missing his flesh and guts.

"You could have just walked up to me," Rosalind said.

"I wasn't sure if I could," Orion countered. Those words seemed to summarize their whole situation at present.

"Well"—Rosalind shrugged—"here is your blanket permission."

He fell quiet. She did too. Orion had turned to face her. Stubborn, Rosalind continued looking out onto the canal. When a few seconds passed, she grew uncomfortable enough to make a small, irritated huff.

"What is it?" she asked. "You're making me itchy."

"Sorry," Orion said quickly. "I just . . ." He suddenly sounded so small—so *wilted*—that Rosalind regretted her tone even before he trailed off. Though she swallowed her wince, taking back her words or apologizing would feel too strange, so she finally turned to look at him. Orion blinked. The breeze had picked up again, ruffling his hair.

Orion Hong had always been *attractive,* conventionally speaking, but Rosalind hadn't been attracted to him—not in the beginning, not in the way that others he ran after could be snapped under his finger in an instant. Now there was a bewildering battle in Rosalind's head, because he had grown on her so thoroughly that it physically ached to be near him without reaching out and touching his face—and yet it wasn't *this* Orion who had grown on her, so how could she reconcile the two split images?

"What is it?" she said again. Nicely, this time.

"I believed you when you called yourself my friend," he said slowly. "But that is not all, is it?"

Oh. Rosalind had known this question was coming sooner or later. She supposed she had had the time to prepare herself, but still, reaching into the full catalog of her memories for an answer that he didn't recall felt like she was baring herself inside out.

"Beloved."

Orion blinked. "Beloved?"

"That was what you called me," she said. "Not Rosalind. Beloved."

A wispy leaf floated down onto Rosalind's shoulder. As soon as she brushed it off, however, it landed on Orion's sleeve next, and he stared at it a moment before picking it up carefully, handling the leaf as though it were some live animal before setting it onto the cold soil.

"I suspected as much," Orion said quietly.

Rosalind stared at him. What was *that* supposed to mean? Was he glad to hear it? Did he hate the idea? She didn't know what she hoped for exactly, but she was ready to overthink the matter all night—until she heard the smack of footsteps in the distance.

Her attention snapped up, toward the stone bridge that connected her cousin's house with the rest of the sleepy township. "What's that sound?"

Someone came into view from the alley on the other side of the bridge. By moonlight, it was hard to see anything until the figure lurched onto the bridge and hurried across it, coming upon this side of the canal.

Rosalind leaned forward, squinting to make sure she was seeing correctly. She was: Celia hopped off the bridge, then paused to catch her breath. They both identified each other at the same time, it appeared, because the moment Rosalind scrambled upright, meaning to help her sister, Celia called, "Oh, good, you're here!"

Her sister rested her hands on her knees, heaving an inhale. "We need to go! Lady Hong is going after Oliver to make her next round of experiments."

26

Inside the house, a frenzy had erupted with the news Celia brought. While everyone scrambled to make sense of what Celia was trying to explain, Rosalind watched her sister's expression. She could see it plainly: no matter what conclusion they came to tonight, Celia was going after him.

"I got this letter in the last town," Celia said, laying a piece of paper down on the dinner table. Six heads crowded around its four sides. "I should have opened it immediately, but the soldiers closed in on us and Oliver got himself captured to lure them away." She paused. Winced slightly, skipping past recounting the specifics. "It wasn't until I was hitching a ride on the back of a truck that I remembered to open it. It's from Priest."

"What is Priest doing sending a correspondence?" Alisa asked. "Telegrams are easily intercepted and spied upon."

"It was an emergency." Celia spun the paper around. "She must have known she needed to get this information to Oliver before his mother caught up to him. It's only that the Nationalists got to him first."

I performed investigation on Lady Hong. She turns soldiers immortal with "seramorine," produced only by mutated gene found in human blood. Cannot be

stabilized unless two types of blood present: original and genetically diversified offspring.

She gave the original to herself. I read her research thesis from start to finish, and she describes an offspring's seramorine supply to be limited. Hong Liwen should be reaching the limits of his use. By the description of its presentation, Hong Feiyi doesn't have the gene. She will be coming after you next if she is to finish her research and make the complete concoction.

Run.

—Priest

Rosalind leaned back when she finished reading, her thoughts spinning at breakneck speed. Lady Hong's first illicit experiment wasn't on Orion after the Nationalists pulled her funding. Her first illicit experiment was on herself, *knowing* she needed to wait to pass it on to her children. By the time she got caught, the main reason she targeted Orion was because Oliver had already left the household and joined the Communists.

"*Huh,*" Rosalind said quietly.

It still didn't wholly make sense. Perhaps Lady Hong had abandoned Orion at the last stop because his blood wasn't useful in her experiments anymore. She needed to go after Oliver instead to continue harvesting this genetic component and continue her terrible research. Only . . . it wasn't as though Orion were deadweight. Short of his blood, he had still been subject to her other experiments. He was her first impossibly strong soldier. An asset regardless. She could have had both her sons—it didn't *need* to be one or the other.

When Rosalind's eyes flickered to Orion, he was already watching her. Her breath caught in her throat on sheer reflex, though she quickly suppressed her reaction. Embarrassing. She had had him back for a day, and she was reacting like this over his gaze alone. Orion lifted an eyebrow, seeming to ask what she was thinking. She shook her head, gesturing that she'd tell him later. He didn't have his memories, but he still remained excruciatingly observant.

"How much do you trust this Priest?" Juliette asked after finishing the letter, the question directed at Celia. Her cousin looked more doubtful than everyone else at the table. "Because this sounds like a lot of intimate knowledge she shouldn't know."

Celia frowned, pulling the letter closer to examine it again. "What do you mean?"

"This part about Hong Feiyi." Juliette tapped the line. "How would she have gotten ahold of that information?"

At Rosalind's side, Orion nudged her carefully. "That's my sister, right?" he whispered.

Rosalind nodded.

"I don't know," Celia, meanwhile, was answering. "But of everyone scrambling for power in Shanghai, I can't imagine why Priest would need to make things up. Oliver is her handler. She must have methods of gleaning information."

Across the table, Roma leaned over to Alisa, whispering, "Do you know who Priest is?"

"If I did, brother dearest," she whispered back, "there would be a lot less doubt and confusion at this table right now."

"I wondered whether it might be you."

Alisa gave him a look askance. "How could I be a sharpshooter when my aim is shit? *You* never taught me."

Rosalind felt as though she were trying to tune in to three hundred different conversations at the same time. In truth, it was only Juliette's and Celia's voices crowding in too while they debated the legitimacy of the letter, but every time she caught sight of Orion's perplexed expression, her attention split another fragment.

"All right—hush, hush," Celia commanded.

The kitchen fell quiet. Orion propped his chin into his hand. "I wasn't saying anything."

"Maybe you ought to," Roma countered. "Out of everyone, you should probably stay here."

"Agreed," Rosalind said, at the exact same time that Orion blinked and exclaimed, "Absolutely not."

Alisa grimaced. Celia pretended to get distracted by the side of the table. Orion, despite barely following the situation, pulled his shoulders back, straightening his posture.

"Oliver needs me."

"You don't remember him."

"He's my brother, isn't he? Memory or no memory, how can I leave my brother to the wolves?"

"Enemy brother, don't forget," Celia added quietly. "Those wolves are *your* people."

An awkward tension drifted in. Alisa mumbled something about wanting to make tea, but instead of rummaging through the cupboards, she pivoted out of the kitchen and into the living room, looking into the other drawers.

Orion laced his fingers in front of him. "I'm not going to claim to know more than I really do," he said. "But I think you need me for a rescue mission because you don't have anyone else here to provide brute strength."

Lady Hong was coming after Oliver, but Oliver was being held captive by Nationalists. If they wanted to keep Oliver out of Lady Hong's grasp, then they needed to break him away from the Nationalists before Lady Hong did. Which, to Orion's credit, did require someone who would perform the outright fighting, because heavens knew a Nationalist jailbreak was not that easy.

But . . .

"Orion, it really isn't that simple," Rosalind said. "Celia is right.

We're split down two factions. When your memories come back, you might find that you would have made an entirely different decision. Going in to get Oliver means actively combating your own side."

There was an unspoken question in Orion's expression. They were both Nationalists, yet only he was being urged to reconsider.

"I thought that entire side believes I'm hanjian."

"Brainwashed hanjian, technically, so it's not like they *really* blame you," Alisa called over from the living room. As soon as they all turned to look at her, she ducked into her shoulders, scrambling to add, "Sorry, sorry, I've removed myself from this conversation."

Alisa did make a good point. Rosalind hesitated.

"They have marked you off as a lost asset," Rosalind said. "But in all honesty, if they knew you were no longer under your mother's control, they would probably accept you right back into the ranks. The Nationalists operate smartly. It's about result more than doctrine."

The web that Rosalind had drawn was still up on the counter. Orion searched for it again, his gaze landing on the information and tracing the names that had been scribbled with arrows and connecting points.

"Until you get your memories back," Rosalind continued, "you probably shouldn't decide yet whether you're going to betray them."

"But you are going on this rescue."

"Of course."

"Then I must as well," Orion concluded. "*You* are my side. It is not betrayal."

Rosalind blinked. He was making his decision under the assumption that they were one combined unit, choosing not by reason but by his faith in her. How could he trust her so easily? What had she done to deserve it, especially now, when he didn't even remember her?

"That's that, then," Celia said when Rosalind remained unspeaking for too long. "Off we go."

No one moved. Except Celia—who strode a few steps toward the door. She stopped. Turned back.

"*I* was ready to leave with you, Celia," Alisa supplied helpfully.

Celia gave her a wry look.

Orion suddenly pushed away from the table, swinging his arms. At once, Roma gestured for him to wait, his frown serious.

"If you are insistent on leaving," Roma said, "then you must come back in a week's time. When Juliette and I got ahold of your cure . . . we never tested it. We didn't know who to give it to or if there was any value playing around with what limited supply we had."

"What Roma is trying to say is that we cannot promise your mind will stay as it is," Juliette interjected bluntly. "Lourens didn't make that cure directly for you, and your conditioning could have been different. If you don't return by the time he's here to get looked at properly, it's not our fault if you lose control again and kill people."

Rosalind's mouth dropped open. Juliette caught sight of her expression, then raised her brow to signal, *What? I'm only telling the truth.*

"I understand," Orion said, nodding. "I will return in a week."

"I will bring him back," Rosalind added.

"Time is ticking!" Celia called from the door.

"Regardless of whether this rescue mission succeeds or fails, you must return." Roma had spotted the paper full of names they left on the counter. He picked it up, eyeing the lines. "It's not only the people around you at risk. It is yourself. Your very mind could crumble."

Orion considered the matter for a moment. "Are you trying to scare me on purpose?"

Roma frowned. "No, of course not."

"If you scare me, I do think it might help. Your eyes are so piercing that I can feel my heart rate picking up, and it's sharpening my thinking—"

"All right, all right," Juliette cut in, giving Orion a push out of her kitchen and toward the entryway. "Stop wooing my husband. Rosalind, keep him under control."

For the first time that night, a bubble of laughter rose up Rosalind's throat. She tamped it down, but by the grin Orion gave her over his shoulder, he had caught it anyway. At the entryway, meanwhile, Celia saw there was movement at last and opened the front door with a flourish, gesturing for everyone to hurry. She stepped out. As did Alisa. Only Rosalind looked back one last time, giving Juliette a nod.

"A week," she said. "I promise."

27

When Silas considered every clue he had gathered up until this point, it felt as though the final answer he sought ought to be well within reach. Yet here he was, staring at the picture on his desk, stumped beyond belief.

Why was it that he could practically track Priest's weekly movement across the city, but he didn't know anything about how she was getting around? Why was it that he could trace the origins of her tapes down to their manufacturer and the ink of her pens to their shops in the French Concession yet he couldn't follow a single lead past that and lost every thread he pulled? The challenge grew mightier in his mind with each passing day. It was as if Priest lived up there, taking residence alongside his thoughts so that she could never be caught, one step ahead before he ever homed in on her.

Silas hadn't thought of himself as inadequate for quite some time now. That used to be a frequent concern of his, back in London when he was growing up alongside Orion and Phoebe. It wasn't that either of them made him feel deficient on purpose—but in comparison to two people who possessed attitudes capable of shaking the world, Silas had always wondered what use he was if he couldn't achieve the same.

He got over that quickly when he started working as an operative. Filled up all that hollow space in his chest with purpose and concrete change.

Of late, he had to admit that feeling was roaring back at full height. Suddenly he was twelve years old again, looking at the vastness of his life ahead and doubting he could make any order out of it. Suddenly he was just a kid, skipping ahead multiple grades in his studies and comprehending enormously complicated concepts without understanding how exactly he was supposed to use any of them. All he knew was that he ought to study hard so that he could leave London and go home early; all he knew now was that he needed to do *something* to help find Orion.

What was the point of mapping Priest out so well if he still couldn't figure out who she was? How was he supposed to aid his city if he couldn't even uncover a *name,* never mind determine whether she harmed or helped the nation at large? He had one job as an intelligence operative. *One* job.

His mother's voice drifted down the hallway. "Lian Lian, are you at home today?"

Silas turned the picture over with a frustrated sigh, hiding it before she could see. "I am. I thought you and Bàba were away until next week."

"We changed our plans." His mother poked her head into his room, smiling. Mr. and Mrs. Wu were not ambitious people—or rather, they took opportunities that showed up at their doorstep but would never go out of their way to make a mountain out of a molehill. It was how his father had gotten into business with the Scarlet Gang those many years ago, when a distant uncle or other was recruiting for more hands in the inner circle, and it was how his parents had easily extricated themselves when gangster work turned official alongside the government. They didn't make enemies, but they didn't make many great friends, either.

Silas liked it that way. It meant that if his parents weren't out for work, they were lounging around at home, reading the papers or helping the kitchen staff bake. He had enough to fret over when it came to his work. His home life was the one thing that had always been peaceful.

"All right," he said simply. "I'm making a social call to Feiyi in the afternoon."

His mother understood that was usually code for his work. Partly because he, too, had very few friends, but mostly because so long as an assignment wasn't confidential, Phoebe was usually wheedling to come along.

Sometimes even if it *was* confidential.

"It's always social calls." Mrs. Wu made a quick *tsk*. "You are getting too old for such frequent outings without intention, Lian Lian."

Silas blinked. "Māma, I'm only eighteen."

"Yes, marriage age."

His cheeks flamed at once. "I need quiet to work now. It was lovely to chat as always."

He could hear his mother's laughter twinkling all down the hallway as she walked off. "Dinner at seven. Be back before then!"

A door closed. She had gone into some other part of the house. Thank goodness.

Marriage age. Maybe that was what Priest was getting at too, giving him this picture of a church. At the printing shop, he had asked for the best quality possible, until each varying shade of gray could be identified from the negative panel. Although he could see every detail on the stained-glass windows now, it wasn't very helpful if he didn't know where the church was. It might not even be Shanghai—with so much architecture in the Concessions modeled on their colonial influences, this could be any old town outside London, outside Paris. Maybe Priest wasn't giving him a meeting place. Maybe it was a sign to get on it and say something to Phoebe before he withered into an old geezer, which was probably his midtwenties in his mother's mind.

"What are you trying to tell me?" he muttered aloud. "Why not just give me an address?"

He leaned closer. He couldn't help feeling like he was being presented a puzzle and that Priest was toying with him until he could solve it. For what? A test? Was he being suspected? As far as Silas was aware, he had done nothing to incite her suspicion, and he *was* careful. Being a triple agent was difficult because there was a whole headache of threads to keep track of, but it was also easier than merely playing double agent, given the Communists expected to see him still running around with the Nationalists. He didn't have to sneak around. He only had to assume both sides thought the best of him.

And they had better think well of him, because he was waiting on so much from every side that he was spread as thin as a crepe. Silas would do anything for concrete action—and at the moment, he hadn't received a report from *any* side.

Silas got up from his desk. He started to pace. The picture showed one side of a church. Walls, windows, door . . .

He stopped. Picked up the photograph again, bringing it to the light. If he stretched his imagination just a tad, he wondered if that splotch of color on the door was tape. And if he really wanted to make a further stretch, maybe it was the barest remnants of tape from five years ago, when the city came down with a particularly nasty bout of contagion. It was called a madness at the time—infecting victims upon contact—so the Scarlet Gang had taped red *X*'s over public facilities in their territories if they were areas of quarantine. Maybe. Maybe . . .

"Māma?" Silas stepped into the corridor, following in the direction where his mother had gone earlier. "Where are you?"

"Here, darling."

He found his mother again in one of the offices at the other side of the house. She looked up, in the midst of dusting the potted plants, when Silas skidded through.

"Where are your old Scarlet books?"

The Wu family owned a few scattered water factories in the city. When there were shutdowns five years ago, surely his mother had made a log of the areas that were hit.

"Third room, second floor. What do you need those for—"

Silas was already hurrying away. Their house was so organized that he knew exactly where to go as soon as he entered the room, running his finger along the thin layer of dust on the lowest shelf and taking out the folders. It would have to be a foreign-controlled area if there was a Western church to begin with. Then it would have to be nearer to the east of the city if there had been a madness outbreak five years ago. So he only needed to compare the streets that his mother had noted to be barred off back then, and then search for which ones had churches. . . .

The phone rang. Distractedly, Silas stood and picked up, already two paces away from the corded receiver on the table.

"Wéi?"

It was for him. Though his attention initially stayed pinned on the folder open in his hand, the moment the voice on the other end started speaking, he almost dropped the folder entirely.

"What?"

Phoebe took a bite of her bun. She had her purse shoved under her arm to hold it in place while her gloved hands were busy with food, each of her breaths blowing visible in the cold. The street was lively around her—outer French Concession that bled into Chinese territory at the south of the city. Overhead, a row of colorful shop lanterns fluttered with the wind, bright in contrast with the dull afternoon clouds.

She was already planning to be in the area, so when Silas called last night and asked if she was free, probably because he felt guilty for abandoning her at the library, Phoebe said she was and to pick her up here. He had wanted to go into the French Concession—she had yet to ask why, though Phoebe could make a guess. In the past few days, she hadn't seen Silas at all, too busy holed up in her room trying to understand a doctoral-level thesis. She had finally sent off her missive yesterday using a safe point. Early this morning, she had checked in with a liaison station nearby to see if there had been returning communication, but there was nothing. Since she didn't want to raise suspicion in case she was spotted leaving the building, she was wandering the street now to make her presence here appear natural, poking her head into the tailor shops and bookstores, perusing the hotel lobbies and greeting the hat makers.

Phoebe finished her bun, scrunching up its paper bag. She hoped her telegram reached Oliver in time. She hoped he would read her warning and hide in a hole somewhere, preferably stay there for a few months, or until their mother did something to put herself into the international spotlight and the government went after her properly. It was only a matter of time given the headlines of late. Every new week brought another riot erupting in a different part of the city to protest Japanese aggression. Even if the Nationalists were slow and overly fond of pacifying methods, they couldn't keep excusing this for long, especially not if the covert branch finally found evidence of Lady Hong making contact with the Japanese military outright.

The question was when that would happen. Whether Lady Hong would make landing in Shanghai first, where all the foreign forces were gathering.

Phoebe retrieved her purse from under her arm, her gloves ice cold when they crinkled against her skin. She had said to meet in front of the Heaven Cinema, so she came to a stop by the two posters out front, displaying the only showings. She waited. The rest of the street bustled on.

Why couldn't it have been *her* that their mother was going after? She knew it was a ludicrous thought, but maybe if it were Phoebe instead of her older brothers, she would have a chance at convincing her mother away from her current path. Their relationship had been good: they could sit down and talk it out. Maybe they could even stroll through a park together like old times. Phoebe could show her mother how great her aim was nowadays—so different from the little girl who had asked to be taught with a wooden pellet shooter when she was eleven—and her mother would be so proud. Proud enough to remember why she had given Phoebe a pellet shooter to begin with. Oliver and Orion wouldn't understand how to talk to their mother like she did; they couldn't imagine how their mother must have been forced into corner after corner, causing her to develop tunnel vision. Phoebe *could*.

But Lady Hong's thesis had been clear. Carriers of the changed gene had accelerated heartbeats, at a degree unnatural to the ordinary person. Phoebe's was perfectly normal. She had taken her own pulse multiple times, going as far as to ask Ah Dou to count too, and they had both concluded the same.

There was a reason why Phoebe was standing here musing about her mother's potential understanding while her brothers were likely to disagree. Lady Hong had told Phoebe once that all she had ever wanted were her three children. *Your brothers are my greatest achievements in this world, built for grand things,* she had said, tapping Phoebe's nose. *But you're my greatest reward, providing happiness at the end like a dessert.*

Phoebe had only laughed at the time. It had sounded so silly, comparing her to a treat. She couldn't have known what her mother really meant until these experiments came into the open. And she couldn't have *fully* known until that very moment she reached the conclusion of her mother's thesis. Oliver and Orion were valuable creations from birth, built for a purpose and raised in the name of science. Maybe Lady Hong hadn't predicted Oliver walking out, but then Orion had still been around to serve as a backup.

You're my greatest reward, providing happiness at the end like a dessert.

Phoebe's shoe scuffed as she kicked it against the pavement. How twisted it was that her mother found her to be a reward, a bonus at the tail end of three children, but that only meant Phoebe got to be treated as any ordinary child might.

A familiar figure caught her periphery. When Phoebe turned, she recognized Silas in the distance, talking to a street vendor. A girl, probably their age, who appeared incredibly enthusiastic about whatever their topic of conversation was.

"Excuse me?" Phoebe muttered at once, heading toward them.

"—immense admiration," the girl was saying when Phoebe neared. She touched Silas's arm. The stall beside her showed a display glimmering with necklaces, and though Silas was looking at the display, the girl was looking at him.

"This was certainly not where I said to meet me."

Silas jumped in surprise. Whether it was at her sudden appearance or because Phoebe had claimed his arm instead, she wasn't sure. Either worked. She tightened her grip, curled around his sleeve like a crawling vine.

"Oh, hello," the vendor said carefully.

Phoebe leaned to look at the display too. She had a bright smile pasted by instinct, but it almost faltered when she registered what the necklaces were.

"What are we looking at?" Phoebe asked, feigning ignorance.

The vendor cleared her throat. She had taken a very small step back. "I was just explaining this new design," she said. "These are catered for fellow Chinese customers, not Westerners. There's interest citywide in supporting those fighting for freedom. No one wants to be accused of supporting enemy parties, so subtle iconography has been selling very well."

Crosses dangled from each of the necklaces. Some small and wooden. Others larger and studded with fake gems. Phoebe had a suspicion that was rather sacrilegious, but it wasn't as though most common people in Shanghai were actually devout. Just as the vendor explained, this was symbolic of someone else, someone prominent in the city.

"I didn't realize Priest had captured public recognition this thoroughly," Silas muttered.

"Of course!" the vendor exclaimed. "Haven't you seen the gossip columns?"

Phoebe tugged at Silas's arm. She had had enough of this. "Surely you can get less cheap-looking jewelry elsewhere," she said acidly. "I want to go now."

He let her lead them away. His vehicle was parked at the end of the street, and Phoebe steered them in that direction quickly, trying to block out the image of the necklaces winking in the light. He must have parked and gotten distracted by the stall. If she had been paying attention, she might have seen him walking toward the vendor instead of having to interrupt the conversation a while afterward.

"How are you?" Phoebe asked, breaking the silence.

"I have bad news."

They approached the car. Silas opened the passenger door for her.

"Oh dear," Phoebe said, climbing in with a rustle of her skirts. She was wearing a pale blue frock today, though the straight hem at her calves deceptively hid the thick fur lining. "I've been doing well too, thank you, Silas."

Silas suddenly appeared chided. "I didn't mean to—"

"I jest." She pulled her door closed. Waited until Silas came around to the driver's side and got in. "You're so easy to tease."

"You . . ." Silas sighed, admitting defeat to Phoebe's quick switches. In a series of rote maneuvers, he turned on the engine and stepped on the accelerator, pulling the car onto the road. "Is *this* a jest? Ought I apologize before I start speaking in case you get angry at me later?"

"That's for you to worry about later. What's the bad news?"

Silas drove forward, watching the tram lines to make sure there wasn't one barreling into their path.

"We've lost contact with Rosalind."

She blinked. *What?* Last she heard from Dao Feng, the preliminary report on the Communists' side was that Orion had been freed from their mother, which Phoebe assumed meant Rosalind had gotten ahold of him. So how had that evolved into losing contact with Rosalind?

"From the tour?" Phoebe asked.

"There was an incident with your mother. Upper command says Rosalind has gone missing, but whether on her own volition or because she was yanked by Lady Hong, they have yet to determine." Silas craned his neck to get a better view out the windshield, checking the corner before he turned. "Orion allegedly made an appearance, though the operatives we had on the scene couldn't see anything when a conflict broke out. Smoke bombs, apparently. I suppose we will have to wait to see if Rosalind makes contact again before we find out what happened. Who knows—maybe she has Orion and they're heading back."

Phoebe didn't buy that, and Silas didn't sound very convinced either. Heading back without making contact with the Nationalists first was . . . strange, to say the least. Unless there had been some other development on the road. What had happened between that preliminary report Phoebe heard and these new conclusions?

"So, where are we going?" Phoebe asked. She could do her own digging later. Maybe Dao Feng had heard more.

"The church off Rue Lafayette." Silas opened the glove

compartment, letting Phoebe reach inside to grab the paper bag herself. It was thin, holding just a photograph. When Phoebe took the photograph out, she pretended it was the first time she was seeing it.

"Let me guess," she said dryly. "Priest, again?"

Silas turned the wheel. "What gave it away? The church as a location site?"

"Sure. Most certainly not that you're obsessed with her." Before Phoebe could let her snarky remark turn into a debate, she flipped the photograph around, finding smooth white on the other side. Her grumbling wasn't entirely feigned when she continued. "What is this for, then? Do I get to meet the elusive Priest?"

"I'm not sure," Silas answered. "I was only given the picture. No details, no time, no meeting date. I had to hunt down the address myself."

"How did you do that?"

Silas braked. In a fit of momentary panic, Phoebe thought she had asked too abruptly and let her true curiosity slip in, but then she realized the car had stopped because they had arrived. A church loomed to the left, enclosed by a chipping brown fence.

"How did I locate the church in the picture?" Silas clarified. "There's tape on the door that puts it among a list of quarantined buildings from five years ago. I only had to go looking through my mother's logs."

Silas surprised her sometimes with how quickly he latched on to the right paths. He was explaining his search process with such matter-of-factness, even though it was a hint that Phoebe hadn't even realized she'd left in the picture. It made her wonder what more she didn't catch from him . . . or what more she had accidentally let slip.

"That's not an easy link." She held the picture up. "I'm sure most people would take weeks to hunt it down by going through each church in the city. *Weeks*."

As she thought he might have needed.

"It took some abstract thinking," Silas agreed. He opened his door, nudging aside a pile of dirty snow with his shoe. "Come on."

On Phoebe's side, the road was clear. Snowfall usually melted quickly in the cities, but if it didn't, it gathered in hardened, muddy lumps at the pavement sides. She was slower than Silas as they approached the fence, dragging behind to survey their surroundings. A row of trees waved with the breeze, their branches spindly with the ice. Phoebe had learned to shoot on trees like those, except piled with far more snow, sending a spray of white down onto her with each successful mark.

"Feiyi, are you coming?"

Silas had proceeded much farther in the time Phoebe was watching the trees. She skittered forward, holding her skirts and coming to a stop beside him at the front door.

Up close, the church appeared abandoned. That little bit of tape was still stuck to the edge of the large double doors, and Silas reached to pluck it off.

"I am still not quite comprehending our presence," Phoebe said. "I don't hear anybody inside."

"If Priest were inside, I doubt she would be calling out a greeting."

Phoebe bristled. He had so much damn *attitude* when it was about this topic—where did all this attitude *come from?*

"Go on, then." She gestured forward, prompting him to knock.

His knuckles rapped on the wood, which echoed with a hollow sound. They waited.

Nothing. Thirty seconds passed. He knocked again. A minute. There was nary a phantom shuffle inside that might have indicated a presence. Coming to the end of his patience, Silas pushed on the doors, and they creaked open with a colossal groan.

Despite the show she was putting on, Phoebe shivered, feeling the hairs at the back of her neck stand upright. She could blame the cold, but her gaze flickered to Silas while he was observing the scene before them, his lips parted in awe to take in the stained-glass windows and the pews that hadn't been cleaned in years.

Look at me, a part of her wanted to scream. *I know you could see me if you tried.*

Silas stepped into the church. "It's empty," he said. Disappointment flooded his voice.

Yes, Phoebe thought, following him in. She blew onto her gloved hands, trying to warm them up. *And so long as you have already been directed toward this one, trying to figure out why, you don't investigate the orphanage two streets away if you eventually hear murmurings of a church hideout.*

"I don't understand," Silas continued, wandering deeper into the dilapidated pews. A pile of rubble had built up in the corner—the church was far more run-down than its exterior had implied. Perhaps it had never even been in use, constructed by missionary money and promptly abandoned when its investors pulled out.

"Silas," Phoebe said quietly. "I think that's for you."

She pointed to the rubble, where a single envelope was balanced on top of the bricks. A thin coat of dust had already settled upon it. Phoebe stayed a considerable distance away, making sure it didn't appear like she could see anything when Silas picked it up and read MAGICIAN on the front. Only once he turned the envelope over and plucked out the paper inside did Phoebe take her opportunity to drift closer casually, sidling up to his shoulder.

The letter only contained a single, typewritten line:

I think it would be best to conclude your tutorage.

"Conclude?" Silas's voice rang loud in the church now, bouncing back multiple times. "We barely began."

Phoebe waited a beat. Then she lifted a hand and gave Silas a small pat on his arm.

"Think of it this way," she said. "Better to be broken up with by an assassin before a real lover. It's like a practice run."

"Phoebe."

Silas had switched to English. That should have been a warning in and of itself. He and Orion had always been different from her in this aspect. Where Phoebe naturally started her sentences in English, they always tried to go whichever route made the most sense in the situation. Landing in London at eight years old meant the boys perceived Chinese as their mother tongue. Being sent off at six years old meant sometimes Phoebe faltered trying to remember her metaphors and idioms, mixing between the Chinese ones and those she had picked up from her British tutor.

She pressed on, ignoring Silas's prompt.

"Remember when Orion moped for a whole month after getting broken up with by . . . What was his name?" Phoebe tapped her chin. "Matthew? Maxwell?"

"Phoebe," Silas said suddenly, and it was so sharp that he might as well have snapped at her. "Could you give me a minute?"

Phoebe rocked back. Absorbed the request. There wasn't much else she could say in response except "of course."

Quietly, she stepped away, trailing over to the other side of the church, where she knew there was a little chair waiting at the end of the pews. It had probably been made for children, but she sat down on it anyhow, examining her shoes and feeling a peculiar burning sensation at the back of her throat.

She didn't like seeing the misery on Silas's face. She didn't like hearing his disbelief when he read the announcement of their severance. And none of these feelings were the professional, sensible judgments that she ought to be making as Priest; all of these were the enflamed, heedless sort of disregard that she possessed as Phoebe Hong. What part of this was Silas failing to understand? Priest wasn't going to save them. Priest wasn't *real.* She appeared in the full image of a girl, but she was a two-dimensional rendering that crumpled the moment someone looked from a different angle and widened the scope. Nothing could be done about the situation to turn her into a savior.

"Ready to go?"

Phoebe's head jerked up, her arms wrapped tightly around herself. Silas was walking toward her, but he had returned the envelope atop the rubble. Though she hadn't been watching him, she had heard the scratch of pen on paper. He had left behind a reply.

"I might stay for a few minutes. I like the feeling here."

The church amplified every sound, every squeak of the small insects running along the stone floor, every creak of another rotting piece trying to break from the ceiling. When Phoebe adjusted on her chair, the hind legs scraped an ugly caw.

Silas pushed his glasses up. "Stay?" A thought seemed to occur to him. "I didn't mean to be rude to you, Feiyi, I swear. I only needed to think, and I couldn't think at that very moment. It wasn't to do with—"

"No, I get it," Phoebe interrupted lightly. She pushed down the truth. Buried the teeming frustration before it could bubble up.

As much as she tossed in distress over Priest being a figment of imagination, wasn't Phoebe Hong the very same? The final child in a family of assets—the girl who was supposed to be the reward at the end and had turned herself into someone to be consumed with one easy bite. If people didn't see sweet, then they were seeing someone else entirely, and she didn't know who that was.

Silas crouched down, putting himself at eye level with her while she sat upon the small chair. He frowned.

Do it, Phoebe thought. *Call me a liar.*

He didn't. He asked, "You are not angry?"

I am furious. Not at him. At the world, for closing her into this lifelong charade where she wasn't allowed to be furious.

"I understand taking a quiet moment to think." Phoebe tipped her head back, gazing at the ceiling. There were so many cobwebs in the corners, showing crystalline reflections where light poured through the windows and coursed through the fine threads. "Just as I want to treasure a moment here now. Let me reflect."

She waved him off. Hesitantly, Silas said, "All right. I'll be in the car whenever you're ready. Don't stay long—we don't know who may come around." He backed away, watching her warily until his shoulder nudged the front doors and he had no choice except to turn around and exit the church.

As soon as the door closed behind him, Phoebe got up, heading for the envelope on the rubble.

"Why would you go hiding a reply from me?"

She slid her finger along the flap smoothly. Plucked the paper back out, flipping to the reverse side, where Silas had written a note.

Phoebe felt her whole stomach drop.

The Nationalists have captured Oliver Hong. If you don't rescue him, he will die.

If you trust me, I can help you get in.

28

"If we're coming from this direction, there's a safe house in the west of the city that should be empty. The only issue is that we have to cross the Suzhou Creek."

"Why is that a problem?" Orion asked.

Celia's expression turned incredulous, as if she were being addressed by a rock that had grown a mouth to speak rock thoughts. At once, Rosalind wound an arm around Orion's head and clamped her palm over his lips, preventing him from speaking further.

"I promise—with my whole heart and soul—that he's usually smarter," she said to her sister. A lurch on the road jostled them, but she held tight on her smothering effort, even as Orion tried to say more against her palm. "You'll see when he gets his memories back."

Alisa snorted. She was braiding a lock of hair away from her neck. "Are you sure about that, Janie Mead?"

Rosalind tried to kick the girl without looking. With a squeal, Alisa snatched her legs closer, hugging her knees to her chest to keep out of Rosalind's range of attack. She was wearing borrowed trousers from Juliette, which meant she was able to crawl about the burlap-lined floor easily. Meanwhile, Rosalind and Celia maneuvered the cargo bed of the truck uncomfortably, shifting every so often to get comfortable amid the straw and sacks. Some of the buttons down Rosalind's back were also misaligned. She had made a rushed effort of undoing her qipao while they were waiting at the roadside last night, just enough so that she could reach for her shoulder and yank out her stitches. Her body had worked through most of the poison by the time they were leaving Zhouzhuang; it was easy to tug one loose edge of the stitching to get everything out, letting her skin smooth over the holes. Celia had witnessed the entire process in abject horror, only blinking when Rosalind tossed the thread away into the trees. There had been little time to discuss it, because then a truck was rumbling down the road, and they had scrambled to stop it for a ride.

The driver was a carrot farmer who had been driving eastward anyway to make deliveries into Shanghai, so he didn't mind four stowaways piled in the back if he could make some extra cash. They had tried to rest through the night, but no one got any sleep—which Rosalind knew because she had been wide awake the whole time.

Now it was late morning, and Celia had pulled out a map so they could prepare for their entry. The driver would have to drop them off before the actual city borders. Any closer and the risk of being sighted was too great, especially in the city center, where there were eyes at every corner.

"To answer your question," Rosalind said to Orion, clamping on his mouth tighter. "The Suzhou Creek surrounds the International Settlement, and most bridges are watched by the Japanese navy. We don't know who will be on the lookout for us."

"There was an incident last week in Zhabei," Celia added. "Public animosity against the Japanese is at an all-time high in Shanghai. There are riots almost daily that the Nationalists are attempting to control." She paused, tapping the map. "Key word: attempting. Foreign relations in the city are no doubt about to spiral into a crisis."

Orion said something. This time, because Rosalind couldn't

guess what his words were, she removed her hand to allow Orion to repeat himself, but she still couldn't understand. He was speaking Japanese.

"I beg your pardon?"

"I just said, *I didn't realize I could speak Japanese*. What else do I speak?"

Rosalind put her hand back over his mouth. Slyly, instead of taking it as a reprimand, Orion set his head down on her shoulder, and suddenly it looked as if she were embracing him instead of shutting him up.

She yanked her hand down. Orion kept his head there. He was sitting directly on the floor like Alisa, so they were at the perfect angle for him to rest comfortably.

"I think we will have the best luck taking that bridge right outside the International Settlement's border," Rosalind said, trying to ignore him. "The one by the oil mill."

"I agree," Celia said. "Maybe if we time our entry to one of the protests, both Japanese and Nationalist eyes will be distracted by the chaos and won't be watching us pass through."

Alisa leaned closer to the map. The corners were fraying because this was an older version that Celia had been carrying around in her belongings.

"Who are we most afraid of right now?" Alisa asked. "Nationalists or the Japanese military?"

"We're not *afraid* of the Nationalists." Rosalind pointed a thumb at Orion. "We only cannot get caught because then they will want to do things their way, which means a thousand hours of processing and putting Orion into a cell until they gather intelligence."

"Technically, we're not afraid of the Japanese, either," Celia added. "Given everything we have learned about Lady Hong, I'm guessing that she's valuable to their empire only if she can make this concoction before they launch a true invasion. So she must have contacts along their military line—we don't know who may report to her from the ground and whether a sighting will cause a unit to come after us."

Alisa waited a beat. Then: "Both of you just described the very definition of being afraid of something. Got it. We're avoiding everyone."

All of a sudden, the truck came to a halt, throwing the four of them forward. Orion was quick to catch Rosalind, preventing her from any collision with the floor; Celia had good balance and steadied herself. Only Alisa went sprawling, opting to stay down once she hit the floor, rolling around and setting her hands over her stomach. Rosalind was certain she had done it on purpose.

"Girl down!" Alisa declared.

Celia smacked her calf. "Stop being dramatic. Be prepared. We might have been stopped."

At once, Alisa got up again, reaching inside her jacket. Celia continued to talk, shuffling closer to the cargo door.

"We have to—oh my God, *where* did you get *that?*"

Alisa had pulled out a very small gun. "We just left my brother's house—why are you surprised?"

"Did he let you take it?"

A nervous laugh. "No."

The door opened, interrupting the rest of Celia's scolding. Rosalind tensed, putting herself in front of Orion, but it was only the carrot farmer peering in.

"Is everything all right?" Celia asked.

"I'm afraid I will have to let you out here," he said. "They're checking papers up ahead. There's a rural station that could take you closer into the city if you walk north."

"They're checking papers this far out?" Rosalind asked, flabbergasted.

"Authorities declared martial law yesterday," the farmer said.

"All the foreign concessions are closing their borders. Barbed wire and sandbags everywhere. It's harder to get into the city itself too."

This was . . . not good. Not good at all.

"Thank you," Celia said to the driver, hopping out. Rosalind followed her sister's lead, waving for Alisa and Orion to hurry along before gathering up the map. At Shanghai's outskirts, the fields went on forever, patches of brown and green growing under the layer of winter ice. Who knew—maybe in a few decades the factories would expand out here too, layering cement and pavement down onto land that seemed to be waiting for interruption.

"A train station is definitely not an option," Alisa muttered as the driver pulled away. "I don't have false papers."

"I do," Celia said. She nodded at Rosalind. "I have two different sets, and one could pass for you."

"Who knew that being twins would come in so useful for fugitive work?" Rosalind mused. "What about Alisa and Orion?"

Celia surveyed their surroundings. They stood at a four-way split on the road, a path extending in every direction. Brief flashes of color appeared ahead on the horizon—a fluttering flag, which the truck driver must have spotted to determine there was a control point. Of everyone, Celia was the one most experienced in lying low and staying out of view from official eyes. Rosalind was far more willing to follow her sister's instructions than try to supply her own opinion on how they ought to proceed.

"Hide out in the last township we passed, due west," Celia decided, pointing the way they had come. "Rosalind and I will enter the city and find a car. Then we will find you two and time our reentry so that we can drive in without hitting a control point en route."

There was no objection. Three heads nodded back at her.

"Fantastic."

Celia waved for Rosalind to follow, departing northward to put their plan into action without any hesitation. Meanwhile, Rosalind paused, turning to Orion.

"Listen to everything Alisa says."

Orion lifted a brow. "If I must."

"I'm serious. I don't want you to get hurt."

He seemed to consider her words more earnestly, the levity in his expression fading. "It'll be fine. Return quickly, and then you can protect me yourself."

"Fine," Rosalind said.

"Fine," Orion echoed.

"*Mèimei, allons-y!*" Celia called from up ahead. She had already proceeded far enough that her voice was faint.

"Excuse me?" Rosalind exclaimed, hurrying after her. "I was born first! That's still jiějiě to you!"

Their surroundings fell quiet as Rosalind and Celia faded into the distance. A bird chirped. The ice creaked.

"So," Alisa said as she and Orion started to walk west. "Do you want to hear all the juicy parts of the story that Rosalind skimmed over?"

Orion grinned. "Oh, *do* I."

29

Rosalind had gotten a brilliant idea for making sure no one questioned why she didn't exactly match the small picture of Celia in the corner of her falsified papers: she clawed her face bloody.

Ten gashes decorated her cheeks like tear tracks. Once those appeared nice and realistic, she had been sure to tend to the other empty space around her face as well, making it seem like she had either been released from surgery at the hospital or had been involved in some disastrous beauty experiment. She had been rather inspired by the poisoned cut that marked up her cheek after fighting Orion at the tour stop. Though that cut had closed up at some point in the previous night, once the poison flushed out and her healing kicked in again, it had been bizarre to observe herself while the injury was there. Each time she glanced into the mirror and saw the slash of red, it was like looking at an entirely different face, one that didn't belong to an immortal experiment.

"This way," Celia said quietly after the conductor checked their papers, steering Rosalind to the left. They entered a third-class carriage, glancing around briefly to take inventory. It was far from luxurious, but that was to be expected. On these sorts of rural trains, running primarily back and forth between two cities with sparse stops in between, every carriage was a third-class carriage. "Watch your step—"

Despite Celia's panicked warning, Rosalind still stumbled on a bump in the carpet, muttering a curse under her breath. The makeshift bandages she had wrapped around her face were actually pieces of fabric she had torn from the lining of her qipao, and they were obscuring her vision. Blood had dried to stick the red-brown bandages against her cheeks, around her forehead, and down to her chin. Though her skin had already healed underneath, Rosalind ought to keep the bandages on until she was safely out of view of the conductor.

"You really could have left your forehead alone," Celia muttered when they sat down. The seats groaned beneath them. Someone had ripped out the sponge padding inside the armrests.

"It's not as though it will leave scars," Rosalind countered, grimacing when she moved her arms onto her lap. The train was terribly rickety. She wouldn't be surprised if this whole row fell apart before they could make the short trip into the city.

Her sister tutted. "But didn't it *hurt?*"

Rosalind pulled at the bandage near her eye, trying to clear some of her vision. The train started to move. Railway schedules never strayed a second from the dot. One man had just managed to board on time, seating himself across the aisle.

"Well, yes," she admitted. "So?"

Celia shook her head. "Sometimes," she sighed softly, "I feel as though you forget that you don't have to take pain just because you can."

The train carriage rocked. Conversation continued in a low hum along its aisles, elderly ladies discussing hair care at the back, a couple arguing over dinner to the right. The space between Rosalind and Celia, meanwhile, fell quiet, and Rosalind swallowed hard. Instead of brushing it off or making a pivot into a lighter topic, she suddenly asked:

"How long have you known?"

Trees and fields flew past in a green blur outside the window. Across the aisle, the man who had boarded last was coughing, heaving up a racket. Rosalind didn't expand further on what she meant; Celia knew exactly what she was asking.

"I was the one who got them out."

Her sister's words were soft. Rosalind took a moment to absorb them.

Celia had gotten them out. Meanwhile, who knew what Rosalind had been doing at the time—probably moping or crying in a corner somewhere. Gathering all that anger and regret that would eventually culminate into what the Nationalists had used to turn her into Fortune. She exhaled tightly, her hands fisting into her lap.

"I'm glad. That she had you."

Celia made an audible wince. "Juliette wanted to tell you, Rosalind. So many times, but—"

"No, it's good that she didn't," Rosalind interrupted. She wouldn't have trusted the girl she was back then with such a secret. She wasn't equipped to handle a matter that needed a friend over a traitor. "I had to catch up with myself first."

She'd had to remember who she was. Lug herself out from the sinkhole of her mistake, walk through the dark for miles and miles.

Truth be told, she wasn't even entirely sure she was out of the dark yet. But her feet were moving, and she could only hope it was in the right direction.

"Sir, you'll have to remove your bag from the other seat. That's a safety hazard."

The train attendant's sudden command gave Rosalind a fright. Warily, she glanced back to check what the problem was and found the attendant talking to the man with the bad cough, only he was acting as if he hadn't heard her. His dark glasses covered most of his face.

"Sir. Do you understand me? Please remove the bag."

Even with his eyes obscured, something about the lack of response struck a nerve with Rosalind. She leaned out of her seat.

"If I have to summon an officer on board—"

"My apologies," the man said. "I will put . . . the bag down."

His movements were halting. And his words were ever so accented, even if Rosalind couldn't be sure what she was picking up.

"Celia," she said slowly, turning back and pressing her head hard against the seat. "Is there any chance we were followed?"

"Followed?" Celia echoed, her voice lowering to a whisper too. "By whom?"

"Lady Hong's men," Rosalind replied. "Alisa and I led them right to Zhouzhuang after abandoning the tour stop."

"We would have noticed tails in Zhouzhuang. That place is too small."

"But what if they'd stayed outside? They could have lingered under the cover of the trees, waiting for the moment we emerged again."

A terrible thought occurred to her. The only time they could have picked up a tail was right before they got onto the cargo bed of that truck. If Rosalind and Celia were followed, then Alisa and Orion were likely also followed when the group split up.

"I'm going to try to draw him away to see if I'm correct in my suspicion," she muttered, rising in her seat.

"Wait, wait." Her sister grabbed her elbow, stopping her a moment before she could get up. "What are you going to do in such a tight space? *Kill* him?"

"He's as good as dead if he's already been brainwashed," Rosalind answered. "It's only the final strike."

Celia shook her head. "That's probably the same thing war generals say about their expendable soldiers. 'They have already enlisted, so they're as good as dead.'"

"Brainwashed is hardly the same as enlisted."

"And yet someone's Orion could be among them," Celia countered. "How do we know if any of them signed on willingly?"

Rosalind hesitated, her mouth opening and closing without sound. She couldn't think about these things. No—*Fortune* couldn't think about these things, because a job well done meant striking without question, and with every question asked about how someone had chosen their side, each face in a war became a never-ending debate. Of course each soldier had their own reasons. Empathy didn't mean mercy.

"I can try," she said, tapping Celia's wrist for release. "But sometimes we might just have to disagree, mèimei."

Celia let go of her elbow, and Rosalind got up.

She pushed through the carriage door, entering the passageway between cars. Wind whistled at a roar through the flexible rubber that wrapped this passageway from the harsh elements. A small mound of snow had leaked through, though Rosalind wasn't sure how it had yet to melt. Instead of idling in the space, she pushed forward into the next carriage. A concession stand operated here, selling small snacks and packaged meals. She took a seat in the first free row she saw, right at the edge of the aisle. While Rosalind waited, she tore the bandages off her face, giving her cheeks a hard scrub with her fingers. Dried blood floated onto her lap, a smattering of scarlet flakes collecting upon her pale qipao fabric. She brushed them off.

The carriage door opened. She knew without looking that the man had followed her in, carefully stepping down the aisle as he searched for her presence.

Rosalind didn't surge up or begin a fight. Quiet as a mouse, she plucked out a hairpin, held it along its middle so only an inch of the metal was available for use. Then, right as the man passed her, she shoved the pin into his leg.

He made a noise, but Rosalind yanked him into her row of

seats in an instant. If any of the other passengers were paying attention, they might have thought she knew the man and was playing around in jest.

The man stumbled. She clamped a hand over his mouth, holding him down as he flailed. Thankfully, he must not have been enhanced in strength, because she managed to keep her grip until the poison kicked in and the man stilled, going unconscious.

There was no reason to interrogate him about when or why he had come after her. Lady Hong's concoction wouldn't give him the free will to answer her questions, if Orion had been any indication. She may as well knock him out cold and see what she could find.

"No killing," Rosalind muttered, as if Celia might be able to hear her from the other carriage. "Be proud of me."

His pockets were empty. Rosalind was quick to abandon her search, setting the man on the seats and extricating herself, shaking the bandages onto the floor and hurrying back into her original carriage.

"What happened?" Celia hissed when she returned. "I saw him get up and—"

"And he left his bag," Rosalind said, plucking it from under his seat. She returned to her sister, unbuckling the bag.

A Japanese military uniform waited inside. Both she and Celia stared at it, working through myriad curse words in their heads.

"We're going to need to find that car fast," Celia decided.

"There's also no more time to wait for a distraction." Rosalind buckled the bag back up tightly. "We will have to make one."

Orion and Alisa had taken refuge at a teahouse, and to Orion's surprise, Alisa knew the owner, waving happily when they approached the front steps and going off to chat. Unless Orion was missing something, he couldn't fathom how she had made contact here before, but the likelihood of Orion missing something was also high.

He tossed the orange in his hands up into the air. Caught it on its way down. Alisa was still at the front counter.

Orion really didn't want to say something unless it was absolutely necessary, but his headache was getting worse. It had started as a mere annoyance when they were in the cargo bed of the truck. On the walk into this township, it had turned sharper at the back of his head. Now the ache was bringing flashes of light in the corners of his vision—glimpses of hallucinated images and snippets of conversations from the past floating through his ears. One would think that would mean his memories were coming back, but he couldn't even begin to discern whether any of these flashes were true recollections or utterly made up.

I'll get you a ring. What do you like? Silver? Gold?

Orion pressed down on his temple. Ever since he woke to Rosalind Lang hovering over him in Zhouzhuang, he had been searching for her in every crevasse inside his mind. The problem was that there were a *lot* of hiding places up there. He traced her shape as best as he could, followed the bright spot that she left from memory to memory. It wasn't that he struggled to find her, though. It was that every time he pressed too deeply on those faint impressions, the rest would dissolve, filled with too many other details that wanted to slip away and too many other people who wouldn't take form.

He knew her, that much was certain. He felt her occupying immense space, the sound of her scoff and the color of her lips, the smell of her hair and the cadence of her voice. He couldn't form the words that described how she existed in his head, but the feeling would balloon in his chest at any invocation—a soft feeling, a sweet feeling, less like sugar and more like springtime's first warm breeze.

Yet despite it all, nothing wanted to come into clarity. No

order came out of the disarray. If his past was a network of interconnections like the one Rosalind had drawn on paper for him, he hadn't so much undergone complete amnesia as he had experienced each connecting line breaking, each name thrown inside a bag to be scrambled into incoherent letters.

"Ouch," Orion muttered, his fingers moving to pinch the bridge of his nose instead.

Start simple, he urged himself. He was working himself too hard trying to put together every fragment at once, so if he went to the very first—

"Puis-je avoir un morceau?"

The girl waiting outside the cinema seemed around his age. Nine years old, or maybe older, if the fact that she was slightly taller indicated anything. At his question, she turned around, wordlessly offering the bag of popcorn in her hands.

She looked him up and down. Her hair was done in two careful plaits. "Huárén ma?"

Orion had nodded. Switched to the common Chinese tongue too. "Did I have an accent? I'm still learning French."

The girl laughed. It was a sound that qualified more as a titter than anything possessing true humor, a one-off *"Hah,"* and Orion was intrigued in an instant. He had a perpetual habit of trying to win people over—the tougher the task, the more satisfaction he gained from it. Some might call it having a dysfunctional personality. He just thought it earned him plenty of friends.

"Sure," she said lightly. "I asked if you were Chinese because it was the accent that gave you away. Not your face or anything." The girl jostled the bag of popcorn, then offered it again for Orion to take another piece. "There aren't many of us here."

He bit into the popcorn. Slightly burned, but nothing that changed the flavor.

"I'm only visiting my big brother. Usually I live in London."

"Oh. *I* live here." The girl didn't sound very happy. Her eyes flicked down the road. She used the popcorn bag to gesture to an apartment building. "With my tutors. Very irksome people."

"That's why you're lurking outside a cinema?"

Her mouth had quirked. Again, it was not an outright show of amusement, only a hint of it. As if to tease that someone *could* make her laugh if they tried hard enough. Only a worthy effort would be rewarded, and nothing prior.

"My sisters are inside watching a picture. I'm not a fan of the tragedies."

"Do you prefer the avant-garde melodramas?"

"Comedies, actually."

Orion grinned. Someone called for the girl from inside the cinema just as someone called for him down the street—his mother or his brother or his sister, he didn't know; that part didn't want to clarify itself. What he did remember was his quick, "Wait!" and the girl pausing between the two heavy doors. He remembered the orange sunlight coming down from the clouds and her brown eyes practically golden in the haze.

This was the age when he had started noticing people. And this girl was the first who had triggered a curious feeling in his stomach and a weightlessness in his chest. Stirrings of interest, the most innocent kind that came with simple yearnings for the brush of a hand or the nudge of a shoulder.

"What's your name?" he asked, switching back to French.

The girl cast a small smile over her shoulder. "My name is Rosalind." She gave a wave. "It's all right if you forget me. Au revoir."

When Orion jolted back to the present, he missed the next toss of his airborne orange. It landed with a thud on the wooden floorboards. He lurched to his feet. That was the *same* Rosalind. Why had that never occurred to him? Though the memory had only returned this very second, he found it absurd that he hadn't made the connection from the very moment he was reacquainted with her. It had been buried so deeply beneath every other event in his life that it had struggled to emerge, but now, with everything jostled . . .

"Alisa!" he bellowed. "I remembered something—"

Alisa wasn't at the front counter anymore. Mystified, Orion looked left and right, but the teahouse had cleared out.

"What the hell?" he muttered. He hurried through the back. One cook was in the kitchen, minding his own business stirring a pot. Orion pressed up to the dingy window there, seeing nothing in the alley, then backtracked into the main area again and rushed out the doors, disturbing the two red lanterns that swung on either side.

"Oof!"

He heard a phantom grunt of breath. Not from the alley to the left, which the kitchen had been facing, but to the right, between the teahouse and a large residential block constructed with stone.

"Alisa?"

Orion ran into the other alley, on alert. He found Alisa. And two uniformed bodies on the ground, a third being pushed down at that very second. As soon as the soldiers went still, Alisa wiped her forehead, clearing her sweat.

"You're welcome," she heaved. "So much for 'you need me on this mission to provide brute strength.'"

Orion gaped. "I didn't even know that you were in combat out here!"

"I suppose these men didn't, either. I took them by surprise. They're only the regular brainwashed kind, no enhanced strength."

"What—you—I thought you were untrained."

"I am. I'm just very good at jumping onto shoulders and smacking hard."

Alisa hurried toward him, frantic as she pushed him along and prompted their exit from the alley.

"Come on. No more teahouses. We need to hide."

30

The 19th Route Army waits in Shanghai.

Impatiently, with every passing day since the Japanese ultimatum. While the Route Armies operate under Nationalist jurisdiction, their sense of concord with the leadership couldn't be farther away. The top of the command ladder wants the country to compromise. Appease. Allow for conciliation. *Wouldn't we prefer to achieve internal pacification before we go forward with external resistance?* The 19th Route Army already fought viciously in Jiangxi before being moved up here. There, it was against the Communists. Civil strife, clambering to control the core while their border is bitten to nubs. The soldiers aren't any less angry now that they're in a new environment. They froth for blood, sick to death of letting imperialists run rampant on the streets.

"Bunch of devils in the suits of men," the soldier with the ripped shoes says. He's trying to stitch up a hole in the armpit of his shirt, because they haven't gotten new uniforms in eons, and besides, there are more important matters.

"Who?" the other soldier asks. This one brought his own shoes as spares. The two men came from the same place, a Cantonese unit, but they are as different as night and day.

"The Japanese. Who else?" the first soldier says. "It's already starting, and they're not letting us fight yet."

Who else? Funny. There are actually quite a lot else.

The Chinese parts of the city are breaking. Zhabei teeters at the tipping point of invasion, its people demanding an exit of Japanese forces, and the empire pressing harder to retaliate. If the soldiers of the 19th Route Army are to be let loose, there needs to be declared conflict. The leadership formally created the 5th Army for Shanghai some few days ago. The 19th Route Army's commanders have shifted around to accommodate it. Each and every one of them can smell war on the precipice, but the declaration has not come. They wait. They itch.

"No military action yet on either side," his friend says. He's echoing what has been passed along the ranks. An assurance, of sorts, as if it is meant to be a good thing.

There might not be military action yet, but conflict started a while back. It started with the city's distaste for the invasion up in Manchuria, an empire trying to claim control over land that didn't belong to it. It started with the volunteer forces forming among the Japanese—the ronin—taking it upon themselves to act as a police force in the Japanese-governed areas of Shanghai.

The soldier finishes stitching his shirt. It'll break again. Just as it has already broken the last few times. Maybe his tighter knot will hold for longer this time, though.

"No military action," he echoes plainly. "But plenty of the ronin going around. Beating. Raping. Executing. No one's going to help the civilians at their mercy when any action is counted as a maneuver of conflict."

A strange rumble sounds in the distance. The soldiers who have been resting perk to attention, wary over the interruption. They are still somewhat in the peripheries of the city. Removed from the areas they speak of, the fear that has shrouded the people unfortunate enough to be located in a pending war zone.

It has to stop. No matter the cost, no force can be allowed to run amok in such a manner. In Zhabei itself, the volunteer corps stir to life, gathering numbers to prepare for what is to come. In the foreign concessions, when the Westerners aren't looking, the remains of gangster rule pass weapons and money, recruit snipers from every corner of the city to be ready.

I'm ready, the city whispers. *I can bleed. I'll drown you with every wound.*

"Must be a truck," the soldier says, shrugging his shirt back on. "Back to base, then."

They walk. The skies come down with a light smattering of rain, erasing their footsteps in the soil, shifting the twigs into place again with every rivulet. The roads wash over, all the mud of the tire tracks spilling to the edges, the gravel undisturbed.

They wait.

31

Without a shadow of doubt, Silas knew that something was wrong.

"Your house?" he asked, shooting Phoebe a glance when he finally broke the silence. They had been driving for some time now, and Phoebe had been eerily quiet since leaving the church. At first Silas thought she might have been carrying a grudge for the tone he had taken with her, but when he tried apologizing again, she had brushed him off easily, opting to resume staring out the window.

Phoebe could be unreadable at times, but letting him drive in complete and utter silence was blatant. The day had turned dark despite the afternoon hour. Shanghai in the winter was already gray; it grew even gloomier when storm clouds drifted heavily in the skies.

"My house," Phoebe confirmed.

Her face was still turned toward the window. Silas continued navigating northward upon the dreary roads.

"You're making me nervous, Feiyi," he said, slowing at a red light. "You may as well come right out and say it."

He wondered if she might ignore him. Brush it off and switch countenances, or laugh like she didn't understand what he was talking about.

Phoebe pulled at the rim of her hat. The circular flap didn't look very warm when she tugged it over her reddened ears, bitten and chilled from their time outside.

"I want to know why you would keep news about Oliver from me."

Silas felt his stomach drop. He wanted to glance over at her, to scrutinize her expression while she spoke, but the light had turned green, so he kept his attention forward, pressing on the accelerator.

"You read the message I left."

Accusation slipped in. As did an air of complaint, because that hadn't been for her eyes, but she had gone prying anyway.

"How could I not?" Phoebe asked. "It would appear I needed to, or who knows when you might have told me?"

"You put me in an impossible position," Silas said, his hands tightening on the steering wheel. "At the end of the day, you are not an *operative,* Feiyi. I'm not supposed to be telling you these things."

"He's my *brother.*"

Silas couldn't understand this. Couldn't comprehend the volatility that always erupted when Phoebe reacted to this. "And I'm handling the situation to save your other brother. Why can't you trust that I can do this job?"

The Hong residence was around the bend. The driveway loomed ahead, that long line of gravel surrounded by rosebushes and sprawling magnolia trees staying evergreen in the winter. He had made this drive so many times, and yet none like this.

"You're trying to lure Priest in with Oliver," Phoebe said coldly. The tone was unfamiliar. Like it was coming from someone else, and yet it suited her voice, so maybe it was only that Silas had always chosen not to hear it. "You're putting Oliver at risk for something that might not have any outcome. Trick her into rescuing him, and then what? The Kuomintang notices an escape happening and shoots them both?"

"I don't want to do this either," Silas said. This city was at war, and in times of crisis, operatives needed to call for their last resort.

"Trust me, I'd much rather go about it a proper way. I'd much rather sit down with Priest rather than hand her in—"

"Are you *serious?*"

Silas pulled into her driveway. Each crackle of stone under his tires rang loud after Phoebe's interruption. "Listen—"

Phoebe shook her head. "I *can't.* I can't keep watching you treat her like some deity. It's absurd—she doesn't deserve any of this."

"*Deserve* this?" Silas braked. Seeing that they had arrived, Phoebe pushed out through her door immediately, but Silas was quick to follow, yelling, "Stop right there!"

Phoebe halted in her step. He was almost surprised. He didn't think she would listen. He had never yelled at her before.

"What . . . ," Silas said now, near breathless as he lowered his tone, each word spiriting into the air around him with a visible cloud of white, " . . . is your gripe here?"

Silas didn't mind if Phoebe didn't love him as he loved her. But this felt as though he were being toyed with. Who was Phoebe to decide what was and was not deserved? Why was she acting as though his faith in another affected her in any way? If they could get Priest, it was a best-case scenario. If they could get Priest, he would have fulfilled an assignment for the Nationalists and taken them one step closer to saving Orion. If they could get Priest . . . Wasn't that enough of a reward on its own? To finally pin down someone who had evaded everyone else in the world for this long?

Phoebe turned to face him slowly. Her lips were thinned, eyes gleaming as if she was barely holding back tears.

"Phoebe—" He circled the hood of the car, coming to her side. Each step was slow. Deliberate. He couldn't send her running. "I promise I have my reasons. I *need* to talk to Priest. I need to get her face-to-face. If I can get through to her, I can help Orion."

"And I promise that you're wrong." Though he had been afraid of startling her, it was Phoebe who surged toward him when he came closer, barreling into him so fast that he gasped at the contact of her cold, gloved hands on his face. She tightened her clutch, forcing him to look at her. "Just *trust me* on this. You don't need her. Leave Priest alone."

Silas pushed her hands off. He could hardly fathom the action when this touch was something he craved, but at this moment, with these words, it felt like a mere distraction, and he couldn't bear it anymore.

"Why are you this concerned?" he asked. "Tell me that, and I will listen."

Phoebe was shaking. He didn't reach to comfort her. She didn't try to touch him again. Instead, her fists clenched tight, as if she needed to gear up for a fight.

"God*dammit,* Silas, it's because *I* am—"

With a heavy thud, the front door to the Hong mansion flew open, striking the exterior wall in interruption.

"Xiǎojiě!" Ah Dou shouted from inside. "You have a phone call from Lang Shalin!"

32

Rosalind ran her marker along the map in her lap, circling their final destination: Zhabei. There, they would make their play. War was nothing but the movement of overgrown chess pieces, after all, using the city as a game board while following rules and orders. In Shanghai, no attack could enter the foreign concessions. Only Chinese land was up for negotiation. If—*when*—war broke out, anyone standing on the banks of the creek inside International Settlement jurisdiction could easily watch the battle unfold on the other side without fearing any consequence.

They would have to avoid the protected areas. They would be safe walking among the chaos, because then they would blend right in.

She put the marker's cap back on. Celia, in the driver's seat, started to brake, slowing in front of the township entrance and peering out the windshield to search for Alisa and Orion.

"See anything?"

"Don't think so."

Celia came to a complete stop. The moment Rosalind put the map down, meaning to get out of the car so she could go look for them, there was a thud on the trunk.

"Jesus—" Celia and Rosalind both jumped in fright, but it was only Alisa getting their attention.

"Let's go, let's go," Alisa said, opening the back door. "Orion, get in."

Orion lumbered into the back seat. Tried to sit properly. "Is this a car for ants?"

"First of all, we are working on a *budget,*" Celia said. "Second of all, Hong Liwen, you should be so lucky that your brother even taught me how to drive. No more complaints before I send us off a cliff. *Ready?*"

Celia stepped on the accelerator as soon as Alisa got in too and closed the door after herself. Rosalind widened her eyes, gripping the handhold with a grimace. Her sister had developed an attitude recently. She liked it.

Orion shifted forward, bumping Rosalind's seat to find a more comfortable position. At the same time, Rosalind craned her head around to face the back.

"Did you stay out of trouble?"

She had intended to sound like she was making a quibble, but instead, her question came out soft-spoken and gentle. Rather like she was murmuring some intimate request.

"We were followed," he answered, "but Alisa handled it before I could lift a finger. Surroundings were clear after that."

"Good," Rosalind said.

It was very possible that their tails had only been the remaining soldiers who were present at the tour stop. Maybe those men were carrying out their previous instructions, and they had disarmed all of them.

But if there were any who had reported back and slipped away, Lady Hong would soon know they were about to return to Shanghai.

"Were you followed too?" Orion asked.

"Only by one. Always easy to shake off."

Orion's mouth twitched. "Confident."

Rosalind gave him a droll look. "Shouldn't I be?"

"Of course you should."

"Oh?"

"I'm agreeing with you."

"Sounds like you're challenging me."

"What? Never!"

"Children," Celia interrupted, "if we are finished flirting with each other, may we discuss the small change in plans?"

Alisa giggled. Rosalind knitted her brows together, feeling rather unjustly accused.

"I was *not* flirting—"

"I was." Orion adjusted in his seat again, trying not to whack his head into the ceiling. Before Rosalind could tell him off, he switched back to business fully, asking, "We're changing our plans?"

"We have to adjust our route." Celia glanced quickly at the rearview mirror. Seemed to confirm that there was nothing concerning in their surroundings. "There's a safe house in Zhabei we can use for our base of operations instead. It's too chaotic there for any eyes to track us."

"Doesn't that mean we have to enter the city from the north?" Alisa asked.

Rosalind had drawn the plan out with Silas on the phone very quickly, so she could only hope that they had not missed anything in the planning. If they had, it was too late now to go making adjustments.

"I know it sounds dangerous," Rosalind said. The skies loomed ominously on the horizon. It was five o'clock. Night would soon set in if rainfall didn't turn the day into shadow first. "But the timing should work. Silas received word that a student organization is marching in an anti-Japanese protest near one of the main roads. He and Phoebe are going to park just outside the vicinity to wait for us, and he'll use his Nationalist identity to usher us through. If we are stopped, any Nationalist unit should be distracted enough to take his word and wave us through. There are more important matters they ought to pay attention to."

"But if they aren't distracted enough and *do* decide to look at our faces . . . ," Alisa countered. "Doesn't that mean we're caught?"

The car fell quiet. The skies thrummed with motion. A single drop of rain landed hard on the windshield. Though the bead slid away at once, its impact was as loud as a bullet.

"The west might be less watched, but it is also more quiet. If we're caught there, we don't have a single route out," Celia said slowly. "We have to follow the crowds. It's our best bet."

Slowly, Alisa nodded her agreement. A tight ball of anxiety had started deep in Rosalind's stomach, and she didn't think it was going to go away anytime soon.

A small tap on her arm. Rosalind shifted her head slightly, and Orion was there, pressing forward into her seat, his hand dangling over her shoulder. He said nothing; he only stayed close as a physical presence.

The car drove forward, along the rural swaths and dilapidated houses. Alisa closed her eyes to rest, Celia focused diligently on the road ahead, and in the quiet, Rosalind reached toward her shoulder, touching Orion's hand with the lightest contact, so faint that it might have been imagined, so hesitant that it could have been easily left unacknowledged.

Orion laced his fingers through hers firmly.

From where they had parked, Phoebe could hear the faintest sounds of protest.

She was in the back seat, watching the corner of the road. The moment she spotted the vehicle that Rosalind had described, they would start driving. There was no time to waste.

"Feiyi." Silas, from the driver's seat.

"Hmmm?"

"Are you going to ignore what we were talking about before Ah Dou interrupted?"

Phoebe stared hard at the road. She was trying to summon Rosalind's vehicle using sheer will. It was pitch dark now. A single streetlamp lit the space above their car.

"What are you talking about?" she asked airily.

"So, you *are* ignoring it."

"I don't even know what I'm ignoring."

Silas went quiet. Phoebe resumed watching the rearview. A solid three minutes later—which Phoebe knew because she was counting—Silas finally took a deep breath. She braced.

"Do you actually think," he asked, "that I believe this act you put on for the world?"

This tension now was her fault for tripping up before. Dao Feng had been clear in his warning about her identity, and she had agreed. Phoebe shouldn't have lost her temper. She was better than that.

"I've known you since you were six years old," Silas went on. "Give me some credit, *please*. It may look the same to an outsider, but I've watched you long enough to tell when you switch between faces. You are not fooling me."

But she was. She had been fooling him for as long as she had signed on to become Priest, and yet he still could not see it, so what did that mean? That he truly couldn't tell? That the face he knew best was far from the person she really was?

Phoebe caught a flash of light around the corner. "They're here."

Silas made a frustrated noise. "Feiyi—"

"No, really." Phoebe clambered into the front. "They're here! Drive!"

He knew not to argue. At once, Silas started the engine and stepped on the accelerator, pulling onto the road in front of the small car that had appeared. The car drove close, tailing Silas smoothly. Phoebe tried to catch a glimpse of Orion through the rearview mirror, but he must have been sitting in the back.

"Our route is through the smaller roads, yes?" Phoebe asked nervously.

"We mapped a route that gets relatively close to the protest," Silas answered, his hands tightening on the wheel. "We're certainly going to encounter *something*. The hope is that we don't raise alarm."

Even to get to the edges of Zhabei, Silas and Phoebe had passed two government control points. The stationed soldiers didn't go as far as to barricade the road and check the papers of each vehicle passing through, but the Nationalists needed to have eyes on city exit and entry points. If it wasn't to control their own domestic populations, to make sure they weren't provoking the foreigners too much to cause outright confrontation, it was to watch for Communists. There was no way to entirely avoid a control point while returning to the city—it was only a matter of whether they would be waved through without close inspection.

"First one," Phoebe muttered. Up ahead, the barbed-wire control point looked as welcoming as a predator's nest.

Silas leaned out his window, slowing near the wooden posts. A large building resembling a cotton mill loomed to the left, while a small crop of trees sat to their right. He made a small, polite wave at the soldier standing closest, signaling too to the car behind, and the soldier distractedly gestured for him to proceed through the narrow path left open between the wooden posts. The sound of the protest was getting louder.

"Don't look so tense," Silas muttered under his breath when they drove through. "They're going to think we're spies."

"Not an invalid assumption," Phoebe returned. She didn't even look that tense; she was only watching the rearview mirror too nervously. There was little she could do except sit in her seat and breathe out when the car behind followed between the posts too.

"Unless the next set of soldiers has taken the night off," Silas said, "there should be one more control point."

Their car rumbled from the rougher streets onto proper, large roads. A rhythmic chanting drifted through the night. When Phoebe rolled down her window, the cries of the protest were close enough that audible words entered the car.

"Boycott! Boycott! No more accommodating Japanese interests!"

"I don't think they *all* took the night off." Phoebe squinted through the windshield. The second control point appeared. Their surroundings were growing nicer, with brick walls that blocked in small neighborhoods and advertisement billboards that waved in the wind, fabric corners flapping under the electric lights. "But surely at least half were diverted for the protest. Look at the numbers."

There were far fewer men than there had been on their way out. Phoebe could only take it as a good sign when Silas rolled his window down, repeating the same gesture.

Except this time, the soldier signaled for him to stop, coming closer to the door.

"It's okay," Silas whispered in assurance. "This is routine."

And yet all that ran through Phoebe's head was *Oh God, oh God, oh God—*

"Good evening," the soldier said in greeting, ducking to get a good view into the vehicle. "Where are you coming from?"

"We drove from Nantong this afternoon," Silas replied. He rested his elbow out the window nonchalantly. "General Yan's orders. I'm on assignment to bring a few trafficking victims back."

The soldier nodded. It seemed he was going to allow them forward, but then another soldier in his unit left a conversation he had been having by the wooden post, asking, "What's the situation?"

"Trafficking victims. Going to headquarters, I presume?"

"Right to headquarters," Silas confirmed. "We'll be out of your way shortly."

While the first soldier was ready to grant them passage, the second soldier was frowning. A terrible gust of wind howled, ripping a string of flags from the restaurant to their left. There was no sign of suspicion on the second soldier's face though; if anything, it was concern.

"The area is turning into absolute pandemonium," he said, looking around. "We can send an escort with you. It'll ensure you arrive at headquarters rather than get stuck in the protests."

Phoebe's heart lurched to her throat. She could sense Silas freeze too, though he recovered quickly.

"There's no need. We don't want to take away from your posting here."

"Nonsense." The second soldier waved for them to proceed. "Drive through and wait at the corner. I can escort you personally."

If Silas argued, it would seem suspicious. There was no reasonable excuse he could give. He could only gulp, then slowly maneuver the car forward.

"This is bad," Silas muttered to Phoebe. "This is really bad."

They were not actually going to headquarters. They couldn't have an escort *following* them through Zhabei into a Communist safe house with an address gleaned from Rosalind's sister.

Phoebe thought fast. She turned in her seat, making sure the vehicle behind them was following too, making sure Orion entered the city successfully. As soon as Silas started to slow again at the corner, Rosalind's sister mimicked the maneuver, though by the way she braked more erratically, she was clearly surprised he had done that.

On the other side of the control point, a military vehicle rumbled to life, its headlights flashing on. Its tires moved heavily, heading their way to add itself as the third vehicle in their procession.

"I will meet you at the safe house."

"Excuse me?" Silas demanded in an instant.

Phoebe opened her door. "I can distract him. Force him off route. Maybe I'll dive in front of him and cry."

To his credit, Silas didn't question her. Nor did he ask how she expected a plan like that to work. He asked, "Are you sure?"

"Don't take any detours, but go slowly if you can." She swallowed hard. "Just trust that by the time you get to the safe house, he won't be following anymore."

Silas nudged his glasses up. Though it would have been hard to see his expression in the dark, the military vehicle pulled in line at that moment, and its headlights flared bright enough to pierce forward. There was admiration in his eyes, and Phoebe didn't know if she ought to be taken aback to see it.

She slammed the door closed, taking his silence for agreement. Before the soldier could spot her, she dove into the nearest alley, breaking into a run. Now that they had entered the city properly, Phoebe could move through the smaller alleys, cutting a quicker path than the main roads. So long as Silas didn't drive too fast, she knew a good street corner to put her plan into action, halfway along their mapped route.

Phoebe pushed herself faster. She reached into her dress pocket. Pulled out a pistol.

At that corner, a clock tower rose high above the other buildings. And the street there was perfect, because it was entirely U-shaped while it curved around the tower, narrow enough that a three-car procession would have to pass through one by one.

Phoebe ran by empty restaurants and empty brothels. Silent, foreboding residential blocks, many with their windows boarded up after hearing warnings about the protests. She could hear the students' chants fading into the wind as she weaved in and out of the alleys, her eyes tracking the movement of the clouds and the street signs on the walls to make sure she was going the right way.

There. She could see the clock tower.

From the other side, in the narrow gap between the clock tower and its neighboring community center, she could also see Celia's smaller vehicle, already rumbling down the turn of the road. *Shit.* She was going to be too late.

With a gasp, Phoebe hurtled past the building and shoved through the walkway along its side, settling into the shadows where the clock tower breached the road. She dropped to the ground immediately to avoid being seen, heaving to catch her breath, her pistol lifting and her hand stabilizing. Her elbow pressed hard to the cement. Her knee was scraped, probably bloodied in her scramble.

The military vehicle came around the bend.

Rumbled by, then turned, presenting its rear to Phoebe's gun.

She fired, shooting a hole into its left back tire. Before she had released her next exhale, she inched her pistol to the side and shot another hole into its right back tire. The vehicle shuddered. It stopped, entirely lopsided, unable to roll forward while its wheels lost air and pressed flat to the ground.

The soldier scrambled out from the driver's seat. He hurried to his rear wheels, letting out a bewildered shout over how they had both ruptured.

With a grin, Phoebe scrambled to her feet and darted back into the shadows, brushing dirt off her skirts.

33

Oliver didn't know what they had given him, but it was fucking awful.

It had to be some sedative, or it wouldn't be this impossible to keep his head up. A cold sweat covered his neck, making him shiver while his skin blazed hot at the same time. The Nationalist soldiers were hauling him forward without much priority toward attentiveness, so it wasn't as though they cared.

They tossed him in the cell. Oliver heard the bars banging shut. He couldn't pry his eyes open long enough to confirm. He felt the rough floor beneath his fingers. Damp. The staccato *drip-drip-drip* of a pipe in the corner signaled the cause.

How long had they been traveling? He couldn't keep track. Since they'd pricked that needle into his neck, he hadn't been able to hold on to his thoughts for longer than a few seconds. For a moment in that dark vehicle, he had been half convinced that it wasn't the Kuomintang who had him but his mother. Since when did the Nationalists go *sedating* their captured Communists? There was no need. Stuff a gag in his mouth and hold him at gunpoint. It wasn't as though he would cause any trouble when he was aware that it meant a bullet right into the forehead.

Yet they had continued injecting him every time the sedation started to wear off. He had been prepared for their end destination to be his mother's facility. His heart had hammered terribly when the vehicle slowed, which was all the more jarring when the rest of him could only go at a snail's speed.

Then he heard the soldiers calling instructions to one another. He had pried his eyes open and managed the barest glimpse to confirm that they were walking into a major Kuomintang base in Shanghai. It wasn't his mother after all, yet he could still feel her presence everywhere.

"Shepherd sent instructions to tie him up."

Shepherd? Oliver thought blearily. That was his sister's friend. The triple agent. The loyal Nationalist. What governance did he have here? Intelligence agents could throw around decent weight along the chain of command, but rarely did that include overseeing enemy prisoners.

"Tie him up?" another soldier echoed. He sounded just as flabbergasted. "How's that going to get him to talk?"

"It's not," the first one replied.

Oliver felt a harsh tug on his shoulders hauling him upright. They pushed him onto a metal table, a freezing-cold slab hitting his back.

"Keep him asleep. A doctor is coming soon."

Before he could try to fight, the next needle was already sinking into his neck, into his bloodstream. He couldn't succumb to it entirely. Who knew what they would do to him? Who knew whether he would survive long enough to emerge again from his slumber?

Something tightened over his wrists. His ankles. They were restraining him to the table, murmuring among themselves. Sweat flashed up and down his spine, turned him freezing cold. For all Oliver knew, the room could have filled with ice, unmooring him entirely.

He thought of Celia. Then he thought of nothing at all.

She had done it. Somehow, she had actually done it.

Silas had been watching his rearview mirrors the entire time, and yet he had no clue how Phoebe had accomplished the distraction. One second the soldier had been driving behind them. The next his vehicle had entirely disappeared.

Fearful that it might be a temporary delay and not wanting to get any closer to the safe house unless he had confirmation, Silas pulled to the side, watching the crest of the road.

Nothing. A minute passed. The soldier had truly been thrown off their tail.

Silas flashed his lights, signaling to Celia that they were continuing. This time he picked up speed. The rest of their route proceeded entirely without trouble, and before the moon had slipped out from behind the thick clouds, he had pulled up in front of the nondescript address of their safe house.

He got out of his car. As did Rosalind and Celia, whispering between themselves when they pushed open their doors. Without any patience remaining, Silas took it upon himself to hurry toward the rear door of the other car and open it before Orion could.

There were plenty of soothing reassurances that he had rehearsed in his head. But when he saw his best friend inside, one hand hovering as if he had just been about to pull the handle, all Silas could do was stare, unable to believe their rescue effort had finally come to some sort of fruition. Nothing about this had been easy, yet it certainly hadn't required the grand sacrifices he'd imagined, either. When Silas was so prone to catastrophizing, anything less always threw him off.

"Hello," Orion said slowly. He climbed out of the car. "I apologize that I don't remember who you are, but as long as we weren't lovers, I am sure I can make amends somehow."

Silas choked on a laugh. "I am far too young for you." He held his arms forward, grabbing Orion in a firm squeeze. Orion, despite not knowing anything about Silas at present, returned the gesture just as strongly. "We're all very glad you are alive."

"Me too," Orion replied quietly.

A wave of motion shimmered on their left. Silas was slow to react, and though it might have been terrible if it had been a threat, suddenly there was another pair of arms wrapped around him and Orion, accompanied by a familiar scent.

"Gēge," Phoebe sobbed dramatically. "I have missed you."

Silas snorted a laugh. He stepped back, which left Phoebe to hang from her brother's shoulders. If Silas had been parched and starving, this sight alone would have been enough to satiate him. Let him lose everything else in the world, and he wouldn't mind. Let the world think of him as discardable or frail or cowardly, he wouldn't care. All Silas needed was the people he cared about, whole and well in front of him.

"Oh." Orion looked startled, but he was quick to adjust. "You must be Phoebe."

"*You must be Phoebe,*" she mimicked. "As if I didn't just put on the performance of a lifetime to get that soldier off your tail. Now carry me up. I'm bone-tired."

The safe house was up on the third floor, the fifth apartment of a long residential block. Only one window overlooked the alley at the back, which Rosalind had instantly been wary about if they needed to get out quickly, but Celia assured her there was another hidden passageway, proceeding straight down into the alley through a secret door in the study.

While Rosalind entered the study to examine the aforementioned secret door, everyone else was near collapse and blinking hard to stay alert. It would do no good to work themselves into exhaustion, so now the safe house was quiet for the night: Celia,

Alisa, and Phoebe had piled onto the bed, Silas was dozing on the armchair in the living room, and Orion . . .

Last she saw, Orion had chosen the bathtub for a sleeping spot. He had mostly clambered in as a joke, but then Rosalind had scoffed and told him that it would be terribly uncomfortable to sleep in a bathtub.

To prove her wrong, of course, he had settled in nicely and closed his eyes.

Rosalind trailed her hand along the bookshelves. The one on the right would open for the secret door, as all the books were glued to the red shelf panels with hollowed insides. The one on the left held real books—a few store-bought Chinese novels and some foreign editions of European classics. It was hard to read the titles properly with only a candle flickering on the table. She didn't want to turn on a proper light because the safe house was small, and having a light flare on would disturb the others. Just because she was incapable of sleeping didn't mean she had to drag everyone down with her.

Rosalind plucked out what appeared to be a children's fairy tale. It felt familiar in her hand as she flipped through, a girl on a quest and the shining prince along the way. *Il était une fois . . .*

A floorboard in the study creaked. Rosalind whirled around with a gasp, slapping the book closed.

"Sorry, sorry, didn't mean to scare you," Orion whispered at the door.

Rosalind blew out an exhale. "The bathtub wasn't a good bed?"

"It was a beautiful bed. The best bed I've ever slept in."

"Wow. That's high praise when you've slept in so many."

Orion was struggling to keep a straight face. He crossed his arms. "I cannot tell if you have just insulted me."

"I would never." Rosalind perched on the edge of the desk, mimicking his stance by hugging the book close to her chest. "Is everything okay?"

"Of course," Orion replied. He walked into the study properly, glancing briefly at the secret door before coming to perch on the desk beside her. She almost wished he wouldn't—not because she didn't want him near, but because she had trouble concentrating when he was, an ever-constant hum of music coming from his presence that she needed to listen to instead.

As if he could read her mind, Orion suddenly adjusted so that he was sitting on the floor, leaning on the desk. But then it felt strange for Rosalind to be standing in contrast, so she joined him, settling comfortably on the carpet.

"I couldn't sleep," Orion admitted. "I keep getting flashes of memories."

Rosalind turned to him quickly. "Isn't that a good thing?"

Maybe the cure had only experienced a delay. Maybe the memories would slide smoothly into place with more time.

"I don't know. It's hard to tell whether they're true memories or not. They all seem to be from early childhood. We have met before, right?"

"Us?" Rosalind echoed. Prior to when they were assigned to be married? She had certainly thought that Orion Hong looked familiar, but she'd only assumed it was because he might have been a patron at the Scarlet clubs when she still worked as a dancer. "I don't know. Maybe. If we did, then it must have been in passing. Elite circles in this city extend only so far."

"No, not in Shanghai." Orion reached over slowly. For the book in her lap, she realized when his finger touched down on the title cover. She watched him trace the gold lettering there, feeling the phantom sensation of each movement. "In Paris. I keep seeing the scene over and over again. I am trying so hard to remember the events you have told me about, but I can't grasp anything about Seagreen Press or your apartment or our screaming matches. All I see is you with your hair in two plaits, wearing a ruffled pink dress and your cheeks flushed from the heat. You, standing outside the cinema, grumbling about your tutors who lived within walking distance down the road and offering me a handful of popcorn."

Rosalind felt her stomach dip. He couldn't have known any of those details unless he was actually there. She didn't think she had ever told him about Paris like this, because by the time he knew that she was not American-raised Janie Mead but rather former Scarlet Rosalind Lang, there was already so much unfolding in their mission that she had little time to tell him much about her true life. It couldn't be his mind confusing details that she had let slip around him; she hadn't let *any* of this slip around him.

"As I said," Orion went on, sounding almost worried when Rosalind stayed quiet for too long, "they could be false memories. Maybe my mind is making things up to try to fill the void."

"No," Rosalind said quietly.

She remembered the cinema too, that hot summer day when she was eating popcorn outside because Celia and Kathleen wanted to see a film she wasn't interested in. Eleven years old, not yet jaded by the world. There had been that boy, slightly younger, his eyes bright and mischievous. Though she had looked around the next few times she went to the cinema, she had never seen him again.

"That was *you?*"

Orion's sudden grin was something radiant. As if he had achieved something by remembering what she hadn't, and for a moment—only a moment—Rosalind wondered if it would be so bad if he never got his memories back, if they simply chose to start again from the very beginning. When he was like this, he didn't feel the hurt of his mother using him, didn't wear that sad anger from fighting his brother at every turn.

"Don't feel bad. It took me total amnesia to go back to it."

Rosalind rolled her eyes, only the thought was truly haunting her now. Forget starting again from the beginning: she could leave

Orion alone entirely—it wasn't as though he *needed* to remember her. She could free him from his conditioning, make sure he was out of his mother's grasp, then let him turn over a new leaf. Why keep him bound to her? Their shared code name as High Tide had disintegrated. Their pretend matrimony was no longer in place. She was an immortal girl who was going to lose him sooner or later if she held on. Restoring their time together only meant he was dragged into the pain too.

Instead, she could exist in his memories merely as the girl who had shared her popcorn on a summer Parisian day. Wasn't that so much nicer?

"What are you thinking about right now?" Orion asked, searching her face. He drew his hand back to his side. "You're wearing a mighty strange look."

"You cannot possibly have learned to read my strange looks already," Rosalind countered.

"It's not so hard. You don't hide them."

The book was starting to slip off her lap. When Rosalind made no move to stop it, the book landed on the carpet with a low thump.

"Don't take it for granted," she muttered. "It definitely didn't start like this."

"How did it start?"

Rosalind lifted a brow. She had told him already. All the mechanisms that had been moved into place by the Nationalist covert branch and the conspiracy they'd needed to investigate. . . .

"No, not the mission," Orion clarified before she could say anything. "Us."

Oh. Rosalind's mouth twitched.

"You were trying to chase me from the beginning. The very moment we were formally introduced, in fact."

"I don't doubt that in the slightest." He shifted, propping one ankle over the other. "What about you?"

"Me?"

"When did I finally win you over?"

Rosalind was looking very intently at a spot just over his shoulder. "Could we not just wait until you get your memories back?"

"I want to hear it from you."

Orion waited. Patient as a gentle stream. If Rosalind were to elaborate, she needed to tell every part of it. Every part of her.

"I'll explain it like this," she said quietly. "Attraction is a foreign language to me. And I could hear you speaking complete gibberish for much of the mission, which annoyed me tremendously when I was only trying to do my job."

Orion was trying to hold back his confusion. She could tell by the small twitch his brow made before he smoothed it down.

"But . . . ," Rosalind went on. "Once in a while, I pick up a few phrases. If you speak it slowly enough, patiently enough. If it's around my ear for long enough that I'm endeared to it, I start to understand what you are saying."

"I have to ask," Orion interrupted. "We are not talking about an actual foreign language, are we? Because I'm still working out if I speak Italian or not."

Rosalind snorted. "No, Orion. I'm trying to tell you that I kept you at a distance because I knew I wouldn't respond to you like other people did, and I had no business playing with fire. Then somewhere along the way, between our last petty argument and the fifth time you decided to sleep on my shoulder, I fell in love with you, and once I've tumbled that deep, I'm trying to understand everything you say no matter which language it's in."

He made a shallow inhale. The candle flickered on the desk. Then it went out entirely, as if an invisible breath had blown it to embers.

"I wish I could remember," he said into the dark. "I wish I could remember the first time you told me this."

Rosalind's heart ached. It was him but it wasn't. There were two split Orions, one of the past, superimposed over the one in the present. If she loved one, did she love the other as well? Where was the line drawn?

"I have good news, then." Her words were barely audible. "That was the first time."

Orion shifted forward. Uncrossed his ankles. "Then I still wish I could remember, because under different circumstances, if you told me you loved me, I would have kissed you."

Before Rosalind could cave and allow it anyway, let herself pretend that there was only one Orion instead of two versions, he leaned back and set his head on her shoulder. It was alike to every time he had done it in the past, and yet there was another layer to the gesture, physically placing himself elsewhere so there was no temptation to lean in.

"Is this all right?" he asked.

She nodded. He couldn't see her, but he could feel the motion.

"You can sleep if you want," she murmured. "I'll be awake the whole night to keep watch."

"Wake me when the sun rises?"

"Okay."

The study turned quiet. Rosalind thought that Orion had gone to sleep. Then:

"Rosalind?"

"Mm-hmm?"

A pause. He was thinking—or hesitating.

"Even if the memories never come back," he said slowly, "I'm going to love you again. I have decided to warn you in advance."

Her throat closed tight. *Don't say that,* Rosalind thought. *Don't make this harder than it has to be.*

"You don't even know me," she managed.

"I know enough," he countered. "From the moment you offered

me that piece of popcorn and told me you didn't like watching tragedies, I knew enough." Orion adjusted himself, leaning closer into her shoulder. "Good night."

Rosalind let out a shaky breath. She thought about her past, about every dark night she had spent alone, believing herself at fault for what happened to her, believing herself to be lacking as a person and punished thusly. Regret would always clothe her in a heavy shroud, change the way she moved and the way she met the world.

But so too did love. And it was warmer, thicker.

"Good night."

34

Morning rose, breaking past the storm clouds. Once Rosalind tapped Orion awake, gentle in her disturbance, she took it upon herself to go around shaking everybody else awake too, which was a rather difficult task. The hour was early. Though everyone rolled upright without complaint, she and Alisa were the only people in the safe house who weren't yawning every two seconds.

"How are *you* so alert?" Rosalind asked.

"I'm a morning person," Alisa said happily.

Of course she was.

Alisa slipped out to find food; Silas left to make copies of facility blueprints that would be relevant to their planning. Now the sun was firmly hanging in the crisp blue sky, and there were bags of yóutiáo on the table in front of them alongside blueprints of the Nationalist military station. Rosalind thumbed along the largest one, trying to make sense of the symbols. She supposed she didn't need to understand their route in—she only needed to engage in combat once someone else navigated. Fortune was an assassin, not an intelligence operative.

". . . so that leaves us here, entering the inner facility through this tunnel," Silas finished, explaining the layout of the station.

With a few phone calls, he had confirmed where Oliver was being kept, just outside the western peripheries of the International Settlement and surprisingly close to the Hong household. The good news was that the facility was very large, which meant lower chances of getting caught if they were to sneak in. The bad news was that it was a major station and therefore also very well guarded, which meant higher chances of getting caught if they were to sneak in.

Orion leaned in. Frowned.

"I'm confused," he said. "Aren't we Nationalist agents?"

Celia took a small step back, putting physical space between herself and the claim. "Don't drag me into this."

Alisa mimicked her. "The last time I showed my face here, the Nationalists arrested me, so . . ."

That left Rosalind, Silas, and Phoebe around the table, exchanging looks among the three of them with more complicated answers.

"I am definitely not an agent," Phoebe said first.

"I suppose I'm a decommissioned agent, now that I abandoned the tour," Rosalind added. She rubbed her eye carefully, trying not to smudge her cosmetics more than the rough night already had. "I think Silas might be the only active Nationalist operative among us."

Silas made a little salute.

"All right, so why this planning?" Orion picked up one of the blueprints, placing it aside for an even more complicated one underneath. "What's wrong with Silas marching in and asking for Oliver to be released because he thinks my mother is coming?"

"Because then I would need to explain where the information came from," Silas answered. "Which—given my current active assignment—means generating evidence and pretending that *Priest* told me, rather than that I heard it through Celia Lang, who I shouldn't be in contact with."

Silas suddenly sounded very bitter. Rosalind winced, looking away so Silas wouldn't see her pity. These last months, he had spent so much time and energy chasing Priest with the assumption that she could help get Orion back, only for Priest to remain entirely uninvolved with Orion's rescue.

"To release Oliver, he would also need to get approval all the way up," Rosalind added, clearing her throat as she peered at the blueprint Orion was holding. "Even if it's easy enough to fake a letter from a source, it took the Nationalists months just to decide they wanted to decommission me. Lady Hong would have come and gone before they even started the process."

"Do we know where she is right now?"

That question came quietly from Phoebe. While the rest of the table debated back and forth, she had wandered off, breaking the circle and going to the window. Its glass was frosty, misted over by the cold and years of inattention. Nothing much of the street outside could be seen except for blobs of color, but Phoebe was still staring intently.

Silas hesitated. "She hasn't been sighted, but possible units under her control have been. My guess is that she's already here."

"We were tailed right until the city," Celia said. She looked to Alisa, who grimaced and tugged her sleeves over the scratches that still remained after their scuffle outside Zhouzhuang. "Probably means that she's in the vicinity too."

Phoebe made a thoughtful noise. She didn't add anything: she only continued gazing out the glass.

"I know there are . . . concerns about how this might work," Silas said. His gaze flickered to Phoebe. She didn't react. "But there's already going to be a distraction at these cells. Priest will be trying to free Oliver at the same time."

Alisa made a horrified noise. As did Celia. Only Rosalind and Orion remained quiet—and that was because Rosalind didn't like her assassin rival by concept, while Orion was entirely confused. Now it made sense why Silas had sounded like that earlier. He was still after her. At this point, he probably wanted her merely for a job well done.

"How did you manage that?" Rosalind asked dryly.

"It didn't take much," Silas replied. He pushed his glasses up. "Oliver has already been captured. It would be a shame to waste the opportunity."

Celia made a noise of disgust. "He's not *bait*."

"No, he's not."

Silas's attention returned to the table, to the blueprints scattered on its rickety surface. Something flickered in his expression: something determined and steady, almost cold in the way it settled. Rosalind always seemed to forget that each of them here was qualified among the highest branches of operative work. Then she watched someone like Silas narrow his eyes, and suddenly she remembered this was not a room filled with people connected by blood relations and proxy family—this was a room that might determine the country's fate.

Her gaze wandered over to the window. Everyone here except Phoebe, in technicality, but even then Rosalind wasn't sure if the girl ought to be disqualified. Phoebe was tracing her finger over the mist of the glass, the movement in perfect mimicry to Silas as he picked up a pen at the table and drew a very large circle over a blueprint in the middle.

"He's the reason the Nationalists will be distracted," Silas went on. "Priest won't let her handler rot in prison. The Nationalists won't let Priest slip through their fingers if she delivers herself to their very doorstep. The moment they hear that a Communist assassin is breaking in, every effort will be focused on her." He put the cap back on the pen and set it down. "Win-win. The Kuomintang finally catches the assassin that has evaded them for years, while we are cleared to get Oliver."

The room went quiet. Silas was right. It was a good plan.

Rosalind, though, didn't voice her agreement outwardly. While her sister sighed and nodded, while Alisa and Orion hemmed and hawed before getting on board, Rosalind pinned her scrutiny across the room, waiting patiently for Phoebe's reaction. This was her own brother trapped in the cells. This was one of her closest confidants coming up with a plan that valued an ulterior motive—that let Silas catch a girl who had evaded him for months—instead of staying a sole focus rescue mission. Surely Phoebe had something to say about this.

Yet Rosalind observed nothing.

Interesting.

"Fine, it will work," Celia finally allowed. "Once we're within the inner facility, there's an electric door on the north end of the cells and a manual door on the south end." She pointed along the blueprint, tracking the straight path with her finger. "Tell Priest that you will lift the north door for her from the control tower and let her take the attention when the guards go to combat her. Then we enter through the south door for Oliver."

"What if there are guards at the south door?" Alisa asked.

Rosalind finally pulled her eyes away from Phoebe, returning to the debate around the table. "You can leave that to me."

"And me," Orion added.

Silas nodded.

"Then we are settled on this plan," he decided. "Upper command is already aware of Priest's incoming presence. I will get in touch with her today on specifics." He looked to the calendar dangling on the wall, which displayed one day per page on the lunar schedule. Clearly no one had been around to this safe house in a while because it was still stuck in the year 1927. "Friday, we make the swap."

"No," Celia said immediately. "Sooner. Each day we leave Oliver in there is a day his mother could swoop in first."

Her sister spoke aloud the part that would convince everyone else present in this room, but Rosalind heard what accompanied the panic. Each day they left him in there was also another day of getting tortured, or worse.

"Tonight, then," Silas said. He grimaced, looking wary over how fast they needed to be moving. "Nine o'clock."

Alisa nodded first around the table. Everyone else followed suit, except Phoebe. As far as plans went, its gears were sturdy: Nationalist operative Shepherd tells the Kuomintang that Priest is arriving like a mouse into a trap, having used all these months to win her trust and trick her into revealing herself. He lifts the north door with official approval, and as soon as she enters the Nationalist compound, the soldiers are ready to descend on her, pulling their attention onto this invader. At the south door, hardly anyone would expect there to be an actual breakout happening.

Rosalind hesitated.

"What if there are consequences for Oliver's escape?" she asked. "You will be attached to it. They could easily suspect you of having a hand in it."

Silas didn't look bothered. "I play the fool and claim I couldn't have known. There are Communist spies up and down Nationalist ranks. No one would be surprised if this plan leaked somehow and a second rescue effort is sent in tandem. I would have already given them Priest. It's not my fault that someone actually came to rescue Oliver outside my trap."

"You don't think a Communist rescue effort would also think to warn Priest if they received word about a trap?"

A low, long creak ran through the safe house. Some neighboring apartment was opening its doors, its hinges groaning along the floorboards and dust-lined walls.

"I think," Silas said slowly, "people are always willing to sacrifice certain game pieces if they want another more badly. And say, if the Kuomintang think Celia Lang put a spy in the Nationalists and heard about a trap for Priest, then of course she would throw us a faceless assassin to get Oliver Hong back. Don't worry. This checks out."

Rosalind glanced at her sister. Hearing her name being used for this hypothetical, Celia looked a little green, but she didn't protest. If push came to shove, then Silas was probably correct.

They were operatives, but they were also people. Just people—capable of selfishness and love, with the same instincts for preservation and group protection as the first wanderers who walked this earth.

"All right, well, to pull this off, we're going to need disguises." Rosalind made a show out of brushing her sleeve, as if there were dust upon the cuff. Then she said, "Hong Feiyi, do you want to come shopping with me?"

Phoebe's gaze whipped over. Surprise flashed through her eyes for a moment before she blinked it away and brightened. At once, Phoebe pranced across the room.

"Absolutely. Let's go, sǎozi."

Rosalind tutted. There was a pistol on the shelf, left behind as a feature of the safe house, and she was quick to pick it up and put it into her coat. Alisa and Celia were muttering to each other about different paths into the larger compound. Silas and Orion were picking through the different blueprints, talking quietly about contingency paths.

"I thought I told you to stop calling me sǎozi."

"Yes, at least not until I propose properly," Orion added from the table, his gaze still scanning the blueprints.

Did he just say—

Rosalind's jaw dropped. A beat passed. With no smart retort anywhere to be found, Rosalind could only pivot wordlessly and push out the door, ducking her head into her shoulders to hide her flaming cheeks.

Phoebe's steps clattered after her into the hallway. "Sǎozi, slow down!"

35

Rosalind and Phoebe played it safe: the first items they purchased were silk scarves and sunglasses, though Phoebe complained about the circular lenses looking funny on her. Rosalind had told her to tie the silk scarf around her head tighter—which did help Phoebe look less funny, because then she looked like a child playing dress-up instead.

"You know what . . ." Rosalind sighed. "Just take them off."

They had hailed rickshaws into the thick of the city, using the regular bustle of Nanjing Road as their cover. It would be very hard for someone to recognize them given the number of people coming into Wing On every morning, and so Rosalind and Phoebe browsed the shelves in the megastore, quickly waving away any employees who wanted to help.

"Oh, good," Phoebe said with relief, plucking the sunglasses off. "They were really hurting my nose."

"We are not wearing them for style."

"Speak for yourself. Not everyone is as naturally glamorous as you are. I would rather get hauled in than look ridiculous."

At the very least, even if Phoebe was recognized, she could extricate herself and make the excuse of being out and about. There was no active search for her in the same way that the Kuomintang were likely scratching their heads over where Rosalind had gotten to.

"We ought to find a few hats," Rosalind remarked. She looked through the paper bags she was already holding on her arm. "You check the shop across the aisle. I'll go to the next one."

"Commencing hat search."

Phoebe marched off. Rosalind went over to the next shop, browsing the mannequin heads and hatboxes.

Ten minutes later, Phoebe appeared by her side again.

"Find anything?" she asked.

"They are either too colorful or"—Rosalind flicked the nearest hat—"covered in feathers. What about you?"

Phoebe shook her head. "I think feathers are in fashion. I found one hat that might look nice on Silas though."

"Silas isn't going in disguised. You need to be finding something for your brother."

"My brother has an abnormally large head."

"What . . . ?" Rosalind thought about it. "That's simply not true."

Phoebe grinned. "The more we say it, the more he might believe it. Play along."

"I am not playing along if you find a hat too big."

"Lang Shalin, why must you ruin my joy like this?"

There was something about Phoebe Hong that persistently gave Rosalind the same funny feeling as that first day she had met her, prancing into Seagreen Press with that basket on her arm: recognition. Some people were very good at leaning into what was expected of them. But do it too well, and it created shimmers in the illusion. A mirror image that overcorrected was just as jarring as one that didn't reflect every part.

"Oh, *now* I'm Lang Shalin and not your sǎozi when I'm telling you off." Rosalind picked up a black hat. It might work for a break-in. "Are you concerned?"

The question had come so suddenly that Phoebe didn't follow Rosalind's topic switch. There came a pause, then Phoebe gave her a confused look, tugging out a hatbox from the bottom of the pile.

"About being told off?"

"No," Rosalind said. "About Silas being fixated on Priest even after Orion has been rescued."

Silence. As soon as Rosalind glanced over, she caught Phoebe smoothing down her expression.

"It's not my business."

"Sure it is." Rosalind moved some of the boxes aside to help Phoebe retrieve the one from the bottom. "It's a little selfish for him to be concerned about his work while Oliver is at risk."

The two sides of Phoebe's face suddenly suctioned in, as if she were biting down on the insides of her cheeks. After a few seconds, she released the clamp and said, "I have faith that Oliver's rescue will be successful."

"Oh, I agree," Rosalind said. "That doesn't mean you can't be upset at Silas's priorities."

"I'm not *upset.*"

Rosalind wasn't buying it. "You are. I saw you."

"I was marginally perplexed at best, all right?" Phoebe huffed. "He's obsessed with her. I've said this before. I find it bizarre."

"You're jealous."

"I'm—*no.* That's absurd."

"Then why is it only Priest that bothers you? He's equally obsessed with maintaining his standing in the Nationalists. I don't see you looking sour over that."

Phoebe folded her arms aggressively. She almost whacked over the hatbox stack with her elbow, and a shopkeeper nearby shot her an irritated glance.

"At least that makes sense," Phoebe retorted. "It's his very career and livelihood. Meanwhile, what's this one task going to achieve? He finally reveals the identity of one assassin. *So?* You're an assassin. You're not any different from the rest of us."

Rosalind lifted a brow. "Actually . . ."

Phoebe's hand snapped up. "Fine, fine—that was a bad example."

There was a small part of this that was just a tad amusing. Phoebe couldn't see how she looked right now: two blots of red on her face and her eyebrows furrowed down.

"Issue an ultimatum if you want him to let go of the matter," Rosalind said lightly. "It's impossible that he will choose Priest over you."

"I wouldn't be so sure about that." Phoebe plucked up a blue hat and put it on herself. It shadowed her eyes, a ribbon trailing over the side. "I didn't think Oliver would abandon us. I didn't think my mother would turn out to be a national traitor more interested in advancing her own work above all else. So I don't know. People have proven me wrong again and again."

Rosalind winced. She started a lofty, "Well—" before halting at once, her gaze catching on something over Phoebe's shoulder. Suddenly their entire topic of conversation seemed arbitrary. She ducked to take herself out of view, and Phoebe, to her credit, followed suit immediately.

"What's happening?"

"Soldiers," Rosalind hissed.

"In Wing On?" Phoebe craned her neck, trying to look into the aisles without jutting her head out too far. "Shall we leave through the back?"

"Give it a second. He's still there."

But the moment the soldier in the aisle turned, putting his back to them, two others appeared at his side, coming into view too. What was happening? Why would the Kuomintang be surveilling a department store?

"Let's go," Rosalind said. "Through the aisle now."

They dove out, hurrying for the back. A sharp left, then a shortcut through the shelves of one store. Rosalind could almost see the doors that led into the alleyway exit before she turned in a rush and rammed right into a soldier.

She froze. A charade prepared itself upon her tongue, but it fell to the wayside the moment she met the soldier's eyes. She could see the difference at once. Though he wore a Nationalist uniform, this was one of Lady Hong's men.

"Hello," he said.

"He's speaking," Phoebe whispered, grabbing Rosalind's arm as they both took a step back. "Why is he speaking?"

"They *can* still speak," Rosalind answered quietly. Would the soldiers make a scene? If they had come dressed in uniform, was it to allow Lady Hong to pin the incident on the Kuomintang when a public fight broke out?

"Yes, but—"

"Feiyi."

Phoebe's grip tightened at once, pulling panicked at Rosalind's sleeve. Rosalind put her hand over Phoebe's, trying to calm her down.

"Feiyi. I hope you will join me of your own free will. Family comes first."

"Oh my God," Phoebe murmured. "That's my mother. Those are her words."

The soldier was speaking English, but it was Japanese-accented with the wrong intonations. The soldier didn't understand what he was saying; he was echoing sounds instead of words.

"He's been fed a script to repeat," Rosalind said. She pushed her bags into Phoebe's hands. "Run. Go, hurry."

"But—"

The soldier lunged. A flash of a knife. Rosalind barely reacted in time to push his arm, throwing his attack wide.

"Run, Phoebe!"

Phoebe dashed off. With a gasp, Rosalind didn't have the time to avoid the next slash, taking a gouge from her neck to her shoulder. *God.* That was a lot of flesh to cut through.

She lurched back, digging into her coat for her pistol. There was a shout from another aisle, which meant the rest of the soldiers were coming. This was no place for a fight—and she was outnumbered anyway. She drew her pistol to shoot once at close proximity, running off as soon as the soldier staggered back from the bullet in his stomach.

"Please don't be poisoned," Rosalind muttered, her hand going up to clasp her shoulder. Her whole arm throbbed and stung. Though the blood squelched when she ran her finger through the tear in her qipao fabric, it seemed that her skin was closing.

Rosalind kept her head ducked, barging past the other shoppers with a one-track goal of getting to an exit. Ignoring cries and concerned shouts, she pushed out through a side door, stumbling into the alley.

"Rosalind!"

Her head snapped up. She spotted Phoebe at the end of the alley, and Rosalind lurched into motion again, lunging for a broomstick by the trash bags and shoving it through the looped handle of the door. It wouldn't hold for long, but it was enough for Rosalind to hurry over to Phoebe, heaving for breath.

"Here." Phoebe tried to pass the bags back. "I'll meet you at the safe house. Covert needs to know that my mother is in the city."

"What?" Rosalind demanded. She didn't take them. "You're going to Kuomintang headquarters?"

"I'm the only one who *can,*" Phoebe said, pushing the bags forward more forcefully and impelling Rosalind to take them, lest they drop straight to the ground. "I know they're practically useless, but my mother's in the open now. They can gather forces. Get in her path. We have to keep her away from the rescue tonight, and they're the best possible resource."

Rosalind cast a frantic look at the side door into Wing On. At either end of the alley, the day carried on per normal, its busyness utterly unaffected by the soldiers who were about to break through the exit. Phoebe was right. Lady Hong being in the city and playing strange games trying to summon Phoebe to her side meant she was ready for her next move. She was going to go after Oliver.

"Merde," Rosalind hissed. "*Merdemerdemerde—*"

The door shuddered. The broomstick slipped. If Rosalind moved now, she could get on a rickshaw and disappear before she was spotted.

"Go!" Phoebe hissed, giving her a push. "I'll see you shortly."

Rosalind started to move. "We leave for the facility at nine o'clock," she exclaimed over her shoulder. "You have to be back before then."

"I will," Phoebe promised. "Go!"

Rosalind turned and ran as fast as she could.

Phoebe hurried in the other direction, though she already knew she'd be spotted. Her pastel skirt flared around her obnoxiously, no help in hiding her when she paused at one of the shop corners to see where the soldiers would go.

A loud clatter echoed through the alley. They had broken past the department store's door. By then at least Rosalind had disappeared. She had either blended well into the mass of shoppers on Nanjing Road, or she had long boarded a rickshaw. They wouldn't be able to follow her to the safe house.

Phoebe took a deep breath. Instead of running toward Nationalist headquarters, she stepped out from the corner, coming onto the street plainly. She raised her hands over her head. Tipped her chin high as soon as one of the men spotted her, his uniform lapels catching the morning light.

"Don't shoot," Phoebe commanded evenly. "I'm coming with you."

Shanghai shivers in the cold.

Its central buildings are well insulated, at least—lined with wool and gold. These theaters and hotels won't feel the wintry temperatures approaching with the darkening afternoon, won't hear the cries from the north, where the currents and gales blow hardest.

Its peripheries are a different matter. Some stores shutter. Others hide away their belongings and gnaw at their nails, considering the costs of moving and the costs of staying, the impending doom that lies on the horizon.

The pages on the calendar have been turning at breakneck speed. No matter how the mayor wills it to stop, the days run and they run, until time is up and the warships press to the banks of the city with a heavy thunk.

"They're trying to take us just as they took Manchuria!" One university student has broken from the rules they set for his shadowing period, finding it impossible to merely observe and jot notes. The meeting ends, and he pulls away from the crowd. He chases after the mayor, his lanyard fluttering behind him, each of his footsteps echoing through the long halls. "How can we agree to this? *How?*"

Municipal buildings will be protected if violence breaks out. It is not the center that will be struck first, anyhow. The doors are heavy; the pillars are stable. The mayor hurries away from the student, and regretfully, he knows any fuss here will be muffled by the smooth walls. It will clash against the echoes already crawling along the ceiling slats: *yes, we will pay monetary reparations for the property loss experienced by Japanese owners; yes, there will be an end to all anti-Japanese protests; yes, there will be public condemnation on Chinese civilians who argue otherwise.*

"Traitor!" the student screams. Soldiers come to escort him out. "You're a traitor!"

The calendar settles on January 28. There's no pretty way for the city to speak about it. No matter what they do, no matter what commands they bend to and how they attempt to prevent the broach, the invasion is here.

36

Despite his best efforts, which included wrapping a small blanket around himself, Orion's headache was back. The safe house had picked up a draft from some corner that he couldn't find, though he had checked the windows and doors. Every few minutes, a breeze blew through the main room, funneling right into his ear and knocking into his brain like an ice pick.

"Won't you sit down?" Alisa asked. She was hovering at the washroom doorway, brushing her hair.

Orion, meanwhile, stood aimlessly, planting himself in the middle of the room and surveying the walls. "I'm looking for a crack," he said. "The wind keeps getting in."

"I think you might be imagining it."

He narrowed his eyes. Before he could make a fuss, Celia gave a polite cough from the table, shutting them both up again. They had done this three times already. Alisa minded his business, Orion insisted there was a problem at hand, and Celia rolled her eyes while she continued fiddling with the earpieces in front of her.

"How is that going?" Alisa asked, gesturing to the earpieces.

Half of the wires weren't working as they should, which was bad if they wanted to be in communication tonight while breaking into the facility. Silas had said he didn't have time to go looking for more earpieces because he needed to go to Kuomintang headquarters and put the last of the double-edged plan in place, so now Celia was in charge of fixing the ones that weren't producing sound.

"I think I know what broke," Celia replied. "Now it's a matter of whether I can put it back together."

Just as Orion was about to suggest yanking out all the wires for a full reset, there was a quick knock on the door: three fast taps to signal someone returning.

Alisa skittered over to open the door. Before Alisa could step back, Rosalind slipped in and closed the door behind her, her chest rising and falling.

"Where's Phoebe?" Alisa asked.

"Headquarters," Rosalind answered with a hitch. "Lady Hong's here."

The faint ringing in Orion's ears got louder.

"What?" Celia demanded. "In the city?"

"Yes. Her soldiers found us. She must have established a secret base to operate from."

Rosalind strolled into the room, dropping the paper bags in her arms and undoing the silk scarf that she had tied around her hair. As soon as that came off, Orion could see the blood splattered on her qipao, a crimson stain that spread from her shoulder to her elbow. Before anyone could remark on the sight, Rosalind was already saying: "I'm fine. Just a knife. We extricated ourselves, and Phoebe was unharmed. She's gone to raise the alarm among the Nationalists."

Orion wanted to go to her. He didn't know whether he was allowed. For a short moment, he wavered with indecision, watching Rosalind frown while she inspected the damp fabric at her shoulder. Then he strode forward, figuring that he could always get yelled at if he was crossing a line.

"Here." He reached into his pocket for a handkerchief.

Rosalind took it, flashing him a brief, grateful look. Warmth moved through his chest in response, the sensation distracting him briefly before the pulsating at his head drew his attention again. He really needed to fix this. Or put an actual ice pick through his other ear—maybe that would help assuage the phantom sensation.

"I thought the complaint we had against the Nationalists was that they're too slow." Alisa crouched down, inspecting what Rosalind had brought back. She was still holding the hairbrush in her hand, so she used it to prod at the bags like there might be a live animal waiting inside.

"They are," Rosalind said, wiping away a streak of blood on her neck. "It's still hugely beneficial if they're on the lookout for her. I wouldn't trust them to be much help, but we might as well exhaust every resource we have."

At the table, Celia put one of the wires into her ear, testing the sound. She didn't seem satisfied. It still wasn't working.

"A prison break is already going to be hard enough," Celia muttered. "We cannot afford to be waging battle at the same time if Lady Hong *also* shows up tonight."

And yet, from what Orion was understanding, chances were high that she would. She was already in the city—what reason did she have *not* to?

"What can we do about it?" Rosalind countered. She leaned closer to a vase on the mantel, using the reflective surface to check how much blood remained. "The priority now is Oliver. Both for the sake of his life and to keep him away from contributing to something terrible. No offense, Orion."

"None taken." Though his voice managed to stay light, his headache operated separately from him, seeming to take extreme offense. The space between his ears screeched with heinous imagined noise, and he barely resisted dropping to his knees entirely. He brought his hand to the bridge of his nose. Clamped down, hoping that the pressure would ease it.

Celia, meanwhile, scraped back on her chair, going to the shelf near the front door. There, she picked up a newspaper, bringing it back to the table with a rustle.

"I was reading today's front page earlier," she said quietly. "Listen to this. 'The ten-day ultimatum issued by the Japanese has reached its close. Though our officials assure there is no conflict to come and the mayor is shutting anti-Japanese boycott organizations, the Concessions react in a way that says otherwise. Over twenty units have organized in the International Settlement, including but not limited to the American Company, the Shanghai Scottish, the Portuguese Company, and a Russian regiment.'" Celia looked up from the paper. Her face was pale. "War is coming. Lady Hong can hear the news just as well as we can. The Japanese are attacking sooner or later, which means she needs to give them *something* on their first offensive wave if she wants in on their side. She's going after Oliver tonight. I guarantee it."

Orion reminded himself to breathe. He had gotten through all of his headaches these few days by riding through them. They always eased once the pain crested.

"Hey."

A small whisper, to his left. He hadn't realized he had shut his eyes until they snapped open again, finding Rosalind at his side. Her hand settled on his arm.

"Are you all right?" she whispered.

Orion nodded. He didn't trust himself to speak. Celia and Alisa hadn't noticed that he was scrambling to keep his wince at bay, and if he could help it, he preferred to keep it that way. They were still discussing the matter at hand, with Alisa announcing:

"I have an idea." She paused. "You won't like it though, Celia."

Celia raised her eyebrows. "All right, then, I don't want to hear it—"

"We should cause an outright melee," Alisa went on as if Celia hadn't answered her. "Let's tell the Communists too. Let's say that

Orion is still with Lady Hong, and she's entered the city. Intelligence will find her in an instant. They'll get in her way if she acts tonight too."

Wait. What?

Briefly, Orion released the clamp he had on the bridge of his nose, a frown forming. "Why would they believe I'm still with her?"

"It was the last thing they heard anyway. No one on our side knows what happened after the attack at that tour stop," Alisa returned. She gestured at Celia. "Our agents never reported in."

"I was going to report in when I got Oliver back," Celia said, setting the newspaper down firmly. "But you want to go beyond omitting information. You want me to outright lie."

"It increases our greater success tonight. We get the Nationalists out of our way by sending in Priest. We get Lady Hong out of our way by sending in the Communists. Set up distractions on every front so that we have a clear path to Oliver."

Celia didn't look very convinced. "Operatives are going to die fighting her."

"Willingly," Alisa replied in an instant. "Central command has told covert to prioritize gaining Lady Hong's inventions. They know it could turn the tide of the civil war."

"But it's still a lie." At this, Orion knew that Celia was gesturing toward him, but he had mostly closed his eyes again. "Orion's not with Lady Hong anymore. They would be going in to die for nothing."

"No, they would be dying for duty. No one fights a war believing every move will advance the battlefield." Alisa shrugged. "Our side wants a scientific discovery never before seen by mankind. Fine. Now they are putting in the work for it."

Celia still seemed hesitant. Rosalind hadn't said anything in a while either, but Orion couldn't tell if it was because she was staying out of it as a Nationalist agent or if she was more concerned with watching him closely. He could feel her scrutiny. He was using every bit of energy to keep his pain off his face.

"We're tricking them."

"We're tricking the leadership," Alisa acknowledged. "But for the agents on the ground, is it really trickery? Ask any of them whether they would prefer to do nothing or prevent Lady Hong from giving weapons to the Japanese, and most would opt to stop her, wouldn't they?"

Orion didn't get to hear what answer Celia gave. The next pang that shot up from the base of his skull was unbearable, and he made an audible noise, almost choking on his exhale. He was aware that Rosalind was saying something to him, something frantic, something terrified, but every sense was drowned out, his vision flashing white and overwhelming his headache into something much worse.

When his focus cleared momentarily, Rosalind was in front of him, hands clasped to his face. He had dropped to his knees. When had he dropped to his knees?

"Come with me now."

She pulled him to his feet, dragged him into the study. His vision swirled. The door thudded shut.

"Is it your head?" Rosalind asked.

Something about this felt familiar. As if Rosalind had asked him this question before. As if Orion had once held his hand in this exact position, clasped to his temple and feeling like he was balancing on the cusp of death because he couldn't catch his breath.

"Okay," Rosalind said when he couldn't reply. "Fresh air, then." He felt her grab his other hand. A creak sounded in the room: the bookshelf opening to reveal the door and the door opening to reveal the stairs descending into the alley. Though Orion could barely see where he was going, Rosalind led him along, forging onward until they pushed outside.

Gray sunlight. A cold, snow-dusted afternoon.

He breathed in and his chest seized. He breathed in and there was no oxygen to take.

"Ros—"

Her lips pressed over his. Suddenly he stopped trying to make frantic inhales—suddenly he forgot that he needed to draw breath at all when there was the softness of her presence and a sharp, fragrant taste on his tongue, spreading as molten gold might. His heart slowed from its usual breakneck clamor. His body calmed like a weapon tempered under heat.

Though neither of them had exhaled into the kiss, Orion felt as if she had moved a vital breath into his lungs.

Rosalind pulled away. Slowly. Warily. Orion's eyes fluttered open to find his vision cleared, the world misty around the edges. Beyond the alley, there was the low echo of what almost sounded like a foghorn.

"I should have just done that in the room," she whispered. She kept her eyes closed. Her cheek pressed into his shoulder.

"In front of your sister?"

Rosalind laughed. Once. That same sound from his memory, the only one he truly remembered.

"In the study after I closed the door, you blockhead."

A breath out. A breath in. The worst of the headache had eased, fading to the dull twinge he had been putting up with since he woke up in Zhouzhuang.

"Orion?"

He had been silent for too long. Without giving himself time to hesitate, he wrapped his arms around her and sent a note of gratitude into the universe when she let him pull her as close as he could.

"Yes?"

Rosalind hesitated. When she spoke again, she was very quiet, her voice muffled against the fabric of his shirt. "There's something I skimmed over when I was explaining the situation in Zhouzhuang. You were one of the earliest recipients of your mother's strength experiments, which means you need new doses of those alterations on a routine basis. Without them, the headaches are a sign that it's eating away at your body. It's slow-acting, but you're deteriorating."

Orion had had a suspicion that this was related back to his mother's work. He wasn't surprised that he could hear recognition in Rosalind's voice. A headache like this had happened in front of her before.

"I would have guessed it was caused by the mind conditioning," he said. "But that makes sense too."

Rosalind sighed, pulling back from his embrace. She peered up at him awhile before lifting her hand and grabbing his face gently. Her palm to his chin, four fingers on one cheek and her thumb pressing into the other, lightly enough that he could feel the warmth of her skin instead of the pressure of her hand.

"Probably related, though," she said dolefully. "If your physical health weakens, it might allow the conditioning remaining in your mind to creep back."

Orion grimaced. He wanted Rosalind close again. He didn't want to think about these headaches, nor about what it was doing to his mind, unbeknownst to himself.

"See anything troubling?" he asked. She was still holding his face, keeping him at arm's length to observe him. His hand, almost absently, traced a flower stitched at the waistline of her qipao. He had the temptation to pluck her up as if she were a bloom too, to hear a proper laugh and store it away in a place no one could ever take from him again. He wouldn't dare, of course—she would probably bite him if he tried.

Which was tempting in and of itself too.

Rosalind searched his eyes. Perhaps she had been expecting to find something worse, because her concern settled. "No. You don't appear to be crying tears of blood or vomiting sludge."

"Terrifying visual."

That earned a smile. "Don't worry. You're still pretty."

The urge to hold her grew all-encompassing. Perhaps he ought to feel embarrassed that the desire was this strong when Rosalind was right—without most of his memories, he knew very little about her. Yet his instincts remembered what his mind didn't, in the same way that he hadn't forgotten how to walk or to speak.

"You've stolen my line. I was about to say that to you."

"I have claimed it. Find something else."

"Fine." He couldn't help it. He started to lean closer. "A jewel, then—"

The hidden stairwell thudded in interruption, its door opening into the alley. Before either of them could move, Alisa had poked her head out, examining the scene.

"Hello," she said. "I came to check if you needed help."

"No," Rosalind replied. Her hand was still splayed upon his cheek. "All is fine. We're only talking."

"Oh, all right." Alisa didn't move. "What are we talking about?"

The girl knew exactly what she was doing. There was a slow grin spreading across her face.

Orion cleared his throat. "Nothing very interesting—"

"I am *so* interested to hear it," Alisa interrupted. "I want the full scoop. Don't leave a single detail out."

"Alisa . . . ," Rosalind warned.

"Yes, Miss Lang?"

Rosalind pulled away from Orion fully, plucking a pin from her hair and wielding it like an axe. "How dare you mock an assassin? I will have you answer for your crimes—"

Alisa shrieked, hurtling back up the stairs. Rosalind shot after her. For a moment, Orion could only blink in confusion. Then he hurried to shove his foot through the doorway before it could lock him out, slipping through too.

"Wait for me!"

37

Sundown drew long over the French Concession, tinting the houses a delicate sort of blue. Phoebe could hear a chorus of birds cawing on the next street over. Seconds later, their entire formation shot up into the violet sky, soaring in the shape of an arrow before disappearing south.

The vehicle stopped. At the front, the soldiers paused for a few seconds before moving to disembark. There were two seated at the back too, but they weren't making any great effort to guard her. She had come willingly.

Phoebe eyed the soldiers as they got out, careful with her skirts when one held the door open for her. In the time they had spent getting across the city, she had been observing the soldiers, and she couldn't determine whether they were all under chemical conditioning or not. They didn't speak much; nor did anyone speak to her. One, though, was humming to himself during the drive. Another had casually adjusted his hair in the reflection of the window. With the way Rosalind had described it, Orion had become an entirely different person while under conditioning. Even prior to their mother inducing total amnesia, he would slip off to headquarters and lose track of reality until the task was complete. Nothing would stir him out of it.

The vehicle doors slammed shut. A pair of birds perched on the closest tree shot off too, blending into the hastening night. They had parked outside a manor, it seemed, though little of the residence was visible from the gate. There were soldiers inside already waiting for their arrival, opening the gates with the low, long groan of its hinges.

"Where are we?" Phoebe asked.

She wasn't sure if anyone would reply. They didn't. She had been keeping track of where they were driving up until the sharp turn five corners prior, and then she had lost her bearings. All she knew for certain was that they remained within the International Settlement, because there had been no control points to pass, and their surroundings remained a peaceful sort of quiet. A battle would never press in on foreign territory, so the streets here would remain idle and beautiful no matter what raged in the north.

Which begged the question: How had Lady Hong established herself here anyway?

The men waited by the open gate, gesturing for Phoebe to proceed. She could run now. Turn on her heel and get as far away as possible instead of risking herself. But that wasn't the attitude of an operative, so Phoebe clutched her hands together and proceeded, her heels clicking on the stone path. A few of the soldiers trailed after her in a loose line. Others remained by the entrance, still and silent to watch over the street.

None of them resembled the sort of mind-controlled playthings Phoebe would have imagined. They only seemed . . . a little subdued. Each soldier clearly remained their own person. If she suddenly took a knife and charged at one, he wouldn't stand there and take it; he'd swerve out of the way. If all were asked to return home and resume whatever routine had been in place before their recruitment into Lady Hong's militia, they could do it.

A harsh wind blew at her eyes, ice-cold upon contact and causing her to tear up. Her heart raced beneath her ribs—wild, frantic.

Careful, a snarky voice whispered in her head. It sounded a lot like Priest. *We wouldn't want her to think you suddenly developed the gene.*

Phoebe continued walking forward. Before she knew it, she was at the door, staring at the beige color a moment before rapping her knuckles against it.

"You may go in," one of the soldiers said behind her. English. "She's expecting you."

Phoebe couldn't wrap her head around this. She pushed at the door, half expecting him to be lying, but it opened without any resistance.

Inside, the foyer was empty, devoid of furniture. A circular rug decorated the floor. Little else here resembled a usual household: no shoes in the corner or frames on the walls. None of the soldiers followed her in, so Phoebe was alone when she crossed the marble flooring and entered the living room, holding her breath. White curtains blew along the open deck doors. Beyond the glass, the manor's grounds extended endlessly, taking up space in a way that definitely signaled outer International Settlement. Where *were* they? And why?

A melodic clinking sounded from the corner of the living room. Phoebe's gaze shot over at once, finding another door that had been left ajar.

She took a step closer. Then another. Though she would have guessed this was some storage space tucked into the side of the main wing, she prodded the door open to find a whole laboratory—gleaming white walls and polished metal tables. And standing by one of the shelves . . .

"Feiyi," her mother greeted her, effortlessly casual, sounding as though she had stepped away momentarily to make dinner instead of leaving Phoebe for *seven years.*

"Māma," Phoebe croaked.

Lady Hong hadn't changed a bit. She looked exactly the same, actually, from the carefully brushed hair to the knowing glint that sparked in her eye. Phoebe used to think her mother could read her mind. That each of her secrets would spill to the forefront the moment her mother gave her nose a tap.

Lady Hong set down the clipboard in her hands. She walked over. Closed the distance in less than three steps. When she lifted her hand, brushing Phoebe's hair back to get a better look at her face, it seemed that even her scent remained the same—the faint whiff of perfume that Phoebe had never found in stores no matter where she looked—and Phoebe couldn't help herself. Despite knowing their situation at present, despite knowing everything that her mother had done, Phoebe reached out for a hug.

Her throat was tight with tears. She clamped herself to her mother, and she was twelve years old again. No time had passed and nothing had gone wrong. Lady Hong wrapped her arms around her, and Phoebe could pretend that it was their house around them instead of a lab, could pretend that Oliver and Orion were about to walk through the doors too and ask who was sniffling up a storm.

That last thought finally gave her the push she needed to step back. She was halfway to a sob before her hand came up to her mouth, locking the sound away.

Her mother didn't try to stop her. Phoebe composed herself quickly, drawing an inhale and swallowing it down. Another curtained area had been roped off to her right, beside the shelves. In the silence, the fabric waved gently, picking up a breeze blowing in from the foyer. There was nothing particularly secretive from what Phoebe could see. Boxes, crates, folders.

"I know you must have a lot of questions," Lady Hong said. "Believe me, Feiyi, if I could have reached out, I would have done so."

Phoebe didn't know what to say for a long moment. There were all these varying versions of herself that wanted to jump to the helm. The Phoebe who kept peace among adults, whose instinct was to match her mother's calm tone. The Phoebe no one would ever suspect of being a Communist assassin, tempted to play the fool and act as though she didn't know what her mother was doing here. Somewhere, dark and deep within, there was also the feral girl stupid enough to play Priest, and *she* wanted to reach for a gun.

Phoebe lowered her hand.

"I have just one question," she said, and her voice was far steadier than she would have expected. "Was it worth it? Was your research worth breaking apart this entire family?"

Lady Hong lifted a brow. At once Phoebe knew that nothing she said here would land; nothing would strike as anything close to an attack. Her mother almost looked exasperated, the same sort of expression she'd worn when Phoebe clattered into the kitchen with her shoes muddy, the same sort reserved for children who didn't know better.

"Hong Feiyi," Lady Hong said. "Do you know where this country is heading?"

"To *war*?" Phoebe snapped.

"Yes," her mother replied easily. "Since long before you were born, this country knew that it was crumbling. If not the Japanese, don't you think another power will try, sooner or later? Look at the land we stand on. Look at the state of Shanghai for the last century." She nudged a clipboard on the shelf, aligning it straight. There was a long column upon the paper, but Phoebe couldn't read what it said. "The government calls me a national traitor. Fine. From another angle, I am only protecting my family. I am choosing the victor before their victory. Don't you remember what I told you?"

Phoebe did remember. The last time she had seen her mother, it was the thick of London's winter. The sky had resembled the one tonight, low and gray and dark. They had stood surrounded by snow at the neighborhood park, and when Lady Hong said goodbye, summoned away by business in Shanghai, she had bade Phoebe to take care of herself and her older brother.

Some people fight for the nation, her mother had said. *We fight for ourselves.*

"'Protecting your family is the most important thing,'" Phoebe echoed dully, recalling her mother's parting advice. "What happened to that?"

"Don't you think I am protecting you all?" her mother fired back. "What happens once Japan takes over? Who do you think survives: the ones who helped them or the ones who opposed them?"

"They would have a harder time *taking over* if people like you weren't helping them," Phoebe hissed. She couldn't believe she was having this argument. She couldn't believe it boiled down to something as simple as her mother doubting their own country might have its own two legs to stand on. Their civil war had been raging for years now without either side relinquishing. Didn't that mean something? Awful as the war was, didn't that say something about the spirit pulsing upon every part of the land?

Lady Hong shook her head. "I won't be made into a villain for being realistic. I have worked to pave our place in the new societal order. I have contributed immense research to make sure we live well."

"You *used* Orion as your personal soldier."

"As he was made for," Lady Hong returned sharply. Her calm was finally slipping. "He is no ordinary civilian, and he shall not be treated as such."

For all these years, Phoebe had been carrying her promise to her mother closer to her chest than anything else. Yet that promise had been nothing more than a gross misinterpretation. She had set out to protect Orion, had believed herself so heroic for it, when her mother had really just wanted Phoebe to protect her *asset*.

All along, the greatest threat Phoebe should have been fending back was the very one she idolized.

"I read your research, Māma."

Her mother tilted her head, eyes narrowing. "You did?"

"Cover to cover. Who knew? Turns out all those years of private tutoring means I'm actually smart." Phoebe scrunched her hands into her skirts. It kept them from shaking. "You began this work long before the empire started creeping in. So tell the truth. You want to discover immortality. Everything else is an excuse."

Lady Hong sighed. "Can't it be both, darling?"

"It can't." Phoebe stormed forward. Her mother didn't stop her from snatching the clipboard on the shelf. From flipping through out of a vehement need to see what was hiding right in front of her. "You either birthed us as people capable of individual thought, or you birthed us as components to be used. It can't be *both*."

Nothing about the pages on the clipboard made any sense. Though Phoebe had enough background to understand her mother's thesis, she didn't understand the numbers and letters drawn up here as formulas across and diagonal.

"It can." Lady Hong, almost gently, took the clipboard back. "You know how Liwen is. If you gave him the choice to experience some pain so that the rest of us would be protected, he would choose to do so."

"But he didn't *choose*. You did."

"Same thing, no?"

"No!" Phoebe snapped. "You abandoned us. You told me again and again that family was the most important thing, and then you left us for seven years."

"And how is that any different from sending you abroad for school?" her mother returned.

"Because we believed you to be *dead*!"

Lady Hong shook her head. "It was a sacrifice I was willing to bear. There is one goal in sight for us, Feiyi. If we want safety in the end, then I can forsake everything that is temporary. Don't you see?"

Arguing about this was a lost cause. Phoebe took a shallow breath, then another, and she felt herself giving up on her mother like the loss was a physical sensation; she felt the illusion of her family shatter into pieces as cleanly as an arrow through the heart. There was no such thing as being utterly safe, just as there was no such reality where Phoebe could have stayed in the shadows forever protecting Orion. Eventually, people had to face their own danger. Eventually, countries had to fight their wars.

"You find it worthwhile." Phoebe could scream that her mother had lost it, could curse and shout and hurl accusations. It would be useless. This had always been her mother. Phoebe had merely been too young to see it. "But I do not. We will have to agree to disagree."

"Regardless of what you think, it'll be over soon." Her mother set the clipboard down. "You will all return to my side when this is said and done. We'll be a family again. Nothing will be able to break us apart when I've produced something so worthwhile."

"We were never a family to begin with," Phoebe said quietly. From somewhere in the house, there came the thud of a door. Had someone else come in? Was that from the foyer? "Anyone who cooperates with you is just as much a hanjian."

"Is that so?" Lady Hong's eyes lifted to the door. Footsteps pattered closer, heading their way. "Feiyi, step behind the curtain."

"I beg your pardon?"

Lady Hong gestured at the curtain, as if Phoebe needed directing. "Go on. You'll see."

Phoebe didn't like this. She had to be getting back soon. They were heading for the facility at nine o'clock—and they were trying to keep Lady Hong away from it. Should Phoebe do something here? Would her mother even let her leave?

Suddenly, showing up on her own seemed like a horribly bad idea. The entire perimeter was guarded. If Phoebe made a run for it, she wouldn't get far at all. Her mother gave her another pointed look, and Phoebe hurried for the curtain, slipping out of sight just as something else came into the laboratory.

"You're late," Lady Hong said.

"My apologies," the new voice replied. "I had a lot of stops to make before this meeting, obviously."

Phoebe blinked rapidly, trying to register the words, trying to make sense of what she was hearing. Something was very, very wrong.

"Is everything set for your end of the bargain?" her mother asked.

"Yes. I have been overseeing each withdrawal session since his capture. There will be enough blood by the time I make a retrieval tonight. You don't need to attend personally."

What the hell? Phoebe thought. It couldn't be. That couldn't be who she thought it was.

Slowly she reached for the curtain. Her fingers curled around the fabric, pulling just enough to show her who had stepped into the room.

No. No no no no no—

"Fantastic," Lady Hong said. "Thank you, Xielian."

Silas nodded, offering a small smile.

38

It was creeping closer and closer to nine o'clock, but neither Silas nor Phoebe had returned.

"Maybe they ran into each other at headquarters," Celia suggested.

Rosalind leaned her shoulder against the wall, blowing her breath out in an opaque puff. One streetlamp stood a few feet away. With the dark, they felt comfortable enough to hover outside the safe house, surveilling the street corner for the first glimpse of either Silas's or Phoebe's return. Thus far, Rosalind had only seen soldiers hurrying past in a rush to get somewhere. Which really felt like a bad sign.

"And then sat down for a leisurely cup of tea?" Rosalind said. "It shouldn't be taking them this long."

Celia had little to say in response. She mimicked Rosalind's shoulder lean against the wall, then turned her attention back to the street corner. The safe house was surrounded by factories and redbrick buildings and barbed-wire barriers. Zhabei was already starting to look like a war zone, and the Chinese soldiers stationed out and about only added to the atmosphere. Most came from the 19th Route Army. Just as Rosalind was wringing at her long sleeve again, another cluster of them hurried by, surely freezing in their thin uniforms. The temperature had only dropped since sundown.

"They look so young," Celia whispered.

Rosalind remained quiet. The front page of the newspaper that Celia had been reading from earlier said the 19th Route Army had brought over thirty thousand men into the city. To amass numbers that large, one really could not be picky. Some in the group didn't even hold weapons. Their uniforms were faded of color after too many washes. Their caps were wrinkled, shoes bearing holes.

"Base to Fortune. Come in, Fortune."

Rosalind rolled her eyes at once, pressing her earpiece to activate the microphone. "Orion, this is a closed radio line. You don't need to use code names."

"Listen, I don't remember anything about being an operative. Go easy on me."

His voice was accompanied by constant static. Celia had finally fixed the earpieces—and by fixed, that meant they worked but not very well.

"We're ten minutes to nine o'clock," Orion went on. He was inside the safe house, so he could have easily stepped out to communicate, but the novelty of using earpieces was clearly giving him amusement. "Alisa asks what our plan is."

"We can't get in without Silas," Celia said, pressing her own microphone. The earpieces were all connected on one line. The moment anyone spoke, everyone else could hear it. "What are we going to do except wait?"

Rosalind crossed her arms tighter. She had released her earpiece, so only her sister heard her when she asked: "You don't think they got caught or anything?"

Out of everyone, Celia was the most anxious about this turn of events, but she didn't show it. The only reason Rosalind could tell was because she knew her sister. She could read the more minute movements: the constant tension in her fingers as she clenched and unclenched her fists, the turn of her head left and right every few seconds to take in her surroundings. Even before Rosalind suggested coming onto the street to watch the corner, Celia had exhibited the same behavior inside the safe house, which told her Celia wasn't watching for danger creeping up on her; rather, she was glancing for Oliver out of habit. Rosalind and Celia may as well start taking turns on whose mission partner went missing.

"Caught for what?" Celia asked lowly. "They're Nationalists. The only people who can catch them are their own. And both Silas and Phoebe belong to that side . . . right?"

"Well, yes," Rosalind said. "But what if Communist covert got to them?"

Reluctantly, Celia had agreed to Alisa's plan. She had made the call to central command, reported that Oliver's status was undetermined and Orion remained with his mother. Without saying it outright, she had implied that Lady Hong was in the city, so the Communist covert branch must have put their feelers out at once.

"I doubt it," Celia said. "Bigger fish to fry, after all." Then, with a wince: "Bigger fights to die in."

The night fell quiet. Faintly, the clouds rumbled with the hum of what sounded like an airplane before the noise faded away. Though Rosalind lifted her head to inspect the stars, she couldn't see anything immediately concerning.

"You did the right thing, you know."

"I do know," Celia replied. She exhaled, running her hand through a lock of hair and pulling it straight. "Oliver would hate it, but Oliver isn't here."

He wasn't. But in an hour, he would be, and then they would have every element they needed to combat Lady Hong. Perhaps they couldn't take down a whole empire, but with seven agents, they could surely take down one major threat.

"He'll be fine," Rosalind assured her. She pushed off the wall. "I promise."

Celia's eyes tracked her movement, sharp and observant. *You cannot possibly promise that,* her gaze seemed to say. Still, Rosalind needed to make the promise, if not to fool her sister, then to fool the very universe into bending to her will. She secured her hair band, prodding around her skull to make sure each of her pins was in place. Other than Rosalind's tight updo and Celia's loose plaits, they looked more like twins in this moment than they ever had. They were both dressed like fugitives in the clothes Rosalind had acquired earlier in the day: dark trousers and thick jackets instead of society-appropriate qipao. Once they neared the facility, cloths would go over their faces to conceal their identities.

"It's me again," Orion's voice sounded into Rosalind's ear.

Rosalind pressed down. "All right, Huntsman. Have your fun. What is it?"

"Are you hungry?"

"What?"

"I found sweets. Are you hungry?"

"Not really, but—"

A flare of headlights came around the corner. At once, Rosalind and Celia perked to attention, waiting to see who was coming.

"They're here!" Celia announced into her earpiece. "Come down now!"

"Wait," Rosalind said quietly. The car stopped. When the door opened, it was only Silas.

"Sorry, sorry," Silas rushed to say, hurrying around the front. "I didn't realize it would take so long to confirm the mission with headquarters. Everything is ready. Let's go."

The plan was still in place. The military facility was also located in Zhabei, a short drive farther out west. Silas would be entering through the Nationalists' control tower as an operative taking part in a capture mission. Rosalind, Celia, Alisa, and Orion needed to find their way through the outer facility on their own after being dropped off somewhere along the perimeter. When Silas gave the signal that the guards were distracted by Priest's eventual entrance, they would be breaking into the inner facility and beelining straight for Oliver.

"Where's Phoebe?" Rosalind demanded. She was supposed to be the getaway watch. The one waiting on the outside to make sure they had a clear exit route.

Silas frowned. "What do you mean? I thought she left with you."

Alisa and Orion emerged from the safe house. In their black clothing, they blended right into the dark, their faces obscured already.

"Here," Alisa whispered, squeezing between Rosalind and Celia, holding two lengths of fabric. Celia took hers. Rosalind, momentarily, was still puzzled, trying to process what Silas meant.

"You didn't see her at headquarters?"

"*Phoebe*? Why would she be at headquarters?"

Something felt off. Rosalind couldn't parse why. Where else could Phoebe have gone? It was possible they had simply missed each other. Kuomintang headquarters was relatively large. But Phoebe had known that Silas was there . . . so surely she would have looked for him once she arrived?

"We need to go," Celia prompted. "Otherwise we're going to miss our cue."

Rosalind's panic built slowly, then shot to its peak all at once. Suddenly she was frantic—what if Phoebe was in trouble? What if she hadn't even made it to headquarters?

Orion touched her elbow. "This rescue will take less than an hour," he said quietly, just to her. "If my sister is in trouble, we can help her afterward. The most likely culprit is my mother, and it doesn't sound like she would hurt her."

"Hold on," Silas cut in, overhearing Orion's remark. "What happened to Feiyi?"

"We don't *know*," Rosalind snapped. "Maybe if you were less concerned about catching Priest, you would have seen her reporting to headquarters. Lady Hong is in the city. Her soldiers tried to go after Phoebe."

"All right, darling." Orion got ahold of her arms at once, running his hands up and down in a soothing motion. "In the car."

Silas blinked. Once. Twice. He was entirely unfazed by Rosalind losing her temper on him. There was no trace of offense in his expression—there was only shock and terror. Maybe he knew that there was no need for him to react in the wrong anyway. It was Rosalind who had left her. Rosalind who had hurried to get back to the safe house, abandoning Phoebe to flee on her own.

"You mean to say her mother came after her?"

"I mean to say she probably *has* her."

"But . . . but how . . . ?"

Celia slapped her hands upon the surface of the vehicle. The sound echoed into the night, as harsh as the gust of wind that followed.

"First we get the sibling she wants to siphon for blood," Celia said. "Then we get the sibling whose last-known location we have. Let's *go!*"

She was right. They had to move, because arguing was only a waste of time. Each of them piled into the car, letting Silas slide back into the driver's seat, his eyes still wide with disbelief. Alisa leaned forward, offering one of the earpieces.

"Do you need this?" Alisa asked.

Silas shook his head. "It'll look far too suspicious. I'll activate a facility-wide alarm for your signal. When we're all finished, I will meet you here at the safe house."

Alisa nodded. As did Celia and Orion. Rosalind must have remained silent for too long because Alisa took it upon herself to thud Rosalind's leg, drawing an "Ow!"

"Understood," Rosalind muttered. "In and out. Let's move fast."

Silas's eyes lifted to the rearview mirror, meeting hers. He nodded to acknowledge her instruction, but there was something uncertain about the gesture. When he pressed on the accelerator, Rosalind's stomach dipped, like it had been left behind on the curbside.

God. She had a damn bad feeling about this.

Phoebe wiped the tears from her cheeks, but new ones replaced them at once, ice-cold against her face in the wind. She allowed herself the rickshaw ride to cry. After that, as soon as she arrived, she needed to stop.

"What was that?" she had demanded of her mother. The moment she'd shoved the curtain away, the laboratory had seemed to grow a hundred sizes with the way her voice echoed. "Why was Silas here?"

She had waited for the front entrance to slam shut, for that echo to travel throughout the manor. She had waited until he left the premises, or who knew what he would do if he witnessed her presence there. Her mother had told her to hide on purpose. She almost seemed to relish Phoebe's shock, a knowingness playing in her manner as if the answer to her question should be obvious.

"Why do you think?" her mother replied. "He's working with me. Getting me what I need."

And what she needed was Oliver's blood. Lady Hong wouldn't even need to compete with their rescue mission tonight—she already had someone on the inside, someone among the Nationalists who could knock Oliver out in the holding cells and siphon the blood from him. Christ. Phoebe felt like she was going to be sick, like she was going to hurl her guts all over the shiny floor of her mother's research laboratory.

"What is he getting out of this?" Phoebe asked. Her voice turned shrill. "Why would he help you?"

Lady Hong paused. Surveyed her demeanor. "That's for you to ask him. I am sure you can guess, though. He determined that it was worthwhile. You may like to learn from him, Feiyi."

Phoebe wanted to scream at Silas. Project her words loud enough to travel through the gardens and onto the streets, reach him while he was getting into his car and driving off. *There is* nothing *worth this. Is this why she released Orion so easily? Because of* you*? Because you offered another promised victim?*

Phoebe had taken a step toward the door. Then another—each thud deliberate, waiting for the consequences that were to follow. All these pieces had been set up at the facility for the break-in, and almost none were necessary. They had practically lost already. There was nothing more for Phoebe to do except slide the last player into place, let Priest make her appearance and get Oliver out.

"I'm going to go," Phoebe stated. "Are you going to stop me?"

Lady Hong gave her a pointed look. "You're free to leave if you wish, Feiyi. I'm not a tyrant. I'm just your mother." She turned around. Her work was calling for her attention again. "But you will come back. I promise you will."

Now Phoebe practically tumbled off the rickshaw, paying the runner before giving her face one last scrub to clear the tears. The safe house was dark. The hour hovered around a quarter past nine, which meant she was too late. They had already left for the facility.

Phoebe sniffed hard. She barged up the stairs, rammed her shoulder through the door into the empty safe house. She had cried enough. Phoebe Hong had no place here anymore. She needed her hands still and her aim precise. She needed her heart slow and her pulse steady, nothing in her way when she leveled her rifle. With haste, Phoebe plunged her hand into the bag that had been left by the door and took out the last remaining set of dark clothes, changing in a blur. Just before she was set to leave the safe house, she caught sight of the earpiece that had been left on the table.

She put the wire in. Tapped it hard, hearing only static. She wouldn't be able to reach the others until she was close enough in range. Wouldn't be able to warn them about the traitor in their midst.

Her heart was sawed in two. She couldn't comprehend any of this.

"Tā mā de," she muttered under her breath. Then, because that wasn't satisfying enough, she pushed out the door and screamed an utterly incoherent noise. "You want me? Fine! *Fine!*"

Priest dove back into the night.

39

Silas drove forward carefully. The entirety of Zhabei was on edge. Though its streets were relatively quiet, the hush was caused by a cloak of nervousness. One could press their ear close to the stores and hear a malevolent thrumming. Its civilians had decided to clamp their mouths shut not because this was a restful night, but because they were afraid being too loud would draw unnecessary attention.

His eyes flickered up to the rearview. Everyone inside the vehicle had been largely silent on the short drive too. They were almost at the drop-off point right outside the perimeter, where the others would use a side door to enter the outer facility. From there on, Silas would continue to the control tower. He would step in as Shepherd.

The moon peered out from behind a cloud. When his eyes went to the rearview again, Rosalind was giving him a strange look, but he couldn't tell if it was that or his own guilt drawing goose bumps at the back of his neck.

They don't know, he thought. *How would they know?*

"It's here, Silas."

Silas braked, almost missing the turn.

"Sorry," he apologized quickly. "My vision is bad at night."

Celia opened her door. "Not to worry," she replied. "Good luck. Come on."

Alisa slid out too. Then Rosalind. Last, Orion sidled over the seats to get to the door, clapping his hand over Silas's shoulder.

"Be safe," he warned.

"You too," Silas returned.

They made it past the facility perimeter easily. Getting into the facility itself would be the hard part.

Orion winced, shaking his fist out. The side door hadn't budged. "What the hell is this made out of? Solid gold?"

"Gold is a soft metal," Celia said plainly. "It can break quite easily. It's only heavy."

When he glanced back, incredulous that he was getting a scientific correction at a time like this, Rosalind gestured over her sister's shoulder for him to ignore Celia and continue.

"Go for the handle, silly," Alisa said.

Orion frowned. When he struck the door again, he aimed downward, onto the handle, and though the door still stayed quite firm, the handle broke off, clattering onto the concrete stoop outside. "I would have worked that out eventually."

"Keep telling yourself that."

He kicked the door hard, drowning out any more of Alisa's lip. It thudded back, making a clatter against the wall. This sector wasn't supposed to be well guarded because it was so far from everything important in the facility, so there was little reason for anyone to have heard their entrance. The moment they entered the base, though, they had to assume they were close to being caught at all times.

Alisa went in first, having been assigned the role of reconnaissance. "I'm much faster than everyone else," she had said when they had planned this out. "Let me check the sector first. Then I will come back with the best path for movement."

When she disappeared, she didn't turn into the hallway like a normal person. She lunged onto the wall for a boost upward and grabbed onto a vent in the ceiling, kicking the grate away and climbing through.

"Mon Dieu," Rosalind muttered, watching Alisa scamper out of view. "Are we sure she isn't superhuman too?"

"Maybe she was born with spider genetics," Celia added.

"I was thinking cat."

"Have we checked for a tail?"

Orion blinked rapidly. "We're joking, right?" he asked. "Please tell me we're joking."

Rosalind patted his arm. "I hope to the high heavens that we are joking."

Alisa kept her breath quiet despite her exertion, crawling along the vents. She had memorized the blueprints when Silas put them in front of her, so it wasn't hard to find the exact paths she needed to investigate.

"Oh, shit—"

Without warning, the panel in front of her almost gave way under the press of her hand, wobbling before she snatched her arm close to her chest and halted in her path. Voices floated through the gaps, bringing instructions from below to guard the perimeter. Reports of movement sighted. That was fast. Hadn't Priest been given a later time?

Alisa reached forward carefully, prying the loose panel from its place. One of the bolts was still firm, but she twisted the panel clockwise, then anti-clockwise, jostling it repeatedly until the bolt fell, landing on the linoleum tiles below with a *clink*.

Alisa jumped down. She still clutched the panel like a makeshift shield, looking around where she had landed. Some sort of boiler room. Maybe the steam had weakened the vents.

She poked her head through the door. There were a few cells here too, but they were empty, their bars pulled open.

Footsteps clattered around the corner. Alisa pressed back into the boiler room at once, waiting for the sound to pass before inching the door open again, watching the soldiers move through the larger cell block and disappear through a set of double electric-controlled doors. All the electric doors operated with signals from the control tower, but there were boxes beside them that Silas said would break the communication line if they were disconnected.

Everything here is rudimentary at best. Just assume that if you break something, it will turn a door back to manual.

If Alisa was still facing north, then going directly past those doors ought to take them into the inner facility. This should work.

She started to run the way she had come, tracing the hallways back.

Celia gnawed on her lip, following Alisa forward. There was a pit in her stomach. A festering pit made of blades, digging around her internal organs and driving her fanatic with worry.

"Mèimei, stop scrunching your sleeves like that," Rosalind whispered from behind.

"What?" Celia whispered back. "I am not scrunching anything."

Alisa put her arm out at the front of their single-file line, signaling for them to pause as voices bounced down the next corridor. While Celia drew to a halt, her sister reached around her, giving her left hand a slap.

"What did I just slap your hand away from then?"

"My *hem*, technically."

"That's still *something*."

"If the both of you don't hush," Alisa said, "I will perform this rescue mission alone."

Celia thinned her lips. The voices seemed to have faded, so she gestured for Alisa to continue onward.

"Some nerve you have speaking to your superior like that," Celia muttered.

"I know," Alisa retorted, moving again. "You don't smack me around enough, so I have grown too bold—oh, *shit*, step back!"

Just as Alisa hissed her instruction, an alarm blared through the corridor, loud enough to give Celia's eardrums a hefty shock. Silas's signal. The north door had been pulled, which meant the south door was clearing of guards. Celia shifted, ducking out of view while a group of soldiers hurried by in pairs, paying no attention to the four intruders hidden by the wall. Out of the corner of her eye, Celia spotted Rosalind communicating with Orion silently, and the pit in her stomach twisted further. The sight was eerily familiar, not because she had seen any of her sister's interactions with Orion in the past, but because it reminded her of somebody else.

"Come on," Alisa said, and though she might have intended for it to be a whisper, she was nearly shouting to be heard over the blare of the alarm. "It's clear until the south door."

They ran into a wider area, where the ceiling rose high and two stairwells on each side led up to a platform circling the rectangular hall. The middle was open—Celia could see past the platforms and into a second level of empty cells. Cobwebs had started to grow along some of the bars, which meant they had been untouched for quite some time. Though that probably should have been a calming thought, a chill skated along her shoulders instead.

"Orion, get the box," Alisa commanded.

"Get it?"

"Break it!"

He smacked a fist into it, hard. The metal crumpled, shortly before sparks lit up at the top of the door. Celia and Rosalind reared back in concern, but Alisa was already searching the vicinity around them, mumbling under her breath. She found a guard's baton. Handed it to Orion.

"Again," she said. "The handle first this time."

Orion gave her a silent look of chagrin. He struck the door handle with the baton, and when the metal snapped off, the hinges creaked on Alisa's push.

In the next hallway, there were soldiers on guard.

All of whom stirred at the disturbance, noticing the arrival of intruders.

"We'll handle this," Rosalind said, reaching into her hair. "Alisa, Celia—forward."

Though Celia hesitated briefly, Alisa did not. She grabbed Celia's wrist, and as Rosalind and Orion split like a creature cleaved into two for combat, Alisa pulled her forward in a straight shot down the hallway.

The south door opened smoothly. No lock, no bar. Only the hinges groaning, and then Celia was peering around the next sector of the facility, trying to make sense of its long layout.

It was dark. Glimpses of the moon peered through the windows, which were not so much windows but rectangular cutouts in the stone walls, lined by metal bars. They had found themselves on an elevated platform: a set of stairs led down onto the lower-level cells. At the commotion, a guard shouted to another below, but it seemed there were only the two of them, left behind on watch while the north door took everyone else's attention.

"Quick," Alisa said. "Before they see us."

Have mercy on my soul. I do what I must when there are greater matters at stake—

Celia drew her pistol, aimed over the railing, and shot the guards dead.

"I have this," she said, already running along the platform for the stairs. "Go back and help Rosalind!"

Alisa nodded, pushing through the door again. Before it could slam closed, Celia heard a faint scream on the other side. She didn't let it slow her frantic descent down the stairs; she could only hope the sound hadn't come from their side.

"Oliver?" She skidded in front of the first cell. Not him. Someone else, clothes tattered and handcuffs holding them to the floor. Most of the other prisoners didn't react to her presence, though none of them looked as if they were on the verge of death. One woman blearily lifted her head, and Celia could only assume that it was exhaustion keeping them to the corners of the cells instead of shaking the bars, wondering what was happening outside.

"Oliver!"

She spotted him at last in one of the farthest cells, the only one with some sort of bed. The guard had fallen dead nearby, and Celia scooped the keys from his belt, jamming each one into the lock on Oliver's cell until something fit. She heard a click. With a quick push, the bars were clattering open with a *thud-thud-thud*.

Why was Oliver *strapped down*?

"Oliver, can you hear me?" She grabbed at the first restraint she saw, trying to tug it free. It didn't budge. Beneath them, the white clothes Oliver had been put in were stained red—not enough to think that they had been cutting him into pieces, but enough to be mightily concerned.

She reached into her boot, pulling out a small penknife. Oliver seemed to come to consciousness while she sliced at the restraints, his eyes struggling to open. His hand jerked. As did his legs.

"Celia?" he murmured. "Am I hallucinating again?"

"No, it's me. Let me get the last one—" She cut through the restraint at his shoulder. Loosened from his hold, Oliver tried to move, but whatever they had done to him, he had turned delirious, almost tipping right to the floor.

"Hey, hey, *wait*—" Celia caught him. He was so warm that it was like touching a furnace. "I'm going to get you out, all right? But you need to tell me your capacity. Can you walk? Can you see?"

"They said . . . they said . . ."

She was going to take that as a no to both questions. It seemed that he had perceived her presence, but he wasn't registering the rescue effort. In fairness, an Oliver who was alert would have told her off the moment he saw her here. He would have given her a whole earful about how stupid it was to break into a Nationalist stronghold, and Celia was incredibly upset that she wasn't getting the lecture because that meant he was too injured to deliver it.

"Oliver," Celia said firmly. "Can you—"

"They ran off to evacuate the outer wings," he murmured. "Be careful."

Celia pressed the back of her hand to his forehead. The heat stung her skin. He was burning up beyond belief. "What are you talking about?"

He lolled onto her. With a gasp, Celia grabbed his shoulders, holding him steady. She could hear him struggling with each shaky breath and every strained effort to lift his head.

"Oliver," she demanded. This was too important to let slide. If he put in this much effort to warn her, she knew she needed to understand. "Why are they evacuating?"

He inhaled. Exhaled.

"Japan," Oliver managed. "Japan is bombing us."

40

"*Hello? Can anyone hear me?*"

Rosalind pressed her wire into her ear quickly, trying to catch that snippet of sound. A guard fired in her direction, missing her by the barest margin. She already had at least three bullets in her torso. It would probably take another minute before the first one was pushed out. In that minute, hopefully they would have won this fight.

"Oh my God," Rosalind said aloud. She shoved close to the wall, taking a moment to breathe so that she could speak into the earpiece. "Phoebe?! Is that you?"

More indecipherable sound. The walls were thick, impenetrable. The earpieces were already faulty on top of how difficult it was for their signal to stay stable.

"*. . . now! . . . my mother!*"

Rosalind slashed the closest guard when he lunged at her. He went down. Over her shoulder, two remained with Orion, but then Alisa burst back through the door and ran toward him to help, so Rosalind stayed where she was, pushing the wire farther into her ear.

"Phoebe, I can't hear you!"

"*. . . I said I'm here! I'm here in the facility!*"

"What?" Rosalind demanded. "How did you get here?"

"*. . . follow him. It's . . . can't!*"

Though the wire transmission was terrible, Rosalind could hear

Phoebe's breath coming short, like she was in a dead sprint while talking.

"You need to go somewhere with better signal." Rosalind dropped the hairpin in her hand, reaching for another. The poison needed replenishing after about five uses. Nearby, Orion took down his final opponent, then immediately grabbed Rosalind's elbow for her attention. He gestured silently to the windows, not wanting to interrupt Phoebe. A low hum was droning closer and closer outside. Airplanes.

". . . distraction . . . control tower."

"Hold on, hold on," Rosalind commanded. She pressed her microphone button hard, as if that might help Phoebe emit clearer. "You're still cutting out. Have you found Silas?"

"SILAS IS THE PROBLEM." Suddenly, Phoebe's voice boomed loud, entering a patch of perfect signal. *"He's working with my mother! She's not coming tonight! Silas has entered some sort of bargain to retrieve Oliver's blood for her—you can't just rescue Oliver; you need to destroy everything they took from him!"*

The fight in the corridor came to an abrupt end when Alisa brought down the last soldier by the door. In utter shock, the three of them exchanged glances, unable to believe what had just blared into their ears.

Celia must have been listening on her end too, because her voice interrupted the line then. First it was only a quiet: "Oh God." Then: "Okay, move fast. Move *now*. The Japanese have marched into Zhabei."

Rosalind's hand lowered from her earpiece. "What?"

Like the cosmic stage taking its cue for entrance, a colossal boom struck the facility. The ground shook. The ceiling rained with bits of rubble. Rosalind gasped, throwing her hands up, while Orion swore frantically, ducking to snatch a gun from one of the fallen soldiers.

"Christ," Alisa exclaimed. "This is such bad timing."

Another boom. There was a red flash from the night outside, as if fire had erupted upon landing. They were being shelled. Bombs were dropping on Zhabei.

"Rosalind!" Celia boomed over the earpiece. "Get over here now!"

They needed to move. They needed to get Oliver out and get themselves out, because if the district around the facility turned into a battlefield *while* they were performing a prison break, they would get stuck inside Zhabei.

"Go, go, go," Rosalind hissed.

They pushed through the south door, skidding onto the elevated platform above the cells. At the lower level, there waited Celia and a half-conscious Oliver smeared with blood.

"I've got him," Orion said once they had hurried down, taking him from Celia easily. "Which way?"

"Back the way we came," Alisa answered.

"Wait," Celia said. She hesitated. "Phoebe said we need to destroy the entire supply."

Alisa grimaced. "It's not in the cell?"

"No. The cell is empty."

The facility shuddered again, more vigorously this time. The shelling was getting closer. What would happen if a bomb landed directly atop them? Would the facility hold?

"I can go search," Alisa said. "I'm fast—"

"I'll do it," Rosalind interrupted. "It's much safer."

Celia was already turning on her heel. "I'll come—"

"No, *no,*" Rosalind snapped. "You make sure Orion gets Oliver out. Wait by the side door we came in through."

"But—"

"I'm immortal. I'll go alone," Rosalind cut in. "End of argument. Get out first."

"Rosalind—"

When the next boom came down, the entire facility seemed to tilt on its side. Though it righted itself quickly—it had only been the shudder of the impact, not the actual foundation shifting—the sensation scared Rosalind enough to draw a cold sweat down her spine.

"Celia, there's no use arguing," Alisa hissed. "You only need one person to smash a few vials."

"Fine." Celia turned to Rosalind. Her lips had tightened to a complete line. "If you encounter danger, you turn around and leave, do you understand? It's not worth risking your life."

Rosalind nodded. She would have nodded even if she didn't understand. Perhaps her sister knew that, because she gave her a glare so fierce it rivaled the bombing around the facility.

"Here." Alisa gave Rosalind her small gun. Rosalind accepted it without complaint. When she met Orion's eyes, he stayed quiet, but he didn't look happy.

"I won't be long, I promise," she said.

Before anyone could argue further, Rosalind bolted in the other direction, deeper into the facility.

Phoebe reloaded her rifle, her hand coming up momentarily to itch her nose beneath the fabric around her face. It was stifling hot in this part of the facility. Or maybe the stress of the situation was getting to her, drawing all her blood to her cheeks beneath the covering.

She pulled the trigger. Cleared another soldier out of the main hall at the north end.

"Phoebe?" Rosalind's voice crackled into her ear. "Where are you?"

Phoebe activated her microphone. "Don't you worry about me. Have you found the supply?"

"Not yet. I'm making my way to the control tower. I'm just not sure whether I can get through the inner facility without trouble."

"Keep going," Phoebe said. "You've got to pass the north door. It's open."

Her voice held a slight echo, even though the rest of the facility was in absolute havoc, alarms blaring at high volume. She was situated on a higher platform, tucked by a door that proceeded eastward. In that short gap when Rosalind and Celia were fighting through the south door and left the communication line idle, Phoebe had made it through the north door. She already knew what their tactics were—it wasn't hard to come prepared with a rifle she had stolen from one of the perimeter guards, to lie in the shadows and pick off the soldiers who were waiting for her.

Phoebe breathed deep, grimacing when the facility shook again. Usually, she never let herself linger long at the scenes she left behind. She was in and out: aim, shoot, run. The work of an assassin had to be quick. Whatever happened afterward was none of her business. Only the initial shot was.

A twitch was starting in her hands now. Phoebe was no soldier. Her training was ill-suited for war, for situating herself in one place wiping out endless opponents. If she kept seeing men fall dead, the images were going to sear into her mind permanently. Each shot left behind fallible flesh and corpses.

Phoebe adjusted her position. Scratched her nose again. A part of her felt like a traitor for shooting inside this facility when foreign enemies were bombing the city from the outside. Another part of her knew this had always been her job. She was a Communist assassin: from the very beginning, she had always been adding to internal strife.

Suddenly, Rosalind appeared within view, crossing through the door into the hall. The cells to each side had been cleared. Phoebe adjusted quickly, putting her eye to her scope again. She heard movement at the north door. There were new soldiers streaming in to close the ranks that Phoebe opened, which meant there would be combatants coming to meet Rosalind. The facility's intruder alarm was still screeching.

Phoebe pressed her earpiece again. "Keep moving."

Rosalind's expression flashed with terror. Her hand shot up to her ear. "There are soldiers."

"I have you covered."

"What?"

Phoebe breathed out. Aimed. When two soldiers went down, she pressed her earpiece again. "Move!"

Rosalind was clearly mouthing expletives below. Without activating her earpiece, nothing made its way up, so Phoebe could only guess what Rosalind was cursing frantically in French.

Rosalind darted forward. Phoebe adjusted on the platform, turning to the other side and directing her rifle toward the soldiers by the north door. She was giving up her position by shooting like this. She fired anyway, counting each shot that struck true. The moment Phoebe stepped into the fray, she had known what she was sending herself into. She had agreed with everyone around the table at the safe house, after all.

This was a foolproof plan to secure Priest and get Oliver out at the same time. The soldiers expected *her* to go after Oliver, and for as long as they were diverted toward this intrusion and combating her, it kept them away from the exit route that Oliver was actually taking. This was a sacrifice she was willing to make. If it meant that he would be safe, she would make the sacrifice a million times over.

A thud came from the other end of the platform. The door blew open. Phoebe scrambled upright at once, exposed on two sides when soldiers crossed the upper platform, closing in from the separate entrance. Though she had put herself in the corner, they sighted her immediately, which meant someone had sent them up there, finally pinpointing her location.

Whether or not she made it out of here alive was up to fate now. Phoebe had made her peace with it—Priest was never supposed to be an eternal deity. She had only been created to serve the people she loved.

Phoebe touched her ear. She said, "I'm going dark. I'll be all right," then pulled her wire out, dropping it to the floor before any of the soldiers could confiscate it. When the soldiers circled her, Phoebe pressed her foot over the earpiece and felt it break in two.

"Hands up, Priest," one said. "It's over."

She didn't reach for the trigger again. She set the rifle down and put her hands up.

I'm going dark. I'll be all right.

Rosalind didn't understand what had just happened. When she spoke into the earpiece again, she didn't get a response from Phoebe, nor from any of the others. They must have gone out of range.

The control tower was eerily empty. Each section echoed hollowly unto itself, the corridors dark and the windows shuttered. The evacuation effort had already cleared most of these rooms. Chances were high that the base would be rubble by the night's end, so there wasn't much point in guarding most of it anymore. The bombs were dropping so loudly that her eardrums were close to bursting, if the blaring alarm hadn't already shattered them.

Rosalind came to an abrupt stop around the corner. A group of soldiers hovered directly ahead. She reared back faster than a blink, pressing to the wall with a gasp. The facility shook again. Their surroundings screamed the song of carnage. When Rosalind was fairly certain that she hadn't been spotted, she craned her head around the corner again, trying to see who these people were. It was too hard to hear what they were saying, but she did make note of their darker clothes, which were different from what the Nationalists guarding the facility were wearing. Half split in one direction; the other half went left, passing Rosalind at the corner. She held her breath. Released it when they disappeared out of view.

Celia had put that call out, so they had known this would happen. A Communist presence had entered the facility too, hoping to secure Orion or come in contact with a vial that they still believed existed. It was rather annoying in retrospect because their mission hadn't needed to add this extra hazard for themselves, but at least it posed no threat. The rescue would continue.

"Keep moving," Rosalind muttered to herself. The Communists appeared to be going wide to search for their assets. She only had to avoid them.

On the first door she tried to open, the lock held firm. She timed her gunshot to another rumble from outside, then kicked the door open, caring little for whether it was obvious there had been a break-in. It wouldn't matter after tonight.

Inside, a cabinet was affixed to the far wall. An equipment cart blocked it, entirely cleared of tools except for a stack of tissues.

The building shuddered again. The bombs were getting louder. Closer.

Rosalind shoved the cart aside. Threw open the cabinet door to find it entirely empty. She was on the move in an instant, stepping back into the corridor and trying the next door.

There weren't too many rooms within the control tower, so she made fast work of her search. Rosalind had studied the blueprints well enough to determine that the lower level was the most likely place Silas could store something. Their actual control room was upstairs, alongside the wires and lights that controlled the doors around the facility. Nowhere to hide a dozen vials. It had to be here somewhere, unless he was *keeping* them with him . . . ?

Rosalind barged in through another room, this one piled heavily with blankets and threadbare prison uniforms. There weren't any cabinets or shelves to search through, so she knew in an instant that there was no chance she would find what she wanted.

Her gaze dropped. By the sink, though, there lay three broken glass shards and a crimson stain. As if someone had dropped a vial and smashed it, leaving it be rather than waste time cleaning it up. Was that blood? Had the supply been here previously and then moved?

Rosalind hovered in indecision. What was she to do? Find Silas? Shake an answer out of him, use force to stop him? He might have left the facility already, for all she knew.

The ground shuddered aggressively, almost throwing her off-balance. That was answer enough: it was time to get out. Everything else could be determined afterward. A terrible noise swept through the facility, cutting over the alarms. The stone walls were coming alive, screeching with a cry drawn from a centuries-old creature's stomach.

"Shit. Shit—"

Rosalind ran for it. The world was shaking without pause. She traced the same route back, keeping far from the walls in case any of them suddenly collapsed. The floor shuddered. Sections of the ceiling started to fall. When Rosalind skidded back into the row of cells where they had retrieved Oliver, she slammed into a wall of smoke.

At first she couldn't comprehend what had happened. She heard a gunshot. Voices. Then she outright tripped on a body in her path and fell, her hand coming down on a bloodied chest. Nationalist uniform. The soldier was dead.

"Retreat! No sign of asset!"

Rosalind had run directly into a battle between Nationalists and Communists. A paralyzing, noxious feeling of dread held her in place. She scarcely had time to back away or find another path when piercing white light suddenly flooded the cells—at last, a direct hit from overhead.

The sound was colossal. Metal and stone and brick tangled together before everything started to crash down, boxing her in.

Rosalind cried out, her arm flying over her eyes. Though the light faded swiftly, her vision was seared with a vivid imprint of the world afterward. Everything was doubled: the part of the cells that had collapsed to the left, the part of the stairs that had hollowed out in the center . . . and the man standing only a few paces away from her, pistol aimed at her head.

"Lang Shalin, get down!"

The facility groaned. Debris flew wide. When the gunshot fired, it was the end of the world and the beginning. At such close range, it should have landed somewhere high. Somewhere near her throat. Blown her head to bits.

But she felt nothing. There was only the sudden appearance of a figure right in front of her, hands clasped on her shoulders, his face obscured by a cloth. He stilled for a second. Then he crumpled.

Instinct kicked in. Before the soldier could aim again—she didn't even have time to determine which side he was on, couldn't read his uniform or pick out the details in the smoke—Rosalind retrieved her own gun from her sleeve and shot him, flinching at the way her arm surged back each time until, on the third, he went down.

What happened? What just happened?

She knew who lay in front of her.

"No, no, no—" Rosalind dropped to her knees. She yanked the cover off Dao Feng's face. "What is wrong with you? Why would you do that?"

"I thought I might find you here," Dao Feng said in reply. Though his breath was labored, he spoke easily, as though he was pleased to see her after a few months away, gone abroad on vacation.

Of course he would have attended this retrieval attempt. Of course he was among the Communists trying to secure Orion—if they were under the impression that Orion was still brainwashed, then it was Dao Feng who knew him, who might be able to get through to him.

"I cannot believe you," Rosalind gasped. What she had intended as a rebuke came out as a sob. "You taught me Fortune could survive anything!" Even though she knew that hit would have been fatal. Even though she knew he had just saved her life. Still, she demanded, "Why didn't you let me take it? Of all people, Fortune can *take it.*"

Dao Feng gave a small shake of his head. Blood bubbled up to his lips. Dripped one line down the side. "I was not protecting Fortune," he managed. "I was protecting Lang Shalin. You . . . are a person first and an operative . . . second. How many times have I taught you that?"

The bullet would have hit his back. There was so much blood. Her trouser fabric was soaking up the growing circle of red. Around them, one side was retreating, but Rosalind had no goddamn clue which was which. The smoke was too thick, muddying the scene.

"How dare you deliver me a life lesson now," she seethed. "You should have found me earlier. You should have explained yourself."

Rosalind had been here before: kneeling in that alleyway over Dao Feng's dying body, screaming for help. This time there was no help coming. This time it didn't matter how much she cried, because there was only her own person for witness.

Dao Feng shuddered. His hand lifted, and she hurried to grab it, squeezing tight.

"I'm glad I have a chance to speak to you," he managed.

Rosalind pressed her free hand to her mouth, trying to keep her tears back. They ran freely anyway, even if she made no noise.

"I *am* sorry," Dao Feng said, his voice dropping quieter, nearing a rasp. "I would have tried to convince you to come with me if it were easy. But you . . . were never meant for that sort of work, and I couldn't take you away from the duty you had issued yourself."

Rosalind tried to pull his shoulder. "Stop it," she commanded. "I'm going to get you out of here, and we're going to get to a hospital—"

"Listen outside, Lang Shalin." His breath snagged. The sound was terrible: the bullet must have hit his lungs. Too much blood trickled from his mouth. "Every hospital . . . piling with bodies. It is all right. It is all right."

"Please—"

Another bullet flew overhead. Rosalind looked over with a gasp, but it was Alisa who emerged in the smoke, her eyes widening when she finally caught sight of her.

"Rosalind," Alisa said, lowering her gun and hurrying over. Her eyes were vivid with panic. "Rosalind, they've got Priest—the alarm has stopped. The Nationalists are reconvening at any moment to clear the facility of Communists. We cannot be caught here."

Dao Feng's eyes closed. He gasped: "Go, Lang Shalin."

Rosalind wanted to hit him. No—she wanted him to sit up and flick her forehead, to tell her he was merely joking and these few months had been a well-designed test.

"How could you do this to me?" she demanded.

Alisa tugged her elbow. "Rosalind."

Dao Feng had stilled.

"No! You can't die! You're supposed to be my handler! Who am I supposed to listen to now? *Who?*"

Voices erupted in the smoke. Alisa made a strangled noise, her head swiveling to search for incoming Nationalists. Rosalind shook Dao Feng's shoulder again, but he was unresponsive.

"Dao Feng! Wake *up!*"

"Rosalind," Alisa said. She grabbed her arm properly. "I'm sorry—I'm so sorry, but we have to go. *We have to go!*"

Rosalind barely heard her. She knew it made her selfish, but the only thing that played over and over in her head at that moment was: *You can't leave me. You can't leave me* again.

"Come on!" At last Alisa managed to get a good grip on Rosalind and yanked her to her feet. Her hand tore from Dao Feng's. Alisa pulled her along, away from the body, away from the cells.

The last thing Rosalind saw among the rubble was that stain of red, and then her handler was out of sight, left behind amid the rest of the ruins.

41

"We have confirmed capture. Shepherd, initiate lockdown from control. Other intruders are attempting a retrieval."

Silas flicked the first few switches in front of him, watching the changes on the display board. Just as he was about to pick up his radio device and verify that they had truly locked Priest in—because she was wily enough to somehow slink away before then—a unit of covert agents returned to the control room.

"Quick, quick," one said. "Begin lockdown before they escape."

There were huge portions of the base hit by the overhead bombing. This timing had been less than ideal, though it wasn't as if the Japanese cared about asking which hour suited its conquests best.

"Of course," Silas returned. The display board winked its lights at him. He knew the other intruders were Communists following Celia's report. The Nationalists thought they were trying to break Oliver out, if the chaos of battle sounding over the radio lines was any indication. The control tower kept track of which doors were open, which were closed, and which were nonresponsive. He could trace the exact path his friends had taken for entry, following the red lights that signaled maintenance on the door. When Silas looked wider, however, there were multiple doors nonresponsive in places he knew his friends had not touched. They required a complete lockdown to cut those paths off.

But he couldn't do that until the rescue mission got out.

"Shepherd, initiate lockdown," his superior demanded again, the radio overwhelmed with static. "What's taking so long?"

With a wince, Silas moved the sliders on the control panels, watching the lights in every sector change color. There was little he could say to buy time. He could only hope that his friends had moved fast. If they were already at the outer facility, then this wouldn't affect them.

He smacked the glass case closed, cutting off access to the main control panel. Now that part was out of his hands. There was another matter, far more pressing.

Silas stood up. Cast a glance at the other operatives, busy with their work. The bombing had reached a lull.

"I'm going to go oversee the completion of Priest's capture."

One of the operatives glanced up. "They put her in the west sector. Infrastructure is most sound there after all the bombing," he reported. "The soldiers said it was like handling a feral animal. Almost bit Jiang's finger off for trying to remove her covering."

Silas frowned. "What was he doing touching her anyway?"

"Hey, don't ask me." The operative put his hands up. "Just trying to make your job easier, all right? You can deal with it."

To tell the truth, he hadn't wanted to give Priest up. He hadn't wanted to turn her over to the Nationalists, at the mercy of soldiers who had full permission to use torture if they weren't hearing what they wanted. But what was he to do? They had assigned him this task. First and foremost, catching Priest had been Shepherd's priority mission. It had been a matter of improving national cohesion, of solving their internal issues before the country could fight off its foreign invaders. It was his own fault he had grown so attached. It was his fault that he had wandered astray somewhere along the line, trying to fill this hole in his chest. National responsibility used to be enough. Now he was turning his head toward personal fascination, acting as if Priest were a friend he needed to care for rather than an enemy to capture.

What had happened to him?

Silas shook off his thoughts, picking up the portable radio in case his superiors wanted to contact him again. He stepped out, taking the stairs down to the ground level of the control tower. The lights had gone out in the corridors. A row of gas lanterns lit the entryway instead, varying shades of gold and white-blue. Whatever battle had occurred here was now over. Still, the hallways loomed ominously in the dark. The stone walls garnered an echo, but the metal-padded corridors were no better, resembling an oversized cage.

Silas greeted the soldiers guarding the west sector. One of them was covered in blood, though he looked uninjured.

"Third cell," the soldier said, gesturing for Silas to proceed. "Shout if you need us."

Silas could feel his pulse pounding in his throat. It wasn't as if he was *nervous*. It was hard to describe what he was, because the culmination of so much work was cresting to this result in front of him, yet if he were honest with himself, he wasn't sure what this result would bring him. Priest's capture wouldn't be any help getting Orion back anymore. Priest's capture alone couldn't help them win the civil war.

He needed to see her. That was all. He needed to know that he had a purpose in this city, and he was capable of achieving it.

Silas walked toward the cell. The radio in his hands buzzed.

"Shepherd, report."

A burst of static. He ignored it.

Priest was in the corner. Dressed in black, just as his friends had been when they broke in too.

"Hello," he said. "You will have to forgive me for deceiving you like this. It was a matter of necessity."

"I could have." Priest's voice was a shock. Much sweeter than he expected. Much more . . . familiar than he could have guessed. She still had her back to him, facing the corner of the cell. "But is this the worst that you've done?"

"Shepherd. Shep . . . come in . . . Shepherd?"

Silas turned the radio off, sheer incomprehension slowing his movements. He knew this silhouette. He knew exactly who was standing before him.

There had been a mistake. They had caught the wrong person, made a mix-up inside the facility when the soldiers were pursuing intruders.

Silas gripped the bars. "Don't worry," he said in a rush. "Don't worry. I'll get you out."

"Why?" Phoebe turned around. "You've worked so hard to put me in here, Magician."

42

Each hallway they barreled through was locking before their eyes, doors switching over to red and fences coming down from the overhead mechanism. Rosalind barely avoided getting a foot trapped under a rolling plate of metal, stumbling forward into safety by a hairsbreadth.

"Hold my hand," Alisa huffed from ahead, extending her arm.

"What? Why?" Despite her confusion, Rosalind reached out anyway and grabbed Alisa's hand. "Do you see something?"

"No." They hurtled past the next hallway. "I'm offering emotional support."

The situation was so ludicrous that Rosalind almost laughed. Except it seemed any sort of strong response triggered the twist in her throat, because she let out another sob instead.

Alisa audibly winced. They were either near or already in the outer facility, if the change in door markings was any indication. Rosalind was relying on Alisa to lead them to the exit. Though she had memorized the blueprints too, she was hardly at capacity to identify which sectors they had already passed, especially when many of the areas were now marred by smoke and dust. The damage had been much worse in other parts of the base.

"I understand wanting to curl up and have a cry. Trust me, I *really* do," Alisa said. "But right now you have to stop sniffling because it's going to mess up your vision. And you need to see properly if we're going to make our way out."

Rosalind wiped her eyes hard. It cleared her sight, but not by much. At least clutching Alisa's hand, holding on to something solid, something rooted in the real world, did help her gather her bearings. "How much farther?"

"Not much. The metal gate that almost cut you in half pushed us into the outer facility."

The walls blurred. Smoldered. Though the worst of the overhead attack seemed to have passed, the floor beneath their feet would still tremble at intervals as it picked up aftershocks from elsewhere.

"Make a left."

Rosalind turned on Alisa's command. She could barely feel each footstep anymore. The world was made up of echoes and shadows, and she moved through it accordingly.

"We're almost—*aaah!*"

They halted just before a part of the ceiling could smash directly atop them, thudding onto a pile of rubble instead. Most of the outer facility was built with steel and metal, which meant the ceiling coming down had also collapsed an entire vent in their path.

"Which way?" Rosalind said, breathless. "We can't go through."

Alisa tried to push at the rubble. It shifted an indiscernible inch. "This is the *only* way through."

Rosalind attempted to help push. They were trying to move a whole hallway: she wasn't even surprised that nothing budged.

"There has to be another route out."

"We would have to circle back." Alisa gave the vent a kick. Something echoed on the other side, though it didn't sound like it was made by the same motion. "*Ugh.* Where's Orion when you need him?"

". . . here . . . be patient."

The faintest voice snuck through the rubble. Rosalind lurched close to the blockage, trying to catch the sound again. "Orion?"

A piece of steel moved out of place. A circular hole opened in the obstruction.

"As I was saying," he exclaimed. "I'm here. Move back, please."

Rosalind and Alisa gave the rubble wide berth at once. Orion pushed with effort, and then a section of the vent fell loose from its cloistered pile, opening the slightest path.

"Come on," he called.

Alisa climbed in first, muttering under her breath as a lock of her hair got caught on a sharp edge of broken metal. On the other side, Orion maneuvered her over a hefty chunk of metal, then gestured for Rosalind to hurry too.

She climbed through. Landed in the pile of debris.

"Hey, hey, hey," Orion said, stopping her the moment she crossed to his side. He tipped her chin up, getting a proper look at her face. "What happened in there?"

Her throat constricted. She shook her head. Orion didn't wait for her to manage an answer. He reached for her and brought her into his arms, clasping her close.

"It's all right," he whispered into her hair. "It's all right, beloved."

"Dao Feng. He's dead." Her tears had dried. There was only its remaining hollowness, gnawing up her insides. "He had to go and save me, that *fool*."

Though Orion had no recollection who Dao Feng was, though he couldn't have known more than the brief few pieces Rosalind had told him to summarize their past mission, his hold tightened like he was sharing her sorrow.

"Old man," Orion murmured, mimicking her description when she had drawn that web of names. "Pain in the ass until the very end."

Rosalind choked out a sniveling laugh. It was pathetic and miserable, but it captured her heart exactly.

"Let's go," Orion said, glancing at the rubble barrier. The building trembled again. "Before this buries us."

Rosalind nodded. It was an exhausting effort picking through the final corridor, and the exit was barely intact. When they finally made their way out, the air felt stifling hot. A thin aura of red lined the night sky. The horizon appeared to glow with light.

Not light . . . fire.

"Thank goodness," Celia said. She was on the grass, kneeling beside Oliver. "I was about to pass out from fright when the passageway collapsed."

"Was it bombed after you got out?" Alisa asked, frowning. Her head craned up, trying to make sense of the situation.

"No, the bombing has passed this area now," Orion answered. "Everything collapsed a few minutes after we exited. There's damage across the whole base that's taking a while to settle."

Rosalind clutched her arms. All the little hairs at the back of her neck were standing straight. Smoke, thick and impenetrable, clogged up the distance.

"Does anyone know what happened to Phoebe? Or how she even knew that Silas sold us out?"

Better yet—*why* would Silas do something like that?

Silence across the clearing. A few moments later, Alisa cleared her throat.

"I was in range by the time I came looking for you," she said. "I heard your last exchange. It sounded like Phoebe is hiding out until things clear. We should do the same."

Nothing made sense. But Alisa was right: they needed to go. They needed to find the vehicle that Silas had left by the perimeter and leave before either the Nationalists caught them or the oncoming war incinerated them.

"How's Oliver?" Rosalind asked.

He seemed alert enough to respond to his own name, waving

his arm for an answer. His head, however, was drooped while he sat upon the grass. If Rosalind didn't know better, she would have said he was either under extreme fatigue or drunk out of his mind.

"One bad wound at his side," Celia reported. She winced. "It needs medical attention, but it's still not enough to cause this state of . . . whatever this state is. I worry that he's poisoned."

"Let me see." Rosalind hurried to him, mimicking Celia's crouch on his other side and pressing her fingers to his pulse. She was an expert where poison was concerned. This didn't resemble the symptoms of any poison she could name.

"Celia," he mumbled, trying to push her away. "Ow."

"I'm not Celia," Rosalind replied.

Oliver continued resisting. Rosalind held on for another few seconds, then put her hand on his forehead. Blistering hot.

"It's not poison," Rosalind decided. "I want to guess that it's blood loss to dangerous levels, but . . ."

"I can do a transfusion," Celia said immediately. "We're the same blood type. They made us test in the event of an emergency on missions, so—"

"Wait." Rosalind peeled back his shirt slowly, taking a look at his wound. They hadn't bandaged him up the last time they took blood from him. The circular lesion itself was angry and red, but the surrounding area was a chalky sort of blue. Celia was right: this was going to need surgery, preferably sooner rather than later. "If it was blood loss, he would be cold, not hot. And his heartbeat would be going fast, but it's perfectly normal at the moment, which . . ."

Rosalind trailed off. Which wasn't normal for him at all, actually. "Orion, come here."

Orion followed instructions. He kneeled down, and Rosalind put her hand to his neck, counting his pulse. Prior to Phoebe's findings, she couldn't believe she had never noticed this detail about him. There had been multiple occasions when she had been pressed up right against his heartbeat, hearing its rapid thudding under her ear, and she had always brushed it off to the situation at the time.

His was going much, much faster than Oliver's. And this time, she didn't think it was caused by the situation. It was his resting heart rate. The resting rate for their altered blood.

"I think they took too much too quickly," Rosalind whispered. "Too much blood, but more importantly, too much of the material created *in* his blood by his mutated genes." His body was reacting to the loss. The normal pulse wasn't normal for Oliver, so everything else was overcompensating. "A transfusion isn't going to help because his body needs to be generating more of that sera-whatever Lady Hong passed on to him, not just blood."

Oliver's head tipped up with effort, trying to join the conversation. As he blinked, however, he finally caught sight of Orion for the first time, and his brow furrowed at once, uncomprehending. *"Liwen?"*

Orion looked stricken. He seemed torn between a friendly smile upon instinct and, at the same time, a snarl given what he had been told of their past history. He settled for something in between, his teeth clacking together to make a neutral grimace. "Forgive me, gē." His grimace grew even more awkward. "I have a rather terrible case of amnesia."

"What?" Oliver murmured. His head tipped forward again. He had expended all his energy for that short exchange.

Celia looked terrified. "If he's in this state because his body lacks his mysterious genetic substance," she said, "how do we help him?"

"I don't know." Rosalind searched for a good answer, for some way to put her sister at ease. She came to a complete blank. "We wait for it to replenish itself, I suppose. The hospitals must be in shambles right now. Our best bet is finding a safe house and bunkering down."

Rosalind got to her feet shakily. She held her hand out to help Orion—more for something to do than because he actually needed the aid—but he took it nonetheless, rising straight.

"I'll drive," he declared.

43

Refugees were flocking to Zhabei's district lines, trying to make their way into the neighboring International Settlement. Most would be stopped—the foreigners wouldn't allow the masses to enter at such high volume for fear of the chaos it would create. It was their land, after all, and they could decide who they did and did not let in. From here, Rosalind could see some of the foreigners milling near their hotels and restaurants on the other side of the Suzhou Creek, curious about what was happening over in Chinese jurisdiction.

Gunfire echoed nonstop around the North Railway Station, traveling down to where they were hiding. Rosalind flinched at every impact and boom, her fists tightening. She peered around the alley corner again, surveying the crowd flocked by the bridge. The scene hadn't changed from the last five times she had looked. The Municipal soldiers were very careful about who they permitted to cross the barrier. Those crossing who were Chinese were always well dressed and likely had property in the International Settlement. Or some connection to the foreigners, making a phone call to pluck them away from the war zone that would devastate those without the means and wealth. Those crossing who were foreign themselves—much fewer in number—were quickly ushered through the moment they approached the bridge's barbed wire, not needing to say a single word.

Even if they attempted to send Alisa over the bridge first, that still left the rest of them. Besides, in this state, a Municipal soldier would take one look at her and see that she wasn't a *Western* foreigner, which was rather necessary for entry into the International Settlement.

"Hey," Celia said quietly, coming to stand by Rosalind's side. She had set Oliver down in the alley, letting him rest with Orion watching him.

Rosalind swallowed hard. "Hey," she replied. "Is Oliver holding on?"

"His bleeding isn't getting worse, but it's not going to get any better, either. We need to get to proper shelter."

"I know." Rosalind's voice had dropped to a whisper, though not by intention. She was finding it so hard to speak. "I'm trying to think."

They couldn't stay in Zhabei. It didn't matter if they went back to the safe house or found a comfortable nook or took refuge in an emptied shop. The bombing wasn't going to stop. Another wave had started in the distance, and the fighting between Japanese Marines and the Chinese 19th Route Army was overwhelming the streets. They had barely made it south by car, taking the smaller alleys, before realizing they couldn't drive farther without encountering some sort of barricade like the one in front of them, clustered with crying civilians.

Pain bloomed across Rosalind's palms. She didn't notice that she was doing it to herself until she looked down in surprise and found nail grooves carved into her skin.

"Can we help them?" Rosalind asked.

Her voice broke on that simple question. Her sister didn't need to ask what she was talking about. Celia folded her arms in front of herself tightly.

"Trust me, I want to as well," she answered. "But we can barely help ourselves. There is little we can do here."

Celia was far better at keeping the quaver back, though it tried to push into her words. Had it always been like this? Was this contrast new? In her mind's eye, Rosalind could picture the days when she went around the world aloof, when she used to press her finger into soft places and never cared to check what bruises she made. It was so much easier back then. Her heart had always felt strange and isolated, but if it also meant she was rid of this terrible *ache* now . . .

"They're going to die," Rosalind whispered. Overhead, a plane zipped through the red-toned night. It whined like that of a murderous insect, only a thousand times louder, looming over the very world with its poison sting. "So many people are going to die."

While this part of the city became a grappling ground, the people took the brunt. Japan marched its claim in and scrambled desperately for land, but it wasn't the soil that would bleed; it was real, living people.

Celia reached out. Carefully, she took Rosalind's left hand and started to pull, urging Rosalind to loosen her terrible clench.

"You have to remember"—Celia kept tugging, one finger after the other—"our job is to minimize. Tamp down fires before they erupt. Build dams before floods break. We are not an army. We are not a government."

"We are not regular people either," Rosalind countered with a rasp. Now that her palm was open, her hand felt detached from the rest of her body. Cold and unfeeling, barely registering Celia's touch. "*I* am not."

At the edge of the crowd, there was a woman trying to push her child forward. Various civilians helped her along, conversation screaming back and forth, words funneling into the wind. It was hard to tell what the resolution of the matter was, because although the Municipal soldiers didn't lift the barricade, one came forward and hurried to walk the woman elsewhere, as if there was an alternate route to take. A clump of the crowd decided to follow. The rest remained, taking their chances with the bridge they had already selected.

"You might be immortal," Celia said, "but you are not an army."

"Celia—"

"No, listen to me." Her sister was firm. Unyielding. "Can you use any of this immortality to get us over the bridge? What are you going to do? Sacrifice yourself in a blaze of bullets and fire? What would that achieve except a great spectacle? War isn't a place for heroes, Rosalind. War is a place for survival until those above us have tired us out."

Dao Feng's face flashed in her mind. His shuddering breath, his final words.

You are a person first and an operative second. How many times have I taught you that?

Rosalind wanted to tear at the sky, rip apart all those who hovered above them. But she was one girl, not an army, and she could do nothing except eye the clouds and hope the skies didn't descend down on her.

"I know we have barely had contact these past few years," Celia said softly, continuing when Rosalind remained silent. "So forgive me if I seem like I am lecturing you. But in the beginning, I had to learn my lesson too. It took Oliver nearly a year to shake it into me. If I am to do some good, then I must make peace with my own limits. I would lose perspective otherwise."

A loud boom rang across the district then, into the alley. When Rosalind closed her eyes briefly, two twin teardrops fell on either side, but that was the extent of it.

"I'm sorry," Rosalind said.

Though she couldn't see her sister, she knew that Celia was confused. "Whatever for?"

"I should have stayed in touch. I had no idea."

The night shuddered. Celia released her hand, but only so she could squeeze her elbow. "You do now, though."

Rosalind opened her eyes. Looked out at the bridge again.

"All right," she said, and her voice rang loud. She turned around in the alley, addressing the others. "The fighting can't cross into the International Settlement unless the Japanese also want to declare war on the Western foreigners, so we should try to take shelter there until we can figure out our next steps."

Alisa tapped her hands against the sides of her head. "I could pretend to be British."

"Alisa Montagova," Rosalind said dully. "You do not seem British."

"I could *pretend*."

"I would much sooner believe you were Chinese before I believed you were British."

Alisa sighed. "It's the eyebrows, isn't it?"

Rosalind made no comment. She glanced at Orion next, who stood with his arms crossed.

"I'm no help—I have little recollection of this city's geography," he said. "I hardly know where the Suzhou Creek runs to."

Oliver said something. His head was slumped so his words became swallowed, but Orion crouched immediately, nudging his brother and asking, "What was that?"

"House. Our house. Right there."

Rosalind blinked. She peered out the alley again, eyeing the bridge and the water banks on the other side. He was right. The Hong residence was *in* the International Settlement, no more than ten minutes past the border from here.

"How did I not think of that?" she said aloud. "We have a perfectly valid reason to be crossing over. And a safe place to go."

"Sure," Celia said. "If every single one of our faces wasn't recognizable for arrest the moment we approach that bridge."

Rosalind eyed the row of shops at the other end of the alley.

Some glass windows were shattered. They would have to move quickly, before more soldiers arrived. Before bullets started flying. While she could scratch herself up again as an excuse, it would probably be rather suspicious if they all did it. But then again . . .

"It's winter," Rosalind said simply. "Who said we had to show our faces?"

The night was incandescent in the north. Orion had never wished harder that he could summon his memory back. Anything—*anything* to be helpful, other than standing guard at the door to the dress shop, letting everyone else do the debating and planning while they rummaged for costumes.

He was concerned about Rosalind.

Eldest-born, some voice whispered at the back of his head. It stuttered, halted, then emitted another person's echo into his ear: *You remind me of Oliver sometimes. The seriousness. The world on your shoulders.*

He blinked, trying to push harder into the vague wisps of that memory. By deduction, it felt as though Orion himself must have said that to Rosalind. Yet his head was such a wreck that it was impossible to tell fact from fiction, the pieces that held truth from the past and the pieces he might have created just to make some sense of their present. He remembered comparing her to Oliver. But if he hadn't had a good relationship with Oliver, then why—

"Shit." A terrible pain danced along his forehead. There and gone, quick as an electric signal. His breath blew a white cloud around him, misting against the cold seeping into the shop. They had barely needed to break in: it had been too easy to reach through the shattered window and open the door from the inside. Judging by the cup of tea still warm on the front desk, the dress shop had only just been abandoned.

Orion turned his head experimentally. The moment he looked at his brother leaning upon the wall in the far corner, however, the pain surged back. His memories pushed to be heard in unison, and as a consequence, he could hear almost nothing except the loudest of flashes. It wasn't that he didn't have a good relationship with Oliver, the roar wanted to tell him. He was angry and he was betrayed, but with every harsh word and threat of violence he delivered, it was because he missed Oliver so badly, because he had been left behind when he wanted the big brother who took him around Paris on his short visits and bought him ice cream—

"Orion!"

He snapped out of his daze. Rosalind was suddenly in front of him, patting his face.

"I called your name multiple times," she said carefully. "Are you okay?"

"Yes," Orion answered at once. He ignored the new burgeoning ache in his skull. "What's going on?"

Rosalind pulled a scarf around him, bundling the fabric close to his neck. She had been funneling clothes over while she searched, dressing him first while the others murmured their suggestions. Thick wool coats and nice vests. A change of socks. Orion had asked what soldier would even see those, but Rosalind had been insistent, saying that the disguise needed to be accurate down to the bone if they were going to claim a residence in the International Settlement.

"The most laughable part," Rosalind had muttered earlier, "is that this is your usual wardrobe, you know that?"

Orion didn't understand why it was laughable. "The items we are presently stealing?"

"It shouldn't even count as stealing. We are reuniting you with your typical fashion. You owned a vest just like this." Rosalind's mouth twitched when she helped him into it. "I should know, since your clothes were taking up so much of my closet space."

She had been quiet since their escape from the base, her eyes shadowed with redness. Orion had a feeling that this feigned sense of normalcy was more for everybody else's sake than her own, to make sure she was the last person anyone needed to fuss over. Even when he tried to offer concern, reaching out to inspect a bit of blood behind her ear, Rosalind shrugged him off, saying that there was nothing that required his attention. If there had been a scratch or an injury, it had long since smoothed over. No mark or scar left behind.

"These are for you too," Rosalind said after securing his scarf. She opened her palm, revealing a set of cuff links. "Wrists, please."

Orion held his wrists out obediently. He felt a flash of a memory. This one, at least, wasn't accompanied by pain.

"You seem very familiar with dressing me," he remarked. "I feel like an overgrown child."

"A man-baby, one might say," Rosalind agreed. She waited a beat, then smoothed her thumb along the inside of his wrist. It drew a shiver out of him instantly, though Rosalind didn't seem to notice. "No, I only jest. You dressed yourself. I just liked helping with the smaller details."

She slid one of the cuff links in place. Orion was trying very hard to interpret what that meant.

"Such as cuff links."

"Yes, such as cuff links." Rosalind put the other one in. "The last time I did this, you said I was fussing like a real wife. It sent me into a great big huff."

Orion frowned. "Did I say it meanly? I apologize."

Rosalind's gaze flickered up. His sleeves were finished, but she still hadn't let go.

"No," she said. "I was angry because you were right, and I didn't want to admit that it pleased me."

Before Orion could respond, Rosalind's sister was calling for her attention, bundling a ginormous stack of hats across the shop. Rosalind clearly wasn't fast enough for whatever Celia wanted her for, because Celia's bundle tipped over just as she reached Alisa, and Alisa squealed, throwing her hands over her face as she became buried under the hats.

"Don't worry about me," Alisa called, her words muffled. "I've always wanted to try being a hat rack for a career."

Celia rolled her eyes. She reached into the hat pile and fished Alisa out.

"We're ready," she decided. She picked up a particularly wide-brimmed hat and stuck it on Alisa's head. Then she selected one for herself. "Best to cover your hair. Tuck in as much as you can."

Alisa nodded, grabbing a fistful of blond curls and shoving them away. Meanwhile, Rosalind sighed, reaching to adjust Orion's wooly scarf again.

"Remember," she warned, "this cannot leave your face. I need you shivering like you might drop into an icicle if a soldier so much as suggests lowering the fabric."

Orion nodded. He would take her lead. Or Celia's, actually, because she wasn't as recognizable as Rosalind and thus less likely to get them caught.

Rosalind lifted her own scarf, covering her face. "Let's go."

They left the shop, one after the other, before Alisa closed the door tightly. Orion felt as though he were moving in a dream, crossing the street again, nearing the crowd gathered by the bridge. He felt as though someone were plucking his strings to work his limbs, tipping his head up at the dark sky, watching crimson-red blood run through the night clouds before it bled onto the pavements.

"You're in charge of him now," Celia whispered, gently pushing Oliver against him.

She might as well have handed Orion a live grenade. He hurried to grab his brother's arm. "Me?"

"Make it look natural. If I hold on to him, it'll be obvious that he keeps drifting off."

"I am *not* drifting off," Oliver grumbled.

Orion bit his tongue. Indeed, Celia was a head shorter, so no amount of balance on her part kept Oliver walking in a straight line. Orion, meanwhile, could haul Oliver's arm over his shoulder and pull him along easily. Like they were as close as ever, clasped in a brotherly embrace while on a stroll.

"I'm not hurting you, am I?" Orion asked.

Oliver huffed, as if that very thought was preposterous. "Do you think I am made of porcelain?"

"Don't force me to test that out."

"You wouldn't dare."

Orion pretended to stumble. Oliver snapped, "Liwen!"

His chiding tone was so familiar. Vivid recognition rippled up and down Orion's spine with the sensation of a chill, the same feeling he got when he looked at these city streets, the same feeling when Rosalind touched his hand. The memories were right *there,* right within grasp, and yet he couldn't seem to reach them without straining himself beyond capacity.

"Tripped on a pebble," Orion said, teasing.

Seeing that they were proceeding well, Celia hurried forward and looped an arm through Rosalind's, getting into character before they approached the crowd.

Orion tightened his hold on Oliver. He glanced at his brother once. Then, again. "Forgive me if this is a silly question." It wasn't the place nor the time to be having this discussion, yet Orion suddenly couldn't stop himself. Before he could think better of it, he continued: "But there was a lot of opposition when I insisted on coming along to get you. Everyone seemed to think that if I had my memories, I wouldn't have done it."

"Yes," Oliver replied in an instant. "They're right."

Orion frowned. "Why?"

"Liwen, the last time you saw me, you threatened physical violence. And the time before that. And the time before *that*."

His brother sounded tired. Maybe it was the situation at present; maybe it was a byproduct of the crowd swallowing them in, frantic and worried and scared. Celia and Rosalind had started to push through, murmuring their apologies for the jostling.

"Why?" Orion repeated. He was having such a hard time imagining himself like that. He didn't feel like the type to anger, especially if it concerned the people around him. All the same, everything he had been told gave him the impression that he hated his own brother.

Oliver was quiet for a moment. He seemed like he wouldn't answer the question, too exhausted keeping up the facade of appearing normal to waste more energy on the conversation. It wasn't until they were almost at the front that Oliver sighed and said:

"Because I abandoned you. I abandoned you once, and then I kept abandoning you over and over again each time I left you to fend for yourself." A pause. "I had always suspected our parents to be more guilty than what the courts concluded. I had always suspected that Māma was more involved than she let on, that Bà couldn't have thought of this alone. You caught me rummaging through his office a few months ago." Oliver winced, turning to see if that reminder rang familiar to Orion.

It didn't. Orion couldn't remember it. "Were you looking for evidence to turn him in?"

Oliver faced the front again. A cold gust blew at them. "No. I didn't care who the Kuomintang did or didn't lock up. I was looking for evidence to show Feiyi. Because if she had proof, then she could convince you as well, and the two of you could pull away. I should have worked faster. I should have prioritized it and kept digging beyond checking the obvious places. I'm sorry—I am. By the time I found concrete proof of our mother's work in Warehouse 34, so much was in motion that it was too late to get to you. I could have prevented this from the very beginning."

There it is, Orion thought suddenly. That was why he had that memory of telling Rosalind she reminded him of Oliver. The two of them possessed the exact same attitude. Holding the entire world on their shoulders and blaming themselves when it felt too heavy.

"We've been carrying this gene since birth," Orion said plainly. "You couldn't have stopped anything."

"And yet you were the one who got experimented on," Oliver countered. "Not me."

"I am literally supporting half your weight right now because you have a hole in your ribs."

Oliver furrowed his brow, set to argue, but then Celia gestured for their attention ahead, and they both snapped to attention, surveying the barrier. Though no one could see his expression past the scarf, Orion was apologetic with his grimace when he hurried forward, adjusting his grip on Oliver's arm to keep his brother moving in tandem.

Celia reached the front. She pretended to trip, coming close to the barrier and grabbing it before rearing back with a hiss. Rosalind pretended to fuss over her. Orion was holding his breath when two of the Municipal soldiers approached.

"Please, Officer." Celia's voice wafted back with the wind. The first Municipal soldier was Chinese, but his companion behind him was foreign. She switched to French and turned her pleading to him instead: "Our father will be so worried about us. We only came here on an outing. We didn't think we would get stranded."

"Who is your father?" the soldier asked. He shuffled forward. His tone was kind, responding in French too.

"General Li," Celia said, lying so smoothly that Orion would have believed her if he hadn't witnessed their plan to pick the most common name and hope for the best. "We live along Bubbling Well Road. We need to get home."

The soldier lifted his gaze, searching beyond her shoulder. "Who are your companions?"

"My siblings."

"All of them?"

"We're a big family."

His eyes stopped on Alisa.

"Lisabeth, however, is a friend," Rosalind contributed, her French much huskier than Celia's. She faked a big shiver, sinking deeper into the fur at her shoulders. "Our next-door neighbor. Your mother is probably worried sick too, no?"

"She's probably breathing into a paper bag," Alisa supplied. "We really must get back."

While the charade was hard at work before him, Orion shifted on his feet, nudging Oliver's arm away the smallest fraction to avoid the appearance of holding him up. Since they were stationary, he had high hopes that Oliver could hold strong—or at the very least, not pitch forward in a heap.

"I am releasing you a tad," Orion warned in a whisper.

"I will be fine," Oliver whispered back. He winced visibly, his arm moving to brace against his wounded side. Though his coat covered most of it, a sliver of the shirt that Rosalind had given him was sticking out from the bottom. The shirt was supposed to be white. Not red-and-white striped.

"Christ, you are *bleeding,*" Orion muttered, reaching over and nudging the shirt back under the coat. While Celia continued talking, one of the other soldiers had come forward to inspect them, and Orion could feel his eyes moving past the girls, coming to rest on him instead. It couldn't look like he was helping Oliver. It couldn't look like Oliver was injured at all.

"It's not bad."

Orion held back his incredulous look. His brother was absurd.

"I am not afraid to hold your hand if you start leaning away, dàgē," Orion hissed.

"It's very hard to sound threatening to someone who used to change your diapers."

The other soldier seemed satisfied by his cursory inspection. He walked away, his attention summoned by an elderly woman leaning over, wanting to speak to him, and Orion tugged Oliver's arm back over his shoulders, hurrying to secure him again. He frowned.

"I might not have any memory," he muttered, "but I can do math. You could not possibly have changed *that* many diapers."

What was taking so long? They had been going back and forth for long enough now that it was feeling suspicious. If they were really children of International Settlement elites, this wouldn't be allowed to stand. The soldiers clearly *believed* them when Rosalind, Celia, and Alisa spoke French so fluently. Yet the soldiers weren't lifting the barrier.

Orion shifted forward. He nudged between Rosalind and Celia, breaking into the conversation. God, he really, really hoped his accent had improved since that memory with Rosalind in front of the cinema—

"Sir, we can find a telephone line and bid our father to call if that is preferable." *Thank God.* His French was tinged ever-so-British but still acceptable. Orion nudged against Oliver, bumping him as if he were getting his attention for agreement. "If he asks why we weren't let through to begin with, though, I worry that causes more havoc on your end, especially when you have so many other people to process. . . ."

Orion waved carelessly behind his shoulder. In support, Oliver made a very ambiguously French sound as the extent of his contribution.

A second passed. The wind blew cold. The sky shuddered with sound.

The first Municipal soldier finally nodded. He gestured for his companion to move the wooden barricade. To pull aside the barbed wire, open a path for them to come through. It worked. It had *worked*.

Orion resisted a premature celebration, keeping his expression neutral. Celia passed through. As did Rosalind and Alisa.

"One second."

Orion froze before he could start walking. His heart lurched to his throat. Threatened to beat directly out of his chest and onto the bridge. It was going to land in the gravel as a rapidly pulsating red organ, and then this whole endeavor would fall apart when the soldiers saw how fast it was going and deduced him to be an altered human experiment.

"You dropped this." The soldier bent down, reaching for something in the ground. When he straightened, he extended his hand to Celia, and the overhead streetlamp showed the item in his palm to be a small earring. It must have fallen from her ear when the scarf nudged at the backing.

"Oh, merci," Celia said, taking it. "That's an expensive thing. It would have been terrible to lose."

Behind them, the crowd groaned with injuries and wounds and ragged clothing. Many held their belongings in fabric bags clutched close to their chest, the extent of everything precious they owned able to be scooped up in one motion and taken out the door.

"Safe travels," the Municipal soldier said.

Orion pulled them through, stepping onto the bridge. Oliver managed to keep his gait straight. Though Orion craned over his shoulder and watched the soldiers push the barrier back into place, he was quick to face forward again while they walked. It felt too suspicious to look any longer. The expectation would be to hurry away, put Zhabei out of view.

"I feel as though we just colluded with the enemy," Orion muttered under his breath. He had done plenty of that in these few months. It was apparently *all* he had been doing, used as a weapon for matters he had no say in. Yet now, even with his agency restored, why did he still feel like he was turning with the grain instead of going against it?

"Suck it up," Oliver replied, not unkindly.

Orion glanced back once more. *Last time,* he told himself, taking in the scene they were leaving behind. Or else the Municipal soldiers really would notice. "I thought you of all people would agree. Look at us. Getting through because we speak French while everyone else stays barricaded."

"Look at us. Getting through because we are agents working toward greater goals for the country," Oliver corrected.

He had just been plucked from a prison cell, and his head was still thinking about work. Or perhaps there was never a moment when their sheer existence *wasn't* about work anymore, because the moment they had been born, they had turned into living, breathing assets malleable for someone else's use.

Orion shifted his brother's arm, holding him more comfortably. "Save your breath. You're really going to bleed out otherwise."

"It's not a crime to be born into privilege," Oliver muttered like he hadn't heard him. "What matters is using it instead of closing your eyes to it."

Orion forced himself to block out the new wave of shouting that started behind him. He pushed forward faster, and then they were across the bridge, inside the International Settlement.

"Come on. We made it."

44

"Is anyone there?"

The street stood eerie. Each thud on the front door of the Hong residence ricocheted into the night, harmonizing with the distant claps of gunfire. Though none of the fighting could travel past Concession lines, its impact boomed through the rest of the city like thunder.

"HELLO?"

While Celia knocked, Rosalind busied herself with breathing warm air into her gloved hands. They needed to get Orion back to Zhouzhuang—to Lourens—so that his mind didn't detonate. They needed to get Oliver to a hospital in case he was experiencing some sort of internal bleeding and Rosalind had diagnosed him falsely.

The problem was that they had no way of knowing when the bombing would stop—*if* it would stop—so how could they plan their next steps? Never mind that Rosalind was also worrying herself sick over where the hell Phoebe was at present or what Lady Hong was doing if Silas had passed her all of Oliver's blood. How long did they have to stop her? How quickly would she work?

"Can't we break in?" Alisa asked in the meantime. "Those windows look like they could shatter easily."

"They have a housekeeper," Celia answered. "Are you trying to give Ah Dou a heart attack?"

"Maybe he's since gone home."

"Home? To the countryside? Who would leave *the International Settlement* for the countryside when we're about to get invaded?"

As Celia and Alisa continued debating over the door, knocking incessantly, Rosalind folded her arms to trap the heat, nervously eyeing Orion and Oliver. Though Oliver claimed to have gained some clarity, able to stand and walk on his own, Orion still hovered around him, frowning at every small movement.

It was incredibly confusing looking at them together. Rosalind was blooming a headache herself at the mere sight. She had noticed Orion wincing too, but each time she asked if he was all right, he maintained that nothing was wrong . . . despite his expression speaking the contrary.

"It's very late in the night," Alisa was insisting. "Maybe he is sleeping through this—"

The door opened suddenly. Celia almost stumbled on the front stoop before withdrawing her next knock, pulling her arm back. An elderly man dressed in pajamas stood inside, one hand still on the doorknob and the other rubbing his bleary eyes. He looked at Celia, then past her shoulder.

"Shàoyé," Ah Dou said, his eyes widening at the sight of Orion. Then his gaze shifted to Oliver beside him, and the old housekeeper did a double take, spluttering again, *"Shàoyé?"*

He put his hand to his forehead. When his attention flickered between Celia and Rosalind next, the housekeeper was clearly doubting his wakefulness.

"Am I seeing in doubles? I didn't think my vision had deteriorated that much recently."

Celia held her hand out. "No, you're seeing correctly. You don't know me, but I am Lifu's mission partner, Lang Liya. Can we come in?"

Ah Dou shook her hand, then pulled her through the door, gesturing for everyone else to hurry too. Rosalind stepped in ahead of Orion so she could nudge the housekeeper aside for a moment, whispering, "Liwen has lost his memory. Don't be concerned if he doesn't remember you."

"He . . . Oh, goodness. Let me make some tea. You are?"

"Lang Shalin."

"Oh, the wife. Lovely."

Ah Dou shuffled off into the kitchen, leaving Rosalind to blink after him in surprise. The timing didn't check out for Orion to have relayed her identity to his housekeeper. Ah Dou had likely only known who she was from reading about her in the papers.

"I think we're in the clear." Alisa closed the front door, pressing up against it for a few moments. "It doesn't seem like anyone is after us yet."

Rosalind nodded her agreement, already taking inventory around the living room. As soon as they entered the foyer, their every word carried a hollow echo, darting in and out of the vases under the clock, landing hollowly over the thin rug laid out by the leather sofa.

So this was where Orion grew up. Or rather, this was where he grew up prior to being shipped off to London, the site of his happy memories before everything turned gray.

It felt rather empty.

"—here!"

Rosalind jumped at the unexpected volume, swiveling her attention to Orion and Oliver. Her every nerve had tensed on instinct, but nothing was wrong. Well, something was clearly wrong, but there was no immediate threat. The brothers were only arguing with each other.

"I'm not telling you to get on my shoulder while I throw you around," Orion snapped. "I am saying—"

"I know, Orion. And *I'm* saying I don't need you clucking after me like a hatchling—"

"A hatchling!" Orion crowed. He lifted his hand to his neck. Anyone else might have brushed it off as an absent gesture, but Rosalind knew better. He was in pain. His head again. "If *anything*, I am clucking after you like the *father* chicken—"

"Enough, enough," Celia chided. "Stop it. Oliver has plenty to deal with right now."

Rosalind flinched. All her defensive hackles rose. "Hey," she cut in. "Orion's not doing anything wrong. He's only trying to help."

Memory or no memory, he was the type of person who needed something to do or say. It was probably driving him nuts that he couldn't plan their route around the city or contribute to an escape plan or, hell, even identify where his own house was.

"I suppose," Celia said. She didn't sound very convinced.

Neither did Oliver, it seemed. He pressed against the couch for balance, one arm propped to the backing and the other pressing around his torso.

"Where's Phoebe tonight?" he demanded suddenly.

The living room went quiet.

"She's there." Orion stepped away, putting distance between himself and his brother. Although Rosalind was observing him, he didn't meet her eyes when he drew nearer; he tipped his head up instead, looking at the clock on the wall, and Rosalind knew he was trying to hide the flash of pain crossing his expression. "At the facility. She came along too."

Oliver's gaze sharpened. "Why didn't she make it out?"

Alisa, now, was sidling in from the foyer—slowly, deliberately. She seemed very interested by how Oliver would react to this news.

"She took a different entrance from the rest of us," Rosalind answered. "I have no clue where she was. There was no time to find her on our way out."

"So you traded Phoebe for me," Oliver intoned.

Rosalind's brow shot up. Resentment crawled up her stomach

and into her throat, itching like a thousand-legged insect wanting to work its way out. What kind of remark was that? They had just risked their lives to get him out, and he responded with blame?

"She shouldn't even have been inside," Rosalind returned icily. "*You're* the one who needed rescuing."

Celia's eyes went wide, like she couldn't believe what she just heard. *"Rosalind."*

"What? If he's going to blame other people, maybe he should take some responsibility too."

"What's wrong with you?" Celia demanded. "Do you think he asked to be in there?"

When Orion crossed his arms, both his fists were clenched so tightly that his knuckles had turned bloodless. "Technically," he said, jumping in before Rosalind could. "*Yes*. He did. When you both picked your sides."

The temperature in the room plummeted. This was getting dangerous.

"That's unfair," Celia said coldly. "I don't need a Nationalist telling me that we deserve to get picked off."

"He's not telling you as a Nationalist," Rosalind fired back. "We just killed a whole unit of Nationalists to get Oliver out of there."

Celia scoffed. "Doesn't change the fact that you're the ones always safe in this city."

"Are you joking?" Rosalind pointed toward the door. "Don't you hear those bombs?"

"And *who* are those bombs going to strike?" Celia returned. "Not the top commanders living on this very road."

"Without those commanders, we'd lose the entire city to the Japanese this very night."

"Without any commanders, maybe I wouldn't have almost died in a massacre five years ago!"

"All right!"

As soon as Alisa barged between them with a shout, Rosalind reared back with a gasp, snapping out of her fury. Celia blinked hard too, as if she had suddenly realized how far she had taken it.

"I am going to need *everyone*"—Alisa flung both her arms out, keeping them at a distance—"to simmer down right this moment. There's a war outside, for goodness' sake. What are you doing going for each other's throats in here?"

Rosalind's lungs were horrifically tight. Alisa was right. They were doing exactly what she always grumbled the nation itself did, sniping at each other and making terrible hits while actual danger loomed shortly beyond. They weren't their factions. She *knew* this.

Yet the taste of frustration had turned her whole tongue bitter. She couldn't bear to stand there and make civil conversation anymore, even if that was the sensible option. Rosalind had nothing nice to say when Celia was being comparative like this.

She pivoted for the stairs instead.

"That's a good idea!" Alisa called after her cheerfully. "Rest is a great option!"

There was a scrambling of footsteps, and then Orion was right behind her, arm on her elbow and pointing forward in guesswork over which room was his. It almost shocked her that she felt profuse relief over his presence instead of further blistering annoyance. Below, she heard Celia murmuring, and then she and Oliver were going off in another direction of the house, a door slamming on the first floor.

"No need for such force in the household!" Alisa continued from the living room, her tone upbeat. "Take deep breaths! Remember, I love you all!"

No matter how jolly Alisa stayed, Rosalind maneuvered onto the second floor like a dark storm. *C'est quoi ce bordel, who do they think they are—*

She halted at the entryway into Orion's presumed bedroom, letting him enter first. Then, in response to her sister, she slammed the door as hard as she could too.

Alisa winced.

They would get over it. Siblings always did. Everyone was only stressed after the night they'd had. And because there were bombs falling from the sky.

"So dramatic," Ah Dou commented. He had just returned from the kitchen, clutching a tray of teacups.

Alisa went to help the housekeeper, putting the tray down on the table by the couch. It smelled wonderful. She reached for the teapot, pouring two cups.

"If you want to see proper dramatics, you should meet *my* brother," Alisa remarked. She set the teapot down. "Have you worked at the Hong household long?"

"A very long time." Ah Dou picked up his tea. He seemed to enjoy the fact that Alisa was sitting with him to chat. "Since before Lifu was born."

"Ah."

She let the next few minutes pass comfortably, drinking her tea. Inside her head, Alisa was silently doing the math, trying to remember how far apart the Hong siblings were in age. She and Phoebe were both born in the year of the ox—that she already knew. Orion, if her memory served correct, was twenty-two years old. Judging by the tiny statues of a horse, a rooster, and an ox that Alisa could see lined up on the mantel, she could use the process of elimination to guess that meant Oliver was turning twenty-six this year. A long time, indeed.

"I don't mean to pry . . . ," Alisa started carefully, "but did you know that he was going to walk out?"

Ah Dou swirled his tea. "Dà shàoyé, you mean?" he confirmed, referring to Oliver. "I didn't know, yet I wasn't surprised. You can feel those sorts of things, I suppose."

Alisa thought of her own household, back in her childhood. It hadn't been an unhappy place, but it had been volatile. If her brother was in trouble, she could feel it like sleet seeping through the walls. If her cousin was angry at the world, she could hear it in every creak of the floorboards, sense heat on her palms if she touched the doors after him.

"Did you ever feel it with Feiyi?"

Ah Dou blinked. "With xiǎojiě? No, of course not."

The memory of their rescue mission flashed through Alisa's mind. When they had emerged, her ears had been ringing with the conversation she caught. While Alisa was navigating the corridors devastated by the bombing, Rosalind and Phoebe had occupied the wire.

"Keep moving."

"There are soldiers."

"I have you covered. Move!"

Rosalind hadn't seemed to think much of it. Once they were safe, she hadn't commented on the gunshots that had followed Phoebe's instructions. Curiously, Alisa had been waiting this whole night to see whether Rosalind would bring it up, but Rosalind clearly had a lot on her plate at the moment.

Alisa was happy to fill in for her.

She yawned. "I didn't realize I was getting so tired."

Ah Dou finished his tea at once. "Let's get you in Feiyi's room. I'm sure she won't mind. Washroom is right next door if you need it."

He ushered her up the stairs, underneath the large chandelier dangling lifelessly from its wires. Alisa tipped her chin to take in the house, the fading wallpaper and the imprints that had been left on the flooring where heavy furniture used to stand. Rectangular shapes remained on the walls too, blocks where the deep green and golden floral patterns were lighter, the perfect size to imply picture frames that had since been removed.

"The house has seen better conditions," Ah Dou remarked, tracking her line of sight.

"I think it is perfectly well maintained now," Alisa insisted.

Ah Dou smiled sadly. "Nice of you to say. To tell the truth, the Kuomintang is most certainly going to seize everything as an asset soon. How can they not?"

Alisa stayed quiet. When they walked past the doors in the hallway, she could hear voices coming from Orion's bedroom in heated debate. Ah Dou opened Phoebe's room, then grimaced at the state she had left it in.

He bade her a good night. Alisa thanked him and returned the pleasantry. When the housekeeper's footsteps faded away, she was finally at liberty to shut the door firmly and yank up her sleeves.

Alisa performed a slow turn to take in the contents of Phoebe's bedroom. There were all sorts of scattered objects around the carpet: tubes of lipstick and hair ribbons and socks with one hole where the big toe needed to go. The room was waiting in an interlude, holding its breath for its occupant to return.

She eyed the vanity. The mirror leaning against the wall. The closet doors. Nothing about those items drew her attention.

Her gaze settled on the clothing trunk at the foot of Phoebe's bed instead. It sparkled in the overhead light, studded with bright pink jewels. Carefully, Alisa wandered over, then lifted the lid with a single finger. She found neatly folded skirts in varying styles, all plucked from the latest fashion magazines.

Then Alisa swiped a hand across them, revealing the box that sat underneath, latched with a simple mechanism. This was the kind of lock that didn't expect intruders. This was the kind of lock someone put in place if they knew no one would ever come looking.

"No way," Alisa muttered. "No goddamn way—"

She unlatched the lock. Inside the long box, there were two rifles, two pistols, and endless cartridges. Beautifully polished. Not a single speck of dust to be found.

"Wow."

Alisa couldn't *believe* she hadn't suspected this from the get-go. How had it taken her this long? For heaven's sake, she had *known* from the Communist grapevine that Oliver was Priest's handler. Somehow, she still hadn't made the connection. Unbelievable!

She propped her hands on her hips. Considered the situation at hand.

With a great sigh, Alisa lugged the box up.

"Phoebe Hong," she muttered, "you owe me for this."

45

Surprisingly, Oliver's childhood bedroom had a first-aid kit that contained everything Celia needed for a makeshift bandaging job, even though the antiseptic looked so old that it might have expired.

But by Oliver's hiss when she pressed the gauze pad into his wound, she guessed it worked well enough. This was only a temporary solution anyway; the wound wasn't going to heal on its own without a doctor performing debridement on the area.

"What did they use on you in there?" she asked quietly. "This looks like the syringe was as thick as a finger."

"I couldn't even begin to tell you," Oliver grumbled. He tried to flinch away from the gauze, and Celia shot him a glare, pressing harder. He was entirely coherent now, at least. Even if his movements were a little slow, his temperature had returned to normal and his pulse thudded at a healthy increased speed. With time to replenish, his blood must have started making its additional components again.

Oliver winced. "Are you trying to torture me further?"

Celia relented, deciding the wound was as clean as it would get for now. She had forced Oliver to lie down on the bed, where the sheets were gray and covered in cartoonish stars. Ah Dou had been cleaning in here regularly, even though it had been years since Oliver was home. With a gentle brush of her finger, Celia prodded around the circular wound, making sure it had dried before she put anything over it.

Goose bumps appeared where she brushed. She drew back for a beat, setting the gauze in the lid of the first-aid box. While she was kneeling beside the bed, she was half afraid she might suddenly lose her balance and topple, though the bed was perfectly low—made a child's height and unchanging through the years. One lamp lit the room in the corner. Its lampshade was moth-bitten, but the pale blue color had withstood the years, as had the miniature wood carvings of three bears that stood sentry around it on the table. Celia kept swearing she could hear gunfire outside, but she knew it had to be her imagination. They were too far from the conflict, too many streets removed with too many beautiful buildings protected by international law.

"I'm sorry to have done that."

Celia's head jerked up. "Pardon?"

"The argument with your sister," Oliver clarified. "I wasn't trying to blame her. Phoebe will be okay. I know her."

For a moment, Celia was disappointed that was what he was talking about. She thought it might have been something else. Something like why he was nursing a wound after being held captive in a cell. Why they'd had to pluck him away from the Nationalists' hold. Why he had even been in the position to experience capture.

"It's fine." Celia prepared clean gauze. Slapped it to Oliver's torso with an audible sound. He flinched, casting her a bewildered look to ask why she was rough-handling him so much, but Celia ignored him, pulling a strip of medical tape and sticking the gauze in place.

"Is it?"

"I just said it was, didn't I?" She reached for a roll of bandages. It was covered with dust, and she busied herself trying to clean it off before realizing she could simply unroll the outer layers and discard the first few dirtied pieces.

"I don't know, sweetheart." Oliver lifted himself onto his elbow. Celia cast him an immediate glare, but he was unfazed. "You're being a little feisty right now."

"I'm feisty because I'm playing nurse and my patient is being difficult. Lie back down."

"Don't I need to be sitting up if you're wrapping the bandage around me?"

Celia paused. He was right. Dammit. She pulled a long length of the clean bandage, then tore it free. She gestured for Oliver to come forward, and he swung his legs over the bed until he was sitting before her.

"Arms up," Celia muttered.

He obeyed. Winced slightly when it pulled at the wound. Celia shifted closer so she could place the bandage correctly, but it felt like a colossal task deciding how to get one end around. Oliver was so . . . shirtless. He had been shirtless before while she was wiping the blood away, but now there was no blood, only skin, and somehow it felt less like she was playing nurse and more like there was just Oliver shirtless in front of her.

Christ. Celia shook herself into focus. She could see little alternative except to lean right in and snatch the other end of the bandage once it was around him, drawing back quickly.

Oliver put his arms down. He watched her adjust the wrapping. Though there was no sign of any hostility from his end, he stayed so silent that it was Celia who eventually caved, snapping, "Are you going to pretend you don't know what you did?"

"Elaborate."

He was impossible. She was going to kill him. Throw him into a ditch and report up to their superiors that he had simply tripped into an enemy trap.

"You"—Celia tugged the bandage hard, tightening it—"gave yourself up for me. *Why?*"

It went against all of their training. Perhaps if Oliver had had a backup plan prepared, it would have been another matter, but he hadn't. The only thing that had mattered to him at that moment was making sure *she* could escape. Training would have bid them to wait it out, refuse to take unnecessarily heroic risks. If Celia were honest, training would have also dictated that *she* be the one to commit a sacrifice if it came to it, because Oliver was doubtlessly the operative they needed more.

"Celia," Oliver said simply. "Why do you think?"

She was having trouble making a knot on the bandage. Her fingers weren't limber enough to tuck the end under itself.

"I have a hypothesis," she whispered. Her voice almost gave up on her. The attitude she had possessed before grew legs and slipped away, scrambling out the window and out of sight. "But I don't wish to be correct."

Oliver's room hummed with an insular sort of quiet, one that rang in Celia's ears when she wasn't speaking. They were on the ground floor, tucked in the hallway behind the living room, surrounded by the servants' rooms and cleaning closets. Any commotion around the house didn't make its way here.

"Why is that?"

His tone was unreadable. He made a noise resembling a wince, but that might have been the sudden press of pain when Celia adjusted the gauze.

"Maybe I worded that a little strongly." She finally managed to secure the bandage. "Maybe it's more accurate to say that it frightens me."

Oliver went silent again. Celia rocked back, pulling her hands into her lap and clenching them tight. This conversation could end here. It didn't have to break them further than they were already fractured.

"Have I ever told you," Oliver said suddenly, just as Celia was about to rise, "that I latched on to this work in rebellion against my father?"

Carefully, Celia set the bandages back into the box. She closed the lid.

"No," she answered. "You haven't."

A different quiet settled into the room. A certain hesitance—as if Oliver couldn't believe he had started this track of conversation, but it was too late to renege on it. He leaned back, biting down on his grimace when he needed to shift his torso. Celia would have snapped for him to be careful, except the bed was short enough that he was already resting against the wall. He met her eyes, then inclined his head to his side. He wanted Celia to sit with him.

"Well, it was a bad year when the hanjian accusations started coming for my father," Oliver went on. "Orion and Phoebe were still in London, but I was old enough to have returned already. Not only that, but my father had taken me under his wing as his protégé: firstborn son with the making to be exactly who he was in higher society. To tell the truth, I don't think I minded it at all."

Oliver gestured for Celia again, more insistently. This time she relented and folded herself down onto the starry gray sheets, tucking one leg underneath her in the neatest, politest manner she could manage. The sheets were soft as silk.

"I did mind when it started going downhill, though. Even if he never admitted it, I could feel his guilt. In every gesture and every word of advice he tried to turn on me at the dinner table, I knew he would brush whatever he needed under the rug if it meant holding on to his place in society. I hated what I saw. He and my mother alike—it was not the family they loved but the ultimate image of what it could be. When we were younger, it was every language shoved into our heads until we were walking, talking foreign society assets. As we grew older, it was career paths placed into our hands and dinner party guests who needed to be entertained in case they would be of use down the road. If I kept following that same line, I would be exactly who they wanted me to be. I would have turned into my father." Oliver's eyes fluttered closed. Though he appeared tired, this wasn't a gesture of rest. "He was cleared of his charges because he found the right people to put in the right calls. That very same day, I made up my mind to ensure I would end up nothing like him. I would be the exact opposite, in fact, and start from there.

"But I know how it goes. There's always the old order with its flaws and the new order that wants to fix them. Then the new order starts to turn old, starts to pick up its own flaws, perhaps turns even worse, and suddenly the cycle begins again."

Oliver snapped his eyes open. Celia felt like she had missed something, that Oliver had jumped from his first point to the third, and she hadn't caught where the leap had happened. She waited a moment to see if he would keep talking. He stared forward instead, his arms clasped loosely around his middle to keep himself warm while his temperature continued adjusting.

"What are you trying to say?" Celia finally asked.

Slowly, Oliver's gaze returned to her. At such proximity, Celia almost wished she hadn't spoken and drawn his attention, because there was something intensely horrifying about the fact that he was looking at her and wasn't looking away—that he was *looking* at her, and she could not hide from him.

"I'm trying to say that I thought it cast me apart from my father if I joined the rebelling side of a war. If I worked for something outside of myself. He only cared about his own standing, so I would never do the same." Oliver's expression had softened. "But then I hear how you see me, Celia, and I fear I'm not so different after all. Why are you so afraid of me? Of *us*?"

"I never said I was afraid of *you*," she protested at once.

"Then what is it?" Oliver asked. "If it is not duty you are choosing over me, where does the fear come from?"

Celia shouldn't have sat down. She should have taken several strides across the room *away* from him to put some distance between them. Only moonlight covered Oliver's shoulders, and even that was weak, too heavily clogged by the smoke in the skies. She wanted to reach forward. Her fingers craved to revolt against reason, to press outward and—

"Just look at what happened," Celia hissed. "You gave yourself up for me, and you got hurt for it. I already have a problem with your secret-keeping, Oliver. I already have a problem with you deciding to shake the world and catching me up afterward. I won't let you do the same when it comes to your life."

By the look in Oliver's eyes, it seemed that he was cycling through a thousand different thoughts at once, trying to choose only one response. Celia had gotten so caught up in telling him off that she forgot to be afraid of his scrutiny, and now she was staring back at him with equal brazenness.

"Why?" Oliver asked.

"Why what?" Celia returned. She really ought to move away. She was starting to lose track of her own thoughts.

"Why won't you let me do with my life as I please?"

Celia wanted to strangle him. She wanted to pull apart his head and take a good look around to figure out why he would ask such questions.

"Because I know you," she snapped. "I know what sort of burden-bearing paragon you are. And I refuse to be the reason you act counter to everything you believe in and end up dead because you put me above everything else."

Celia shifted to stand up. At once, Oliver scrambled to stop her, both hands on her arms. He was no doubt jostling his wound in the process, and Celia started to tell him off, except he was already shaking his head, quieting her.

"Is that what you think?" he asked. "That loving you is a death sentence?"

All oxygen had left the room. Nothing remained except the void of Celia's own lungs.

"I make you weak."

"No, Celia, tell the truth." His grip tightened on her. One hand rose, sinking into her loose hair. "You spoke correctly the first time. You're afraid. I tell you over and over again that I want you, but you generate excuses for me. I tell you that I refuse to worship my father's image of respectability, but you make it a matter of safety. I will love you if I please. I will make you my altar, I'll put you above everything else in this world, I'll revel in every morsel you are made of. It's simple—just tell me you don't feel the same, and I'll let you go. But I won't accept anything else. I won't accept your refusal on the make-believe grounds of our work."

He was impossible. Absolutely impossible, and maybe Celia was just as bad, because she looked at him under the moonlight, his very presence like some sort of plea from the universe, and she couldn't stop herself from suddenly leaning forward to press her lips to his with every feeling she didn't know how to convey—*for goodness' sake, Oliver, I love you. I love you so much that I would die if you did, and that's precisely the problem.*

She pulled back in an instant. Eyes wide, lips humming with the brief contact. The moment she drew distance, though, Oliver made a noise in his throat and yanked her close again, muttering, "*God,* it has taken you long enough, sweetheart."

Then he was kissing her properly. It wasn't their fleeting contact in the hideout, frantic and desperate on death's door. His hands moved to her waist, his hold tightened, and though Celia would have thought she had no clue what she was doing, her response was as easy as an exhale. On assignment, she knew how to anticipate Oliver's next move and keep in tune, and kissing him was no different. He was warm and he was safe, and when they paused for breath, Celia didn't even think to fret. She hovered there, on the edge of the bed, on the precipice of something unfurling into unknown territory.

"Maybe I *am* afraid," she whispered. "How do I live with myself if there ever comes a day you get hurt because of me?"

Oliver smoothed his hand over her cheek. Brushed right at the soft space beneath her eye, like he was dusting off the stars that had fallen between them.

"You accept it," he replied simply. "Because that's what it means to be alive. That's what it means to fight for something—to love something. The country is good enough for us to die for. Why wouldn't you be?"

Celia breathed out. Shuddered. Oliver seemed to find that funny because his mouth quirked.

"That's terribly morbid," Celia muttered.

"It is only the truth," Oliver returned. "Either accept it or resign the both of us to live miserably forever."

Celia tried to glare at him. Oliver didn't appear fazed. He waited—waited because there was clearly more on her mind. Somehow she'd had the bravery to kiss him, but words were lodging in her throat now. She felt as though she needed to loosen her pendant. She felt as though she needed to run and hide, to find some corner to tuck into, but this was *Oliver*, and if she couldn't answer Oliver, then what more could she do in this lifetime?

"You know," Celia said very carefully, her voice almost hoarse, "that being with me would be different from being with another woman."

Oliver didn't hesitate before grasping her chin, holding her in place, keeping her from diving out of sight.

"Good," he said. "It should be different because *you* are the woman I am in love with, not another."

Oh. Okay.

"Oh" was all Celia could manage aloud too. "Okay."

His responding grin was utterly new to anything he had ever shown her. Unabashed. Almost shy, perfectly suited for the boyish nature of his childhood bedroom.

"Okay," he echoed. "Have we settled that? Can I kiss you again?"

Oliver tugged her higher, careless with his wound. She shot him a stern frown in warning. The moment he gave her an aggrieved look in return, she relented with a small huff and reached for him, biting back her laughter. There would be plenty of time to be afraid on the battlefield. A whole lifetime to be afraid.

"Kiss me. Please."

46

Phoebe hugged her knees close to her chest, trying to resist the urge to rock back and forth. She knew there were guards posted outside the cell block, but she couldn't see them from inside the bars. It felt like she had been left here to die.

Phoebe got up again, brushing off her trousers and shaking out her legs. She had been alternating between sitting and walking, always in motion—or however much motion she could manage in the tiny box of a prison cell. She could pace from one wall to the other in two steps. It wasn't satisfying in the slightest. If they were going to do something, she wished they would go on and do it faster. Was the purpose of leaving her in here some sort of psychological torture?

The moment Phoebe had called Silas "Magician," he had spun on his heel and exited the cell block. No questions, no pleas, nary a single request for information. He'd just . . . left.

Phoebe didn't know what to think. Didn't he *care*?

As if summoned by her thoughts, there was a sudden clang in the cell block. Phoebe lunged for the bars, pressing up against the metal. So far none of the other Nationalists had come to speak to her. Her identity was still intact—her face still covered by a swath of fabric.

A figure approached. Silas. He was back.

Phoebe's grip closed upon the bars tightly. She squeezed tightly enough to send sparks of pain shooting up and down her arms.

"Keep it shut," he was saying to the guards at the door. "Don't let anyone else in."

The door thudded behind him. It was only them in the cell block; it was Phoebe and Silas, both of whom knew nothing about each other, apparently, despite all the years together stacked behind them.

Silas had changed. Swapped out the uniform for civilian gear. Had he left the facility? Reported to her mother, given her Oliver's blood?

When he stopped in front of the bars, Phoebe's first instinct was to reach her arm out, ask for comfort. She stayed pressed close, playing a game with herself to see how long she could delude herself. She could pretend that they were about to go on an outing. That she was not waiting in a prison cell but at the end of her driveway, letting Silas walk up to her with an endearing smile.

"You have multiple charges of killing state officials," Silas started in lieu of a greeting. "That's high treason, Feiyi."

Phoebe stayed quiet for a moment. Then: "I know, Xielian. That's kind of the point of doing it under a secret identity."

His gaze sharpened. The moment their eyes locked, there was no chance of shaking loose.

"How can you act so flippant about this? You committed *treason*."

"Are you really speaking to me about *treason* right now?" Phoebe exclaimed. She had never felt anger surging to life like this before, nor had she spoken to Silas with such intense wrath. In a sudden motion, Phoebe lunged her arm through the bars, but instead of a tender request for comfort, she was practically frothing at the mouth, her fingers flexing in hopes that she could grasp his neck and claw blood out of him. "You betrayed us! You're working with my mother!"

Silas reared back. He didn't deny it.

"We're exchanging crimes now, are we?" His volume was rising too. "Warehouse 34 was you. Each of those notes was you. You let me believe in Priest when all along you knew better."

"And didn't I try to tell you?" Phoebe returned. "I warned you off her from the very beginning."

"You could have said *why*."

"No, I couldn't." Phoebe snatched her arm back. The inside of her elbow was stinging, but she didn't know where she had scratched it. "You would have turned me in. You would have gone running to your superiors immediately."

His jaw twitched. He almost appeared offended at her claim. "I wouldn't have."

"You goddamn"—Phoebe kicked the bars—"*liar!*"

Her echo rang through the whole cell block. Silas turned away then, facing the other wall and sending his arduous sigh in that direction.

"Fair that you don't know me," he said. He was trying to keep his temper in check. He was trying not to break apart the dynamic they had known their entire lives, but Phoebe had arrived with a hammer, and she was intent on shattering it utterly. "Apparently I know nothing about you either. How much was feigned, Feiyi? How much more have you lied about?"

Phoebe's breath was coming fast, practically heaving in her small space. These questions had no business here, as if he were actually owed some explanation. Her entire eighteen years of life was built from cobbled-together pieces. Was that what he wanted to hear? She knew what she liked and disliked. She enjoyed slotting puzzles together; she was good at being an illusion for other people. She didn't want to spend her life straitlaced, nor partaking in respectable society. Her favorite food was strawberries. Her least favorite color was orange. She had enough of a personality to make something that felt real, but when asked who she was and what she believed in, Hong Feiyi was only one part of a constructed picture, split again and again for different people to the point that she had lost track of where she placed each individual fragment.

No whole picture existed. Because no one would care to like her like that.

"*All* of it was feigned," she said meanly. "You don't know a thing about me."

"False," Silas said in an instant. He pivoted sharply, facing her again. "I know Priest."

Phoebe bit down hard on her teeth. "She is a creation."

"And she is you. You never let me communicate what I thought of her. If you had heard me talk about her, you'd believe me. Maybe I don't know Phoebe, but I know Priest."

Silas walked forward slowly. He approached the bars of her cell, rippling with intensity, his manner entirely at odds with the boy she was used to, the boy she was always helping fix his glasses. Did he wish to scare her? He had always treated Phoebe too preciously to tell her off, and Phoebe had always been too committed with keeping up her untroubled persona to raise her voice at him. Now both illusions had shattered. Bombs were falling from the sky, a forward march was trying to raze the city, and yet somehow it was this—it was Phoebe with her insides laid in full view before Silas—that threatened to undo her.

She hated this feeling. She might as well be a child again. Some sniveling, peevish toddler who didn't know when to stop crying, who couldn't control how other people perceived her.

"To tell the truth," Silas said, "at some point I stopped thinking about bringing Priest in as a matter of the mission. A fanatic, twisted part of me just wanted to meet her. The girl who kept slipping from my grasp. The girl who laughed at a joke she told while passing classified information." He paused. Swallowed. "You were right. There was no reality where finding Priest would have helped us get Orion back. I was trying to fool myself. Justify my own longing."

She felt no satisfaction hearing him admit this. Phoebe had told him, after all, and it hadn't been *enough*.

"Right," she said. "Priest was a dead end. So you turned to working for my mother instead."

Silas didn't flinch. If anything, he only bristled, his arms folding behind him. "You can work for the other side, but I can't?"

"What are you talking about?" Phoebe demanded. "I was protecting Orion!"

"And I was getting Orion back."

"By betraying our *country*—"

A door slammed loudly at the other end of the cell block. Though Phoebe barely registered the sound, Silas looked up quickly, a flash of fear crossing his brow.

"Keep that on," he hissed, gesturing to the fabric over her face. "Don't say anything. Understand?"

Phoebe remained silent. Another man came within view, and she inched farther from the bars, creating distance as if she were the one outside the cage and there were barely contained predators prowling the other side.

The man wore a uniform. Some general, Phoebe decided, gauging by his medals and ribbons. He looked an awful lot like her father, though they all did. Beyond their stature, they tended to share the same demeanor, too. The same glaze in his eye when looking at a mere girl on the other side of the bars.

"Any findings yet?" he asked Silas.

Silas took a moment to gather himself. To any other observer, he was only slow in his reply. Phoebe, meanwhile, caught the clench of his fists. The double inhale before he breathed out.

"No. You can leave this to me."

Her torture, he meant. Information extraction in the way the Nationalists were best known for.

"All right," the general said easily. He eyed Phoebe again. She resisted the urge to move, to do anything that might indicate some sort of discomfort. "Shouldn't be too hard. You'll want her out for the count first, of course."

Before Phoebe could step away, the man withdrew a metallic instrument from his belt, shaking it once to bring out its electric end. The weapon hummed. Her heart dropped into her stomach. Though she had thought herself prepared, the moment he shoved it through the bars and made contact with her arm, her world turned white-blue, entirely unfathomable.

Phoebe held in her scream. She took the pain, as silent as the shroud of death, as soundless as the mists floating into the city.

Then she dropped to the cold cell floor.

47

Morning light crawled through Orion's bedroom window a few minutes after sunrise, on a sluggish delay with the gray clouds. Rosalind watched its shape take form on the wall, the faintest haze of orange brightening a pale cream paint color. She didn't know if she was surprised at Orion's decorating choices.

Orion stirred in her lap. The blinds hadn't been drawn during the night, and his eyes opened slowly, prickled by the light. Though Orion had insisted he wasn't tired at all, he had lain down while Rosalind remained sitting cross-legged among his pillows. She had simply become another one of his pillows when Orion's eyes started drooping, protesting between yawns that he was only going to rest for a brief moment, nothing more.

"When did I fall asleep?"

Rosalind snorted. "Sometime during our debate on whether there are penguins in the northern hemisphere."

Orion lumbered upright. His hair was sticking up in all directions at the back. Rosalind reached out to tame it down.

"Have you been awake this whole time?" he asked, startled.

"Yes." She finished getting his hair down, so easy to put back into order. Of course someone like Orion had hair that always complied. "Orion, *I* don't sleep."

His expression remained vaguely bewildered. Like he had left half of himself behind in his dreams, tethered by a short string that wouldn't yank properly until the sun was higher in the sky.

A clatter sounded from downstairs. Rosalind shuffled forward on the bed, giving Orion a small prod so he would recline again. "Get some more rest. You need it. The morning is early still."

Rosalind stood up. Before she could step away, Orion grabbed her hand, and although it was a casual motion—more an instinct to get her attention than an indicator of anything urgent—she paused with concern.

"You won't go far?" he asked.

"Of course not." Rosalind tilted her head to the door. "I will only be downstairs."

Orion released his grip on her hand slowly. There was a look in his eyes that had Rosalind wondering if she ought to ask whether he was all right, but at this hour, the morning turned soft things harsh and pulled new colors into existence. When Orion blinked, he looked entirely normal again. Rosalind offered a small smile. Everything was fine—she had probably imagined that look. She slipped out from his room, her footsteps silent as she descended the stairs.

The sound was coming from the kitchen. Under the bare-bones dawn, she would have expected it to be Ah Dou rummaging around. Instead, she found her sister putting the kettle on and peering around the cupboards. "Hey."

Celia whirled around with a small shriek. "Oh my goodness," she hissed when she saw Rosalind. "Can you make some noise when you walk?"

"My enemies don't call me a shadow of the night for nothing, mèimei." Rosalind leaned against the kitchen doorframe, crossing her arms. She looked closer at her sister. Something was different.

"You're up so early," Celia remarked, turning to adjust the kettle flame.

"To be fair, I am never not *up*."

What *was* it that had stirred her notice? Celia's clothes were the same from the previous night. Nothing of her general appearance had changed, but *something* . . .

Celia, absently, tucked a loose piece of hair behind her ear. "I know," she said softly. "You ought to get more rest, though."

Rosalind put it together. She couldn't resist the smile that spread across her face. "Celia."

Celia looked over her shoulder suspiciously. Her sister knew her too well: she could hear the puffed-up tone that entered Rosalind's voice the moment she spoke a single syllable, the signal that the topic had switched.

"What is it?"

"Are you competing with me to see who can marry into the family first?"

Celia grabbed the nearest wooden spoon at once, tossing it in Rosalind's direction.

Rosalind shrieked, dodging out of the way. "You *are!*"

"Not so loud! The house is sleeping!"

Rosalind pretended to hurry into the living room. "Alisa! Alisa, get the flowers ready!"

Celia caught up to her, wrapping an arm around her head and clamping a hand to her mouth. "I should have absorbed you in the womb."

Despite her threat, Celia was resisting her laugh, and they struggled in good humor for a few moments before she finally released Rosalind, letting her gain her bearings with a snicker. They looked at each other for a moment before Rosalind sobered, remembering the last conversation they'd had in this living room.

"I was hoping to find you down here," she said quietly. "I wanted to apologize."

Celia leaned against the wall. "We're sisters, Rosalind. You don't have to apologize to me."

"Of course I do." She mimicked Celia, leaning a shoulder to the side. When she made contact with the wall, there was a dull thud, like the sound of a body hitting the ground. Like the aftermath of a massacre, corpses falling and falling and falling. "I know what you went through. I plucked you out of the carnage—I should know better than anyone. There was no reason for me to argue with you like that."

Nearly five years had passed since the revolution, but Rosalind still had long scars down her back, and Celia had a puckered bullet scar on her left side. When the Nationalists broke their alliance and turned on the Communists, they had fired on the protesters, uncaring about the civilians who were caught up in the game between faction leaders. Celia had been among them. She had been on the verge of bleeding out before Rosalind found her and pulled her toward help. The upside to never sleeping was that Rosalind wasn't subject to nightmares anymore—in the weeks shortly after Celia's recovery, before Rosalind had been turned into Fortune, she had dreamed about the incident relentlessly. About picking through the piles of the dead, her shoes splashing down in bloody puddles, finding faceless corpse after faceless corpse, none of them her sister.

"If you're apologizing, then I am too," Celia said. "I know where your heart was. I clearly just wanted to pick an argument because it felt better to scream than to sit there doing nothing at all."

Rosalind made a little smile. Celia did the same, then held out her hand for Rosalind to take. They could fall apart and split onto sides at two different ends of the universe, but they would still find their way back here. There was nothing that could truly pull them far from each other.

The front door thudded open.

"Shàoyé?" Ah Dou's voice floated in. He was already calling out for Orion before he had rounded the corner, a note of panic in his voice.

"No, it's us," Rosalind supplied. "Everything all right?"

The old housekeeper hurried into the living room, a shopping basket full of vegetables hanging from his arm.

"Terrible news," he said. "Nationalist vehicles are coming up the road."

A sharp knock pulled Alisa from her sleep so abruptly that her neck cricked when her head lifted. She made an indecipherable noise.

On the other side of the door, Rosalind somehow understood her. "Yes, now! Hurry!"

The sun wasn't even fully up yet. Alisa would have thought they had until daylight rose before someone was on their tail again. She scrambled out of the bed, pushing off the frilly sheets. In the reflection of the mirror, she flipped her hair once before tugging the door open, hurrying into the hallway.

She was right in time to see Orion exit his room next door as well and stumble to his knees.

"Hey!" Alisa exclaimed. She hurried to him at once, dropping to a crouch. "What's wrong?"

"Do you hear that?" he gasped.

The only thing Alisa could hear were Celia and Rosalind's concerned conversation downstairs. Somehow, she didn't think that was what he was referring to.

"Hear what?" she asked. She looked around the hallway.

"Voices." Before Orion could go on, his hands flew to his ears, clamping down hard.

Alisa reared back. "Hong Liwen," she said frantically. "Please don't be succumbing to the conditioning already. That would be so terrible. We don't even know if we can get out of the city."

Orion wheezed something. Alisa didn't catch it the first time, but on his second try: *"Get . . . Rosalind."*

Alisa was moving at once.

"Rosalind!" She skidded down the staircase. "Rosalind, help!"

The moment she reached the landing and turned for the living room, Alisa slammed right into someone. Two hands shot out to steady her. When she looked up, she was blinking at Oliver Hong, who returned her confusion.

"Why is everyone shouting and running?" Oliver demanded.

"Because we need to go," Celia answered, appearing from the other end of the hallway. "Kuomintang soldiers are scouting the end of the road. They're going to come knocking at any second."

That doesn't seem right at all, Alisa thought. She had been running from the Nationalists for months at this point. She knew how they worked. Never had she witnessed a unit forming this fast, especially if they didn't know where to go. Unless someone in this household had made a phone call—and she doubted it, because even if anyone here had reason to make a summoning, she had slept in the room next to the telephone, so she would have heard it.

Oliver's eyes flickered up the stairs. He wasn't looking for the telephone like her. He was looking directly at Phoebe's room, a wariness in his eyes.

"I got rid of everything."

His attention snapped back to Alisa. "I beg your pardon?"

Alisa didn't think this was a safe place to be elaborating. She merely feigned devout and crossed herself, as if she had suddenly adopted religion.

"I got rid of everything," she said again. "Don't worry. You need to check on Orion—he's acting strange."

Oliver nodded, both to signal understanding for what she was hinting at and for what she had declared outright. Rosalind hurried into the hallway too, hearing the tail end of Alisa's instruction. Without asking for further detail, she followed Oliver up the stairs, which left only Celia in the hallway with Alisa.

"Ah Dou said there are two vehicles in the garage, so Rosalind and I are splitting off," she said. "I assume you want to go with Rosalind back to your brother."

"No," Alisa replied.

Celia looked bemused. Meanwhile, Alisa's train of thought continued darting from one conclusion to the other at the speed of light, trying to jam a web together and failing at every turn. Sending a military unit into the International Settlement was horrifically risky. If the Kuomintang suspected their own outlaws to have returned home, they would have sent covert. A single agent, lurking on the rooftops to confirm a hunch before reporting back. They wouldn't be sending *soldiers*. For a faction who defined their time in power by small, inoffensive movements, why would they risk accidentally setting off the foreigners?

"Are you taking Oliver to an underground hospital?" Alisa asked distractedly. There was something here. Complete understanding was hovering right outside her grasp.

Celia nodded. "He needs an actual doctor, as much as he insists otherwise. The bleeding is starting and stopping too frequently."

A thud sounded upon the staircase. Alisa and Celia both looked over. Oliver was certainly going to cause further bleeding if he kept launching himself around like that, dragging Orion after him.

"Into the car, into the car," Rosalind was saying, her voice frantic as she hurried behind them.

"Rosalind, can you even drive?" Alisa asked.

"Of course I can *drive*." She opened the door into the garage, pushing Oliver and Orion through. "I know what everything on the dashboard does. In theory."

That definitely meant the Nationalists had taught her how to drive once and she had never tried getting on the road. For the love of God, Alisa was tempted to go with them just in case they crashed.

"If you're not going with Rosalind," Celia continued, "are you coming with me?"

"No," Alisa said again. She tipped her head to the side, listening. Military trucks, rumbling closer. "I'll regroup with you afterward. Check in with the liaison stations once you're on the move—I'll contact you that way."

Celia hesitated. For a moment, Alisa feared that Celia would insist on bringing her along anyway. Her superior must have realized, though, that taking Alisa somewhere she didn't want to go would be the equivalent of wrangling with an upset cat, so she nodded.

"Be careful. Check in later today even if there's no news."

Alisa quirked an eyebrow. "Why do you sound like Roma?"

Celia reached for her hand. "Because when people care about you, they hold on to you." She squeezed once, then placed a small orange into Alisa's palm. "I ask out of concern, not restriction. Be careful, okay? And eat this before you go anywhere. You'll starve otherwise."

Alisa nodded. Content, Celia hastened for the garage, tugging open the driver's door into the first vehicle. Rosalind, meanwhile, got into the second vehicle, giving Alisa a quick farewell wave.

Alisa watched Celia pull out first. Rosalind followed suit, with far more starts and stops, but she maneuvered onto the path and made a large turn to take the route along the back of the house, avoiding the soldiers incoming on the main driveway.

In the silence that followed, Alisa didn't return inside the house. Celia's words were still playing in her head, rattling about while she peeled the orange and popped the segments into her mouth. Alisa was a slippery person by nature. She needed unrestricted parameters to run wild. That was just how it was.

She hummed. Popped the last segment of the orange into her mouth. For certain people, though, she supposed she could allow *some* reporting in.

Just as the military trucks rumbled into view and started to cut through the gardens, Alisa cleaned off her hands and stepped outside the garage, getting a deep gulp of morning air. Then, she found a good foothold on one of the pipes and clambered up quickly.

Alisa hid herself behind one of the chimneys. She waited, eyeing the first truck as it pulled up outside the Hong residence, eyeing all the others that followed suit. Though she was some distance away, she didn't need to get a better look at the men who poured out. They knocked on the door, asked Ah Dou to step aside so they could survey the house. When they fanned out to make a search, their movements told her enough.

Of course. This wasn't the Kuomintang at all. This was Lady Hong's forces.

Alisa jumped from the roof silently, landing at the back of a truck and tucking herself into the corner.

48

Rosalind crashed right before Shanghai's border.

She was under no mistaken impression about her driving abilities, so she couldn't say she was surprised when they slammed roughly against a telephone pole and the vehicle wouldn't start again. Really, she was just grateful that it had been a random pole on a quiet street in the west of the city rather than one of the barbed-wire fences at the control points.

"How are you doing?"

Orion blinked. They were standing over the crumpled vehicle, trying to decide whether there was any chance they could salvage the situation. The front hood had turned utterly concave. One of the wheels appeared flat.

"Me?" Orion replied. "I'm uninjured. I'm more worried about you. You practically flew into the windshield."

"Okay, don't exaggerate. I did not *fly*."

"You flew. Flapped your cute little wings and launched yourself face-first into the glass."

Rosalind glared at him. No one in this sleepy neighborhood seemed to have heard their collision with the pole and come investigating, but it was only a matter of time before a witness wandered by. Any time spent in the open meant an opportunity for one of their myriad enemies to descend upon them. If they were abandoning the vehicle, then they ought to get moving.

"I was asking after your head. Better?"

Orion shoved his hands into his pockets. She suspected that he knew what she had been asking the first time she asked it; he was only playing the fool. Orion hadn't been jostled around too severely with the crash—which likely had something to do with the fact that he had been sitting at the back, nursing his headache.

"It's not debilitating," Orion managed. That didn't address her question, per se, but it was an answer.

Rosalind watched the skies. She could sense the rumble of warfare. Even if they weren't anywhere near the site of battle while they stood this far west, the feeling coursed through the city overhead, every whirr of its fighter planes echoing through the thick clouds. She had taken this direction on purpose, opting to stay in foreign territory for as long as possible. Eventually, though, they would need to pass a control point, and to do that they could either hide in a vehicle already cleared to pass, or they could outright attack the soldiers guarding the city's borders to make their exit.

"I have an idea," Rosalind said.

There was an inn at the end of the road. It looked homely enough. Maybe it was a family business, passed down through the generations.

She extended her hand.

Orion didn't move at first. While his eyes immediately latched on to the offering before him, *his* hands stayed in his pockets. Wariness and yearning alike darkened his gaze. He stared forward the way first-time thieves observed prize jewels under glass, wanting to make a hungry taking while remaining somewhat nervous of the risk.

Rosalind flexed her palm more forcefully. It was just her hand.

"I don't bite," she said.

"Yes, you do." Still, his internal dilemma seemed to have settled. Orion removed one hand from his pocket and slipped it into hers slowly. Rosalind felt her palm prickle with the motion. Their fingers laced together; their wrists whispered a greeting. Although she had been the one to offer this proximity, the slow and intentional matter they had made of it felt entirely too intimate for the gray morning, standing in the middle of the street next to a wrecked vehicle.

"Tell me if your headache gets worse," she said.

"I have it under control," Orion assured her. He feigned confidence, but Rosalind felt the thrum along her fingers, felt the involuntary quiver that had tensed down his arm. He was scared. Not for himself—*of* himself. "A perfectly sound mind."

"All right," Rosalind said. She started walking in the direction of the inn, pulling him along. "Then you're playing the part of my husband again."

With every abrupt turn the truck took, Alisa was almost thrown out of her hiding place between two wooden boxes. She would have slipped multiple times if her upper-body strength had been slightly less adept, but thankfully she managed to hold on to the barest sliver of a lid, staying tucked in the back.

Alisa Montagova had memorized a map of Shanghai years ago, but this driving was making it very hard for her to trace their route. They would make a sharp left, then two rights that directly counteracted the previous maneuver. She couldn't tell if it had been a particularly long drive, or if it only felt that way because they had been going in circles to avoid picking up a tail.

The moment the truck stopped, Alisa was quick to move. She flung herself over the side, pressing close to the tires and waiting to see if anyone had spotted her. Most of the soldiers disembarked normally. No one shouted out in alarm.

Alisa hadn't thought she'd get this far. She didn't even know where she was. They had come in past a set of tall gates. A manor loomed up ahead.

Movement shuffled around the other side of the vehicle. Despite her confusion, Alisa needed to act fast, because hesitating would only waste time. With a muttered curse, she shot forward in a dead sprint. If they spotted her, then so be it. What mattered was getting to a hiding place afterward. She had never lost a game of hide-and-seek in her life.

"Hey!"

That was fast.

Alisa winced, throwing a glance over her shoulder. She allowed herself one cursory inspection to count how many soldiers were stirring to attention; then she turned around again, pushing forward. The manor was built on an angle, the back end rising higher than the front. The rooms seemed to be positioned slightly above the ground to accommodate the sloping hill. As soon as Alisa skittered along the side of the manor, she leaped up, grabbing ahold of a balcony railing affixed to the first floor. She swung herself over the ledge and through the open window. Easy.

While the soldiers made their pursuit, she landed in a dusty bedroom with its contents cleared save for a single chair in the corner. Overhead, its light fixtures were bare of bulbs, showing only exposed wires. Alisa dove for the walk-in closet, waving around her face vigorously to clear the dust.

The annoying thing about nice houses out in the Concessions was that they were built well, with carefully measured floor plans. Much unlike the sort of houses she had grown up in, where apartments were mushed and fused together by nature of urban center architecture, leaving gaps and crawl spaces between floors and walls.

At the very least, nice Concession architecture could be trusted to have insulation space between its levels. And those were usually accessible from the first floor to allow for maintenance.

Alisa spotted the small rectangle on the closet ceiling. She heard a shout in the hallway. With frantic speed, Alisa hurried for the lonely room chair, lugging it into the closet too. She clambered onto its seat, then its backing. Finally within reach of the small rectangle, she shoved her hands up and removed the covering, opening a tiny hole for her to pull herself through before kicking the chair out of the way so it didn't point to her route of escape.

"Success," she muttered, dragging herself into the crawl space. She set the covering back in place. Breathed out.

Alisa took a moment to listen. The soldiers entered the room she had just departed. Fanned out, calling to one another in confusion. Rarely did anyone think to check crawlspaces. Rarely did people even know that those *existed* in any house. She heard shuffling. More shouting. Then footsteps leaving the room to check the other parts of the manor.

Slowly, she started to move as well. Alisa picked her way along the raised wooden beam on her knees, careful to shuffle along the sturdy part instead of applying pressure on the ceiling plaster. It was nice to know that she hadn't lost her gift for squeezing through tiny spaces. She used to spend hours as a child doing this. Eavesdropping on everyone in the household. Learning all of her older brother's secrets because he always spoke out loud when he was writing his private letters.

Alisa paused after a few minutes. Judging by the direction she had been crawling in, she was just short of the foyer, somewhere near the main atrium. There was activity below. Voices wafting up the lines of the ceiling. Alisa couldn't hear what was being said, so she carefully lowered herself off the beam and pressed closer to the ceiling boards. She put her eye against the lines. The room took shape, forming smooth floors and metal tables . . . and the soldiers strapped down to them.

"Oh no," Alisa whispered.

One woman stood over the soldier on the very right. Three men dressed in dark suits surveyed the scene from the doorway. The woman was injecting the soldier with a syringe, and Alisa squinted to catch the last of a green concoction disappearing into his arm—a familiar deep green, like the one Alisa had been carrying for months while she was on the run. When the woman pulled the syringe away, she was quick to cross the floor, explaining something hurriedly to the men in suits. As Alisa listened harder, she realized the reason she couldn't understand anything wasn't because she wasn't catching enough words. The woman was speaking Japanese.

This had to be Lady Hong. She looked like a lecturer in the last ten minutes of a lesson, scrambling to finish the topic at hand, a single strand of hair slipping out from its tight clasp.

Despite Alisa's lack of understanding, she could tell by tone alone that Lady Hong was defending herself. She gestured once to the soldier she had just injected, and when one of the men asked a question, she shook her head vigorously. She gave a deep sigh. Before she could elaborate, the soldier jerked to life.

He started to scream. Alisa barely held back her gasp of surprise, her hand clapping to her mouth. Everyone in the lab below, though, did not look surprised, as if this had happened a few times already. When Lady Hong returned to the soldier's side and reached for the equipment cart, she looked resentful. Her hand hovered over the contents before going past the green vials and picking up a clear vial instead. Alisa would have assumed that vial to be empty until Lady Hong unplugged the stopper and took a syringe to collect the liquid. A colorless liquid, but viscous, judging by the way it moved up the syringe.

She turned and injected it into the soldier lying before her. Seconds later, he stopped screaming.

There, she seemed to be saying. Alisa strained, trying to catch anything she could, trying to decipher the situation with any similar sound she could pick out.

Hanten shi ta, Lady Hong had said before. It sounded a lot like hòutuì in Chinese. She wasn't saying *reversed,* was she?

As Lady Hong reached for the cart again, Alisa leaned harder into the ceiling. The boards creaked suddenly, protesting underneath the exertion. The noise caused one of the men to look up . . . and his eyes went right to where Alisa was hiding.

Shit.

49

First and foremost, Rosalind had needed some way to bypass the fact that her face was plastered on every second poster from here to the Huangpu River. She considered her every option. She could bandage herself up again. She could pretend to have a particular nasty cough and hold a handkerchief over her mouth.

But that didn't solve the fact that Orion was identifiable too. Hence what she ended up doing was so blatantly obvious that she was rather surprised it worked.

"That is the third time someone has mistaken me for that assassin girl this week," Rosalind bellowed when they entered the inn. "Do we look so alike to them? I don't see it."

"I think it's your hairdo, qīn'ài de," Orion replied. "I don't resemble the hanjian in the slightest. I merely get dragged in by association standing next to you."

They had put on horrifically Northern accents. Orion's attempt could use some work. Rosalind's, on the other hand, was polished albeit grating to the ear—a result of her evenings lounging around with Celia and Juliette in the past, nothing better to do except speak to each other like they hailed from a family of Beiping mistresses. In Shanghai, there was no easier way to stand out as an outsider than by speaking differently. And the moment someone marked themselves to be different, it was hard to think of them as a Shanghai native, hard to push past the inherent, puffed-up sense of self this whole city possessed—for better or for worse.

"A room, please," Rosalind simpered when she approached the front desk. Before the silver-haired innkeeper could say anything, Rosalind sniffed with displeasure and turned to Orion with: "Why did your sister insist on moving here? Look at this mess in Zhabei. We're going to get stuck inside city bounds *forever.*"

"You think I want to be here?" Orion slipped a little. A hallmark of Northern accents was the curliness of their words, extra *er*'s added wherever they could go. Shanghainese, meanwhile, was too flat, and the tail end of his sentence curved back down. Rosalind stomped on his foot subtly; his wheeze of air disguised the mistake. "I blame that little bastard she married. Some mèifū he is, kicking us out like that."

"I can open a room for you," the innkeeper said at the desk, looking sympathetic. She glanced at the log book in front of her, tracking a finger down the page. "You will certainly have trouble leaving anytime soon though. Do you have anyone you can ask a favor of?"

What she meant was, *Do you know anyone in the Kuomintang who can make a call?*

Rosalind shook her head. "We're unimportant. The most we can hope for is a ride." She pretended to consider the matter. "I don't suppose you know any traveler who comes in and out often?"

"*I* do not." The innkeeper grabbed a key below the desk, then gestured for them to follow her. "You may like to speak with my niece when she returns. She knows lots of people."

Rosalind nodded. They couldn't rush this. Messing up now was the difference between getting out safely and getting hauled into a Kuomintang cell. They trailed after the innkeeper into a small room, stepping in and chorusing gratitude. After pointing out where their amenities were located, the innkeeper closed the door after herself.

Rosalind turned to Orion.

"What's wrong?" he asked immediately.

"Why do you assume something is wrong?" Rosalind marched to the window, pulling at the curtain and peering out onto the roadside. The inn was very quaint. Watercolor paintings for decoration and half-burnt candles for light. Low ceilings and creaky floorboards, which meant it would be hard for people to sneak around because their footsteps would be audible from miles away.

"Well . . ."

Orion trailed off, gesturing vaguely—almost awkwardly—in her direction. She knew why he asked: her entire demeanor was on edge. But perhaps he decided against speaking it aloud in case it was offensive, and the thought gave Rosalind a peculiar surge of warmth. Despite the scramble in his head, he remained overly considerate. Despite everything, this was just who he was.

Orion's awkward wince suddenly turned into a sound of pain. Rosalind let the curtain fall into place, striding toward him and grasping his face.

"Bad?" she asked.

"No," Orion replied. He had closed his eyes. "No, it's fine."

"Orion."

His eyes snapped open. It was brief, yet Rosalind caught that flicker, that moment of absence when there was no one looking back at her. As soon as his gaze adjusted, though, he returned to normal, and those dark brown irises glowed once more by the daylight streaming through the curtains.

Rosalind couldn't help herself. She sighed, putting her arms around his neck and burying her face into his shoulder. Orion's arm wound around her waist on instinct, resting against her in return even as he said: "I'm all right. Really."

"I know," she murmured. And she knew that he would try his best to keep it to himself even if he wasn't. That he was the type of person to hate appearing troubled because he had gone his whole life without being allowed to, even if he couldn't remember any of it.

She needed to get him back to Zhouzhuang. It wouldn't solve the headaches until there was some fix on his mother's strength experiments, but it would eliminate the possibility of him sinking too deeply into one and his mind snapping into blankness permanently. Lourens needed to help him. She had a terrible feeling that she was going to lose him otherwise.

Slowly she withdrew, pulling away from his warmth, from his steady, raging heartbeat. Orion didn't release her immediately, so for a moment they stood nose to nose, his head tilted down without moving farther, her head tipped up to hold time still.

Rosalind exhaled softly. "Get some rest," she said. "I'll find us a way out."

The question, then, was whether Rosalind would discover an exit route first, or if the Nationalists would find the vehicle they had left on the road. It could take some time to trace the vehicle's ownership, even if they had hauled the wreck in already. And once they traced it back to the Hongs, who was to say they would find this inn?

The innkeeper's niece didn't return until the next day. Though Rosalind was already asking around for her in the morning, apparently the niece kept strange sleeping hours, and Rosalind ended up checking back every ten minutes until she woke up.

"We're looking for a way out of the city and we're not fussy in the slightest," Rosalind said, both her elbows propped up on the desk when she finally got the chance to speak to the girl. She was young—definitely younger than Rosalind. Late-afternoon storm clouds had darkened the inn, robbing the day of its hours and teetering toward evening early. The radio droned continuously about the invasion. Distantly, Rosalind caught a snippet talking about the country's capital moving from Nanjing to Luoyang; the Nationalists were worried that Japan's willingness to attack Shanghai meant Nanjing might be next. Western powers, meanwhile, were trying to negotiate a cease-fire, too worried about their own interests to stand back while the city raged with battle.

"You aren't in trouble, are you?" the girl asked casually.

"Of course not," Rosalind returned without missing a beat. "We're only trying to go home. My husband has a condition. He needs his own bed. Plenty of rest."

She wasn't really *lying,* to be fair.

The innkeeper's niece was leaning back on her chair, balancing on its hind two legs. She hardly seemed to be paying attention to this conversation, head tilted for the radio instead.

"Which direction?" the girl asked.

Rosalind hesitated. She was still faking that Northern accent. The better answer would have been northward, just to see who could get them through the city's control points. But time really was of the essence.

"West," she said instead. "Toward Suzhou."

If the girl found it peculiar, she didn't voice it. She tapped a pencil on her nose, thinking.

"Oh, easy. Our grocery deliverer brings produce from his farm in Suzhou every week. I imagine he would be willing to take you with him on his way out. Our inn is always his last stop."

"When is he coming next?"

"Wednesday." She peered at the logbook on the desk. "February third, if we're looking at the Western calendar."

Rosalind hesitated. Wednesday would make it a whole eight days since they had left Zhouzhuang. The longer they remained here, the more likely it was that they would get caught. Yet if Rosalind cast her inquiry wider, if she kept poking her nose around asking other sources for faster routes out of the city, that might get her on the Kuomintang's radar anyway. This would have to do. At least they could hide at the inn until then.

Rosalind pushed away from the front desk. "Thank you," she said. "That's great."

"You look familiar," the girl said suddenly. It was an offhand observation, one made while still balancing on those hind legs, but Rosalind froze all the same. "Do I know you from somewhere?"

"I can't imagine so." She imagined every possible outcome of this. The worst-case scenario played like a reel behind her eyes: the Nationalists hurrying to the inn, hauling Orion away, keeping him locked until he deteriorated beyond saving.

The girl shrugged. "All right. If you need me again, my name is Millie."

It wasn't the Nationalists that came knocking a day later. It was a messenger. And though Rosalind lunged back in an instant when she opened the door to the unfamiliar face, the boy threw his arms up, signaling goodwill.

"*Waitwaitwait*—someone sent me!"

He turned over a slip of paper in his hands, showing Rosalind before she could grab the coatrack and hit him with it. Two characters were written in small, squished strokes: 姐姐. Celia's handwriting.

"What?" Rosalind demanded, quickly veering away from the coatrack. Orion heard the commotion and got up from the table, hovering over her shoulder when she took the paper and unfolded it for the message inside.

Safe. Stitched. Yours? Have you heard from Alisa?

It was like speaking in code, except rather than following a cipher, Celia knew that Rosalind would understand exactly what she meant no matter how much she shortened her message. *Stitched* meant that they were at a hospital and Oliver had been under surgery for his wound. *Yours?* was to ask about Orion.

"How on earth did she find me?"

The messenger appeared sly. "We have our secrets. Do you want me to take a reply? I have a few minutes to spare."

Rosalind shuffled for the table at once, searching for a pen. "Yes, yes. Stay there."

> ***Also safe. Trying to leave. No—have you heard from Phoebe?***

Her sister's reply came a few hours later.

> ***No. I'm worried.***

So was Rosalind. When the same boy asked if he could take anything back, Rosalind shook her head. There was nothing they could do except wait.

On Monday, Rosalind ventured outside with a scarf over her head. Their mangled vehicle had been removed. Two Municipal police officers stood at the site of the crash, investigating the glass pieces on the road.

Rosalind hurried away, stepping inside a small fruit shop. She bought a bag of apples.

On Tuesday, Orion had almost gotten through the entire bag.

"You're ridiculous," she said when he started peeling the last one. "That's way too many apples."

"I keep telling you to eat as well," Orion protested, as if that were the issue at hand. He had rolled his sleeves up, cuffing them at his elbows to get them out of the way.

"I will have one apple a day, and that is quite enough."

"Then why did you buy a whole bag? Hmmm? Checkmate."

Rosalind scoffed, turning in her chair to resume reading the newspaper the innkeeper had delivered earlier. Out of the corner of her eye, she saw Orion grin at her, and though she fought with great effort to maintain her frown, she lost.

"Hah." Orion shoved his arm out, offering the peeled apple. "Bite."

"You're ridiculous," she said again. Nevertheless, she leaned in and took a bite.

Wednesday arrived. She and Orion waited patiently at the back of the inn, having paid for their lodgings with a necklace. Neither of them was carrying enough cash—Orion wasn't carrying any, understandably—and going to a bank would summon the Kuomintang faster than a spotlight into the sky. Rosalind wasn't going to miss the necklace anyway. She had acquired it years ago with Scarlet money, and the only sentimental value was the fact that it had even lasted this long before she found some better use for it.

"There," Orion whispered, spotting the truck pulling up around the corner.

Talking their way onto the farmer's truck was a breeze. Rosalind put on her best teary eyes, asking if the farmer was perchance driving west in the direction of Zhouzhuang. Her husband had an injury, she sobbed, and they needed to get to a specialized doctor outside the city.

"Come on, come on," the farmer said easily, fetching a handkerchief from his faded denim overalls and practically throwing it at Rosalind. "No need to cry. There's plenty of space to accommodate an emergency."

Rosalind shot Orion a satisfied look, dabbing at her eyes with the handkerchief. Though Orion had been pinching the bridge of his nose before to emphasize the injury she claimed he had, she suspected that some of that tension in his expression wasn't feigned anymore. His head really was starting to ache, as it had been doing in waves these past few days.

"Will they check papers, do you think?" Rosalind asked when the farmer finished loading his groceries for the inn. Her tone stayed demure. Posed the question out of curiosity, rather than worry.

"Ah, no one bothers on this route," the farmer said. He slapped his knee. "As long as you're not a criminal!"

Rosalind laughed nervously.

So they hadn't needed to get into the cargo bed at the back. The truck had room on the long seat at the front, and Rosalind had sidled in beside the driver, pulling Orion next to her. She made idle conversation with the farmer. Orion leaned his head against the side. There was no window; he could only close his eyes and brace against the brutal winter cold rushing against him.

Hours passed on the road. Now they were almost at their destination, and Rosalind couldn't believe how close they were . . . so of course that was the point when trouble started to arise. She felt it first in the sharp inhale Orion made. The farmer was heartily distracted, talking about his chickens, answering every question Rosalind threw at him. Rosalind, however, had been splitting her attention with monitoring Orion at all times.

"What's happening?" Rosalind whispered when the trees turned dense overhead. The road was scattered with branches that snapped under the truck's wheels, filling the space with sound and making the driver grunt with complaints as he focused on proceeding forward. "What are you hearing?"

"So many things," Orion mumbled. "I will be fine."

He didn't sound like he believed it.

"Are you sure?"

He didn't answer. When Rosalind touched his shoulder, forcing him to look at her, his eyes went blank. She jolted in her seat; Orion blinked, his focus returning. In that split second passing between them, his panic flashed starkly in his expression, knowing that he had just barely suppressed whatever was about to come over him.

Oh, shit.

"Is there any chance," Rosalind said brightly, turning to the farmer, "that you could drive a little faster?"

"I am going as fast as I can, tàitài," the farmer remarked.

"I do understand and appreciate that," Rosalind said. She was keeping her voice so falsely happy that it had the potential to grow wings and flutter off. "However, if there's a chance of speeding up—"

Before she could finish her sentence, there was a gust of wind to her side. She whipped around just in time to catch Orion kicking the door open wide and diving out from the truck.

She gaped. "What the *heck*—"

Rosalind followed suit and jumped after him, barely bracing before she was rolling on the sharp gravel. The truck kept driving forward—perhaps the farmer had scarcely registered the series of events and didn't have time to stop, or perhaps he didn't have the willingness to halt for the two city dwellers who were foolish enough to dive from a moving truck.

Rosalind's shoulder hit a large rock. She came to a rough stop.

"Are you out of your mind?" she shouted at Orion, lifting herself onto an elbow. A slow trickle of blood obscured the vision in her left eye. Her forehead must have gotten cut on the rock, but she wiped it away, barely paying it any attention.

"Yes!" Orion shouted back, some distance away. He had stopped near a hanging tree branch that poked onto the road. "That's why I threw myself out!"

Another car sounded as though it was approaching along the road. Rosalind hurried to Orion, then grasped his shoulder in an attempt to get him up.

"Orion, come on."

"I can't," he said tightly. "If I move, I'm going to lose control."

"That's fine." Rosalind gave him another tug. "You can stab me again. I don't care."

"*I* care."

The hum of an oncoming vehicle got louder.

"Come on, come on," Rosalind said, frantic. "We're going to get run over."

Too late. The vehicle rounded the turn and barreled toward them. With a curse under her breath, Rosalind grabbed Orion immediately and threw an arm up, as if her one mere limb could counter the impact. Though she had accepted that the car would not see her in time, there came a deafening screech of its brakes.

The echo bounced through the forest, through all the trees.

The car's bumper halted inches away from contact.

Rosalind lowered her arm, the motion slow and hesitant. She breathed out shakily, adrenaline rushing like a torrent in her body.

The rear door of the car opened; the man who stepped out looked incredibly familiar. It took Rosalind a prolonged moment to remember that the last time she saw him, she had been tied to a chair in Zhabei, waiting for the world to strike her down.

"Hello," Benedikt Montagov said plainly. "Any reason you're in the middle of the road?"

Rosalind gulped. When Orion shifted under her touch, there was an edge to his manner.

Hold on, she pleaded. *Please. You have resisted for so long.*

"Don't come any closer," she warned. "He's—"

Another door opened. Rosalind couldn't believe her eyes when Lourens Van Dijk stepped out, peering over the car carefully.

"Oh," the old man said. "Hong Liwen. I remember working on him."

. . . *What?*

"You what?" Rosalind asked aloud. Her grip tightened on Orion. Whether she was trying to keep him back or keep the others away, she wasn't entirely certain.

Lourens took a step forward. In haste, another man pushed open the driver's door to stay with him, his dark hair in a frenzy. This was Marshall Seo—despite her rare encounters with him in Shanghai back when the gangs were around, Rosalind had to assume the person always accompanying Benedikt was his now-husband.

"Wait, Lourens. You probably shouldn't—"

Rosalind didn't have time to second his warning. Orion stood so quickly that Rosalind was forced to release him, reeling in surprise. One second he had been sprawled on the gravel, and the next he was lunging for Lourens. Acting on pure instinct, Rosalind kicked her leg out, striking the back of Orion's knee. He teetered off-balance, his attack averted only a mere hairsbreadth short of striking the scientist.

"Get back!" Rosalind shouted.

She didn't wait to see if Lourens would listen. With a huff of exertion, she dove for Orion, intent on pinning him to the ground. The moment her hand closed down on his shoulder, however, he whirled around to face her. He barely brushed her elbow in his wide hit; still, he was so strong that Rosalind went sprawling into the gravel, landing hard enough for the bits and pieces to cut into her flesh.

"*Ouch,*" she spat. "Orion!"

He didn't hear her. He wasn't listening anymore, lost in what had come over him. Perhaps lost utterly, but Rosalind couldn't think like that or she would stop fighting, or she would splay her arms wide and accept whatever was to come while he loomed over her. At least she had his attention now.

In her periphery, she could see Benedikt drawing a pistol.

"Stop it!" Rosalind shouted immediately. "Put that away!"

"Miss Lang, he's going to *kill* you—"

"Put it"—Rosalind retrieved a pin from her hair—"*away.*"

Orion surged forward, but Rosalind was prepared this time. She didn't swerve out of contact; she met his offensive maneuver head-on, catching his wrist before it could strike and using his own momentum against him when she twisted her leg around his ankle, taking his balance out from underneath him once again. She couldn't match his strength, fine. She only needed him within range for one moment to get her sedative in.

Rosalind stabbed her hairpin into his shoulder.

"God," she wheezed. "Do you know how *lucky*"—she tore the metal out—"you are to have me?"

For a second, it seemed Orion might possess enough energy to attack before the sedative kicked in. Then his eyes fluttered. Rosalind finally relaxed, hurrying to slide her hand forward and soften the impact when his head lolled onto the ground.

Footsteps crunched through the gravel on her left. Lourens came to stand behind her, observing Orion quietly.

"I'm not carrying him," Marshall declared by the car.

Rosalind needed a second to catch her breath. When she looked over her shoulder, Benedikt had put his pistol away, warily observing the scene with his arm held before Marshall to forbid him from going forward.

"He's out cold," Rosalind said. Bitterness put an acrid taste on her tongue. "You don't have to worry."

She clambered off Orion, but she didn't step away. She was

unwilling to relinquish him until she had some answers, so even as she turned to Lourens, her hand remained encircled around Orion's arm.

"Before," she prompted, "what did you mean when you said *working on him?*"

Lourens didn't respond for a long moment. He had aged tremendously since Rosalind last saw him. A weary sort of exhaustion had settled over his features.

"Same as how I worked on you," Lourens replied. "I helped his mother with her research before I left the country."

50

There was too much happening inside the house, so Rosalind had forcibly removed herself to stand by the canal, her fists clenched and tucked under her arms.

Lourens had brought a whole luggage case full of concoctions and chemicals, everything he could possibly need to fix Orion. It was that alone keeping Rosalind from lunging at him even now, that alone which had reined her in after he had casually admitted to his part in the experiments that had changed Orion.

Well . . . and the fact that Juliette had arrived on the scene just in time to physically yank Rosalind back the moment she released Orion and sprang forward with her arms outstretched. Her cousin had held her in place with a death grip, barely comprehending what was going on and why on earth Rosalind was trying to attack Lourens until Benedikt and Marshall yelled their quick explanations, voices overlaying each other. With a muttered curse, Juliette had taken one look at Orion on the ground and understood, then told Rosalind, "You need to let Lourens make his cure *first*. Then you can decide what he deserves."

Juliette was right—that needed to come first. Beside the canal, Rosalind breathed out, keeping her eyes closed against the cold flutter of wind. Everyone else was inside. This wasn't supposed to take long. Lourens hadn't seemed to fret in the slightest when he'd opened his case. Either he had a fix that would already work, or he didn't. Either there was something already invented that could bring Orion back, or Lourens would require a whole lab and years of research time.

"Rosalind."

Juliette's voice. When Rosalind ignored the summons, resolute only to listen to the elements and the low rumble of an incoming storm moving across the afternoon clouds, her cousin cleared her throat. The sound carried a layer of warning. Rosalind opened her eyes.

Juliette tipped her head into the house. "Come in."

"Must I?"

If Lourens declared that there was nothing he could do for Orion, she wouldn't even know what to do. Go back into the city? Hide Orion somewhere to keep him out of his mother's grasp? And what were they to do about Lady Hong anyway—go after her before she provoked them, knowing that *eventually* there would be some move made, or wait until trouble rolled in?

"Lourens says—"

"Do you have any errands for me to run?" Rosalind interrupted suddenly.

Juliette appeared confused. "What?"

"Letters to drop off, groceries to get, enemies to kill . . ."

"First of all"—Juliette put her hands on her hips—"I have people for that. What's going on with you?"

She couldn't stand here.

"I can't," Rosalind managed. She turned on her heel. The urge to run thrummed from her bones, prickled discomfort along every inch of skin. *I can't,* she'd said aloud, but the unspoken continuation of that sentence was *I can't face him forgetting me a second time.* It was so much worse to be waiting in anticipation. So much worse to be cold and shivering and left behind than already hiding away somewhere in the shadows. At last, at the end of the road, where there was no more room to muse about whether he was better off without her, she had to admit: getting him back meant everything. How could she bear it if she remained nothing to him?

She hastened toward the bridge.

"Could I at least finish what I was saying first?" Juliette bellowed after her. "Lourens says he's *awake*."

Rosalind whirled around, one hand already on the railing, one foot raised onto the first stone ledge. Her attention refocused on the doorway, on her cousin waiting, just in time to see Orion emerge from behind her, his eyes wide and hair disheveled, half the buttons on his shirt undone and no coat anywhere to be found.

She wasn't breathing. Maybe when Lourens changed her five years ago, it wasn't only the lack of sleeping and the lack of aging; maybe she simply hadn't noticed that she would survive perfectly fine never fulfilling her lung capacity either—

"Where are you going?" Orion shouted.

Rosalind took a step away from the bridge. In the time it took her to turn properly, Orion shot forward, colliding with her and wrapping her in his arms before she could register what was happening. It felt like she'd had new air injected directly into her lungs. Like she had leaped off a precipice expecting to hurtle to her death and grown the ability of flight instead.

"Is it you?" Rosalind asked, though she knew, she'd known the second his arms came around her.

"I love you," Orion said in lieu of a reply, in perfect replacement of any straightforward answer. "I love you, I love you, I'm sorry I said so many stupid things. I can't believe I asked why we couldn't cross the Suzhou Creek."

Rosalind choked on her laugh, her arms finally lifting to clutch him. She allowed herself a few seconds of absorption, focusing on the sensation flooding into her chest and the solid existence of Orion under her fingertips. Then, knowing that they were being watched, Rosalind pulled away, peering back at her cousin in the doorway.

Rosalind jolted. Where did Juliette go?

"Did she return inside?" Orion asked without looking, reading the surprise in her expression.

Juliette's voice floated out from the house, getting fainter and fainter.

"Roma, my love, fetch the letter opener for Ah Cao's messages. He's sealed them too tightly. And keep Marshall away from Hong Liwen—I'm afraid for the state of this house if they befriend each other. . . ."

It was such an offhanded statement that Rosalind couldn't resist a single laugh, looking up at Orion to see if he had heard the same. Orion, though, didn't seem to be paying attention to what was going on behind him. No longer observed by witnesses, he leaned in, and then he was kissing her to make up for every day they had lost, every week that had been stolen, every month spent torn apart. Just as Rosalind had known that his memories had come back by the tone of his voice, it was clear at once that there was a difference in *this,* the hum of her skin where there was contact, the sheer familiarity when he touched the back of her neck and she rose to the tip of her toes.

They drew back slowly, putting an inch between them. Orion breathed out, but he didn't move farther.

"Sorry," he whispered. "I couldn't help myself."

Rosalind had always thought of herself as a performer—a pretender. When she let herself laugh, let herself grab Orion and draw him close again, for once in her life it felt like she had found the curtain into backstage, allowed her to shed her mask and show her true face.

"I do hate to interrupt."

That was a new voice: definitely not Juliette. Rosalind pulled away, looking over Orion's shoulder right as he turned too. Benedikt Montagov leaned in the doorway, his arms folded over his chest casually and a slight lift in his brow. Despite his words, he didn't seem to hate interrupting at all. If anything, he enjoyed being the one to barge in.

"Do you?" Orion asked, catching the same tone.

Benedikt's lips quirked. He pushed off the wall so he could return through the door. "If I don't, everyone else here is too soft to do it. Come in—there's been a message."

The message was from Celia, sent along to Juliette and Roma's city contacts and brought in as an urgent missive. With the state of the border, however, any urgent missive was half a day old at least, which meant Celia's message was even more dire.

> ***Alisa got in touch. She found Lady Hong's base of operation in the International Settlement. Her experiments have succeeded—there's a new concoction. If you can get back into the city by sundown, I'll find a way to disperse her militia for you.***
> ***7 Arden Road.***
> ***P.S. Alisa also says "я не хочу принимать ванну."***

Rosalind blinked at the last line in the note. She looked at Roma. "Did you transcribe this?"

He shook his head. He also seemed to be puzzling over it, turning the note over and around as though there might be an explanation at the back. "It came in as is. I didn't get lazy and start writing in Russian."

Why had Celia suddenly switched to Russian to tell them that Alisa didn't want to bathe? Or had Alisa herself relayed only that line in Russian? What a bizarre thing to include.

"What does it say?" Orion asked, leaning over the table.

Rosalind shook her head. There was no time for what would probably turn out to be a trivial joke. Her cousin and Roma were deep in thought, mulling over the situation at the table. Benedikt and Marshall, on the other hand, appeared very puzzled, entirely out of the loop by the kitchen counter. Only Lourens remained in the living room, dozing on the couch.

"Orion and I need to head back," Rosalind decided. "If we leave in the next hour, it'll time us roughly for sundown."

Juliette took the note from Roma. Her hands were gentle when she laid the paper down flat on the table. "We'll go with you."

A wave of horror lurched through Rosalind at once. It might as well have been a physical sensation for how viscerally she felt it rip through her organs.

"I beg your pardon?" she demanded. "I thought I just misheard you say you were coming too."

"That's exactly what I said," Juliette replied.

"Absolutely not," Rosalind countered. "Are you kidding me? The city is being invaded. The north is being bombed without pause."

"That actually increases our chances of blending in without trouble," Roma said plainly.

"*No,*" Rosalind snapped. "The last time you were both in Zhabei, you *died.*"

When the kitchen went quiet this time, it was an awkward silence, compounded by Marshall making a squeaking noise and Benedikt giving him a light kick to shut him up. Rosalind huffed. Juliette watched her, waiting for her to give in.

"I won't pretend to know what happened in the past," Orion said, trying to break the tension. "But this could be all-out war within a war. My mother has the fighting force of a militia. She is one arm of the Japanese invasion effort."

"That's why you need us," Juliette said. "No more arguments. I won't hear it."

Rosalind was slick with dread. She had *just* managed to accept that her burden wasn't as big as she had believed these past few years. How could they be so careless now as to follow her back?

"I have a question," Benedikt said suddenly. Though everyone in the kitchen turned to him, he was looking into the living room. "Lourens."

"Hmm?" Lourens replied, jerking to attention.

To Rosalind's surprise, Benedikt tilted his head toward her next. "You altered Miss Lang, right?"

"*Altered* is not quite accurate." Lourens cleared his throat. He could sense the glare that Rosalind had turned on him. She didn't care if it made her ungrateful. No matter what good he had done in the past, his work with Orion canceled it all out. "That sounds as though I was performing a routine experiment. I was not. Miss Lang was dying. I had to find whatever would act fast and keep her heart going."

"Sure." Benedikt reached across the counter, plucking up that original missive from Priest, the one sent to warn Oliver that Lady Hong was after him. "Then I am only curious why we keep talking about the danger of this Lady Hong's new invention when yours already exists. Hers is stabilized by putting"—Benedikt scanned one of the lines—"*seramorine* in a person and taking the mutated version from their children to be used. Why is she spending twenty years and two generations trying to harvest an ingredient before making immortal soldiers? What did *you* use?"

Rosalind's fists closed tight. From her side, Orion reached over and smoothed his hand over hers, his thumb brushing the inside of her wrist. There was no pomp accompanying the gesture; in fact, she almost suspected he didn't realize he was doing it. He had merely sensed her aggression and wanted to put her at ease, too familiar with her small tells.

"Did you know"—Lourens hobbled to his feet, coming to read Priest's telegram too—"I became acquainted with Hong tàitài because we were both working on this sort of research? I read her thesis when it was published. Fascinating findings."

"Lourens," Roma said dryly. "That wasn't the question."

"It had been exceedingly difficult to find her because she published under her maiden name, and by the time I'd identified who she was, she had left the city for the countryside," Lourens went on. "She thought a spy might have sent me. Eventually it was only an exchange that won her trust. She sat down to talk about her thesis when I started sharing my own. She was very interested in what was achievable through chemical conditioning of the mind."

Orion flinched. Now it was Rosalind's turn to clutch his hand in reassurance, interlacing their fingers together. Out of his periphery, Roma must have noticed the motion, because when he looked at the scientist again, he was frowning with disapproval.

"Lourens," he prompted again, much sharper this time.

Lourens started. He peered up from the telegram with his eyes wide, as if he were surprised to find that there remained others in the room while he waffled on. "Pardon?"

Benedikt rapped his knuckles on the counter. "The immortality concoction," he reminded. "What did *you* use?"

"Ah. Right." The old scientist pulled on his beard. "There is only so much known science in this world, you know. I had the same base ingredients, but the entirely wrong method. With twenty years and two generations, Lady Hong's invention is—as Benedikt said—stabilized. True immortality." With a grimace, his eyes dropped to Rosalind. "Mine was not stable. Rosalind Lang only has a few years of borrowed time before it kills her."

51

No one else was panicking as much as Orion was, and he couldn't fathom why.

Everyone had dispersed through the house. They had determined their timing, put into order how they were reentering Shanghai. Benedikt and Marshall were going to drive west to begin their journey home to Moscow, passing a black-market rental shop on the way and sending a hired driver. Along with the driver, the shop knew how to provide falsified government papers, a quick fix to make sure the car could ferry people back into the city while it was under guard.

Rosalind had excused herself into the washroom to fix her hair. Predictably, Orion had gotten up and followed her, and though Rosalind cast him a look that said *Really?* she did not bid him leave. He paced the washroom. Rosalind calmly redid her small plaits in front of the mirror, pinning each of them in place.

Perhaps she was making an effort to suppress her reaction. Lourens had told her she was going to *die* soon. That, at best, she had a few years left as the unaging, unsleeping Fortune, and, at worst, she could keel over right this moment. Prior to this piece of information, they had believed her to be *immortal,* and now suddenly it had never been true. Suddenly it turned out the experiment had been wearing away at her this whole time. How could Orion accept that?

"There has to be a cure," he had demanded. While Rosalind had remained relatively stoic, Orion had lunged forward. "Isn't there?"

"To erase something, one must begin with the stable element before making the counteragent," Lourens had replied. He hadn't been bothered by Orion's aggression, nor seemed particularly intimidated. "I can cure your conditioning of the mind because whatever your mother used was derived from my work, so I have the materials to create a counteragent. Meanwhile, your mother never shared her full work with me after inventing her strength concoction. I have no ability to reverse that. Similarly, I cannot cure Lang Shalin when I was never successful with the initial element."

"You can't cure something that doesn't technically exist," Rosalind muttered, almost to herself.

"Yes," Lourens replied, clicking his fingers at her like she had contributed something to class. "You are in half existence."

Orion made a horrified noise. "Why would you *say* that—"

Rosalind grabbed his elbow, shaking her head in warning. It wasn't worth the debate, she seemed to be saying. She didn't know that Orion was willing to argue with a literal rock if he suspected it had insulted her in some manner.

"If you're asking for a cure, the only way forward is obtaining true immortality first," Lourens continued. He had returned to the couch tiredly. "Stabilize the temporary solution I put there five years ago, then erase it. At this point in time, the only person capable of doing something like that is your mother, Hong Liwen."

Christ.

Now Orion could do nothing except stomp up and down the washroom. His mother was the only one who could save Rosalind. Acquiring her completed research was the sole hope for Rosalind's continued survival. This was so twisted.

"Orion, would you quit pacing?" Rosalind said.

"I will combust if I don't pace," Orion replied. "How are *you* so calm?"

Rosalind slid a pin into place. "I already died once," she answered quietly. "I think I have always accepted that I was on borrowed time."

Orion marched toward her without warning.

"You listen to me," he said, grabbing Rosalind's face with both hands. "You are bound to me in matrimony. If you break it and descend into another plane of existence, I *will* chase after you and snatch you back."

For a long moment, Rosalind only stared at him, eyes wide. The pause went on for so long that he started to wonder if he had taken it too far, if he had sounded too threatening, but then she gave a loud snort.

"You know that we're not actually bound in matrimony, right?"

"Says who?"

Rosalind smoothed her expression down, feigning nonchalance. She might have fooled him when all his memories were scattered, but she couldn't fool him anymore. He had their every moment together ready on file. Every shared joke when their eyes met across the office space at Seagreen Press; every vulnerable moment in the half-dark of her French Concession apartment, when the sun was setting but they weren't yet willing to get up and turn on the lights. As infallible and brave as she was, Rosalind still needed him. She needed him as any person needed their burdens borne by another from time to time. Just as he needed her—and now that he had her, he refused to let go.

"Says the government, maybe?" Rosalind retorted.

"Since when did you care about what the government says?"

"The other option is religiously bound matrimony, and I don't think either of us believes in anything."

I believe in you, Orion thought. *Before I put my faith with anything, I would put it with you.*

"My point stands," he said firmly. "You're not dying. We're going to fix this."

Rosalind only scrunched her nose. "Well, I'm worried about you too. Your mind is free, but your body is not. Your headaches are going to worsen with time."

"We can figure it out," Orion said easily. Now that the headaches weren't going to make him snap and attack her, he was hardly concerned. He had suffered worse spells in the past.

"How?" Rosalind asked. "It is the same, no? Your mother holds the fix. Either that or Lourens stabilizes you with what he used on me."

"We can figure it out," he said again. "Mine is slow-acting. Your situation is our priority."

Rosalind didn't refute him, but she didn't agree, either. Her gaze wandered away, settling elsewhere in the washroom. Orion tightened his grasp upon her face to politely request the return of her attention.

When her gaze flickered back, Rosalind looked slightly amused by his prompting. He managed to hold on to that glint in her eye for a mere moment before she was looking at the same point over his shoulder again, and he finally released her face, turning too.

"What is it?" he asked. "What are you looking at it? The bathtub?"

"No," Rosalind replied quickly. "Just thinking. Step out a moment, would you?"

Orion was immediately suspicious. Rosalind, seeing his furrowed brow, pointed to the extra clothing she had brought into the washroom, borrowed from Juliette's closet.

"I need to *change,* darling."

"Fine, fine."

He stepped out. Closed the door behind him, then tried not to fret. Orion needed to get ahold of himself. Resolute to keep his breath under control, he strolled along the hallway, coming into the living room again and leaning against the entryway.

"There you are."

The man who had introduced himself as Marshall was speaking to him, rummaging through a small briefcase on the coffee table. When Orion looked around the hallway, as if there might be someone else instead, Marshall rolled his eyes and gestured for him to come closer.

"Me?" Orion said.

"Yes, you. We are soon to depart, so I thought I would give you this."

Marshall tossed an item at him. Orion caught it smoothly, then looked into his palms to find a stamp.

"I stole it from my father a while ago, and I don't think he ever worked out that I still have it," Marshall said. "He's a Kuomintang general. It's yours now. Slap it over the falsified papers, and it should help."

"Thank you," Orion said, meaning it. His father had had one just like this. Though they couldn't exactly go putting *that* on their papers when General Hong was currently imprisoned.

Orion put the stamp in his pocket. Out of his periphery, he saw Benedikt Montagov exit the kitchen, having organized what he needed.

"We've met before, haven't we?"

Marshall blinked in surprise at Orion's sudden question. Benedikt's expression turned immensely curious too. He paused beside Marshall, his hands in his pockets.

"Have we?" Marshall asked. "Am I the one with amnesia now?"

Orion dug through his memories. With his entire past restored at once, some parts were jumbled, bringing forward his earlier years and making it hard to determine how the linear sequence had occurred. He needed to think deeply about the details in each scene to place when exactly it happened, but he felt like he remembered Marshall Seo from much earlier, when the White Flowers were still around and he had newly returned to the city. . . .

Orion snapped his fingers, landing on the memory. "At the Podsolnukh. You bought me a drink."

In the kitchen, Roma suddenly snorted, and Juliette slapped her hand over his mouth to prevent him from laughing any louder. Orion didn't realize what was so funny until Benedikt turned to Marshall and gave him a look, at which point Marshall most certainly remembered what Orion was talking about. He held still for a long moment. His expression froze, as if he were mentally running through the night *after* the drink.

"Oh, thank goodness," Marshall breathed a moment later. "We played a game of cards, didn't we?"

"Won high earnings," Orion confirmed.

"Let's play again when this is all over. The Trans-Siberian Express is a short journey. You're invited anytime." Marshall hauled his bag up then, with that sufficing as his farewell. He grabbed Benedikt's wrist to drag him along, saying, "Wipe that frown away, nae sarang. It's tarnishing your beautiful face."

"Is my face so beautiful?" Benedikt retorted. He collected his bag too, then waved at Roma and Juliette. It seemed neither he nor Marshall were wanting to make a big matter out of their goodbye. "Was it beautiful that night you were off in the White Flower cabarets instead of at home?"

"You were a full *year* away from saying anything to me—"

"So now it's *my* fault you were off flirting with other men?"

"Jealousy is adorable on you—"

The front door closed after them. Orion felt a little sheepish.

"Of course you would be responsible for causing a fight."

Orion jumped. He hadn't heard Rosalind exit the washroom. She was eerily silent when she wanted to be.

"Don't worry. They do that all the time." Juliette got up, hovering around the stove. "Does everything fit?"

"Like a glove." Rosalind surveyed the living room. Frowned. "Where's Lourens?"

"He stepped out to take a quick walk," Roma said. Though he had answered absently, more focused on perusing the map laid out in front of him at the kitchen table, his head lifted after a moment, as if registering his own response. "Strange. It's been a while."

They weren't taking the scientist with them anyhow, so it didn't matter if he had gotten lost somewhere around the lakes. All the same, he had left his bag here. He couldn't have gone far.

"Hope he stays away," Rosalind grumbled.

No one argued with her. The others were more familiar with Lourens than Orion was, and it appeared it was a discomforting experience for them to find out exactly how much Lourens had contributed to this terrible science.

"What are you going to do about him?" Juliette asked. She was addressing Rosalind, who shook her head.

"What am I to do? Call the authorities? I doubt the Kuomintang cares much about putting him on trial."

"I was rather referring to the fact that I very narrowly stopped you from killing him outside the township earlier."

Orion jolted, surprised. After he had thrown himself out of the farmer's truck, he had little recollection of the events that followed. There was only nothingness in his memory until he jerked back to consciousness in this house with Lourens hovering before him, holding a syringe.

"Don't worry, I'm not plotting his murder," Rosalind said darkly. "I should, but I won't."

"We won't blame you if you're considering it, I suppose," Roma contributed. He grimaced, and when he continued, he was speaking to Orion: "If it's any consolation, he seemed to have realized his wrongdoing while he was in Vladivostok. But it doesn't change the fact that he invented this chemical conditioning business."

Perhaps Lourens was only partly guilty for what had happened to Orion. Perhaps Lourens was ultimately responsible for bringing him back and erasing what his mother had put in him. Still, that didn't endear him to Orion one bit. In his experience, the truly neutral players were the most unpredictably dangerous, and Lourens Van Dijk was exactly that.

Orion said nothing in reply. He let the topic peter out, switching back to their preparations.

"Anyhow, come have some tea," Juliette said. "We're leaving soon."

Orion drifted closer to the kitchen. As did Rosalind, though she walked more purposefully, going to help her cousin fetch teacups.

"Xièxiè, mǔqīn."

Juliette rolled her eyes. "I'm not *that* old."

"*Come have some tea, children,*" Rosalind mimicked, setting the teacups on the table.

"Hilarious."

"I know."

Her cousin didn't seem to pay Rosalind's tone any particular mind, tapping Roma's elbow to signal that she was setting a coaster beside him and asking him to shift the map closer into the center. Orion, though, caught that something was off in an instant, like a single flat note played during a symphony.

What's going on? Orion silently asked. Rosalind couldn't see his expression, so she couldn't reply. No matter how hard he stared at her from the kitchen entryway, she didn't look over at him. She only concentrated on pouring tea, careful not to splatter any droplets.

"So, we have to avoid the area around the North Railway Station or we're simply asking for trouble," Roma said, tracing a red pen through the map on the table. "But Arden Road is on the east side of the International Settlement. We may have to circle outside the city and enter from the south."

"We're still going to encounter garde municipale," Juliette mused, sliding into a chair, "but I suppose it's better than Japanese Marines engaging in active invasion."

Orion finally got closer to the table too, pulling his attention from Rosalind to look at the map. "Then we move through Xujiahui, I presume?" He frowned, bringing his nose close to the small writing—so close that he almost brushed up against the paper. "Does that say *Siccawei*? What sort of map is this?"

"It's old and it's British. Don't judge," Roma said, flicking him away. "Xujiahui is tightly French controlled even if it's under Chinese administration. The moment we enter, we should assume we will be stopped and questioned at any point."

Rosalind put a cup of tea in front of Roma. Then in front of Juliette. When Orion drew away from the table and offered to help her, Rosalind skirted him expertly, shooing him off and pulling her elbow close to her side.

His suspicion shot sky-high.

"Beloved," he said at once. "What are you up to?"

"What do you mean?" She set the kettle where it had been. Busied herself with putting the tea leaves away in the third cupboard to the right.

Orion's mouth opened and closed. He was watching her elbow. It was as if she was trying to shake something back into her sleeve.

"You were—"

A quiet thump sounded behind him. Orion whirled around to find Roma to have pitched forward onto the table. Seconds later, Juliette slanted forward too, her arms laid out already and acting as a pillow when her forehead sank down.

Orion understood. His heart ached at the realization, at the sense of care that Rosalind had even when it was something as underhanded as dropping sedatives into the tea just so they wouldn't accompany the mission back into the city.

The kitchen fell quiet. The stove was still on, boiling the kettle to a low whine, so Orion reached to turn the flame off. Suddenly the silence was overwhelming, suctioning smaller and smaller until it was seconds away from implosion.

Rosalind sniffled. Her eyes were wet. She pressed a hand to her mouth, her complexion almost verging on green.

"I couldn't let them do this," she whispered. "They got out even when I almost ruined them. I won't let them risk it again. This is my problem to fix."

Orion took a step toward her. "It's mine too," he corrected gently.

At first he didn't know if Rosalind heard him. She was still, deathly so. Then she set her head on his shoulder gently, whispering:

"Am I making a mistake?"

Her voice was a mere rasp. Fear shook her words, shook her whole frame, but she didn't let the glistening moisture in her eyes well over. It must have started snowing outside, because the kitchen dimmed a few shades, bringing the cover of a sky veiled in gray.

"If you think you did the right thing, then you did. It is as simple as that."

The clock on the wall chimed. Rosalind lifted her head, casting a glance over. Orion watched her.

"Okay," Rosalind said. Her spine straightened, and in that one motion, she pulled herself together. In that one motion, she became an operative again—Fortune, who did what her country needed. "We should go."

Orion nodded. "Let's go."

Juliette woke up first. She coughed to clear her throat, unable to swallow past how dry and scratchy it had gotten. There was a hint of orange bleeding through the window. Almost sundown.

"By God," she wheezed, lifting her head from the table. Blearily, she reached out to give Roma a shake, seeing double. "Did Rosalind *poison* us?"

Roma stirred. His eyes fluttered, then flew open at once, taken aback over why he was lying on the table. "What time is it?"

Too late to give chase. Hours had passed, which would have been exactly Rosalind's intention. Juliette cursed under her breath, then immediately regretted it when she needed to cough again. Her head was as heavy as stone when she stood up. She stumbled.

"Careful, careful," Roma said, lunging off his chair to catch her.

Juliette exhaled, trying to clear her thoughts while she had Roma to lean on. Then she found her balance again, shaking herself into coherence. She hurried into the living room. Rooted around the desk looking for their contact booklets. "They must be arriving in Shanghai now."

"If we drive fast," Roma suggested, "we could still make it late."

Juliette shook her head. "It would be no help to get there late. The fight would be over, and someone would have won or lost." She took a deep breath, finding the booklet. It was filled with old telephone numbers. Gangsters and businessmen. Drivers and former national soldiers.

As soon as Roma saw what she had picked up, he headed for the bedroom, fetching the second booklet on the shelf there.

"I hope no one needs the telephone for a while," he said, emerging with it in hand. "Where are we sending people? Rosalind's location or general surveillance?"

Juliette steadied herself, worry swirling in her chest. She was going to have a very stern talking to with Rosalind after this.

"Rosalind's location," she said, pushing down the hitch in her voice. "Even if she shakes us off, we're not leaving her on her own this time."

52

Phoebe awoke to a heinous shrieking in her ear.

It took her a moment to realize that it was coming from outside, not from within the cell. A facility-wide alarm was blaring again, different from the one that went off during the rescue mission. Her shoulder was numb. Her eyes weren't focusing yet, showing only dark colors and the bars of the cell.

What was happening? They had mostly left her alone these few days. That electric shock had packed a punch, and even after Phoebe stirred back into consciousness afterward, it had felt exceedingly difficult to make sense of her surroundings. Everything spun. She could do nothing except shut her eyes again and curl up into a ball, fading in and out of fretful sleep in a bid to ease her dizziness. The few times she lifted her head off the floor were when they slid food and water through the bars, and she had consumed the slop with the vague fear that they might just call it a day and slip her poison. It was bizarre that no one was coming to interrogate her. Bizarre that she would hear faint voices arguing by the corridor doors but no further torture.

"Are you awake?"

Suddenly Phoebe could feel a presence in the cell with her. A hand touched her arm. Her eyes bugged wide, her entire body jerking away. Yes, she was awake—finally, when she sat upright this time, her head wasn't spinning anymore.

"It's me, it's me," Silas hissed quickly.

"That doesn't make me feel much better," Phoebe croaked. The skies were alive in warning, which meant they were getting bombed again. "Are you here to torture me?"

Silas muttered something under his breath. While Phoebe tried to push past the wave of nausea pressing at her throat and sit up, he kneeled closer, his hands splayed to show he meant no harm.

"I have been keeping them *away* from torturing you."

"Oh, my *hero,* how can I ever thank you?"

A grimace. Silas glanced over his shoulder. "We don't have much time," he said. "I've been waiting for this next wave of shelling before trying to get you out. The soldiers are evacuating. We have to move at the same time while the doors are open."

Phoebe was having a hard time believing that this, too, wasn't some trick. Doubt had crept into her mind, had colored her very perception of him with the rancor of betrayal.

"I'm not going anywhere with you," she whispered. "You hurt Oliver."

"I had him sedated—"

"You've given something horrific to my mother! The Japanese are going to invade us because of you!"

"I tainted every vial!"

The alarm got louder. It must have been shrieking at half volume before, because its full capacity was deafeningly loud, almost drowning out the first shell when it struck the base's vicinity. The walls shuddered.

"What?" Phoebe whispered.

Silas shook his head. Seeing that he wasn't getting her cooperation anytime soon, he grabbed her arm, hauling her to her feet by force. He had rolled his sleeves up. When Phoebe scrambled for balance, her eyes latched on to the crook of his elbow, where he was wearing a bandage.

"Here's what happened," Silas said, tugging her through the door of the cell and into the corridor. It was empty. The guards were gone. "Yes, I contacted your mother. Intelligence coming through both Nationalist and Communist covert determined that she kept trying to get in touch with Oliver, but no one could figure out why. I took a risk. Early in the tour, I'd heard from Rosalind that Oliver was off the grid and on her tail. Anywhere Rosalind went, Oliver would be present too. So I acted the traitor. I made a bargain with your mother—I promised I could get her Oliver if she let go of Orion."

A monstrous shudder swept through the corridor. Just as they were turning a corner, a section of the low ceiling detached, crashing into their path and ripping the pipes out from the walls. Heat blew into the tight space. Phoebe coughed, her arm coming up to block her nose from the smoke, and Silas cursed, pulling them backward onto another route.

"At first she said she would consider it. I hadn't understood what she was actually doing; I only knew that she was trying to get to Oliver, though it wasn't her priority yet. It wasn't until the last vial was destroyed during the tour that she switched gears and agreed. She would release Orion to us as long as I could get Oliver into captivity and take a certain amount of blood from him."

Another boom rocked the facility. Phoebe could barely catch her breath with how quickly they were moving. She almost tripped on something in her path, but Silas maneuvered her smoothly, letting her recover her balance.

"If you must be angry at me, be angry that I was willing to risk Oliver's safety to get Orion back. But I am a double-, triple-, quadruple-crosser by nature. I was never going to aid her fully. I was going to get what we needed, give her the illusion of cooperation, then tug the carpet out from beneath her."

With another shudder, a crack ran through the wall to their left.

There was shouting when they passed an offshoot corridor, and Silas picked up speed, his grip tightening.

"I am," Phoebe muttered. "I *am* angry at you for that."

Yet she couldn't deny that without him they probably never would have gotten Orion back. Without him Lady Hong could have easily held on to him forever, kept him under her control.

Silas paused at a turn in their path. He looked along the two options, then at her. His mouth pinched into a pained expression, and then he was hurrying them forward again, taking the left. Phoebe suspected a fire was burning somewhere in the facility. She could smell it, pungent in her nose and bringing tears to her eyes.

"My point is," Silas concluded, "I was taking a small amount of blood from myself every time the soldiers took from Oliver. Once they handed the vials over to me, I'd mix the blood together." He pulled them down the corridor faster; gauging by noise alone, they were nearing the outer periphery. "Your mother may have the supply now and it may seem like everything is going fine when she tests for the presence of seramorine, but as soon as she uses them to experiment, nothing is going to last. Ratio's all off. Perfect sabotage."

Another collision rocked the facility. Silas was explaining himself as though the matter had been so simple. As though he wouldn't have been killed immediately had either side caught on to him.

"You should have told me," Phoebe said. Her voice was hoarse. "I could have helped."

How much easier could their jobs have been if they had worked in tandem instead of against each other? How much quicker could they have found what they needed, put together the pieces? It was too late for the thought. It was an impossible one anyway, because at no point could Phoebe have ever suspected that Silas was capable of *this*.

Silas halted by a door. There was already a bag waiting. "You'll leave through here."

Phoebe looked at the bag. She couldn't fathom what was inside—it was long and bulky, strangely shaped at one end. "What?"

"I'm getting you out," Silas said slowly, and she needed every bit of emphasis he applied to his words, because they were not registering in the slightest. He had worked so hard to finally secure Priest . . . and now he was throwing it away?

"What about you?"

"I have to stay." He reached into his jacket and withdrew a pistol. Before Phoebe could be frightened that he was about to shoot her, he gave it to her handle-first. "Hit me."

Phoebe gawped at him. "Excuse *me*?"

"Make it look realistic. I'll tell them you forced me to find you an exit and then discarded me. Hit hard."

"You are *insane,*" Phoebe hissed.

"Come on," Silas prompted. The facility shook. If they dawdled any longer, the whole thing might collapse overhead. "Priest would do it."

Phoebe's jaw dropped. He did not just say that. He absolutely did not. "Do *not* tell me what Priest would or wouldn't do."

"Why not?" Silas challenged. He almost looked humored. "She would. That's why she's so likable."

Phoebe resisted the urge to stomp her foot. "I can't believe," she seethed, "how stupid you are to think you like her."

"I do."

"You're mistaken!"

A low, persistent whine was seeping down the corridors. Though Phoebe and Silas practically had to scream to be heard, their conversation felt enswathed, unaffected by the world falling apart. Silas watched her for a beat. Seemed to register that she was genuinely offended by what he was saying.

"Are you being serious?" he finally asked.

She drew her spine dead straight. "Obviously."

Silas shook his head. Scoffed. Then he stepped directly in front of her, saying:

"Hong Feiyi, don't you see why I couldn't let go of Priest? I'm not some unerring operative. I tried to convince myself that I was simply devoted to the country, but then I saw you in that cell and everything finally made sense." His eyes dropped. "Of course I was committed to her beyond what was acceptable for the mission. I was so fascinated because I could see the parts of *you* in her. I've loved *you* this whole time, just split in two."

Phoebe, for once, had no retort at the ready. Her mouth opened and closed. When her grip tightened on the pistol in her hand, she finally followed Silas's instructions, and hit him hard across the face.

The metal made contact with a vicious clunk.

Silas reared back, his hand immediately coming up to touch his face. Purple bloomed along his jaw, the color already showing after mere seconds. A splotch of blood appeared at the side of his lip where the impact had split his skin. When he lowered his fingers, they were smeared with red.

"Christ, I know I asked to be hit, but a warning would have been nice—"

Phoebe kissed him in apology. Though she was still holding the pistol in one hand, her other dug into his hair, holding him as close as she could, her lips pressed right where she could taste blood. For a moment, Silas was frozen, unresponsive.

Then he leaned in too, his hands coming to both sides of her face. His lips captured hers with an uncharacteristic ferocity, but Phoebe supposed this whole undertaking was full of uncharacteristic behavior, both of them finally peeling off skins they had been wearing and finding they were the same underneath. He kissed her, and she recognized the tune even if the pitch was different. She kissed him, and the feeling was as electric as picking up a real pistol for the first time.

Phoebe drew back. Took a shaky breath. Silas was watching her with his glasses skewed, and she reached to fix them. "Will they punish you for this?"

"It doesn't matter," he answered without hesitation. "My mission has never been more important than you are."

Her heart was making a racket against her ribs. "Don't die," she whispered. "I'm not done hitting you."

Silas huffed a pained laugh. "Noted. Now go. Get out of Zhabei." He pulled away to pick up the bag, handing it to her. As soon as Phoebe took it and heard the clatter, she realized what he had prepared inside. It was a rifle. Plenty of cartridges, too, if the heavy weight was any indication.

She looked up at him. Silas was already smiling, pleased with himself as he opened the door, letting in the blazing night outside. The horizon was engorged in red. Fire, burning endlessly from the bombing.

"Go!"

Phoebe nodded. She ran out the door, crossing the short section of the facility perimeter and looking around wildly, taking the road out. She ran and she ran, ducking when she caught sight of crowds of people, veering away when national soldiers and enemy soldiers alike moved too close in the night.

Phoebe had a whole battleground to cross before she could make it back into the International Settlement. She could hear yelling in every direction, loud enough to echo past the roar of the planes overhead. Across the whole neighborhood, civilians were being rounded up by the invading army and urged not to resist, even when their neighbors remained locked in buildings being torched aflame to eliminate resistance before it could erupt.

Phoebe paused. She slowed down around the corner of a street, watching a group of militiamen at the intersection. The ronin—Japanese auxiliaries to the army—were marked by their armbands, taking it upon themselves to order the streets of Zhabei. She eyed the group as they hooted into the night, heading for the cluster of civilians with their bags over their shoulders. The civilians were clearly seeking safety. Hurrying toward the border into the International Settlement, intent on fleeing.

She unbuckled her bag. Loaded her rifle. The first ronin didn't even make a sound before he was going down, a bullet studded into his head.

Phoebe Hong had somewhere to be, but that didn't mean she couldn't clear out her path while she was moving along. She exhaled, calmed her raging pulse.

She took aim again, and fired.

Even the underground hospital was filling beyond capacity. Celia took another glance at the clock, biting her bottom lip. Though this location remained a secret by official catalogs, the sheer chaos rippling through Zhabei and Hongkou at present was likely spreading its word as a last resort, knowing the proper hospitals were complete mayhem.

"Fine, you're discharged," the doctor said hurriedly, coming back with a bottle of something in his hands. He was terribly young. Freshly out of school, or perhaps still studying. It wasn't as though these sorts of places could be picky about qualifications. "You have to stop exerting the wound, though. Stay off your feet for at least a week. Disinfect twice a day." He passed the bottle to Oliver, who took it, then looked at it as if he had been handed something alien.

The doctor left the room. There was another patient in the corner who had been groaning for the past ten minutes, but he was probably very low in the queue. The hospital was no bigger than three rooms, and Celia had counted only two doctors. She had barely gotten Oliver here in time to be tended to. His bleeding had worsened exponentially on the car ride, and the doctor had put him under a sedative the moment they arrived. It took another two days before they acquired the materials to get him into surgery. Though he had awoken shortly afterward, feeling fine, the doctor had forbidden him from leaving until he was able to stand on his own again, which he managed today.

"All right," Oliver said. He got up from the makeshift bed, raising his voice to be heard over the hubbub in the room, over the fretting parents and frantic elderly, the crying children and the civilians shouting just to get the panic out of their system. "Let's go."

"Did you not hear what the doctor just said?" Celia demanded. "You have to stop exerting the wound."

"I'll be perfectly fine."

Celia crossed her arms. Oliver winced, as if he knew he had misstepped somewhere.

"What is the alternative?" he asked. "Sitting out entirely?"

"No. Of course not."

A plan was already forming in her head. She had kept the earpieces from the rescue mission, had held on to Rosalind's, too, when she'd needed somewhere to put it while they were raiding that dress shop. Celia knew what she had up her sleeve when it came to causing a distraction into the International Settlement, as she had promised Rosalind. The only problem was that she had another point of concern too.

"Take this," she said, bringing out one earpiece. Before Oliver could protest, she put it into his ear, securing it tight. "Go to the liaison station three streets down. Your next objective is figuring out where Alisa is."

Oliver frowned. Earlier in the day, Celia had been the one to check in with the nearest liaison station, finding that Alisa had left a message for her. Celia had passed it on, moving as quickly as she could.

It was only now, after musing on it awhile, that she was starting to get confused. Where had Alisa made the call from? She had to have found a telephone somewhere, which meant she couldn't still be surveying Lady Hong. Where did she go afterward? Why hadn't she found her way here?

"What does Alisa Montagova's location have to do with the trouble at present?" Oliver asked. "She said my mother is generating soldiers. That should be the focus."

"And as we speak, my sister is making her way over to combat your mother," Celia returned. "I can help her. I can do our part. I just need you out of it. Please, Oliver."

He hesitated. It went against his every instinct, she could tell. He wanted to brush his health off. He wanted to insist otherwise so long as it meant he was on the battlefield. In that moment, Celia was terribly afraid that she couldn't get through to him.

Then he reached out and brushed her cheek lightly. A gesture of acceptance, waved like a white flag.

"You," he said with distress, "are making the most pleading eyes at me right now, you know that?"

Celia pretended she had no clue what pleading eyes he was talking about. She grasped his hand, her own palm sliding against his fingers.

"If this is going to work between us, you have to let me decide what's good too," she said quietly. "You can't keep me out of matters. You allow me in, and you accept it if I disagree. If I want to draw the plans instead."

A beat passed. The hospital roared with noise, suddenly more raucous than ever when a plane swooped overhead and gunfire sounded in the distance. Others in the room shrieked with terror, but Oliver and Celia remained still—watchful, waiting. Maybe he wouldn't accept it. Maybe it wouldn't be what he wanted after all.

"It's going to work, I promise," Oliver finally said. It was so gentle that Celia's heart prickled in reaction. She could feel the promise sink deep, burrowing into the very marrow of her being. For that one vulnerable moment, she could see every fear and worry in his expression, but still he was allowing it.

Celia rose onto her toes and stole a kiss. The world shook, flashing light into the hospital. Overhead bombing, resuming once more.

"Be careful," Oliver whispered into her ear. He pressed another kiss to her temple. Then he exited, moving quickly before the next round of overhead planes could cause havoc outside. Celia waited a minute in case there were enemy operatives watching to catch them. Once enough time has passed, she hastened an exit too.

As she was passing the front desk, though, the secretary waved for her attention, spotting her in an instant. She was holding the phone line, the receiver dangling loose.

"For me?" Celia confirmed.

The secretary nodded wordlessly. Everyone here was on the same payroll—the hospital was in direct communication with the liaison station. Celia picked up the phone and pressed the receiver to her ear.

"Wéi?"

"Report landed two minutes ago from the liaison station in Xujiahui," the voice on the other end said. "Fortune has been sighted coming in. Resume your mission. Secure Huntsman when he surfaces."

Celia acknowledged receipt and put the phone down.

Yes—she did have a mission to resume.

There was no trouble getting into the International Settlement with their forged papers. Slowly Rosalind drove past the control point and rolled her window up again, her eyes flicking to the rearview mirror. "You can come out now. We made it through."

Orion emerged from underneath the back seats, blowing a huff of air. "I can't believe I had to hide when I *have* perfectly forged papers."

"It's not to hide from the Kuomintang at the control point," Rosalind muttered, squinting out the windshield and picking up speed. "There are going to be faction eyes watching every border. I don't want the Communists noting your presence here and trying to come after you. We can resume civil war after this threat is eliminated."

If only it were really that easy to push off domestic matters while an international one was pressing on their city. Orion climbed back into the front seat.

"Do you want me to drive now?"

Rosalind braked chaotically, letting a flock of birds take flight from the intersection before she accelerated again. "No, I've got it."

Orion grimaced, looking terrified for their safety. Wisely, he didn't voice it. It wouldn't take long to get to Arden Road, even if Rosalind couldn't stay within the lines of the road. The real tribulation came with their next steps. They weren't crossing into Zhabei, but they were still entering a war. Lady Hong possessed a militia, most of them more dangerous than ordinary soldiers when they were conditioned to follow her commands no matter the cost.

They drove past a group of girls. It had to be some volunteer force, because they were wearing medical personnel armbands, carrying what looked like sheets in their arms.

"I'm worried about Phoebe," Orion said.

Rosalind turned a corner too fast. The tires screeched.

"Chances are high we will find her with your mother as well. And if we don't . . . that would probably mean she's safe in a Nationalist room."

Orion grimaced. His fists curled in his lap. "When this is over, she's in so much trouble. There's no reason she had to enter the facility and put herself in danger."

But at the moment, there was very little they could do about the situation short of putting out a citywide call for Phoebe Hong. And since Lady Hong was so close to destroying the very world with her research, they needed to make that their first priority.

"We play this out first, and then we worry about what comes next," Rosalind decided, keeping her voice firm. Whether she was trying to convince herself or Orion, she wasn't sure. "Again—we may find her there."

"I'm not sure whether that's a good thing."

Rosalind glanced over at him. She had thought she was taking her eyes off the road for merely a second, but then a great bump rolled beneath her right side, and she quickly focused her attention again. What had that been? Did someone leave their shoe out on the road?

"Do you think she would hurt Phoebe?"

Orion leaned against the window. "No. That's never been a risk, especially given that Phoebe has no use in her experiments. I'm more worried that my sister is going to involve herself." He grimaced, then removed his forehead from the glass. Rosalind's driving was too erratic to rest gently. "She's a live grenade. Did you hear her on the communication line?"

Rosalind stayed quiet, more concerned about watching for their next turn. Orion, meanwhile, continued mumbling to himself, mimicking, "*I'm going dark. I'll be all right.* Why would she say that? She sounded just like an operative."

A chill skated down Rosalind's spine. They fell silent.

"Speaking of sisters," Orion said after a while, returning to his normal tone, "how is yours getting in contact with you?"

"She'll find a way," Rosalind replied. Outside the window, most of the French Concession seemed to be carrying on life as normal. There was no indication whatsoever that some of the foreigners strolling these streets even knew there were bombs falling in the north. Her jaw clenched, her grip tightening on the steering wheel.

"Hey."

Rosalind flicked another quick glance over. She thought Orion was going to tell her to ease up on her driving, but as she passed the boundary from French Concession into International Settlement, Orion wasn't watching the road. He reached over, tucked a piece of her hair behind her ear.

"What is it?" she asked.

"Whatever happens," Orion said, "I love you."

"Oh, shut up."

Orion blinked. "*Rosalind—*"

"Don't say anything that sounds like it could substitute for *goodbye,*" Rosalind interrupted. She pulled the steering wheel. They almost collided with a corner before she course-corrected, speeding again. The buildings whipped past. Between the alleys, flashes of the Bund were visible, warships and battalions pressed up against the boardwalk.

"That's not what I meant."

Rosalind tried to relax her shoulders. It was an impossible task. They might have become permanently melded into her terror-stricken posture.

"Then we have a whole lifetime for you to tell me," she said quietly. "Let's fight this first."

Rumors of a sniper in Zhabei spread in an instant.

"Do you know anything about this?" Celia asked. She pressed

hard on her earpiece, relaying what she was hearing from the crowds that rushed past in evacuation.

"Yes," Oliver replied instantly. "It's Priest."

"Your instructions?"

"Not mine. There are other snipers at work too, hitting back at the Japanese militia. Scarlet Gang sent them. I think Priest is just the most effective."

Celia frowned, moving through the streets with haste. For all intents and purposes, the Scarlet Gang was dissolved, operating as a mere arm of the Nationalists. It was only when it came to underground activity that they brought the term back out. The Chinese army needed to follow official governance. As did the Japanese army. But when auxiliaries like the ronin ran rogue, the city needed to hit back with the same energy. Just as Celia paused by a shop front to take inventory of the pandemonium, she heard a series of gunfire from one of the windows, taking out a group of Japanese militia.

This had become an utter war zone.

"Definitely more than one sniper at work here," Celia muttered. "Find anything yet?"

While Celia picked her way to her destination, Oliver was behaving, staying put at the liaison station to investigate. The matter had certainly captured his attention more than he had expected. Half an hour ago, he had reported to Celia about finding the operative who answered the call from Alisa—he only needed to trace the log at the operating center now.

"Give me a moment. A call is coming in about the inquiry I sent out."

Oliver went quiet in her ear. Celia finally arrived at the safe house: the same one they had been holed up at to plan the rescue mission. The paper bag remained by the door. When Celia peered in, she made a curious noise, realizing that the last set of clothes there were gone. So Phoebe must have come by before she appeared at the facility. Celia supposed that made sense. Phoebe had to have gotten her hands on the last earpiece too if she had been communicating with them once she arrived, and that had been left here on this table.

Celia pushed the table aside. There was a storage space in the floor, visible only if she pressed hard on the floorboard and popped the latch out. She hadn't told any of the others while they were here because it was unnecessary for the mission, but it was certainly necessary now. With effort, Celia lifted up the storage space, revealing the case hiding underneath. Her cousin wasn't the most infamous weapons dealer in the area for nothing.

"Still there?"

Celia nudged her ear into her shoulder, hitting the microphone. She needed both hands to tug the case out. "Where else would I go, Oliver?"

"Only making sure you didn't get plucked away, sweetheart. I have confusing news."

Celia frowned. She started to peruse the explosives, picking the ones she thought would work best. "What does that mean?"

"Did Alisa sound at all distressed when she was reporting in?"

"I have no idea." A few of the explosives needed assembling. Celia moved fast, screwing halves together or pulling off safety mechanisms, putting them into her bag one after the other. "When the liaison station passed her message to me, they didn't say anything about that." Celia paused. "The only strange thing they noted was that she slipped in a line of Russian at the end. The liaison station transcribed it phonetically. I was the one to put it together before sending it off to Rosalind."

"Was it anything important?"

"Not at all. Something about bathing. It was the rest that needed attention. I passed most of it on to Rosalind. *'I found Lady Hong's base of operation. 7 Arden Road. She's succeeded with her experiments. Go as soon as you can.'"* Celia zipped up her bag. She was ready. Her earpiece had gone silent. "Oliver?"

"Well," he said slowly. "My findings say that the call originated from 7 Arden Road. So unless Alisa Montagova was so sneaky as to use a telephone on my mother's own base, I have to wonder if this message actually came from her."

53

Arden Road had been blocked off.

"I think we're within the Japanese residential area," Orion whispered. Though they remained inside the car, driving forward slowly to take in their surroundings, he kept his voice quiet.

"We must be," Rosalind said. She craned her neck, squinting ahead. There were barriers erected along the entrance to Arden Road, guarded by uniformed Japanese soldiers. Her stomach twisted at the sight. "They're legally allowed to be here for protection while the battle is ongoing."

On the map, the Japanese residential area spanned from the eastern edge of Zhabei down to a portion of the International Settlement, pressing on the bend of the Huangpu River. They were close enough to the fighting that its sounds could be heard faintly. Still, the streets here possessed an inherent sense of safety, knowing that the imaginary lines between jurisdictions restricted the entry of conflict.

"Legal or not," Orion muttered, "how do we get through?"

Without warning, a *boom!* shuddered in the distance, lighting a flare into the night. Rosalind jolted in her seat, swiveling to survey the disruption. It was coming from the border of the International Settlement. Which . . . wasn't allowed.

"Oh," Rosalind said suddenly. "That's got to be Celia."

The soldiers at the end of Arden Road hurried to survey the

threat. Though there weren't very many civilians around these residential parts, a few vehicles on the street slowed to see what was going on. Rosalind took that opportunity to pull onto the side of the road and halt the car naturally, hoping it wouldn't draw attention. The other cars passed. She nodded at Orion; in tandem, they both exited, stepping into the night.

"What the hell is Celia doing?" he whispered. He reached for her hand, feigning a leisurely stroll. The explosion had come from behind them. Arden Road sprawled ahead, extending toward the south. Though the pavement was on a slight incline, the trees to either side loomed forward, eager to grow against the grain.

Rosalind glanced over her shoulder. Another series of explosions followed the first, though they weren't loud in the way that the overhead bombing was. The skies remained dark at the site—no fire hurtling up to the clouds. It didn't appear to be an attack on the border. If Rosalind had to take a guess, Celia was meddling with the control points and breaking up the barriers that were keeping people out of the International Settlement.

"I know what she's doing," Rosalind said, hurrying their walking pace. "Get ready to run."

First the roar of noise was faint—then it got louder and louder. While Rosalind and Orion proceeded along the side of the road carefully, a crowd appeared from afar, moving forward en masse. Civilians from Zhabei. Refugees and escapees, some lugging all that they could carry while others left with only themselves.

Many decided to swerve upon sighting the blockade on Arden Road, breaking from the group and taking the crosswise roads once they had entered protected foreign territory. A large majority, though, kept pushing forward, completely overpowering the ten or so soldiers that had been posted to protect the Japanese residential area.

Taking the distraction, Rosalind tugged on Orion's hand fast, joining the masses. She didn't know whether the crowd would disperse or if they would continue down Arden Road for the fastest route of escape. They needed to make use of the distraction while they had it.

They moved quickly. Made decent progress, passing beautiful houses and shiny fences.

Then a gunshot flew along the street.

"Stop, stop," Orion hissed, hauling Rosalind close.

The crowd screamed. Her heart in her throat, Rosalind hurriedly scanned their surroundings, trying to see where the bullets were coming from in the absolute pandemonium. Orion, meanwhile, yanked them behind a letterbox, taking temporary shelter.

A cluster ahead of them cleared. Over the crest of Arden Road, a new line of soldiers had arrived to stop the crowd. There was one man dressed in a Western suit, and he held the gun, walking two paces ahead of the uniformed soldiers. When it seemed most of the civilians were scared enough to turn back and take an alternate route, he lowered his gun and spoke something in Japanese.

"What's he saying?" Rosalind whispered.

"He's telling the soldiers to hurry up and clear the street—they can't have trouble here," Orion replied warily.

Rosalind's hand tightened. "I don't suppose Celia has a second distraction up her sleeve."

"That would be too much to hope for." Orion winced. He risked a glance back where they had come from. The masses were starting to disperse. He must have realized their predicament at the same time as Rosalind: if they wanted to chance something, they needed to do it now while the pan was still hot and chaos choked the air. "Okay. How do you feel about forcing our way through?"

There were only two of them. At least fifteen soldiers up ahead.

Instead of relying on her hairpins, Rosalind pulled a poisoned knife this time. "Stay behind me."

Celia was intent on striking every control point east of the Huangpu River.

She waited for the sound. The moment her explosive erupted into the night, the moment the Nationalists or foreigners guarding the barbed-wire control points reared back with alarm and shouted for order, she was on the move. The crowds always handled the rest. They only ever needed the slightest waft before biting down on the offering—before rushing through and taking the opening. The control points would be recovered shortly, of course. They were too well maintained to be caught off guard for long and usually needed only minutes to recover order. By the time the officers blew on their whistles and blocked the control points again, though, enough people would have gotten through to create a flock moving into the International Settlement.

Celia could only hope that was enough. She threw another explosive. Timed it, then rounded the corner, getting out of sight.

". . . come in. Sweetheart?"

She pressed her earpiece. "I'm here."

"Reports from the ground about the ronin starting to shoot at random. Now is a good time to get out of there."

Celia muttered a curse, looking around. She was somewhere near Hongkou. By what she was witnessing, she guessed this area was going to experience the most evacuation. Civilians here had no other way of protecting themselves short of fleeing outright and hoping that was enough to spare their lives.

"Send more operatives into Hongkou to help our line of resistance," she instructed. "I need to get into the International Settlement."

"Can do." A crackle of static over the wire. "Are you going after your sister?"

"Not yet."

Celia needed to bring some sort of defense if she was going to join the battle with Rosalind. Alisa's call had come from the base, so Alisa was still there. And if she was still there, then something was awry, something had been orchestrated two steps ahead of what Celia could see and indicated that Rosalind and Orion were possibly walking into a trap. Still, it wasn't as though they could *not* show up at Lady Hong's base of operation when the completed experiments were under threat of being disseminated. But they had been summoned, and *why* would they be summoned . . . ?

Gunfire rang above Celia's head. She crouched down, taking cover for a short moment, before an idea occurred to her.

"Oliver," she said suddenly. "Can you put me in contact with Priest?"

The wire stayed quiet. It stayed quiet for such a long time that Celia thought she might have lost signal until Oliver activated his side again, clearing his throat.

"I can do that," he said. "She's, uh, she's actually already heading that way. Don't freak out."

Celia blinked. "Why would I freak out?"

"Let me just start off by saying I *am* a responsible brother. . . ."

As long as Rosalind could keep the bullets away from Orion, they could move through this unit quickly.

There was no denying it: there was no chance any gun could beat someone capable of flinging a soldier across the road. Orion didn't need to incapacitate anyone outright. They fell into an easy pattern: Rosalind only needed to slash shallowly with her knife, getting in an opponent's way for long enough to take the initial attempts at firing bullets. The moment she ducked to allow him to take over, Orion had them down and eliminated, moving on to the next.

Rosalind thought they were making good progress. She pulled her knife fast, right through the shoulder of one soldier, swiveling to give Orion room.

Then she felt something cold press to the back of her neck, and she froze in an instant, her breath catching in her throat.

"Orion," she warned.

He spun around. Swore under his breath, raising his hands at once to show himself disarmed.

"I think," the voice behind Rosalind said in English, "that is enough."

The soldiers stopped. The street would have fallen quiet if not for the battle in the distance. Though Rosalind couldn't see who had her at gunpoint, by the sound of the deep, accented voice, she had to guess it was the man in the suit.

"You could have walked up to the manor," he continued, speaking to Orion. "All of this is quite unnecessary."

Orion's eyes stayed on Rosalind. He looked as though he was seconds away from lunging, and Rosalind silently bade him to stay where he was instead of risking it.

"I have trouble believing that," Orion said carefully. He switched to Japanese, and though Rosalind couldn't understand what he said next, she knew he was asking for her to be let go.

The man, predictably, did not move his gun. A cold sweat crept down Rosalind's neck. Her healing had a limit, and being shot point-blank far crossed it. Still, better that he was keeping the gun on her than turning it on Orion.

"Your mother has been waiting for you," the commander said, continuing to speak in English. "We all have."

Orion hesitated. His brow furrowed, trying to gauge where this was going. "She doesn't need me anymore."

"Ah, but she does. Some trick your friend played."

Silas, Rosalind realized in an instant. "What the hell does that mean?"

The man didn't answer her. But that alone seemed an answer in and of itself: if there was some trick in Oliver's blood, then the experiments hadn't been successful yet. They still didn't have the completed concoction.

So why had Alisa said otherwise?

A heavy pit was opening in Rosalind's stomach. It turned even worse when she and Orion exchanged a glance, and she watched a flash of defeat cross his expression. His gaze was soft.

"All right," Orion said slowly. "If she needs me, she can have me."

"*Orion,*" Rosalind said, appalled.

"Tell my mother I have a trade," he went on. "Give Rosalind the cure to her experiments. Then I'll be your test subject for however long my mother needs. I won't protest. She won't even need to force me."

"Absolutely not," Rosalind snapped. "Orion, are you out of your mind—"

The man grabbed her neck from behind. Before Rosalind could do a thing to resist, before she could snarl or fight or grab a pin from her hair, there was a terrible pain in her shoulder. He had injected her with something ice-cold.

And her world snapped dark in an instant.

54

Her arms had been bound behind her back.

When Rosalind managed to drag herself into consciousness, she didn't know whether she was more surprised to see Alisa staring at her from across the room, similarly bound, or that her eyelids still felt heavy, as though she were lacking sleep.

"Alisa?" Rosalind wheezed.

"Good, you're finally awake," Alisa said. "I've been waiting for you. We need to get moving soon. I think Lady Hong is about to take Orion and evacuate from the city."

Each part of that statement seemed more incomprehensible than the last. Rosalind winced, trying to gather her bearings. Her outer coat was twisted uncomfortably with her arms like this, cutting off her blood supply. When she shifted, the fabric didn't move, but she almost lost her balance, veering against the wall that she had been propped upon.

"My entire throat feels like cotton," Rosalind grumbled. "What happened? What do you mean *finally*? How long was I out?"

"I'm just exaggerating. No more than fifteen minutes. I think you burned off their sedative much faster than they expected. This is ideal. We can take them by surprise."

Outside the window, night had fallen completely. It was pitch dark, the clouds dense and immovable, showing no stars. Rosalind tried to pull at the rope on her wrists. Nothing budged—she could feel the strain extending up her arms too, looping not only a simple knot around her hands but clasping her entire torso in place like she were about to be gutted and served at the table.

"What?"

Alisa tipped her head toward the door. She seemed impatient with Rosalind's immense confusion, as though she should have been paying attention while she was unconscious during those fifteen minutes. Rosalind couldn't hear any noise in the hallway, but she could hear yelling from outside the exterior window. It sounded like there was a crowd on the streets again.

"They've been arguing. Orion has been asking for some cure . . . for you, if I'm not mistaken. His mother has said it'll take time because 'you're not her work.' The last thing I heard was his agreement to leave with her."

"Leave with her?" Rosalind echoed, horrified. Her arms started to prickle with more feeling. Her blood was rushing back now that she was moving around, pins and needles darting up her elbows and into her shoulders. "*Where?*"

"I don't know. But out of Shanghai, it seems—somewhere for her to continue working fast without being caught by the Nationalists. They're fighting back on the invasion with more success than expected. The Japanese are going to mobilize harder soon. If she doesn't bring them results before then, they'll stop funding her."

Rosalind tried to ease herself further upright. It wasn't only her arms that had lost feeling. Her legs seemed so weak that she wasn't sure if she could stand up, though they had left her ankles unbound. She wondered for a moment why they weren't afraid that she'd get up and run out, only to turn over her shoulder and see that her rope was tied to a metal loop in the floor.

"Merde," Rosalind muttered. She yanked her shoulder hard. It did nothing to loosen her rope. "Are you okay? Are you hurt?"

Alisa shook her head.

"Sorry to have lured you in like this." She looked at her lap, the gesture uncharacteristically sheepish. "They caught me sneaking around a few days ago. I've been quietly sitting prisoner until they forced me to make contact at gunpoint this morning."

Rosalind shook her head. "We would have shown up as soon as we got wind of her location, even if we knew Lady Hong was trying to get Orion into a trap. I'm just glad you're safe."

"Safe is a bit of a stretch. I did get pistol-whipped a few times."

Rosalind grimaced. "You don't look like you got pistol-whipped, if that makes you feel any better."

"It does, actually. I'm sturdy." Alisa pursed her lips, examining Rosalind up and down. "At least I was allowed to make that call myself. Did you find it? Behind the bathtub?"

Rosalind, carefully, leaned her shoulder back against the wall. She felt the pressure of glass pressing into her arm—smooth, unbroken glass—and sighed in relief.

"Yes, it's in my sleeve."

She hadn't been able to figure out why Alisa had included the line in Russian until Orion had asked her what it said. He couldn't understand it. Which meant, for whatever reason, Alisa had intended it only for Rosalind's eyes. Though it hadn't made sense initially, she'd gotten a sneaking suspicion when her eyes landed on the bathtub in Juliette's washroom. After she'd kicked Orion out, she had approached the bathtub cautiously, not sure what she would find. What a surprise it had been to see the vial hiding there, very much not shattered into pieces, very much whole and intact, its green liquid glistening.

"You trickster."

Alisa snorted. "Thank you. Now listen: I think Lady Hong already has a cure."

Rosalind furrowed her brow. "What? How?"

"I don't know what it *is* exactly, but I saw her experimenting on a soldier before I got caught. The moment it went wrong and he started screaming, she gave him a clear liquid that stopped everything."

Rosalind didn't recall seeing any clear liquid back when they were investigating Seagreen Press or searching Warehouse 34. It had to be new.

"I've been trying to make sense of why she would be arguing with Orion about needing more time to help you," Alisa continued. "I keep circling around the phrase she used: *she's not my work.* Rosalind, a cure must exist. It is only that you're not her invention, so she's telling Orion that to cure *you,* he needs to let her use him indefinitely. Allow her to make her concoction again, give it to you, and then cure you."

Understanding sank in like a mallet, knocking the breath out of her. It was just as Lourens said: *If you're asking for a cure, the only way forward is obtaining true immortality first. Stabilize the temporary solution I put there five years ago, then erase it.*

"Did Orion sound like he was leading up to some plan?" Rosalind demanded. "It's got to be a plan, right? He can't be willing to just let her experiment on him. If she makes her invention, we have lost. The nation is going to fall."

Alisa remained quiet for a few moments. Then: "I think he is, Rosalind. He didn't sound like he was lying."

This was unbelievable. Rosalind's life wasn't worth this much. He couldn't give his mother the material for complete *immortality* just to save Rosalind from hers. It would be used for terrible purposes. World-ending purposes. He couldn't choose her over the world.

"I can't let him do that."

"To be fair," Alisa said, "if you bring out that vial now, that's all she wants. It's the only completed version with strength and immortality combined successfully. She could hand it off to the Japanese. Her mission is achieved."

"No," Rosalind said at once. "Out of the question."

Alisa nodded. She didn't push the matter further, so clearly she had only made that suggestion to test how Rosalind felt about it. There was a reason why Alisa had left the message for Rosalind alone. The same reason Alisa went on the run for months instead of passing the vial to Celia when she suspected Oliver might intrude—Alisa trusted who she trusted, and wasn't often swayed to open that circle. "Let's stop them, then."

That was easier said than done. Rosalind heaved a sigh. She strained against her ropes. "How?"

"I suspect we have help on the way." Alisa used her chin to gesture toward the window. "Do you hear that?"

Rosalind listened harder. It was the same noises as before: faint yelling, albeit drawing closer and closer. "The battle in Zhabei?"

"No. If it were coming from Zhabei, it wouldn't be slowly getting louder. While you were unconscious, I heard two projectiles hit the manor, too. There's a crowd approaching. I think they're about to attack."

Rosalind wasn't comprehending what Alisa was saying, and this time she didn't think she could blame the sedative still in her system. A crowd trying to attack the manor meant it would be people on *their* side, not Lady Hong's. It meant people battling against the Japanese soldiers and units standing guard outside.

"Who would be attacking?" Rosalind finally asked. She rose onto her knees, trying to see out the window. Despite her best attempts, the scene was pitch dark. It couldn't be the Kuomintang because they had another war occupying their attention in the north. But it couldn't be the Communists, either, because their numbers weren't strong enough to be concerned with something like this. Who else was left?

Alisa shrugged. "I don't know. But once they get in, then we make our move. I'd give it five more minutes."

The manor suddenly jolted, like something had struck its side. Another projectile, just as Alisa had said. It didn't have the effect of something as immense as the bombs that the Japanese were dropping, but it felt hefty nonetheless, knocking at some of the higher turrets.

"There's still the problem of"—Rosalind shook her arms, gesturing to her ropes—"this."

"I've been unbound for two days, actually."

"I beg your pardon?"

"Yeah." Suddenly, Alisa lifted her hands, and all the ropes around her shrugged to the floor. "I kept up the pretense because I didn't have a route out, so I figured I may as well play helpless."

Rosalind didn't even want to ask how Alisa had managed that. It would only make her feel bad about her own operative abilities.

Standing quickly, Alisa scuttled near, then examined Rosalind's hair, musing for a moment before plucking out a hairpin. "Is this one poisoned?"

"Only at the sharp end. Be careful to hold the middle."

Alisa held the middle, then angled the hairpin to stab at Rosalind's ropes. She made quick work, sawing through the threads and flinging away the pieces that came loose. The moment Rosalind was free, there was a cavernous thud that echoed through the manor. Then: voices spilling inward, vibrating along the floors in accompaniment with gunfire.

Alisa helped Rosalind up. Rosalind, subsequently, barely had time to scramble for a hairpin and arm herself, too, before Alisa flung open the door, looking left and right to survey their situation. No guards remained on watch. Voices echoed down the long corridor from the left.

Alisa gestured to their right. Rosalind followed her, sticking close. Around them, the manor felt labyrinthine in size, each turn extending for miles and the walls crawling with endless white. She could hear gunfire inside the house.

Another shudder vibrated along the ceiling. Alisa glanced up momentarily, frowning. Though Rosalind paused, meaning to ask what she had noticed, Alisa shook her head before Rosalind could get the chance, gesturing forward. A wooden banister curved into view around the corner. They took the stairs down.

The moment they landed upon the second-floor atrium, they became fully enveloped by the roar of battle, finally entering the fight. Alisa ducked low when she proceeded forward; Rosalind had no clue what she was doing, but she mimicked Alisa nonetheless . . . right in time to avoid a spray of bullets going exactly where their heads had been.

"Mon Dieu," Rosalind muttered. *"Mon Dieu—"*

Alisa yanked her hand, hurrying her along. A scream echoed beneath their feet. Over the banister onto the first floor, there came the synchronized clatter of new soldiers lifting their weapons. "Come on, come on, have some survival instinct, would you?"

"Survival instinct?" Rosalind hissed. "I am not a spy! I am an assassin! I am suited for the shadows!"

Right on cue, a grappling fight exited a nearby corridor and slammed into their path. Alisa squeaked, rearing back to get out of the way. There was another staircase that descended ahead of them. A man wearing a black hat kicked one of the Japanese soldiers, letting him tumble down the steps. When the man wiped blood off his face and charged down with his rifle, Rosalind stared after him, a wisp of recognition striking in her mind. A moment later, she realized where she recognized him from.

"That man in the hat," she said, her voice quavering with disbelief. "He's former Scarlet Gang."

Alisa's brow furrowed. As if a thought had just occurred to her, she gazed out beyond the railing onto the first floor, onto the war zone beneath.

"Former White Flower over there. And there."

Rosalind understood now. She understood who had sent the battalion for them. This was blatantly Roma and Juliette's work. And Rosalind almost wanted to cry out of the gesture, because she had pulled the most underhanded move to shove them back, and still they had sent every resource they could manage to her aid.

Below, the glass-paned doors on the first floor opened out into the vast gardens. Just as Rosalind was running a scan over the chaos indoors, she caught sight of Orion and Lady Hong outside. Though the gardens were dark, the manor had thrown all of its lights on, casting a bluish glow far enough to reach the tree line. Lady Hong clutched a box in her hands. Orion had planted his feet solidly in the grass. Rosalind couldn't hear what he was saying from here, but she knew him well enough to read his manner. He was furious, mid-argument.

"I'm heading that way," Rosalind announced.

"Wait, wait," Alisa hissed, grabbing her arm before she could take a step. "What's your plan? Shouldn't we go for the blood supply?"

"Silas already messed with it. I don't know how. I only know that they couldn't use it. That's probably why you saw Lady Hong reversing the experiments—she'd rather use her soldiers non-enhanced than have them end up dead like the chemical killings." Rosalind's eyes flickered briefly to another door near the glass panes. There was a stack of paper at the threshold, scattered across the floorboards, some corners stained with blood. They must have been pushed over in a rush. "The only way we stop her now is to stop her from leaving with Orion."

Just as Alisa let go of her arm, one of the glass doors shattered entirely, a stream of bullets hitting its middle. There was too much going on to determine who had been shooting, whether it was coming from the inside or the outside. Rosalind, taking the disastrous sight as a prompt, hurried down the stairs at once, pausing for a moment to pick up a discarded pistol lying beside a dead man.

"Sorry," Rosalind muttered. She turned over her shoulder. "Alisa?"

Alisa suddenly inclined her head, listening to something in particular. When Rosalind paused for a beat, she heard it too: sirens. Police sirens, sent by the Municipal Council, most likely. It was no surprise given that the manor had turned into all-out war and this was foreign territory. Some neighbor or another was bound to call the police. The Kuomintang would be here soon too, and when that happened, no one here was going to escape unscathed.

"Get Orion," Alisa instructed, coming down the steps. Her eyes were on the internal door, scattered with bloodied pieces of paper. "I'll clear the manor. Destroy every piece of her research."

Rosalind nodded. At once, they split. Alisa pushed her sleeves up, muttering a curse under her breath while she avoided a gangster with a blade. Rosalind ducked, making herself small while she crossed the floor.

The moment she emerged through the glass doors and stepped out into the night, Lady Hong caught sight of her.

And Rosalind raised her pistol.

55

"You're not going to shoot," Lady Hong said immediately. She set down the white box in her hands. It was latched with a metallic buckle, the sort that surgical nurses might carry around in hospitals.

Orion swiveled at once, his eyes wide. Rosalind didn't bother trying to reason with his mother. Whether she would or would not shoot was not the matter at hand. The threat only needed to be present. In the stillness, all she said in return was:

"Orion. Let's go."

But Orion didn't move. Rosalind's breath came out in a cloud. For several moments, he merely looked at her—he looked and he looked like he was trying to commit her to memory. Then Orion shook his head.

"I can't," he said evenly. "I can't walk away from this when it's the only way to save you."

"Yes. You can." Her grip tightened on the gun. Lady Hong's hand shifted, and Rosalind lurched forward a step. "*Don't* move."

The sirens were getting louder. At the front of the manor, a scream tore into the night.

"We must go now, Miss Lang," Lady Hong said calmly. "If the Nationalists arrive on the scene, they will take Liwen away. Is that what you want?"

It was if it would keep him safe. It was if it would keep him away from his mother. Rosalind could easily stall until then.

"Orion," she said again. "My life is not worth that much. You cannot give yourself up. Too much is on the line. The *nation* is on the line."

Rosalind could hear commands being given from inside the manor. Directions for retreat, figuring that enough of Lady Hong's militia was devastated and defeated. No former gangster could be caught here when authorities arrived. Gunfire ricocheted loudly from the front of the house, then quieted with a frightening quickness.

"How can I say this in a forgivable way?" Orion said quietly. "If I do this, I know the consequences will weigh on my conscience forever. But my conscience will be much worse off if you drop dead without warning when I could have prevented it. The country might still have a fighting chance if I go"—he swallowed hard—"but I am scared that you will not if I don't."

The night was bone-cold, but it wasn't the temperatures that sent a chill down her spine. For so long, she had wanted to be a priority in someone's eyes. She had craved the embrace of being irreplaceable. But *this* . . . this bore too high a cost.

Rosalind reached for her sleeve. She had urged him to walk away, but in return, she could not let go of Orion, either. If their circumstances were switched, she would have done the same thing he was trying to do now, and if that made her conscience equally dark, then she would have accepted it. The two of them were never meant for nation-changing responsibilities. Mere individual people were not *meant* to make decisions this grand.

"Fine," Rosalind said, but she was no longer speaking to Orion. She was speaking to his mother when she pulled the vial out, letting it catch the cold light sluicing from the manor. "Does this change matters?"

Lady Hong blinked. Then again, as if she couldn't believe what she was seeing.

"How . . . ?"

"I'll make you a bargain above all bargains," Rosalind went on. "You get the vial back. Your final vial, the only successful run of your research with seramorine. But you can't give it to the Japanese. Leave them forever and go off the grid. That's all you wanted, isn't it? To create new science? Now that you've finished using their resources to discover this, there's no clause in there that says they have to benefit."

"Lang Shalin," Lady Hong said calmly. "Do you know what you're doing?"

"I am very aware." Rosalind wondered if it might be easier to pull the trigger. No creator, no new science. No creator, no invincible soldiers who were horrifically strong and could heal any wound. Yet this was Orion's mother: How could Rosalind be the one to shoot and do that to him? "Make your decision. Before I destroy this one too, as I should have done a long time ago."

"Beloved," Orion whispered. "Don't—"

Footsteps echoed behind her. Rosalind wasn't going to get distracted, not while she held the vial in her palm, but both Lady Hong and Orion looked over her shoulder at once.

"Mr. Akiyama," Lady Hong said, and the slightest hint of concern entered her voice. "We are set to depart."

"Oh?" Mr. Akiyama said. Though Rosalind didn't turn around, she recognized the voice of the same man they had encountered on the street outside. The one who had put the sedative in her neck. By sound, she could sense him standing by the glass doors. "It doesn't look like your son is complying."

"A minor logistical concern." Lady Hong's eyes drew farther back. More footsteps scattered outward, streaming past the doors and into the grass. Rosalind didn't look away from Orion's mother, but her periphery showed soldiers suddenly surrounding them. What was going on? Didn't Lady Hong control these remaining soldiers?

"There's no need to force him," Mr. Akiyama said. "Look, isn't the solution right there?"

Tā mā de, Rosalind thought. He was talking about the vial in her hand.

"Regardless of what we have now," Lady Hong replied tightly, "we ought to seek safety first—"

Orion's sudden gasp was the only warning Rosalind got. There was no time to even register the threat before the night rang loud with gunshots, and then Rosalind felt blistering pain explode through her body. One bullet struck her shoulder. Another landed near her hip. Her vision detonated into complete black; her ears hummed with nothingness. When she fell to her knees, both the vial and the gun dropped onto the grass. She barely registered their landing.

"Rosalind!"

"No," she rasped, only Orion didn't hear it. He lunged in front of her, sliding to his knees so that he could clasp her arms.

"Ros—"

"I'll heal," she gasped, trying to push him away. Mr. Akiyama had been firing from a distance before, but if he got closer . . . "I'll heal, it's okay, it's okay, get *away*—"

A shadow fell over them. She knew, in that terrible moment, what was coming. She felt danger looming like another throbbing wound, and still she couldn't stop the man when he swapped weapons inside the pocket of his jacket; still she was helpless when he reached for Orion and stabbed him so viciously that an arc of red splattered on the blade's exit, landing in a horizontal slash across Rosalind's neck.

No. Nonononono—

Orion's hand wrapped around his torso. Blood seeped through his fingers instantly. Poured to the grass, coloring it a muddy scarlet.

"What are you doing?" Lady Hong demanded. Though she didn't

move, horror cracked her voice, took it high-pitched and terrified. It seemed incongruous from the rest of her usual demeanor, at odds with the negligent mother Rosalind had long pitted her for. When Rosalind looked around, at a loss for action, she realized that Lady Hong remained where she stood not because she didn't want to rush forward. It was because the soldiers were training their weapons on her, clear-eyed and alert while waiting for Mr. Akiyama's commands.

Callously, Mr. Akiyama nudged his shoe at the vial. It rolled a small distance. "Go on," he said. "Fix him."

"That is my *son*—"

"Who you can fix. Inject him. Then he heals. Then we've finally acquired a subject who has succeeded, and we can ship him abroad for study."

Orion made a terrible inhale. He clutched his side tighter, his eyes on the vial. Though Mr. Akiyama could have used his gun on Orion too, he had switched to a knife on purpose. He wasn't trying to make a quick kill; he wanted a lethal wound with time to force Lady Hong's hand.

"Rosalind," Orion gasped. "Get it."

"Don't move," she urged in response. By then her own wounds had already mostly healed. Memories of Dao Feng's death flashed in her mind. Dao Feng bleeding out before her, studded with a bullet that he didn't have to take.

"Get it!" Orion demanded, growing more incensed. "Or—"

Rosalind cursed under her breath, lunging before Orion could finish. It felt as though someone else had taken over her body. Fortune was at work, proceeding despite the pain. A second later, Mr. Akiyama snarled and reached for the vial too, but by then Rosalind had closed her hand around the glass again, its surface freezing on her palm.

Mr. Akiyama, with his hand clutching empty space, pivoted

even before he straightened up. He grabbed her dropped pistol instead.

"Stop this!" Lady Hong exclaimed. "Stop—"

Mr. Akiyama pressed the gun to Orion's head. Though Orion froze, his eyes were ablaze, latching to the vial in Rosalind's hand. It was one matter to be speaking about this substance in the abstract, peering into a hypothetical future. It was another to be handing it over plainly.

"What are you going to do, shoot me?" Orion spat in threat. "There won't be any more of those vials. My mother can perfect the mixture however much she wants, but she cannot make the most critical component without me."

"We are patient," Mr. Akiyama said. "Once we have one vial, we can easily make the materials ourselves."

Lady Hong clearly did not like this. "You cannot," she gritted through her teeth. "It would take decades."

"That is no amount of time when it comes to building an empire." He looked down. Peered over his nose, as if holding Orion at gunpoint were a matter akin to sniffing at soiled tissue stuck to his shoe. "But if you wish to make this easier for everyone, then ask your mother to take out a syringe. Ask your lover to hand over the vial."

"No," Orion said. "Kill me."

"Liwen, enough," Lady Hong demanded. She was reaching into her box already, bringing out a syringe. "Lang Shalin, please hand it over. For his sake."

Rosalind's breath was stuck in her throat. There was no way around this. The pistol was pressed right to his temple. She couldn't push Orion aside and take it in his stead. Not without prompting the trigger.

"Okay," Rosalind whispered. Her arm extended. Slowly, each of her fingers pried free from the glass, though it felt horrifically wrong. It felt like handing over the blueprint for the end of the world.

Lady Hong took the vial.

"I won't receive it," Orion snapped. "I refuse."

The soldiers around them bristled. They were running out of time: the sirens had pulled up directly in front of the manor.

"Liwen, shut *up*," his mother demanded.

But Orion did not. If anything, he got bolder, pressing right against his mortality and screaming in its face. He met Rosalind's eyes. The softness in his gaze didn't match his tone; his gaze was for her alone, to apologize for the sacrifice he was willing to make.

Stop it, Rosalind wanted to urge.

"Kill me!" Orion demanded. His own hand flew up to the gun. Grasped the place where Mr. Akiyama was holding the trigger, trying to press it himself. "Do it! Shoot!"

Stop. Stop it stop it stop it—

A gunshot boomed into the night.

Rosalind screamed.

56

Mr. Akiyama didn't collapse immediately.

The bullet made a perfect circle in his forehead. At first it was only a dark ring. Then a single bead of blood dripped down onto his nose, onto his lip, before gliding off to land on the grass.

In the moments after, when blood started to surge through the hole and trickle in rivulets, he finally collapsed where he stood, unmoving. It didn't end there: as soon as the first bullet fired onto the scene, more followed in rapid succession, each striking true again and again. The soldiers who were encircling the scene fell where they stood. No bullet was wasted; each bullet made landing to take out an enemy in a single blow.

"What the hell?" Orion whispered, craning his head in search of the shooter. It was coming from above. From the rooftop of the manor.

A final bullet struck the space beside Lady Hong's feet. She gasped, darting back, but the bullet had clearly missed on purpose. The garden fell quiet for a scarce few seconds. Then tremendous shouting began around the other side of the manor, signaling the arrival of police. Their sirens pierced through the night. Their vehicles flashed colors into the dark. Rosalind would give it mere minutes before they came into the garden and found them. Less if the Nationalists were present alongside them, because the Nationalists would know who they were looking for.

"That wasn't the police, though," Rosalind muttered, almost to herself. She finally spotted the shooter. A small figure, hovering by one of the turrets. When they stood, they were quick to slide along the slate tiles, perching on the edge of the gutter before grabbing ahold of the pipes and sliding down.

Even in the dark, Rosalind recognized those ringlets.

"Priest," she uttered aloud, confounded. She remembered the rescue mission at the Nationalist base. The combatants dropping in a path that cleared only for her. She remembered Warehouse 34, how she and Orion were left alive despite every reason to kill them.

When Phoebe turned around, she lifted her rifle again at her mother, keeping her where she was.

"How is he?" Phoebe asked, walking closer. She was addressing Rosalind.

"Bad," Rosalind answered simply.

"How am *I*?" Orion struggled to mimic. "Are you *Priest,* Feiyi? Oh my God, I'm going to kill you—"

"Save your breath," Phoebe demanded. "Worry about surviving before you worry about killing me."

"And then I'm going to kill Oliver," Orion went on, practically heaving to finish speaking. "The fact that he's been your handler this whole time—"

"I can save him," Lady Hong interrupted. "I only need to give him this."

At some point in the chaos, she had put the vial into a syringe. She held the instrument in her hands carefully, its needle pointed to the sky.

When Orion breathed in, it sounded as though there was air escaping through his lungs, as though they had been punctured a thousand times over.

"Let me give this to you," his mother begged. "*Please.*"

The sirens stopped abruptly. In its place came shouting as units were instructed to disperse and search. How much time did they have left? Would the Nationalists find them like this—fugitives and enemy operatives alike, a family broken down the middle?

"All right," Orion finally agreed. His eyes flickered to Rosalind. "Can you come closer?"

Rosalind was already only a few paces away, practically splayed on the grass while Orion hovered more neatly on his knees, his left arm clutched around his wound. She didn't question the request; she moved nearer, her hand outstretching to touch his shoulder for comfort. On his other side, Lady Hong crouched down, bringing the syringe to his arm.

Rosalind didn't register what he was doing until she felt the pinprick on her arm. Didn't register the sudden motion of him grabbing the syringe from his mother's hold and plunging it into *Rosalind* instead.

Lady Hong made a noise of abject distress. Rosalind could only stare at the emptied syringe in disbelief. A second later, she tore it out from her arm and threw it onto the grass, shattering it down the middle. One last drop spilled out into the soil. It sank into the ground.

"Why would you do that?" Rosalind was inside a waking nightmare. Somehow, her hands were covered in Orion's blood already. It had left a print on the glass of the broken vial. "Orion, what did you just *do?*"

"No more science," he decided. "It doesn't solve anything."

"It would have solved the fact that you're bleeding to death right now," Rosalind snapped.

Merde. He was so *stupid*. And selfless. Stupid, selfless Orion. *God*—

She could feel the concoction moving through her body. This one didn't burn the same way Lourens's experiment did; this one felt like her blood was rising to the surface, overwhelming every part of her body until she was entirely made of liquid.

A shout came around the manor. Another.

"Get him help," Lady Hong demanded suddenly. "Go now, or the Nationalists won't let you leave."

She was right. The Nationalist presence was arriving. They would want to arrest Orion alongside his mother before they did anything else. By the time they got around to helping him, he would be long dead.

"Which way?" Rosalind asked. Her voice stayed steady. She clutched Orion's elbow, ready at a moment's notice to leap up and haul him with her.

"Through the house and down the corridor on the very right. It'll take you out a side door. Stay close to the fence, and you will be able to reach the front gate without trouble."

"Over here! Circle all paths!"

Rosalind bit down hard on her teeth. She shifted on her feet.

"Feiyi, you need to put that gun down in ten seconds, or you'll be exposed," Lady Hong went on. It was shocking how matter-of-fact she sounded. If it weren't for the slight shake in her hands when Rosalind took Orion out of her grasp, Rosalind might not have thought there was any love left in his mother. But there was. Rosalind had seen it, and she didn't like that she had, because that made it harder to believe they had ended up here purely because of Lady Hong's traitorous self-interest.

"Oh, sure," Phoebe sneered. Despite her words, she looked like she was on the verge of crying. "I'll put the gun down. So then you can escape too."

Rosalind pulled Orion to his feet. He winced. Blood poured the moment he changed the clasp he had over the wound. She shouldn't have been surprised at how easy it was to tug him up, but still, she almost stumbled over her own feet.

"She's right, Phoebe," Rosalind said. It was a matter of trust now. Entirely undeserved trust, and yet they had been backed into a corner where there was no option otherwise. "Put it down now. Or they'll know you're Priest."

"There!"

With a glance over her shoulder and a stifled curse, Phoebe tossed her rifle into the grass. She'd barely put any distance between herself and the weapon, but at once she seemed entirely separate from it, as though it was a mere coincidence that it sat so close. There was no time to stick around and see what Lady Hong would do without a weapon pointed at her anymore. Rosalind gave Phoebe a single nod. Then she muttered, "Quick!" at Orion, pulling him back into the manor.

"I don't mean to alarm you," Orion wheezed inside the corridor. "But I can't feel my arms."

"I am *plenty* alarmed."

Rosalind turned the corner. Slammed right into someone. Before she could panic and try to use her newfound strength to fight, the other person squeaked, throwing their hands up.

"It's me!" Alisa exclaimed. "What the hell happened out there? Why are you covered in blood?"

"Good news," Orion supplied from behind her. "It's mine."

If it weren't in utterly bad taste to throttle someone who was grievously injured, Rosalind might have done it.

"The Nationalists are here," Rosalind reported in a rush. "Did you get rid of everything?"

Alisa nodded. It likely took one glance at the situation for her to figure out what had happened in the time she was purging the manor of its research. Rosalind was tugging Orion without any trouble; Orion had walked free from his mother.

"Final step is pouring gasoline over the papers and books for safe measure," Alisa reported. "Other chemical materials—liquid or solid alike—I destroyed. Except . . ." There was movement along the floor above, and Alisa's eyes shot up. Quickly, she leaned forward, pressing cold glass into Rosalind's hand. When Rosalind looked down, she was holding a vial filled with a clear, colorless liquid.

"He did all this to make sure it works on you," Alisa whispered. "Don't waste it."

She darted away.

Rosalind gave herself a second to swallow hard. Then she put the vial in her pocket, hurrying Orion forward again.

"How are your arms?"

"Rosalind," Orion said, ignoring the question. "Use the cure."

"Not right *now.*" They hurtled into an atrium, where Rosalind finally spotted the side door. When they stole into the night this time, it felt monumentally colder, the air prickling painfully on Rosalind's face. She breathed shallowly. At the end of the fence, Nationalist forces were streaming in from the front gates. How were they to get out? There was no chance in hell that they could *climb* the fence with Orion in this state.

"Jiějiě!"

The summons came faintly, but it reached Rosalind's ear with pointed quickness. Celia emerged from a cluster of trees, her expression horrified. There was a bag dangling from her shoulder and a pistol in her hands.

"Did Phoebe get to you in time—"

"Of course you brought Phoebe," Rosalind said in return. "I need to get Orion—"

"Go to the car. Hurry, hurry."

Rosalind barely needed to finish any sentence before Celia already knew what she was saying. Likewise, Celia didn't need to conclude a thought before Rosalind had caught the gist. Her sister took one look at Orion and pushed at his other shoulder, hurrying them along the edge of the manor grounds.

"I swear I can still walk on my own," Orion wheezed.

"Shush," Rosalind and Celia said at once.

They moved as quickly as they could. Came to a stop just short of where the Nationalists might see them.

"How are we supposed to get out?" Rosalind whispered.

Celia pointed beyond the gate. A small vehicle hovered on the other side of Arden Road, away from most of the chaos streaming in. "That's the car I drove here with Phoebe. It's unlocked. Move fast."

"And you—"

Celia reached into her bag. "I can't be spotted helping you, first of all, so I'll find some way out. I have two more explosives left. On my mark. Go!"

This time Rosalind didn't let Orion insist that he was holding himself up fine. She pulled, skirting along the gate in the dark, timing their movement to the frantic roar of fire erupting before the manor. Gravel crunched where the concrete pavement was more loosely constructed. When Rosalind glanced back, she could see that Orion was leaving behind a faint trail of blood.

Rosalind shoved him into the passenger seat.

"Rosalind, I—"

"No," she interrupted, slamming the door on him. When she came around the driver's side, she continued: "Save your breath and your energy. Don't say a single thing."

"I'm only trying to—"

"Love confessions and marriage proposals are *forbidden,*" Rosalind snapped, and her tone could have been a death knell itself. She stomped on the accelerator. The car hurtled forward at once, away from the military trucks driving in the other direction. "Are you *trying* to die?"

Orion made a noise that almost sounded like a laugh. "I'm getting too predictable," he managed.

It was only that she knew him too well. And if she knew him this well, then she also knew that he was strong enough to hold on.

"I will find you help." She swerved fast. "Tell your heart to stop pumping so fast."

"I can't," he replied weakly. "It swoons when you're around."

Rosalind tightened her hold on the steering wheel. Her throat twisted, tears threatening at her eyes. She couldn't lose her composure. Orion was relying on her. She could cry her heart out with all the terror racking up inside her lungs when he was patched back together.

But not a second sooner.

57

The Japanese diplomat Phoebe had killed lay facedown on the ground beside her.

She didn't know if she needed to get more distance in. Whether the Nationalists would be able to smell the gunpowder on her hands when they loomed nearer.

"We could go."

Phoebe stiffened. The absence of her rifle made her feel exposed, as though she had stepped out into the night without a coat on.

"You will always be stifled here," Lady Hong continued. "You are my daughter. I know exactly how your life will draw out ahead of you."

"Māma," Phoebe said quietly. "Please. Enough."

The police constables had spotted them. They were cautious about their approach. Weapons raised, eyeing the bodies littered across the garden. When they took inventory of the scene, who would they blame for this? How would they explain away these perfect wounds when it was at odds with the rest of the battle that had raged here?

"You found one thesis and understood my whole research," her mother went on. "You took on an interest in shooting and turned yourself into an unparalleled assassin. Your potential is limitless. Why stay in the bounds of city society? Why stay somewhere that is going to be consumed by war for the next few years?"

Phoebe's fists tightened. This time, when her attention wavered to the dead man again, she realized the pistol that Rosalind had dropped was still lying upon the ground. Half the barrel was hidden under a tuft of grass.

"It's not as bad as you make it seem," Phoebe replied quietly.

For so much of her life, she had bent over backward to get her mother's approval, had perceived her mother's outlook on the world—and Phoebe's place in it—to be perfect. Whether it was age or the sheer shock of these last few months that had booted her out of this impulse, Phoebe wasn't sure. But she knew now what her younger self did not. She had seen the blight that grew under her mother's hand—and all for what? The pursuit of power? Because she didn't think the bounds of this city were good enough?

"We could go," Lady Hong said again. She was looking somewhere over Phoebe's shoulder, which meant she was watching the inside of the manor through the glass doors. "What is stopping you?"

"Must you even ask?" Phoebe answered in a fury. "Because I don't *want* that. I don't want your aspirations. I want love. I want safety. I want to feel as though my world won't crumble around me at any second, which, by the way, began when *you* walked away from us."

Slowly Lady Hong dragged her gaze back. Glass crunched at the manor doors. Though the police constables had been slow-moving at the periphery of the garden, whoever was making their way toward them from the doors was keeping a constant pace.

"I left for the sake of our family," Lady Hong said. "I made a sacrifice so that you could be close with me later on."

Phoebe shook her head. Her hair blew into her face, each ringlet remaining in shape despite the days it had been since she made them. Her mother was the one who had taught her how to do her hair like this. She had spent hours letting Phoebe try it herself; it wasn't only the technique that she taught but the patience afterward to make sure that Phoebe had truly picked it up.

"Don't you know what damage you did?"

It was a question she had wanted to ask from the day her mother left. It had festered in the darkest part of her heart, the shadowed arena that perpetually wondered if it had been a matter of choice, if—when it came down to it—what remained inside the city simply was not enough for her mother. Like her children.

Lady Hong's eyes flickered once again, then returned to Phoebe. "I suppose I did not consider," she said softly, "that although you are my children, you do not pause when you are out of my sight. That is my wrongdoing."

"Hong Feiyi."

The new summons echoed calmly from behind. It sounded familiar, so despite her best judgment, Phoebe turned away from her mother and toward the source. A uniformed Nationalist stood without coming too close; his face scratched her memory immediately. A beat later, when his backup spilled out from the manor, a name rose to her mind.

"I would tell you to be careful," Jiemin continued. "But, actually, I'm not sure what you're doing here to begin with."

Suspicion steeped through his disposition, from the tone of his voice to the stance he held, his hands behind his back. His soldiers snapped to attention when they fell in line beside him. One reported: "We've searched the rooms. There is nothing left save for a few fires. Mass casualties."

"I see." Jiemin considered the report, then tilted his head at Phoebe. "Please step away, Miss Hong. It's over."

Phoebe exhaled. It was. This was the end of the line.

The moment she took a step away from her mother, however, she felt a grip on her arm, then the cold press of a muzzle upon her neck. Phoebe froze. Her eyes bugged wide, landing on Jiemin in a silent cry for help.

Jiemin's expression changed. He had gotten lax. He hadn't

expected this, not when the Nationalists had already surrounded the premises so thoroughly that any resistance was a futile fight. At some point Lady Hong had bent down to reach for the pistol, and no one had noticed.

"Phoebe!"

Silas's voice, coming from somewhere to the side. Phoebe couldn't turn her head to find him, but he sounded out of breath, newly on the scene.

"Māma, please," Phoebe whispered in a rush. "They're going to kill you. They're going to shoot in retaliation if you don't stop."

Her mother ignored her. "You will let us leave," she demanded.

"You are surrounded," Jiemin called steadily. "Where do you think you will go?"

"You may get out of the way, no?"

Phoebe risked the slightest turn of her head. There was Silas, silently signaling for soldiers to fan out, to get behind them. She trusted that he would act when it came to it; he would give the instruction to shoot the moment they could find an angle on her mother.

"Ah, there he is," Lady Hong said suddenly. She had tracked Phoebe's gaze. She was looking at Silas now too. "I suppose you are very proud of yourself."

"I am not," Silas replied dully. "I did what I needed to do."

"You did." Lady Hong grabbed Phoebe harder. "You have Liwen back. You won't mind if I keep my daughter."

Silas stepped forward. It appeared to be an instinct more than something he was conscious he was doing. His mouth was firm. While he searched frantically for a way out of this, scanning across the garden and determining who was least likely to let a bullet fly astray, Jiemin shook his head and waved a hand to signal all the soldiers.

"I am afraid this is not a situation where we will negotiate. If you wish to put your own daughter's life in danger, then so be it. Take aim."

Rifles lifted in every direction around them. Phoebe gasped; Silas lunged forward. "Don't you dare—"

"Shepherd, step back right now—"

"You have a *civilian* in the crossfire—"

"Māma," Phoebe wheezed. "How do you think this will end?"

"I told you, didn't I?" The cold metal of the pistol disappeared suddenly. In its place brushed a soft touch, so light that it might have been imagined if Phoebe didn't recognize the gesture. Back when she taught Phoebe how to shoot with a wooden pellet gun, she used to adjust Phoebe's head like this. Her thumb on one side, middle finger on the other. A subtle angle shift, appearing no different on the outside but making all the difference in her aim. "I'm not a tyrant. I'm just your mother." And in a lower voice, barely audible if Phoebe hadn't been standing so near: "And now they won't suspect you anymore."

Lady Hong dropped the pistol in the grass, lifting her arms high above her head. Phoebe didn't move as police and soldiers alike surrounded them, as they surged forward and took ahold of her mother. They left Phoebe alone. They left Phoebe standing there, sparing no interest even as Lady Hong turned over her shoulder, getting one last look at her.

"Be good," she said simply.

They put her in handcuffs. Led her around the manor, yelling about whether it was foreign or Chinese jurisdiction's responsibility to process her. In the aftermath, no words would form on Phoebe's tongue. No thought would take shape in her mind. There was only the desire to run after her mother. Only the acceptance that perhaps she would always exist in this space where she both loved and hated her.

"Feiyi!"

Phoebe released her terror in one shaky exhale. Her gaze snapped up, searching for Silas, the sound of his call. He was trying to push past a cluster of soldiers, and she reached for him at once.

"She did that intentionally," Phoebe said in a rush, colliding with Silas and clutching him close. He grasped her shoulders as soon as she leaned back a fraction, examining her all over. "She threw them off my involvement by doing that."

"Are you hurt?" Silas demanded.

Phoebe shook her head. The crash of adrenaline struck hard. Her lip wobbled, an onslaught of tears filling her eyes.

"Oh, no, no, no—" Silas wrapped his arms around her again, pressing her tightly into him. "It's all right. You're all right."

"I know," Phoebe sobbed. "But no one else is. Orion got badly hurt. Oliver was already badly hurt. What the hell are we supposed to do?"

Silas let her cry. They remained where they stood even as the soldiers in the garden started to disperse, yelling to check the rest of the perimeter for suspected Communist agents on scene.

"I caught sight of Celia and Alisa leaving the scene before I got in," Silas said quietly. "It's finished here. There is nothing more we can do."

Her mother was going to be put on trial for her crimes. The experiments were done. The chemical concoctions were gone.

Nonetheless, every time Phoebe blinked, she saw Orion, his hand clutched to his side, blood spilling onto the grass.

"It seems the invasion wave is still going," Phoebe said, her head tilting for the skies. She couldn't hear anything, but she could feel the smoke that drifted through the city, could smell the tainted air of war.

"This new onslaught may last awhile," Silas replied. A thought seemed to occur to him. He glanced over his shoulder as if to check whether there were any Nationalists observing them. "Feiyi . . . I suppose Zhabei could still use your help."

Phoebe choked on a single laugh. When she wiped her eyes, her tears cleared, allowing the night to come into blistering clarity. "You need to get me more bullets."

"Done." He kissed her temple, and the sensation overrode everything else that tried to cling to her with heaviness. "I'll get you the world if you need it."

58

Rosalind was afraid that driving on the main roads might mean getting stopped. She navigated the smaller streets instead, flinching anytime there was the rumble of a police car or flashes of military patrol. Foreign concessions were safer, but it didn't mean they couldn't be hailed down and arrested.

"Where is it?" she muttered under her breath. "I could have sworn . . ."

She knew that it was panic messing with her navigation. She had thought there was a small hospital on this corner, but now she was driving along the bend, and it was nowhere in sight. She didn't have time for this. Orion didn't have time for this. All the same, no matter how much Rosalind fretted and sweated and searched, she couldn't summon a hospital out of thin air.

When she had rescued Celia all those years ago after the massacre, she had pulled her to the nearest clinic. She had walked south, trying to find familiar bearings. Here . . . it had been here, right? This was a familiar area. In the past few months, she had been nearby too, albeit last time she had been walking up from the south after those men had tried to kill her. . . .

So this was where Lourens's old lab was located too. There it waited, right in the middle of the street with its shuttered windows and papered doors—and the light inside was on.

Rosalind slammed on the brakes at once. Orion winced, tossed around on the back seats.

History was repeating itself.

"Stay there," Rosalind commanded, pushing open her door.

"Fortunately I don't have anywhere else to go," Orion called after her.

Rosalind rushed to the lab doors. She pushed hard at the glass. She had expected it to be locked. She had thought she might need to slam hard to break it open. Instead, the doors opened under her hand smoothly, as if she were a welcome guest.

"What the hell?"

Her first guess was that perhaps the Nationalists had taken over the lab in search for what Alisa was destroying back at the manor. Her next guess was that the Communists were here instead, making a grab for assets.

When she entered the foyer, however, nothing could have prepared her for the fact that it was *Lourens* who poked his head out from the lab, blinking.

"*This* is where you came?" Rosalind shrieked. "How did you even get into the city?"

"Lang Shalin, I am an old man." Lourens stepped out, squinting onto the street. "Anyone is willing to let me come into their vehicle."

There was no time for the rest of her questions. Rosalind reversed back out. Returned to the car and opened the rear door, helping Orion out.

"Are you still conscious?" she demanded.

"Keep sweet-talking me and I'll be just fine, beloved."

Rosalind wanted to shake him. She hauled him forward instead. It was harder to get him those few steps into the lab than it had been to tug him the whole way here. How much blood had he lost? How long had it been since the knife went in? It felt like years had gone by. Whole eons, passing at the speed of light.

"He's bleeding from a stab wound," she told Lourens when she stepped through the doors again. "Help him. Please, help him."

A flash of concern passed Lourens's expression. He didn't argue; wordlessly, he only waved for her to hurry inside the proper workspace. Rosalind remembered walking out of here. She didn't remember being brought in, already too lost to her fever, but she had been fully recovered by the time they were exiting, the world carrying an extra sheen of saturation and the air strange on her skin.

"You understand that I am not a doctor."

"You are a scientist with enough understanding of human anatomy to be inventing things that should never be invented," Rosalind countered crossly. "You can save him. I know you can."

Lourens grumbled something under his breath, not sounding like any language Rosalind knew. He put a sheet down on the table. Orion was pushed on top. With barely any word of warning, Lourens injected him with a syringe, then another into his torso, right onto the site of his wound.

"What are you doing?" Rosalind asked, panicked.

"Sedating him so he can rest," Lourens answered.

"Wait, Rosalind . . ." Orion's eyes started to flutter, his voice trailing off. Rosalind felt panic close its hand over her throat and squeeze with all its strength. This was all wrong. Everything was being performed so unceremoniously, and though Rosalind knew they needed to move fast, the possibility that Orion might close his eyes and never open them again struck her like a slap across the face.

She hadn't heard him finish what he wanted to say. Nor had she said what *she* needed to say.

Orion fell unconscious, his head lolling to the side softly.

"But—"

"Then I'm freezing the wound so I can stitch it closed," Lourens continued. "This is risky, Lang Shalin. This isn't the fever you had.

This . . ." The old scientist dragged over a tray, the metal tools inside clanking against one another. Scalpels and needles and scissors. "He is likely not to survive."

"Don't *say* that."

"Do you want a medical opinion or not, young lady?"

She dragged her hands through her hair. Tore at her little plaits, plucked at every knot that had grown tangled in the cluster at the base of her neck. Lourens was examining him rapidly, taking his heart rate, measuring his vitals.

"In truth, it is necessary to get him to a real hospital," Lourens said.

"That's impossible right now," she returned. Her voice was taking on a terrible pitch. She couldn't help it. "There's a new wave of fighting in Zhabei—most hospitals in the vicinity don't have open beds. What happens if we need to try several before there is space?"

"But he needs a blood transfusion." Lourens gestured around him. "We don't have any blood."

Rosalind picked up a scalpel. "Use me."

Lourens blinked. "Absolutely not. For one, we also don't have the equipment to do a proper transfusion. Moreover, if you are not a compatible blood type, you will kill him."

"We are."

"What? How do you know?"

Rosalind waved the scalpel. "Because I am the same type as Celia, and Celia said she is the same as Oliver, so I'm willing to hedge a statistical bet that he and Oliver are the same as well. *Use me.*"

Before Lourens could say anything in response, Rosalind took the scalpel to her arm and slashed down. She barely flinched, watching her skin split open. Blood poured from the cut. But it had been too shallow. In seconds, the cut sealed itself again.

"Dammit," Rosalind hissed. "Dammit—"

She lunged for the next table, pulling at the drawer Lourens had reached into before.

"What are you doing, Miss Lang?" Lourens asked.

Rosalind didn't reply, retrieving an unused syringe. She stared at it a moment. Her pulse pounded almost painfully in her throat. If she did this, she lost every bit of safety she had garnered over the years. If she did this, there was the possibility that she might simply drop dead where she stood or return to her body's last state when she had been brought into this lab five years ago, delirious and feverish.

"Okay," Rosalind whispered beneath her breath. She took the clear vial out of her pocket, shoved the syringe into the liquid. Yanked up the plunger. Poised the needle over her arm.

Lourens cleared his throat. "Is that . . . ?"

"If it's looking like I won't survive this," Rosalind whispered, "save Orion first."

"*Excuse* me—"

The scalpel was still poised between two of her fingers. The other two held the syringe. "Get ready."

"Miss Lang, be very certain about this—"

Rosalind pushed down.

The cure moved into her bloodstream with the sensation of ice. It shoved its way into her cells with the suddenness of a downpour. Rosalind barely stopped herself from falling to her knees, from pressing her forehead hard against the floor and screaming into the ground. But she held it back. She held herself tall.

And without wasting any time, she dragged the scalpel along her arm.

Pain flared with a wicked intensity. . . . Then the cut opened with a brilliant scarlet. Her blood ran. And kept running. There was no indication that the wound would close.

The cure had really worked.

Rosalind wasn't Fortune anymore.

"Tiān a—" Lourens flailed for a moment before rushing to a cabinet along the back wall, wrenching open a drawer, and pulling out a clear bag. He hurried back to her and split the top of the bag open wide, then held it beneath her arm to catch her streaming blood. "Hold this," Lourens said, pushing the bag at her.

Though there was an intravenous line attached to the other end, it was short. Rosalind looped her other arm up and clutched the top of the bag on Lourens's command.

Lourens picked up the intravenous line and wiped a sterile cloth over it. He huffed. "You had better be right about this." Without any fanfare, he shoved the line into Orion's arm.

Rosalind was trapping her exhale. Though she wouldn't know whether she was right until the blood had time to flow, she didn't have the capacity to breathe normally until Orion was safe.

"Keep holding that bag," Lourens instructed. "I will tell you when it's enough."

Lourens labored through the night. He had asked Rosalind to bandage herself up after an hour of bleeding into a bag, warily eyeing her from the corner of his eye and seeing how pale she had gotten. At first she had been losing too much blood from her uncontrolled slash. But when she'd slapped a piece of gauze over the wound, she had slowed the bleeding enough to turn it into a slower, steadier stream, letting it drip into the bag and move through the intravenous line into Orion's arm.

"Pull the bandage tight," Lourens had said when Rosalind finally stepped away. "If you faint, I cannot help you."

Then he turned right back to his stitching, a light strapped to his forehead.

Rosalind was hovering now, the gauze thick over her arm. She had forgotten what it was like to need a bandage. She kept accidentally disturbing it and reopening the wound, which then prompted her to go wrap another layer of gauze around her arm.

A sharp metallic sound echoed from Lourens's worktable. He had tossed a scalpel onto the tray, letting it float to the bottom of the disk of water. After a few seconds, he stood up and took the light off his forehead, stretching his arms.

"I have done all that I can."

"What does that mean?" Rosalind demanded.

"It means that he is not bleeding anymore, internally or externally." Lourens pushed away the tray full of surgical equipment. "It means that it is entirely up to Hong Liwen now whether he pulls through."

There had to be something more. Something to help, something to aid, something to—

Lourens was shaking his head before Rosalind could make any desperate suggestion. He pulled his gloves off and said, "Keep him company. If he wakes, it'll be before morning. You must remember that he is already weak without new doses of his alterations. Even if he heals from the injury, his body could drag him back down."

"Why must you—" She cut herself off. She didn't know if she was grateful that Lourens was so blunt or if she hated how little hope he had. If there was no faith that he could be saved, then how could they count on Orion to save himself?

Lourens exited the lab, mumbling to himself about finding a sink. For a few minutes, Rosalind continued to pace the linoleum floors. It had only been earlier in the day that she was telling Orion off for his incessant pacing in Juliette's house. Now here she was, doing the very same.

She hastened toward him. Braced against the side of the table, making every effort not to collapse onto the floor and stay there.

"You were the one stubborn enough to say you would descend into another plane of existence to fetch me if I died," she snapped, as if he could hear her, as if he stood in front of her healthy and well to take her chiding. "This wasn't how it was supposed to go, Orion. What are you doing swapping our places?"

He had the heart of gold. She was the cataclysmic mess. If asked to turn it around and choose Orion's life over hers, she would do it, but she didn't know *how*. She wasn't built to be the savior—she was only a girl afraid of the world, and then Orion had come along to pull her out of the pit she had dug herself.

A flash of pain spirited down her arm. Rosalind winced. Reluctantly, she eased away from the table, putting less strain on her limb and shifting on her feet. She pulled forward a chair. Planted it firmly by Orion.

"So help me." Rosalind took his hand. Clutched their fingers together. "I am never going to forgive you if you traded our lives."

There was nothing more to do except wait.

"Don't leave me," she whispered into the silence. "Please don't leave me."

In Rosalind's dreams, she stood between the pews of a church, staring up at the stained-glass windows. She didn't know where she was, but she guessed Paris.

The pipe organs rang into the summer air. Each note carried long, low, drifting through the church with all the time in the world. Something smelled sweet, and when Rosalind glanced down, she found a bouquet of daffodils in her hands. How lovely. Fragrant and yellow.

Except for the drop of blood on the side. Rosalind wiped at it. The blood didn't come off. It only spread, and smeared, and when she made a frantic attempt to rub it off on her dress, she found that her entire torso was covered in blood too, staining the white fabric a terrible crimson.

Rosalind whirled around. The pews were filled with bodies. Corpses piled up on the seats and onto the aisles. Spilled one over the other, eyes staring up at the ceiling and bullet holes gaping from every part of their body—

Rosalind woke up with a gasp, her head lifting off the side of the table. It had carved an indent into her forehead. She was woozy, discombobulated; logically, she knew that she sat in Lourens's lab, watching over Orion through the night, yet still she smelled the faint scent of blood that had migrated out of the scene in her head.

It had been years since she dreamed. She hardly remembered what it was supposed to feel like.

"It's not real," she muttered to herself. "None of it was real."

Still, the images remained, haunting her.

"This isn't good."

Rosalind jerked awake again with a start. Though it was hard to tell with the lab's fluorescent lighting, the haze of dawn pressed into the hallway outside. She hadn't thought she would be able to sleep again after that terrifying dream. Yet somehow her body had dragged her back down anyway, too tired to resist. She wondered if it would be possible to get used to that again, or if she would forever be shocked each time her dreams dissolved and she remembered she didn't live in two realities, that normal people always hovered in that thin line between make-believe and waking.

"What do you mean?" Rosalind demanded.

Lourens was standing over Orion with a stethoscope. He moved it slowly.

"He started to turn pale half an hour ago," Lourens said. "I thought it might have been the light."

"And is it not?"

Lourens frowned. Rosalind didn't like that look one bit. She felt a cold sweat break out across the back of her neck. What had Lourens said—that if Orion were to wake, it would be before morning? The sky was brightening. Enough time had passed to drag night away, to lessen the sound of war outside.

"His heart is slowing down."

Rosalind's heart, on the other hand, surged to her throat. "*What?*"

"Get the wires at the back of the lab."

Rosalind was frozen. "What do you mean—"

"Now!"

The urgency in his tone snapped her into action. She dashed for the back of the lab, making a frantic search before spotting the loop of red wires and figuring that was what Lourens meant. However, when she grabbed them and brought them to Lourens, he grimaced, shaking his head.

"Did I get the wrong thing?" Rosalind demanded.

"No," Lourens replied. "This is right. But they're frayed. Too many years of inactivity have passed in this building."

Rosalind sniffed hard. Christ. When had she started crying? She hadn't even noticed.

"What were you trying to do?"

"Run an electric current through his heart. It will stop otherwise."

Rosalind searched desperately around her, as though she would be able to identify another tool even if there were one lying around.

"Stop?" she repeated. She had heard him perfectly fine. It was only that she couldn't digest it.

"Yes, Lang Shalin." Lourens took his stethoscope off. "Cardiac arrhythmia. He keeps missing beats. He will enter failure very soon."

"Hospital," Rosalind managed. She took a wheezing breath. "At this point we can find a hospital."

"How close is the nearest one?"

"Ten minutes. Near the fire station."

Lourens shook his head. "He won't make it."

No. Rosalind refused to believe it. He had held on for this long, and it was *here* he didn't make it? Orion was not the sort to languish away in a small lab that had been abandoned for years. Orion was bright fires and burning stars, and when his time came, it would not be *here* by a mere stab wound.

"I'm taking him," Rosalind snapped. She eased her hand beneath his head. Leaned in and told him: "Your life is mine as mine is yours—do you understand me? You are not *allowed* to die."

Lourens tried to stop her, his expression marred by defeat. Only as soon as he placed his hand on Orion's chest in an effort to keep him down, to prevent Rosalind from acting wildly, he paused, his entire demeanor changing.

Rosalind froze too. A moment passed. "Lourens?" she asked shakily. "Why do you look like that?"

He blinked. Lourens didn't respond for a while, as if he were considering whether he might be mistaken. Then he said, "He's stabilizing."

He hurried to fetch his stethoscope again. Pressed it to Orion's chest, listening. "Oh," Lourens concluded quietly. "Oh, I understand."

And then . . .

Then Orion's eyes opened.

"Who was yelling at me?" he rasped. "I heard it all the way in the afterlife."

Rosalind was glad she had left the chair lingering around. She practically collapsed right into it, so many various emotions rushing through her chest that she could articulate nothing except a long, silent scream.

"Who do you think?" she managed.

"It sounded like my wife."

If he hadn't just awoken from his deathbed, Rosalind would have reached out and shaken him. An iron claw was slowly loosening its hold on the inside of her throat, melting into liquid and sliding into her stomach.

"You need to conserve your energy," Lourens warned, shining a light into Orion's eyes. "You almost didn't wake up."

Orion flinched from the light. That seemed to be a good sign, at least.

"What happened?" he asked, his voice weak. "I feel strange."

"That might be the giant stab wound at your side," Rosalind supplied.

"It might also be your new blood."

Rosalind blinked. Orion would have if he wasn't still squinting against Lourens's light.

"New . . . blood?"

"Miss Lang here cut open her arm so we could perform a transfusion. I had only been thinking that your body was experiencing blood loss. I hadn't realized that the cure would transfer over as well." Lourens switched his light off. When he put it down, he looked satisfied with himself, having solved the mystery of what had happened on his worktable. "The cure is quick if injected in liquid form, but your body was cycling in blood possessing its materials instead. It must have been replicating all night, taking its time to set in. I feared that you would be too weak while lacking a new dose of your mother's strength alteration and wouldn't be able to recover from a severe injury. But once the cure kicked in, it restored your body before it could try to destroy itself. You don't need new doses anymore. Your mother's experiments are gone."

Rosalind was swimming in her bewilderment. *Gone.*

Orion reached his arm out. Almost absently, Rosalind extended her fingers to meet him, and he grabbed her wrist, looking at the bandaged section.

Fortune unhealing. Huntsman without the strength. The very world seemed to hold its breath at this change in its nature, but no skies were falling, and the ground remained even. Now they were mere people, civilians plucked off the streets.

"I must fetch some more clean bandages," Lourens declared. "I will be back shortly."

He exited the lab. Rosalind barely knew how to react in the silence, nor what to say—whether Orion would mourn the absence of who he had been for so long.

"Didn't I tell you I wasn't going to leave?"

Rosalind drifted closer. "You heard me earlier?"

Orion shook his head. He sighed, bringing her hand up and pressing her fingers to his face. "I didn't hear anything before I woke up. I'm talking about what you said to me after I'd lost my memories. *Eventually you're going to leave*. I won't. I won't ever. I just defied death itself to prove my point."

Rosalind didn't see regret in his expression. Only contentment.

"Phoebe and Silas are going to want to know that you are all right," she said. "Oliver, too. And Celia and Alisa, while I'm at it."

"They're not going to know what to do with me," Orion said, appearing pleased. "I feel like I have been birthed into the world anew."

Rosalind's mouth twitched. "I suppose you have. Which means you'll need a new code name. Do you want to make your decision before I go make the phone calls?"

Slowly, Orion reached up with his other hand, taking care not to strain the stitches at his side. When he wiped at her face, she felt her tear tracks fade away. For once, she hardly cared that he could see them.

"No more code names," he said seriously, gently. "This time we start with the truth." He held his hand out for her to shake. "I'm Liwen, but I also go by Orion. Enchanté."

Rosalind breathed a small laugh. She met his handshake, palms clasping tight. "I'm Shalin," she said, "but I also go by Rosalind."

EPILOGUE

MAY 1932

The streets spilled with May's summer flowers—magnolias, blooming on the whispering trees. It hadn't been this warm in quite some time, which meant everybody was out and about, moving along Nanjing Road to enjoy the day.

Rosalind stood on one of the corners, waiting. She was lying low these days. Most of her time was spent at her apartment, reading or listening to the radio, keeping pace with the city's affairs. The Battle of Shanghai ended in March, letting the rubble shift into place and the fires extinguish up in Zhabei. They had finally signed the official cease-fire yesterday, which Rosalind heard through the quieter channels before she heard it on the news.

"Fresh flowers, xiǎojiě?"

A bouquet popped into view on her left, carried by a young girl selling them by the bucketload. Rosalind shook her head nicely, and the girl moved on, soliciting other potential customers waiting at the busy corner. If anyone were to take in the laughter and activity bustling about the main road, no one would know what had been sent off in the government offices only some short distance away.

They hadn't lost, but they hadn't exactly won, either. All Chinese troops had been pulled out of Shanghai. They said the city had been demilitarized, an effort made to let it thrive without conflict, to let businesses operate without fear. The British and the French and the Americans didn't have to worry about havoc on their profit-earning endeavors, not like the terrible strain they faced while the fighting was going on outside their concessions. They didn't want to think about the casualties at the hands of the Japanese military, nor the violence from their auxiliary militias, and so the solution was for the League of Nations to declare the whole zone neutral and forbid the presence of troops.

All the same, some Japanese units had been allowed to remain. As if their idea of neutral was to let the invader hold on to a little bite and figure that it made everyone happy. It was unfair—horrifically, sickeningly unfair—after the damage and the bodies left behind in Zhabei, but there was nothing that could be done, certainly not by one agent, not even by a whole branch of operatives.

Rosalind had left her Nationalist work entirely. Even if covert hadn't already wanted to abandon her, she couldn't stick around for any of it. The world would spin on without her, and she had to allow it. She might never loosen her shoulders again if she insisted on hauling every bit of rubble onto her back.

In truth, the parting hadn't been as terrible as she'd expected. Some nights she was kept awake thinking about the deaths and the war and the next time invasion would appear on the horizon, but Rosalind *could* sleep now, and eventually those thoughts were forced away when she reached for comfort from the person next to her and closed her eyes. It was not an utter resolution—far from it. But it was a moment forged out of sweat and blood, carved painfully from the ground that whispered maybe she ought to learn to forgive herself, and Rosalind was trying to listen.

A work in progress, but a work nonetheless.

"Xiǎojiě."

The flower seller was back, holding a pink bouquet out to her.

"I'm all right, really," Rosalind said. There was nowhere in the apartment to put it. She would have to buy a vase. "It's beautiful, though."

"No, it's for you," the girl insisted, pushing it into her hands. "Someone has paid for it already."

The girl trotted off. Rosalind blinked, staring at the bouquet in her hands.

"You don't like it?"

The voice behind her had called out from some distance away, but Rosalind still heard it as though he spoke right into her ear. She turned over her shoulder, spotting Orion crossing the road with one hand in his pocket and the other clutching the edge of his suit jacket, carelessly tossed over his shoulder.

"You don't have a high-paying job anymore," Rosalind said when he stopped before her. A ruckus passed around them: a crowd of cyclists merging and zipping along the rest of the traffic. "Are you sure you should be spending so recklessly?"

Orion was quick to grin. It had taken him some time to gather the nerve to go to headquarters today. Understandably, given that it had been the site of his brainwashing. They hadn't rushed him to come in, at least. After Lady Hong was captured, after her militia dissolved and her ties to Japanese diplomats across the country severed, after all the paperwork was submitted and the higher-ups had gathered around a table to discuss how her charges of national treason would be laid out, Orion had been cleared from fault. While Lady Hong awaited a trial that Orion was doing his very best to block out, the Kuomintang told him he could resume his duties when he wished. Become Huntsman once more when he was done resting—even if he was always going to be under suspicion by the high society he used to spy on, given that the newspapers had plastered his covert work in full detail.

"Office admin still *pays,* beloved," Orion said, swinging an arm over her shoulder. "Maybe not as much as your fancy new salary, but I uphold a commendable effort nonetheless."

Rosalind snickered. He hadn't wanted to leave entirely. Not

when the other option was mingling through high society without spying, and Orion still seemed to think he needed to keep *some* sort of eye on the nation. So today he had officially transferred into the administrative end of government work, trying to manage what he could, but ever wary in case the landscape changed. He and Rosalind had made an exit plan already. The moment things started to worsen, the very moment the city started to murmur about war again, they would leave. The matter was nonnegotiable.

"Whatever you say." She lifted the bouquet to her nose. "Thank you."

"Of course," Orion said softly. His eyes latched on to the other item in her hand: a small note card. "What is that?"

Rosalind gave it over without explanation. It came in this morning from *her* new employers. Alisa had brought it to her door, because enough disruption had sent shock waves through the city that no one was paying attention to her coming in and out of Zhouzhuang, working as a traveling assistant for Roma and Juliette after withdrawing from the Communists. In classic Alisa fashion, she had decided that she wanted to see more of the country rather than doing work she was already good at, and now, whenever the illegal weapons ring business needed any correspondence or stock delivered across the country, she was moving like a speed machine. Thankfully, Rosalind had a far different role: she was their Shanghai representative. After all, there was no need to waste resources by employing eyes and ears from various sources when they could just plant one person they trusted.

"What is this?" Orion asked, squinting at the card. "Is this supposed to be a drawing of two people? What is one holding—*oh.*"

When she first opened the envelope, Rosalind had thought it was a task letter, similar to the previous few she had received, but there was no writing on the card. Only two hand-drawn people with sticks for limbs, holding what she determined was supposed to be a baby.

"I think it's an announcement," Rosalind said, plucking the card back. "But with Juliette's drawing skills, I really can't be sure."

"Maybe they're having a pumpkin."

Rosalind nodded in mock seriousness. "I'll be sure to ask about the pumpkin the next time I see them." They started to walk along the road, moving farther from the looming headquarters that Orion had just exited. She hesitated before returning to the prior topic, asking: "Did everything go okay? With the transfer?"

Orion's arm tensed slightly. She felt the strain along her own shoulders, and on instinct, she reached to lace her fingers through his, her thumb moving back and forth.

"I don't think they expected me to come in with that request," he said. "After months of sitting idle, they probably assumed I was preparing to resume work."

"They are careless if that is the case." A surge of righteous anger stirred in Rosalind's stomach. So many of their superiors hadn't *noticed* Orion being brainwashed with every visit to headquarters, and they had the audacity to wonder why it had taken him this long to step foot back into that building again.

His finger tapped the back of her hand. As if they were taking turns for who needed to reassure the other.

"It's all right," he said. "There were a few questions about Oliver, but I feigned ignorance. No trouble otherwise. The fact that Silas remains highly trusted in covert is a big help."

They could not go a few days without hearing from Silas, which amused Rosalind greatly but had Orion scratching his head. It wasn't that they heard from Silas frequently for no reason: it was because Phoebe was the biggest handful and made it her mission to mess with him. Priest was still at large, though the Kuomintang hadn't blamed Silas for her escape when they knew how tricky she was. Every time there was word about her movement in the city, Silas was sent after her. Whenever the trail seemed to be getting too warm, Silas panicked and tried to warn her. Whenever Phoebe ignored his warnings, Silas would ask Orion to please tell his sister to behave, and then Orion would roll his eyes and say he had absolutely no control over what she did.

The last time Rosalind asked Phoebe about the nature of her and Silas's relationship, Phoebe had given a very sly shrug. It was complicated, Rosalind assumed. Phoebe wouldn't put her gun down, and Silas was still tied to the government. Yet when Phoebe had free time, she was sneaking into his house. When Silas was working, he was conveniently misplacing the evidence that passed in front of him about Priest's activity. The last time Rosalind asked Orion what *he* knew about their relationship, he slapped his hands over his ears and said it was better if he didn't know *anything* about what his sister and his best friend got up to in their spare time.

Rosalind smiled a little at the thought, and Orion cast her a look as if to ask why Silas still being in covert was so amusing. She wouldn't say anything when it wasn't her place, but she could guess there was only one reason why Phoebe didn't leave Shanghai to work, despite the risk of being exposed. Oliver was permanently established in a small township outside of Shanghai these days, after all. The girl could go live with him if she wanted. But she stayed because Silas was here, and sooner or later she would have to admit it.

"What did they say about Oliver?" Rosalind asked. "Nothing concerning, I hope."

Orion shook his head. He skirted around a puddle on the pavement, nudging Rosalind a distance away from the water too so that she wasn't splashed.

"The usual. What they don't know won't hurt them."

Though Celia and Oliver still worked for the Communists, they were no longer mission agents either, but rather the people behind an operation base. Which meant they weren't being held responsible for matters like their famously Nationalist siblings. It also meant they didn't move around anymore, and Rosalind could visit her sister easily, bringing Orion with her and forcing his reconciliation efforts with Oliver by mere proximity. He couldn't show up and *not* talk to Oliver.

Though their brotherly relationship remained dented and marred by the weight of the past, its frozen heart was thawing slowly. Rosalind had caught Orion on the phone with Oliver only today. Of his own volition, no less.

"What don't they know?" she asked, sidling closer to his side and peering up at him. "What secrets did you exchange on the phone this morning?"

A quirk appeared at the corner of his mouth. "Not information relevant to the state, that's for sure," Orion returned. "He was asking when we would be available to attend their wedding."

Rosalind stopped dead in her tracks. "*Excuse* me?"

Orion halted with her, confused. "Wouldn't Celia have already told—" He blinked, then realized his mistake in an instant. "*Oh.* Oh, so he hasn't proposed yet."

"Hong Liwen, you are in so much trouble. . . ."

"Don't tell, don't tell, pleasepleaseplease," he begged in theatrics.

Rosalind bolted forward. "I'm going to tell."

He tugged her close at once, lifting her off her feet entirely without breaking his stride. "You are absolutely not."

At times like these, Rosalind was mightily impressed with herself for holding her own against Orion when he'd had enhanced strength. Because even here, when he had returned to being a regular person, he hauled her around like it was no matter in the slightest.

"Orion," Rosalind said. "You are carrying me like a handbag."

"Swear to secrecy. Then I will put you down."

Rosalind mimed zipping her mouth and throwing away the

key. With a sigh, Orion set her back on her feet, though his hand remained at her waist.

"You know," he said, "we could steal their thunder."

"Oh?"

In the fallout of all that had happened in this city—his parents locked away and awaiting a trial from the Kuomintang that was sure to go on forever and ever—Orion had inherited his house and whatever assets remained. He had brought in people for its maintenance, which meant Ah Dou had real help and people to talk to when he watered the gardens or polished the walls. It was no longer the old housekeeper alone in the big estate but rather a big estate bustling with life and noise . . . though Orion himself was still rarely around. Phoebe's room was always carefully tidied so that she could come and go as she pleased, but Orion was consistently lured over to a building in the French Concession, to an apartment on the second floor.

In technicality, Rosalind's apartment was a Nationalist assignment, but Lao Lao was still the owner of the building, and she told Rosalind firmly that she was not to move . . . unless it was to relocate somewhere larger, which Lao Lao always said with a blatant nudge in Orion's direction. They had abandoned High Tide however many months ago, and there was no assignment that kept them bound together, but all the same, Rosalind and Orion acted as if they were still married, which wasn't quite proper by societal standards.

They had yet to speak about the matter plainly. Which was fine for Rosalind. Really. It wasn't like she *needed* a real proposal. Or a real marriage certificate. Or, hell, even a ring.

It would, however, be nice to have all those things, because no matter how many times Orion asked her to move in with him so they could run a household, it felt rather peculiar to go into their courtship backward. She knew how he breathed when he slept, but she didn't know which term of address to use for him. He kept her amused in the mornings, monologuing about his eternal undying love, but they had never gone to a café in the Concessions together for breakfast because their faces were too recognizable, and chances were high that someone would approach their table in curiosity. Fortune had many enemies, too. Though that part of her was gone, Rosalind still endured the consequences of her past work. If she showed her face in public too often, it might just prompt revenge seekers into the open again, which was less than ideal now that the papers had finally gotten bored with writing about her.

"*Oh?*" Orion mimicked, sounding amused. "What was that supposed to mean?"

"It means exactly that," Rosalind replied. "A prompting noise for you to continue talking. Are you proposing, Orion?"

She had never asked outright like this. In the first month after he'd almost died, the focus was on making sure he was healing properly. Their days were occupied by worry over Oliver and Celia making it out of the city and settling somewhere safe. Then to Phoebe and Silas and their frantic movements on the game board that was this everlasting civil war.

As the weeks warmed, matters seemed to calm. As summer swept in, suddenly Rosalind was thinking more and more about the two of them, the last ones left to tend to once everyone else had their own lives in motion.

"Maybe." Orion had a funny grin on his face. "What would you say if I was?"

Rosalind rolled her eyes. "You clearly are not."

"No?"

Something rumbled in the distance. Rosalind's first instinct was concern, recalling the screech of warplanes screaming above the city and dropping bombs onto the streets. When she lifted her head, though, she spotted only a single plane flying across the bright day, and her nerves eased. The sky shone so clearly, a blue vivid enough that not a single cloud could be seen—at least not until the plane started to leave behind long arches of smoke where it had flown.

The plane did a loop. Rosalind frowned, tilting her head.

"It's a little late for me to reschedule now," Orion said, and Rosalind still wasn't comprehending, "so I should probably clarify that I had this planned far in advance, and the thunder-stealing comment was a joke."

Words. The plane was using its trail of smoke to write *words*, beautiful calligraphed strokes emitting one character after the other, each appearing at rapid speed.

我愛你 . . . 你願意嫁給我嗎?

Rosalind gaped at the sky. The plane did a final loop, then disappeared quickly, flying away to leave the question floating in the bright blue.

I love you . . . Will you marry me?

The crowd around them was starting to notice too. Elderly ladies pointing up in excitement; little children clapping their hands as they tried to read aloud.

"What a coincidence," Rosalind managed. "Someone in the vicinity must also be discussing proposals."

Orion barely held in his laugh. He grabbed her shoulders, tipping her head down to look at him. "Beloved, it's for you."

Rosalind blinked stubbornly. "No, it isn't."

His hands pressed into her face, along her cheeks. The motion was so tender that Rosalind's breath snagged in her throat, her eyes turning up again to read the words. The smoke hadn't blown away yet, though it had fuzzed a little at the edges.

"It's for you," he said again, quietly this time. His amusement faded for earnestness. He must have known that she wasn't being contrary in an effort to be difficult. She had lived a long past life being hidden as a secret, and the habits were hard to shake, the expectations hard to rebuild. Rosalind stared and stared and stared, but the words didn't fade away; nor did the murmurs and the soft squealing from every part of the street, shoppers turning and searching to locate who the question was addressed to.

Rosalind's gaze drifted back down. Orion was still looking at her, patiently waiting.

"I'm sorry this took so long," he said, and Rosalind wasn't sure if he meant since this past January or since the moment they were assigned together as High Tide, when Orion asked if she wanted silver or gold. He let go of her face and held forth something between them, glinting in the daylight. "I wanted to get it custom-made. The center opens with a tiny hidden compartment—see? You can put powders or liquid in here. I know you're not Fortune anymore, but it would be a shame to waste your talent."

He was holding a ring. A glimmering, dazzling ring, with a thin gold band and a circle of rubies surrounding the diamond in the middle. He *really* wasn't joking. The understanding finally set in.

It was beautiful. The most beautiful ring she had ever seen.

"I know too that you would hate it if I got down on one knee, because it would end up in the papers," he continued. "I'm settling for a compromise. I will refrain from being an attention-seeking menace if you let me be very public. The sky itself says I love you. I have loved you since we weren't actually married, and I can't bear another day living in a falsity. Please, Rosalind, put me out of my misery."

She inhaled. Exhaled.

"Of all matters you think I would hate to end up in the papers," Rosalind demanded, finally finding her voice, "do you think I would mind this?"

Then she lunged forward, startling Orion. Fortunately, he caught on in an instant—he caught *her* in an instant, the bouquet clasped between them.

The moment she kissed him, there was no hiding from the world. She wound an arm around his neck, he lifted her off the ground, and then suddenly there was commotion in every direction. Perhaps there was a flash, perhaps there was someone capturing the scene so they could speculate how the city's former covert operatives ended up here, identities exposed and making a rare public appearance before they disappeared again. Whatever they were to say, Rosalind could hardly hear them.

"That's a yes, then?" Orion whispered when they drew apart.

At any moment the alarms could blare, could bid them to pick up their bags and flee. The ground could break under their feet, the sky could wash out its blue, descend into ash instead. The next month lay uncertain, as did the very next day, but no longer was it time spent in the shadows, hidden without love.

"Yes," she whispered. "It's a yes."

AUTHOR'S NOTE

In *The Norton Shakespeare*'s introduction of *As You Like It*, Jean E. Howard writes that "The ending [of the play] does not so much lay out a plan for social reform as celebrate a utopian moment of forgiveness, reconciliation, and hope." When I was planning the events of *Foul Heart Huntsman*, I typed out that quote and stuck it at the bottom of my document, because this was the finale of an alternate world I had been playing in for five years, and this was how I wanted to conclude my story. I can't change the decade that is to come. I can't take away the eventual outbreak of war, nor the destruction that's about to enter the city when the next invasion arrives. But in all darkness there are moments of recovery, a happy-for-now, and that was the truth I saw for these characters too.

As established in the *Foul Lady Fortune* author's note, the backdrop to this duology is a true era of history: the Japanese invasion of Manchuria and the empire's subsequent push into the rest of China. *Foul Heart Huntsman* opens in January 1932, when the political unrest was reaching a breaking point. Anti-Japanese protests and boycotts led by Chinese student organizations and trade unions furious over the occupation had been occurring in Shanghai since the Mukden Incident in September 1931, and Japanese representatives wanted these boycotts stamped out.

Chapter 9 describes the breaking point that would eventually lead to the January 28 Incident in the climax of the book. What proceeds is directly from the pages of history. Lady Hong is a figment of my imagination (and her forces did not exist in history to exacerbate the problem), but Shanghai indeed entered crisis mode on January 18 after Japan issued their ten-day ultimatum. On January 26, Chinese authorities declared martial law and mobilized to defend against the Japanese forces docking into the city. Although the mayor accepted the terms of the Japanese ultimatum on January 28 and attempted to shut down Chinese efforts of anti-Japanese boycott, the Japanese were not satisfied, and under the grounds of wanting to protect order, they sent a force into Zhabei to take the North Railway Station.

The military facility that the characters break into during Oliver's rescue in Chapter 39 is made up, but the chaos in Zhabei that night was real. The time line in *Foul Heart Huntsman* is condensed to include many quick waves on the first night, but in history there were heavy artillery attacks and bombers overhead for weeks, razing Zhabei to the ground and killing thousands of civilians with indiscriminate bombing. Also true to history, Chapter 43 follows refugees trying to escape into the International Settlement because it was "safe" as soon as you entered Western jurisdiction—the foreigners on the other side of the creek were said to have watched the battle from the International Settlement as though it was a sporting event.

The snipers that Phoebe joins in Chapter 52 are adapted from true history. To avoid military confrontation in the foreign settlements, Chinese soldiers needed to stay out of certain areas, and snipers were sent in instead. Among these, many were from the Green Gang (the inspiration for the Scarlet Gang in *These Violent Delights*), so I adapted this to include former Scarlets entering the fray of battle. The Japanese "ronin" mentioned here are taken from history too—vigilante groups who were assigned peacekeeping over Japanese civilians and, subsequently, were infamous for brutal violence against the Chinese civilian population. When battle broke out, if they suspected a Chinese sniper within a building, the entire place would be torched.

Finally, Chapter 53 unfolds on a place called Arden Road; this wasn't a real street in Shanghai but rather a reference to the Forest of Arden in *As You Like It*. Otherwise, places in the book like Baoshan Road or Seymour Road were real and still exist in Shanghai (with different names). The Shanghai East Library in Chapter 23 that Phoebe and Silas go to was also real—it was bombed during the Japanese invasion of Zhabei and destroyed.

The epilogue takes place in May 1932 at the end of this conflict. The League of Nations demanded a cease-fire on March 4; fighting continued while negotiations went on for a few weeks. On May 5, the Shanghai Cease-fire Agreement was signed, which meant Shanghai grew peaceful and business boomed once again. Though the Secret Shanghai stories end here, there's no such thing as happily-ever-after in history: in 1937, the second Sino-Japanese War began with the Battle of Shanghai, which also brought the start of World War II in Asia. Chinese civilians would endure horrific atrocities. We leave our characters during a period of peace, to continue onward with their lives even if they are soon to be surrounded by tragedy: as we all must do to some degree during our time in this world.

Of course, I must emphasize that *Foul Lady Fortune* and *Foul Heart Huntsman* are works of fiction using history to explore its own story, not to provide a textbook account of the era. I would highly recommend nonfiction resources if you're interested in learning about the events that take place in this book and beyond. The Virtual Shanghai Project is also a great resource, accessible at virtualshanghai.net. Shanghai of the 1930s may not have had super soldiers and chemical concoctions, but there were spies and factions and politics aplenty that are incredibly fascinating to learn about.

ACKNOWLEDGMENTS

We made it! We're dead but we survived! It's the end of an era, and I can't begin to express how grateful I am to have the privilege of writing these acknowledgments . . . because it means the book is done. This universe of four novels plus one novella collection is complete, sent off into the world to decorate bookshelves, which has been made possible only with the support and dedication of the following wonderful people.

Thank you to my agent, Laura Crockett—it's been half a decade since we started working together and this fictional universe has blossomed into what it is because of you. I can't wait to send more worlds out together. Thank you to Uwe Stender, Brent Taylor, and everyone at TriadaUS—I am eternally appreciative of the work you do to get this book and its predecessors into its different forms and translations. Thank you to my editor, Sarah McCabe—you're the expert handler to my scrambling operative. By which I mean working with you to get my manuscripts into shape is an exercise in you always saving my life, and I'm very grateful. Thank you to Anum Shafqat, too. Thank you to my publicists, Nicole Russo, Anna Elling, and Lindsey Ferris. And thank you to Justin Chanda and my publishing team at Margaret K. McElderry Books, including Karen Wojtyla, Anne Zafian, Bridget Madsen, Elizabeth Blake-Linn, Michael McCartney, Chrissy Noh, Caitlin Sweeny, Lisa Quach, Bezi Yohannes, Perla Gil, Remi Moon, Amelia Johnson, Ashley Mitchell,

Yasleen Trinidad, Saleena Nival, Lisa Moraleda, Christina Pecorale and her sales team, and Michelle Leo and her education/library team—and a special shout-out to Emily Ritter and Amy Lavigne in digital marketing, who put up with me committing heists in the office every few months. Thank you too to the Hodderscape team in the UK, the Hachette Aotearoa New Zealand team at home, and to every team translating and getting *Foul Heart Huntsman* out in its different languages.

As always, I wouldn't be here without the support of my parents, my family, and my friends. Thank you. I won't go down the list of names because I'll be here forever and you know who you are, but some special shout-outs: This book is dedicated to Tashie Bhuiyan, who has shaped the course of the series in the ideas shouted across our Astoria apartment and in the unprompted "does rosalind know she's my favorite CGO (chloe gong original)" texts I get at 2:00 a.m. I don't know how I would survive publishing without you, and this book is infinitely better with your influence. If we could print emojis I would insert that hand-holding one with the customizations. You know which one. We'll always be roomies in my heart. When it comes to people keeping me sane too, thank you to the d.a.c.u., and to Alex Aster and Dustin Thao—there will never be such a thing as too much Happy Hour for us. And, finally, to Jackie Sussman, Kushal Modi, and João Campos—I love you all for reading these books to support. Thank you for joining me until the very finale.

I'm forever in the debt of booksellers, librarians, teachers, and literary advocates who get these books out into the world. Thank you for everything you do. Finally, I'll end with the biggest thank-you for readers everywhere—those who have newly joined with *Foul Lady Fortune* or those who have been here since *These Violent Delights*. I had the time of my life being gangsters and spies with you. Thank you, thank you, thank you for reading.

Georgina Public Library
90 Wexford Drive
Keswick, ON L4P 3P7